the Half
that you See

Edited by Rebecca Rowland

www.DarkInkBooks.com

First Published by *Dark Ink Books*, Southwick, MA, March 2021

Dark Ink Books is a division of *AM Ink Publishing*. *Dark Ink* and *AM Ink* and its logos are trademarked by *AM Ink Publishing*.

www.AMInkPublishing.com

for the fiction writers,
who spend countless hours planting and pruning their landscapes
so that, for a short while, others may be treated to an extraordinary view

"You are young yet, my friend," replied my host,
"but the time will arrive when you will learn to judge for yourself
of what is going on in the world...

Believe nothing you hear, and only one half that you see."

-The System of Dr. Tarr and Prof. Fether
by Edgar Allan Poe (1845)

Contents

Chalk
Elin Olausson

It was night before he found the house. Dirty big-city rain washed over his glasses, blurring and distorting the quiet suburban street. He had to stoop low to read on the letterbox. The name was written in minuscule, cursive, old-lady handwriting on baby blue paper. He thought again of the notebook he had dropped somewhere, most likely in the backseat of that cigarette-stinking car. The lady's name and address had been in there, along with everything else he needed to remember. But thinking about the notebook only made him anxious, so he forced his eyes toward the house instead. It was a gloom-grey, two-story building at the far end of the street, away from lights and traffic. The garden was overgrown with weeds and the untrimmed hedge rose high above his head, though people often told him he was tall. He didn't look forward to spending the night in a place like this, but he hadn't looked forward to anything in a long while. Pressing one arm to his forehead to keep the whipping rain out of his face, he opened the gate and slipped inside.

His knocks were loud and rude, but his windbreaker was too thin for rainy late-fall nights and he had never liked being wet. There were no lights on inside, not even the blue glow from a TV. He knocked again, then wiped the glasses with his dripping sleeve.

No sounds but the drumming rain, no footsteps or voices. Nothing until the door was unlocked, hurriedly, and that woman stood there. Her eyes reminded him of the snarling Rottweiler that had bitten him as a child. They were small and inky and brimming with accusations of this kind or that. He was much taller than she but she was firm and fat and seemed carved out of alabaster. While her face was round and moon-like, the top of her head was oddly small and pointy, her scalp covered with sparse, coffee-colored hair pulled into a knot the size of a baby's fist.

"Yes?" Something about her deep voice unnerved him.

"It's about the room." He reached into his soggy front pocket, then remembered the loss of the notebook. "I wrote to you... Sorry, I should have come earlier but the man in the car took the wrong turn."

"I see." Her mouth twisted as if she had a cherry-stone in there. "You have money?"

He let the words roll around in his head a few times until he realized that she had a foreign accent. That explained the name. "Yes, I do."

"All right." When she moved away from the doorway the house sighed. "Room is in the basement. Breakfast between six and eight. No guests."

"Understood." He tipped his head backwards to look for damp stains, but there was nothing to see except the bleary ceiling fixture and a pair of drowsy flies circling it. The image was as depressing as the woman in front of him. "Do you live alone?"

"No." She turned her head, barking out a monosyllable name. Her booming voice made the flies scatter. "The girl is upstairs." Lower she added, "She's sick."

He didn't have anything in particular to say to that information. He wished he still had the notebook.

A door opened and closed somewhere on the second floor. Soft, slow footsteps tickled the skin inside his ear.

"Sick," the woman said again. "Don't mind her."

The sounds from the stairs made him wonder what the girl looked like—her legs in particular, if they were bent or broken, or if she was extremely obese like some of those people on TV. Heavy thuds filled the house as if there was a fight. The beginning of the stairs was at the far end of the hall, in a windowless corner. The woman kept watching him, as if the unsettling sounds were everyday occurrences to her. *Thud-drag-thud.* Part of him would enjoy it if the girl turned out to be plagued by some rare, disfiguring illness. But when she showed, emerging from the shadows by the stairs, she was a short and scrawny thing with no visible faults. As pale as the mother, with the same dark hair, but her face might almost have been pretty. If it weren't for her slack, open mouth and the vacant stare in her blue eyes. The hanging arms and slow, strained walk.

"Sleepwalker," the woman said sharply. The girl stopped dragging her feet forward at the sound of her voice. She blinked, once, before her head slumped forward. "Disease. Called something, can't remember what. Now you know. Don't disturb, don't talk to her. Makes her upset."

"She can hear you," he said. It troubled him how the girl's flat, unwashed hair hid her face. "How?"

The woman shrugged. The movement seemed to pass through her body like slow, dark water. "Go back upstairs," she commanded, then scratched at a large red mark on her neck as the girl turned around. "Is sad," she muttered over the sound of arduous walking. "She used to be like you and me."

He nodded. "I should go see the room."

She pointed to a closed door with her alabaster hand. "Basement stairs. There's a bathroom down there, towels, linen. Goodnight."

Rubbing a droplet of water from the tip of his nose, he thought of asking her how old the girl was. But her eyes barked at him, tired of questions. He went down the steep basement stairs and found a square, brick-walled room lit by a naked bulb. The bed was narrow and there was a crack in the bathroom mirror. It was perfect.

Whiny house sounds tore up his dreams. Sounds he wasn't used to and didn't like, but he didn't like his dreams either. They made him sweat. He sat, eyes shut as he inhaled his own stink. There was an air vent somewhere, making a noise like a choir of insects screeching. Maybe he could talk to the woman about that in the morning.

It took him a while to discern the other noise. The *creak-pause-creak*. Opening his eyes, he felt for his glasses on the nightstand. The room wasn't completely dark—there were two narrow windows high up on the wall, twin slits allowing the moon-glow inside. He pushed the glasses against the point between his eyes, counting quietly. *Creak, pause, creak.* Someone was walking through the hall upstairs. Someone was coming.

The insect noise sank to the floor and died when the basement door opened. The stairs were concrete; they swallowed the footsteps without chewing. He watched the end of the stairs, expecting the alabaster woman—but it was the sleepwalking girl. Except she was awake.

"Mister, you have to help me!" She pattered over to the bed, barefoot, polka dot pajama sleeves covering her hands. "She's sleeping now. Finally."

He pulled his knees up as she sat down on the edge of the bed. Her eyes were like marbles, too pale for real life. "I thought you couldn't talk," he said.

"It's only because…" She sighed. "You are not her friend, are you?"

"No." He liked how small the girl was. Her voice was small too, breaking here and there as if she didn't trust it. She was like one of those tiny glass animals his grandmother had collected, the cats and does and velvet-eyed horses. Kept high up on a shelf where he couldn't reach.

"You can't become her friend," the girl said. "She's evil."

"Then I won't."

She gnawed at her bottom lip, wine-colored like his mother's roses. Her skin made him think of chalk. "Why did you come?" she asked, her fingertips slipping out of the long sleeves to press against each other.

"I had to go somewhere."

"I suppose." She didn't sound interested. He didn't mind. Her fingers moved like earthworms writhing on a wet road. "But you can't stay here long. It's a bad house. It steals your dreams." Her milky eyes prodded his own, as loud as her voice was quiet. Her eyes screamed.

"It can have mine." He laughed at the image of a house with a sour, sagging face. The girl gasped, motioning for him to be quiet.

"You don't understand! She…she doesn't like laughing. That was why she started punishing me in the first place."

He remembered what she was like in the hall. A broken toy. "How does she punish you?"

"You know." She shook her head with unnaturally large movements. "I'm only myself at night…like in a fairy tale. It's horrible. She's horrible."

"Is she your mother?"

The girl started crying. She didn't bother to wipe the tears away. "You have to help me. Please. You have to do something."

He lifted his arm but wasn't sure what he wanted to do. When he woke up in the morning he couldn't remember more than that. His lifted hand, and her distorted face stitching itself into his memory.

Breakfast was bitter tea and a hard-boiled egg with toast. He ate fast as usual, alone at the kitchen table while the woman stood with her back to him, doing dishes. She looked the same as the night before. Sturdy black dress, dark slippers. As if she hadn't gone to bed at all. He hadn't seen the girl, and the woman hadn't mentioned her. She had only spoken to him to ask how he preferred his egg.

"It's a good house," he said, trying not to think about what the girl had told him last night. "I slept well."

"No talking." She didn't turn to him. "Is unnecessary."

Her back was a square of resentment and stiff muscles. Had she fed the girl some drug? She looked like a poisoner, though he'd never met one before. She had those dog-bite eyes he didn't like. When he was done eating he went downstairs, wishing he still had his notebook. There were plenty of empty pages left when he lost it. White as chalk.

The girl returned to him that night. He woke from one of the angel dreams and she stood there by the bed, hand waving. He sat up, thinking about poison.

"I had to see you," the girl said. "It's the only thing that makes me happy." Her pajamas had changed color: they were pink with tear-shaped buttons down the front. She was so small, a doe made of glass. A velvet-eyed creature. "I like you," she said. "I like your stories."

He nodded, absent-minded. That noise from the air vent was back, stronger now. He had to speak with the woman about it.

"Tell me something then." The girl giggled, her mouth full of teeth. "You haven't told me anything yet, remember? About you. I want to know about you."

The pink stung his eyes. "There's nothing special about me. I needed somewhere to stay, that's all."

"But you have to have a name. A family. Something."

The family question seemed less dangerous. "I've got a family. My father is away a lot, but he always brings back treats. My mother loves flowers. Grandma does, too, though she likes anything pretty."

The girl's eyes seemed to have grown a size. "I love pretty things too. Don't you?"

"Yes." He winced. The air vent whispered around their conversation like a broken echo. "Then there's Cassie as well. She's the prettiest girl you've ever seen."

The girl huffed. "Prettier than me?" Then she shrugged, smiling. "It's nice that you love her so much. You're a great older brother."

"Thank you."

"I don't have any brothers." Her smile was gone. The shadows stuck to her face like dirt. "There's no one who cares for me. There's no one who can help me get away from her."

He reached out to pat the back of her hand. It was as cool as glass. "I care. I'll help you."

"And then we'll be together forever," she said, and the whispers grew until the world was wrapped in pink cotton.

He slept late the next day, missing breakfast. When he came upstairs, the woman was gone, and there was a note to him on the basement door. *Gone shopping. Back soon.* He didn't know when she had left or where the nearest grocery store was. He didn't care. The one thing on his mind was the girl.

The stairs to the second floor whined, every inch of wood slippery as ice. There were three doors upstairs, all closed. He opened the first, the second, the third. She was in the third room. On her back, fully clothed, empty eyes open. Matte hair spilled over the pillow like dead leaves.

"Oh, no." It pained him to see her like that. He didn't want to. "How can she do this to you?" He sat down on the bedside, the way she used to do at night. He touched the back of her hand, and it was warm. "I'll put an end to this," he said. "I'll make her pay for what she's done."

The girl blinked, but there was no other reaction. Nothing but a girl on a bed in a dark room, her eyes going *blink-blink-blink* like a sparrow's heart. He wanted her to smile but she didn't, so he left her there and closed the door. Went back to his basement whispers, imagining that he filled his notebook with thick black strokes.

When she came to him that night, she was crying. "I don't want you to see me like that," she said. "Like how I am when her poison has taken me." She wiped her cheeks with her sleeves, refusing to look at him. "That's not who I am."

"I know." The whispers prickled his skin but he pushed them back. "You're a pretty girl. You deserve to be free."

"Do you really think so?" She sniffled. The sound tugged at a memory somewhere, and he pushed that away too. "But I'm nothing special. Not even my own mother thinks so."

"Spread your wings," he said, drawing in the air. White shapes, white strokes all around her. "Angel."

He was up in time for breakfast the next morning. The woman boiled the eggs, put the kettle on. No talking, because that was how she wanted it. No air vent whispering. Bitterness slipped down his throat, egg yolk painted the inside of his mouth. He cut one slice of bread, two, three. The woman stood by the counter sipping her tea, back turned. She didn't notice when he rammed the bread knife into her throat. But she made a sound, a gurgling scream that shot into that stinking dark corner of his mind and tugged at his hideaway things. The things no one could know. Her cup crashed into the floor a moment before she did. It was ugly, nothing like that other time. It was sticky tiles and broken china, it was limbs going in the wrong directions. The blood clawed its way toward him but he stepped aside, dropping the knife. No more need for it. He was done.

When he turned to the doorway, the girl was there.

"Angel," he said, and for the first time since that day when they took him away, he felt calm. He had put things right now. Even without the notebook he was fine. Doctor Stein would never have believed it, but he would never ever meet Doctor Stein again.

The girl made a noise. It wasn't words, it wasn't anything like their nighttime conversations. She shook, hands fidgeting while her mouth hung open and all that came from it were those raw, strained sounds. Her eyes stayed glazed over as if she wasn't there. As if she had never been there.

See now what you've done, his mother said. *She's distraught, poor thing.*

"Not now, Mother."

It's like I've always said, Grandma cut in. *He can't be trusted.*

"Oh, shut up."

He closed the door in the girl's face, that pasty, lifeless face he couldn't bear to see. The noises wormed themselves through the keyhole, animal noises, noises almost like the ones Cass had made. Cass in her pink cotton pajamas, playing hopscotch by herself out on the street despite the autumn chill. Chalk lines around her. Chalk wings spreading from her body, and sirens howling like wolves in the distance.

Cassie. Angel eyes.

Don't look at me like that, freak, said—no, that was a false memory, one of those that Doctor Stein had put into his brain with his pills and his electric shocks. "You wouldn't," he said as Cassie jumped from square to square, too focused on her game to notice him. "Never."

"I loved her just like she was," he told the door. "That's why I didn't want her to grow anymore." The girl on the other side grunted. The woman was dead and the blood clung to her legs like a demanding toddler. He went over to the phone on the wall and it rang, one sharp signal before he lifted the receiver.

The call came from far away, a sea of static and a male voice drowning in it. "Is this Mrs.——?" The phone line chewed up bits and pieces of his voice. "I'm sorry to disturb this early in the morning. I'm Chief Inspector——and I——" There was a wind howling, tossing the man's words here and there. "Your name and address were found in a notebook that we believe——and it's of the utmost importance that——"

Notebook, he thought.

"This man is a highly disturbed individual and——ran away from a mental institution on November 10th."

The wind tore through again. The thin line of waves and wires between the policeman's voice and his own auditory canal swayed and shivered like a skipping-rope slapping the asphalt, *thud-thud-thud.*

"He is very dangerous. I don't want to scare you, but——his own little sister——"

The girl had stopped with her noises, but there was a different sound now. Slow, unsteady knocks on the door. *Bang, bang, little fists.*

"Keep your door locked, and don't invite any strangers inside," the Chief Inspector continued. "And if you notice anything out of the ordinary, don't hesitate to give me a call. My number——"

"Thank you." He pressed the receiver to his mouth, blowing hot, stale air into the transmitter. "It was nice of you to call, Chief Inspector." He saw Cassie in front of him, her wings glowing in the sun. She was smiling. The banging on the door continued, but it wasn't important. He would take care of it in a while.

The Chief Inspector shouted something, but that wasn't important, either. The girl made a sound like that of a dog drowning.

"I've got something to attend to now, if you'll excuse me. When you're done with my notebook, can I have it back?"

Winnebago Indian Motorhome by Tonka
Eddie Generous

The silver bell jingled from the top left corner of the heavy wooden door of Cooper Collective as Josh Dolan hipped his way back to the sidewalk, the two-foot box held against his chest, hands pinching the nine-inch wide ends. His eyes bounced up and down from the street to the Winnebago images on the box. He shifted the box to his left forearm and dug his keys from his right pocket.

The box slid into the passenger's seat and he hurried around the front end. He'd left his cell phone stuffed in the cubby behind the shifter, auxiliary cord attached and music still running on random. He turned the key, but not far enough to jog the starter into life. For a moment, there was no music, only the ominous rustling of paper before the piano and horns picked up in David Bowie's *Dollar Days*.

The song was an ode to the eventual and a dying man's recognition that conclusion was beyond his control. Like the lines of Bowie's bucket list could go unticked, no trouble.

"But not this one," Josh said and touched the wrinkled and soft Winnebago box, thinking of his own bucket list. He'd inherited a 1974 Winnebago Indian Motorhome by Tonka as a boy, played with it for three summers before his father dragged him from bed, shouting that the house was on fire and they had to get out.

Strangely, he'd forgotten all about the toy until a few years back when he and Claire admitted they'd been facing down their own eventual. He moved into the den and she said nothing. They ate no more than three meals together a week. They hadn't had sex since she went off the pill.

She wanted a baby—not a child, a baby—of that he was certain. A cat didn't fill the void and the one they'd taken in lasted only a year before a Honda Civic made crow food of the thing. The book club, the knitting, the yoga, the tea outings, nothing scratched that particular itch. He'd tried to get her into other hobbies and in the process, got himself into nostalgia. There were posters and records. He had a small collection of reissued horror movies from his childhood—available for the first time since their VHS releases.

The Winnebago was better than perfect. As a kid, he didn't have either the husband or wife dolls, didn't have the box, and his Winnebago had been rusty with paint nicks and chips. This one had the husband and the box and was showroom mint.

He turned the key and the music silenced for a second before reconnecting. The blinker clicked, but before he could pull into the Sunday afternoon traffic, the music silenced again while his phone trilled a ring.

Claire. She had a work thing in Vancouver for a few days. That she was calling suggested abnormality. Typically, it was a single line of text that came with no expectation of response.

The shifter went back to park and the blinker ceased blinking. "Hey?" he said.

"Is this Josh Dolan?"

The voice was that of a man and Josh sat up straighter in his seat. "Yeah?"

"Your wife is Claire Dolan?" The voice sounded everyman normal, not aggressive or snobbish, no out of place accent.

"Yeah, why?"

"She collapsed this afternoon during a...conference, I guess. At the Radisson."

"What?"

"I'm a nurse at Vancouver General. She collapsed shortly after lunch and hasn't regained consciousness. We need to know if she's on any medication."

The world beyond the windows of Josh's Chevrolet Sonic darkened to nothing and the atmosphere in the cab grew harsh. "No, I don't think so...not since she went off the pill."

"Any prenatal medications?"

Josh closed his eyes and sneered at the impossibility. "What? No. Why would she?"

"Oh. Um. According to her bloodwork, she's pregnant."

Indignant, Josh blurted, "That's impossible we haven't had sex in like two years," and then immediately blushed as an echoing facsimile of his voice said *you haven't had sex, you, you, you; who knows what she's been doing, who she's been doing, who, who, who.* "Oh. Wow. How pregnant? I mean, can you tell how long?"

"No. Hmm, well." The nurse cleared his throat. "She's been unconscious for nearly two hours, but so far we know nothing. You're in Kamloops, correct?"

Josh didn't hear this, wasn't sure how he felt. "I'm coming. Driving. If she wakes up and is going to leave, tell her to call me." He hung up as the nurse began speaking.

He pulled the shifter and streaked into traffic. A truck, one not exactly cut off, but close, honked at him. He took a left at the lights and hopped onto the highway.

Two hours into the trip, he stopped in Hope for gas and coffee. A man coming from the storefront, on his way to the Jeep parked in front of Josh's Sonic, slowed as he pocketed a fat, brown leather wallet, looking into Josh's car. "Hey, I had one of those as a little guy."

Josh, in a state of mild shock, said, "Do you have the wife? I'd like to get him for the husband."

The man jerked his chin in a bird-like reaction and said, "Huh?"

"The wife for the husband. The dolls that go with the camper. You know?"

The guy pouted his bottom lip and shook his head slowly. "Man, had that toy back in the seventies, maybe even nineteen-eighty. I don't remember anything about it beyond that the wheels squeaked like a bugger and my little sister broke the awning—oh, and our cat stole the dogs."

"Dogs?"

"Sure, it came with two dogs. Now that I think about it, might've been kids, too."

"Kids?" Josh scrunched his face. "Would you sell them to me?"

"Man, I told you, I had them when I was only little." The man was shaking his head much faster, eyes widened, as if to say, *Ain't you listening, you wack job?!* "Real small. The seventies."

Josh tutted at this and finished his transaction at the pump.

"She's still out, sir." This nurse was not the nurse Josh spoke with over the phone. This nurse was a woman. She double-checked that the contact information on file was correct. "We'll give you a ring when she awakes. You can stay, too, for a little while."

"I'd like to see her," he said. Deep down, a thought, one probably belonging to the owner of that echoing voice, suggested that he'd know who had impregnated his wife once he saw her face.

"Yes, of course." The nurse stood on the ledge of her stool and pointed down the hall. "Three-two-nine. Please be quiet: there are three other patients in the room with your wife."

Josh began walking, quickly. The waxy floor shined and the dull white walls bounced a soft blue hue onto the nurses and visitors and the milling patients. The place was busy with motion, but most were respectfully hushed. In 329, Josh passed two very elderly women and a teen surrounded by what appeared to be her family. Tears streaked through a powdery foundation on their way to the teen's jawline and abrupt end to the makeup. A curtain circled the only remaining bed and Josh peeped around. It was Claire, but he had no idea who'd put the baby in her and immediately forgot the strange inclination. "Claire?" he whispered and then shook her by the big toe of her right foot where it peaked the bedsheet. She didn't move and the beeping machine kept a constant rhythm. He sidled up to the nightstand next to her and opened the drawer. Her purse was not inside, nor was her phone. He shook her once more before returning to the nurses' station in the hallway.

"Where's Claire Dolan's things? Her purse, cellphone?"

"We have them?" The woman he'd most recently spoken with rose to her feet.

"Somebody called me with her cell, so you must."

The woman disappeared behind a partition and returned swinging a bulky plastic bag by a string. "Claire Dolan. Here you go."

Josh leaned against the island's countertop and began digging with fingernails into the tight knot on the drawstring— made tighter by how the nurse had swung the bag. She was no longer looking at him but had Facebook open on a desktop computer, eyes turned onto the blue grey glow.

The knot finally let free and Josh dug around the bra and blouse, the slacks and shoes. He found the purse and then the cellphone. He held both in his right hand and the bag in his left, as if unsure how to proceed.

"Squeeze tight for me," a janitor said behind him and Josh leaned in, letting the bag fall back onto the countertop, solving his conundrum by needing space for a garbage cart. "Thanks, bud."

Josh transferred the phone to his left hand and opened the purse. The Radisson key card and sleeve were in with the cash in Claire's wallet. "Only one Radisson here, right?"

The nurse didn't look at him. "Yep."

"Better take this back in case she wakes up and wants her bra or purse."

The nurse looked then, reached for the bag and tied the knot, then yanked the bag by the strings as she returned it to whatever lay beyond the partition. "You going to be weird about that phone?"

Josh put Claire's phone in his pocket. Right then he understood a gossip mill had gone around to the on-duty nurses about his conversation, about Claire's infidelity. "No. I'm just—no."

The urge to investigate the phone was strong, but parking tolls ran by the minute at the hospital. He searched out the hotel on his phone and let Google lead him to his destination. Her car was at the airport in Kamloops—she'd flown on the company dime—and the Radisson was right by the airport.

He didn't go to Vancouver often, but little changed. It was a drab and dirty city. Everything was old and disorganized. Half of the houses appeared empty with mossy roofs and crumbling masonry. Windows boarded up, doors broken open. He'd heard there was a squatter problem, but it looked more like there was a problem with land investors driving market values beyond liveability—something else he'd heard.

Once nearing the airport and the hotel, civilization thinned out. Long buildings and gas stations and outlet shopping filled his peripheries as he drove, mind throbbing with that nettling need to know.

He parked at the Radisson, next to a pair of Enterprise rental Mazdas and a lamppost. He stepped out, got halfway across the expansive lot, and turned around. He jogged to the car and grabbed the Winnebago box. Door kicked closed, he started out anew.

The room number was on the sleeve around the key card. He rode the elevator to the eighth floor and found Claire's room. He set the box on one of the two queen beds and withdrew Claire's phone from his pocket. All he had to do was wake it up, look at the messages, and know the truth.

"Ugh," he said and set her phone on the nightstand. He read the instructions at the base of the landline telephone, just below the number pad. He dialed zero and it rang three times before a young sounding woman answered. He explained that he needed to register a car to his wife's room.

That done, he picked up the phone. He touched the button on the side and swiped the lock screen—she didn't password protect, and if she had, it would be her childhood phone number, her pin for everything. He swiped once more and his thumb hovered over the loaded message box. His heart quickened its pace—did he still love her, did he care, what the hell was she going to do with the kid? His eyes hovered away and settled on the Winnebago.

The phone returned to the nightstand and he withdrew the huge tin toy from the box. The husband figurine was on his back, arms out, knees bent. Josh put him behind the wheel. A smile played across his face.

From his pocket, he took out his cellphone and snapped a shot, ignoring all the messages and calls he'd missed while driving—he'd put it on silent when he saw Claire's mother's number pop up.

He lay back and turned to face the TV. They didn't bother with cable at home, so watching bad television was always a treat when on the road. He found *Jeopardy!* and grabbed his phone.

He sent a text to his superior and explained that he wouldn't be in for at least a few days, *Claire's sick in the hospital.*

Before Trebek broke from play for the show's first sponsor, Josh picked up the Winnebago Indian Motorhome by Tonka and set it on the bed next to him.

Josh opened his eyes. He'd slipped down and curled on the spacious bed; the motorhome's passenger's window was eye level. The little man behind the wheel was pale, wore blue pants and a yellow and grey sweater.

"Almost dressed like me," Josh mumbled into the stiff white bedsheet. His t-shirt was yellow and grey, but those distinctive seventies' lines...

Josh rolled to his back and reached for his phone. He had several text messages and a handful of missed calls—all the calls came from Claire's mother, none from the hospital. He dug into the front pocket of Claire's suitcase and found her phone charger. The zipper around the main compartment seemed to tease him: *Look in me, I'm hiding her lingerie, I'm hiding all the good stuff she saved for the other man.* Teeth clenched, jaw strained, Josh jerked the zipper around three rounded corners and flipped the lid. Plain underwear, plain undershirts and bras, yoga pants, slacks, blouses, the bag with her toiletries, everything went to the floor until all that remained was a lacy, silky, red teddy.

He swallowed. She'd never...never in the whole time...

The clothes returned to the suitcase and the zipper closed. Josh plugged in his phone and took Claire's bag of toiletries to the washroom. Working in that same state of mild shock from the day before, Josh stepped into the washroom and stripped. He removed towels and hung everything he'd worn over bars: steam cleaning. The shower ran and Josh sat and stared blankly at the running water until the room fell under a heavy fog, despite the effort of the small ceiling fan. The water temperature lowered and he stepped in.

Fingertips and toes gone to raisin, Josh came to and turned off the shower. Dried but not dressed—he hung the damp clothes in the open closet—and smelling of Crest Whitening and Secret antiperspirant, he went to his phone. No new messages.

"What the hell?" Josh spun and looked around. "Hello?"

The Winnebago's awning was open and the little man sat in a lawn chair. Next to him was a beer cooler, and a few inches from that was a hibachi grill, tiny hotdogs roasting. How the…? Where did…?

"Well, ain't that something?" The roof of the motorhome had been slipped out and stood on an arm as an awning, leaving the top wide open. Inside was the bench seat in the kitchen area, set on the table, revealing a storage compartment. The salesman at Cooper Collectables didn't even know about this, how cool was that? "But, who…?" He gave his head a little shake, lips pursed. The simple answer was obviously the right answer, a bed-turner came in and couldn't help themselves, had to play.

And how could he be mad? They'd revealed a secret.

He put everything away and put the man back behind the wheel. The toy returned to its box and he placed it on the desk. Somebody would come in to make the bed when he was gone.

Before he left, he spun Claire's cellphone beneath the index finger of his left hand, the little blue light at the top blinking, *pregnant* with message. He put it in his pocket.

"No change," the nurse said. This was a different woman, short and wearing the intrigue all over her face. "And she hasn't had any other male visitors."

"What?" Josh said, but knew, got it clear as a mountain stream.

"Some women from her conference, but no men." The woman's eyebrows disappeared behind her curled bangs.

Not thinking, no reason to do so, but doing so anyhow, he leaned in close and said, "I found lingerie in her suitcase. I've never seen her wear it."

The nurse curled and tilted her head while straightening her back. Her eyes wide and her mouth in a tight pucker. If an illiterate's audio dictionary existed with photo explanations, this expression would define the word SCANDALOUS.

Nothing better to do, Josh went to the theater in the mall. He thought maybe he'd see something horrific or at the very least, something thrilling. Nothing showing until four, so he went to the toy store and looked at all the plastic junk. By noon, he was back in his room with a large pizza and a plan to watch the very worst television had to offer.

"What in the hell?" The Winnebago Indian Motorhome by Tonka was back on his bed, out of the box. He set the pizza next to the TV and crouched to look at the man in the little bedroom, mounting a little woman, her legs spread in a V. Both the man and woman wore pants. "What in the hell?"

Someone was...the simplest answer...the same person who'd entered when he was in the shower had the toy at home, or parts of it anyway, and was filling out his accessories. He should be mad at the invasion upon his privacy and belongings, but how could he be?

The hibachi was back beneath the awning by the cooler, and Josh said, "Better hurry or those dogs'll burn." He then sat back and grabbed the TV remote, found the show *Relic Hunter* and settled in.

Josh awoke in the early evening from a pizza coma. The stink cloud of expelled gas seemed to eat the light and for a few moments, Josh had no idea of where he was. He leaned to his left and found the lamp switch. Halos blinked away, his eyes settled on the motorhome. The man and woman sat beneath the awning, next to the hibachi and cooler. A grey cat sat next to the woman.

This was too much. He lifted the landline receiver and dialed the desk.

"You tell whoever came into my room that it's not cool to screw around with my stuff."

"Excuse me?" It was a man minding the desk. "Sorry?"

"Someone came in my room and moved my things." Josh's grip on the phone was white knuckle tight.

"I'm sorry, sometimes housekeeping has to move items in order—"

"I know that! But tonight, tonight somebody came in and played with my...things!"

"Tonight?"

"Yeah, or maybe this afternoon. I was sleeping and they moved my toys!"

"Your toys?"

"What? Yeah, toys. What does it matter what?"

The person at the desk sighed audibly. "How long are you staying? I can put a note—"

"My wife is in the hospital," Josh said, letting his grip loosen and his head fall back onto a pillow.

"I'm sorry, sir."

"She's pregnant, but it isn't mine."

"Okay."

"She was going to see him sometime this week. I found her lingerie."

"Uh, that's not...what do you need me to...what room are you in and I'll make a note—"

Josh cradled the telephone. His pocket suddenly seemed on fire and he heard that voice, *he's calling, calling right now, now, now.* He grabbed Claire's phone and swiped past the lock screen. No incoming call, but there were dozens of missed calls. Aside from Claire's mother was a contact labelled Pharmacy. Pharmacy had called her fourteen times.

"Pharmacy?" It had to be fake. Josh lifted his face and looked at the motorhome. The barbeque had been packed away—*how? how!*—and the people and cat had retreated inside. The husband and wife in the bed, flat on their backs and the cat curled up on the driver's seat. "But." The cat was hard plastic, immoveable, and hadn't been curled. The thing sat upright before. Josh wiped his eyes and jaw, his guts began clenching and he hurried to the toilet. Claire's cellphone in his hands, elbows on his knees, ass on the toilet seat, he expelled something hot and awful, but not as hot and not as awful as the traded messages between Claire and Pharmacy.

"Mr. Dolan, visiting hours are over. There's been no change, come back tomorrow."

The nurse was a man this time, tall and muscular. Josh wondered if this was him. Somehow. He pulled Claire's phone from his pocket and dialed Pharmacy. It rang six times before reaching an automated mailbox.

The nurse was frowning at Josh. "So, come back tomorrow?" he said, making it both a question and a demand.

"You have your cellphone on you?" Josh said.

The nurse grabbed his pocket. The cellphone shape stuck out on the leg of the man's light blue scrubs. "Why?"

Josh shook, sneered and spun on his heels, made for the elevator.

Instead of heading back to the room, he returned to the theater. The latest of the *Fast & Furious* franchise was about to begin and he sat just in time. Usually, the movies dealt with high octane cars that nobody ever owned in the real world, but this one...The Rock was behind the wheel of an old, white with green accents, Winnebago motorhome.

"Hey baby, you get rid of that loser yet?" he said and raised his right eyebrow.

Claire came from the back in the red lingerie and purred, "Soon."

Josh squinted tight and put his hands over his ears. The end credits were rolling by the time he opened his eyes. He looked around the dim seating area. The sparse crowd made for the exits. He inhaled a deep popcorn and candy breath before rising to his feet and following the designated route.

With each step, the fog of shock drifted over him. At the snack counter, he bought a bag of Snickers Bites and a blue slush Fanta; in the parking lot, his car shifted into gear; in traffic, a left-turning cab driver flipped him off for running an orange; in the lobby of the hotel, a beautiful woman invited him for a drink at the bar while she rubbed her breasts on his arm; in the elevator, a man asked him if the hooker tried to get him too; in his room, he stood over the motorhome in the dark with Claire's cellphone in hand. He flipped the main light switch and was not surprised to see the woman in the bedroom and the man asleep on the bench behind the kitchen table. The cat was gone.

He clicked open the last message from Pharmacy and typed *I thought we were meeting?*

He set the phone on the nightstand and grabbed the comforter blanket from the bed he hadn't used and cocooned himself next to the Winnebago Indian Motorhome by Tonka, careful not to disturb the sleeping man and woman. For hours his eyes remained pinned, trying to catch movement in the lifeless toys, before he finally drifted off to sleep.

Josh blinked at the light overhead and rolled to his left. He picked up his phone to find more messages from Claire's mother. He then picked up Claire's phone to find the same, but also one from Pharmacy: *I'm so happy you're out of the hospital, can I tell people at the conference, we're all so worried.* Second message: *And baby if you're up for a visit I'm more than willing to oblige.* The third message was a picture of an average-sized, white, upward-hooking erection. Fourth message: *Baby?* Fifth message: *Claire?*

Josh typed, *How about tonight in my room?*

Pharmacy replied immediately: *I called the hospital when I didn't get a reply. I understand this looks bad but please respect our privacy and space.*

As if a sour taste suddenly invaded his entire face, Josh vibrated and twisted his head backwards to escape the sensation. His eyes fell on the motorhome. The man was on the kitchen bench, while in the bedroom, the woman stretched out, legs in a V as a new man pumped into her.

A knock landed on the door and a voice said, "Housekeeping?"

Josh tried to shout the woman away but couldn't form words—only his vowels were working. He slipped from the bed and unravelled the wrapped blanket. Across the stiff grey carpet, he crawled to the door, got to his knees as the housekeeper's key card opened the mechanical lock.

"Oh!" Josh wailed and flopped his body against the opening door.

"Sorry. Sorry. I'll come back in an hour. Sorry."

He remained there, gathering himself until her heard tiny metallic pinging and an even smaller squeak. As far as he could tell, nothing moved in the motorhome, but…he crawled back to the bed and looked through the windows—the canopy had been closed. The woman was in the back with two babies held to her chest. The other man sat behind the steering wheel; he wore a captain's hat and a matching white sailor's suit. The husband stood a foot away. He wore a ball cap and a rumpled suit, looking as if a localized storm had drenched him, in his hand was a small leather suitcase, the tail of a plaid shirt jutting from a seam. The wee expression on his wee face was of sorrow and loss as he stared back at the motorhome that was once his.

"She took it from him and gave it to someone else," Josh whined into his palms, pressed tight to his mouth. He couldn't let her do it, he couldn't.

No fog; his mind was clear. He got to the hospital, stepping past three nurses who recognized him from the gossip mill, and went into the room that his wife shared with three other patients. The curtain circled Claire's bed, so they'd checked off one step for him. He unplugged the heart monitor attached to her finger, silencing the beeps of her heartbeat. He then yanked the pillow out from behind her head.

Her eyes opened and her lips smacked. She blinked at him. "Josh? Why are you here?"

He faltered, pillow clutched in his hands. "I'm not letting you take anything away from me. Not one damned thing."

"It's already done," she whispered and smiled a mouth full of gold teeth. "And it feels good."

Fury roared inside. Outside, Josh exhaled heavily through his nose and pushed the pillow against his wife's sleeping face and kept tight a 300-count after the twitching muscles in her arms ceased their languid movements. He grabbed her hair and pulled her scalp forward to place the pillow behind her head. Not a word to anyone, he jetted from the hospital, jogged to his car, drove through the city, parked in the Radisson lot, and hurried up to his room, so focused that he saw nothing outside the narrow path he followed.

Claire's cellphone in hand, he typed *I HOPE YOU CAN SWIM!* and grabbed the man in the sailor suit from the Winnebago and charged to the bathroom. The man sank into the great abyss of hotel waterworks when Josh flushed the toilet.

"I hope you can swim!" he shouted and laughed. Licking his bottom lip, mouth open, eyes stretched wide, he ran back to the bed and wrenched the little babies from the woman's arms— they were really snug in there—and took them to the microwave. He tossed them in and put twenty minutes on the timer. "Gonna be a warm one!" He laughed harder, his chin pressed to the top of his chest in the universal maniac expression. He grabbed the woman and looked around the room. Back and forth, his head jerked until he saw what he needed. He unwrapped a water cup and wound the plastic over the woman's face. "This won't hurt, you're already dead." As he set the woman on the bed, plastic around her head like a mummy wrap, someone knocked on the door.

"Mr. Dolan, are you in there?" the voice was mannish, deep, and for some reason Josh thought it sounded as if it came from behind a moustache.

He quietly crossed the room and checked the peephole. Two cops, both big, fat men—sans moustaches—and a small man in a Radisson button-up stood in the hallway. Josh flipped the U-lock over the ball and backed away. His plan had no more steps, but this wasn't how it was supposed to end.

"Mr. Dolan? Open this door."

The electronic key card beeped and the door pushed open an inch and a half. "He's in there if that lock's engaged, right?" a voice said, heavy mannish, but not the same one who'd said Josh's surname.

Josh began breathing fast, faster.

"Josh Dolan, open this door! We need to talk to you about your wife!"

Faster, faster, hyperventilating.

"I can get it open," the man from the desk said, his voice was TV show host smooth. "Just take a card like this and close the door a smidge."

The door moved a hair and a card wiggled against the U part of the lock. The door closed more.

Josh stopped breathing, grabbed the Winnebago Indian Motorhome by Tonka and set it on the floor.

The arm of the U-lock swung, freeing the ball end.

Josh picked up the little man, tilted his head back, and dropped him down his throat. He fell to his hands and knees, pressing his face hard against the open roof of the motorhome as the door burst open.

The cops charged in, both had hands on their gun holsters. "Where is he?" one said, "Not in the bathroom," the other said, "Maybe under one of the beds?" the concierge said.

They checked everywhere and decided the U-lock must've engaged accidentally.

Shauna Amry grinned from ear-to-ear as she stood by the storage unit with the others picking up their winnings from the online police auction. She scored an amazing Winnebago Indian Motorhome by Tonka for twenty bucks, and if it was half as nice as the pictures suggested, she might just flip her lid. Her thirteen-year-old niece had recently gotten into retro toys—she had a four-foot dollhouse, a horse track, a few cars, a tractor, and the better part of a train set.

The door went up and the three officers began doling out seized prizes.

An hour after that, Josie Amry was bouncing on her heels, shouting, "O-M-G! O-M-G! It's amazing!" In her bedroom after supper, she plucked the little man from behind the wheel and a slip of paper fell onto the driveway she'd painted on the dollhouse platform. She picked it up and turned to let the light fall on it directly. *Help I'm stuck in here.* She scrunched her face and set the little sheet aside. "Weird."

Shauna came up to kiss Josie goodbye. "I'm so glad you like it."

"I love it," Josie said.

Josie's mother shouted from down the hall, "Bedtime!"

Shauna smiled, patted the girl's dark brown hair, and headed for the door. "Goodnight, sleep tight."

Josie finished, "Don't let the bedbugs bite."

The room was dark and the house was quiet as quiet got, which wasn't very quiet, not since he'd changed. Everything was loud, but he understood the types of loud and saw this as his best chance.

Josh Dolan climbed down the beveled leg of the table and sprinted from shadow to shadow. He grunted and sweated as he pulled and kicked his way up the dangling bit of duvet hanging from the little girl's bed. Leaning on his knees, back bent, he caught his breath. It was better that he hadn't gone to prison, but it had been a long six months trapped in the Winnebago, that toy.

Ready, he continued on, weaving over and under the girl's splayed and bent arms and up onto her pillow. "Sorry," he said and wiggled in between her lips.

Josie jerked upright, gagging as the little man that came with the motorhome travelled down, down, down. Her stomach clenched and she ached, hands pressed tight at her bellybutton. She moaned and rolled to the floor. She felt her body shifting, changing…shrinking, but then the pain shifted.

She began gagging anew.

Something was coming, something hard and painful.

She convulsed on three dry heaves before the little toy clanked plastically on the hardwood floor. It was a little brown girl—a tiny facsimile of the body Josh Dolan now occupied. He picked her up and started down the hall, stopping at the first open door. He found a light switch and spotted exactly what he sought. He—no, *she*—lifted the toilet seat and dropped the little girl toy in.

Josh-cum-Josie whispered, "Sorry. I hope you can swim."

Sepia Grass
Sam Hicks

My father was a drug dealer and I know that sounds bad, but it wasn't. It was nothing heavy, just a bit of cannabis resin and grass (he hated calling it weed). Money was tight when I was born and tighter still when Mum died, too young, a few years later, and after that, it became clear that Dad's part-time job wouldn't bring in enough to keep us. My father was a clever man, but he'd messed up his education and didn't exactly have first choice of lucrative careers, so in his hour of need, he turned to his one transferable skill—getting high—for help. It was drugs that paid for my school uniform, for holidays and birthday presents. It was drugs that saw us through, and we owed them thanks for that.

Dad wasn't stupid about it, though. He kept his job in the supermarket as cover and his clientele small, and he resisted the temptation to upscale. The universe had, he said, always found ways to stop him overreaching.

When I was six I ate a lump of resin that had rolled beneath the coffee table. Dad was very careful to keep his stock out of reach, but this runaway piece, like a chocolate in its shiny pink wrapper, managed to evade him. Knowing I probably wouldn't die, but that in all likelihood I'd be taken into care if he took me to the hospital, Dad chose instead to sit with me while I underwent hours of intense hallucinations, heightened, no doubt, by the plasticity of my unformed mind. Eventually I returned to earth, dazed but incredibly hungry, and in the aftermath, I'm told, consumed half a packet of Cocoa Pops, two bananas and most of a jar of pickles.

I have little recall of what I said or did during those drugged hours, only the one memory of Dad's big hand holding mine, and the little blue swallow tattoo between his first finger and thumb detaching and flying free. But in the following years I experienced what I believed were flashbacks to my childhood trauma. Visions would tumble into my mind in the last, liminal stages of sleep, visions that were as vivid and as strange as dreams, but marked apart from dream by a sure sense of remembering. In the first act, when the curtain rose, there would appear before my eyes a crazed batik, feathered streams of purples and reds and indigos and greens. Then teethed feelers and furred spikes rose, and trilobite curls, baroquely alien, self-propelling. A storm of parts raged then: compound eyes and rough mouth-hollows, a close pulse of primitive wings, and then the clawed and frantic movements of countless limbs, spurred and sharp like fractured arrows. And at the demented climax of all this, at the finale, I would step abruptly into a place where the light was speckled, brown, streaked. An oatmeal sky hung low over land that glowed in a light of amber-toned antiquity, a land which flowed and circled and sighed and lifted itself with the undulant sway of a billion faded blades of grass.

Dad had told me that "sepia grass" were the only words I said, again and again, throughout my pre-pubescent trip. I must have heard that word, *sepia*, somewhere, so that it surfaced as I tried to tell him something of the washy hues that colored my hallucinations. But I have no original to compare, and I don't know if my later half-waking visions truly mirrored what I thought I saw back then. I wonder if my six-year-old self could have so easily recovered from the same moments that, for me, always heralded awakening. That terrible shuddering of the air. The sudden shunt of pressure, immense and inescapable. The thing unseen, unheard, but felt.

The strange thing is, I felt only a calm acceptance during these hypnagogic states—an acceptance of what was and what was about to be—and it didn't occur to me to talk about them, about their striking imagery and atmosphere, no more than it would occur to anyone else to talk about the untranslatable chaos that plays out in their heads. And anyway, I was prone to strange and unreadable moods which troubled those around me, and it would have been reckless to feed the growing doubts about my mental health.

My dad was always solicitous of my welfare, barring the occasional mishap beyond his control. Perhaps he saw a certain mental instability in my bouts of uncommunicativeness, and maybe he even blamed the childhood accident for that, but whatever the motives, he always tried his best to shield me from the more worrying realities of our lives. I had a fair idea who Dad sold to—no one had that many friends visiting at night—

but he took great pains to conceal the workings of his illegal business, and I didn't know where he obtained his supplies nor where he stored them, nor how much money he brought in. But, despite the suspected fragility of my psyche, my tendency towards a kind of internal freezing, he wasn't hypocritical enough to stop me trying his wares when I became of age. Dad believed in the curative power of marijuana, a gift from the earth, and I can't say it ever (except once) gave me a bad experience, although, unlike him, I could take it or leave it. It used to give me a hazy feeling, which I liked but didn't crave.

Above all, Dad conducted his affairs with complete discretion, and so when one day, out of the blue, he seemed about to give away some vital information, I immediately suspected the worst.

"You'll never believe it," he said as he made a roll-up cigarette to round off his breakfast. "About my latest score."

I looked up from the book I was reading—I was in the middle of exams and the last ever term of school, a good student headed for a good university. His latest score? What was going on? Was he in trouble? Were our lives about to fall apart?

"Don't look so worried, Dan. It's its name, that's all. This new stuff I'm getting. Sepia grass, it's called. You know—like you kept saying when you were little and ate that hash. Remember that, how I've told you about it? *Sepia grass*, you kept saying." He did a little mime of what I suppose was meant to be the six-year-old me, goggle-eyed and pawing at the air. I didn't laugh.

"Tripping off your little head, you were, but I knew you'd come through OK. That stuff was pure. Mother marijuana doesn't hurt her friends, so long as you don't hurt her—haven't I always told you that? I always wondered, you know, where you'd picked up the word *sepia*. TV? At school? What do you think?"

I shrugged.

"Kids pick on up things, and you've always been a bright kid, but I mean, it isn't a six-year-old's word, is it? Weird coincidence though. Bloody weird."

It was more than weird, what Dad had just told me. I had predicted the future. Might it be that, after all, like him, I received messages from the universe?

"That's mad," I said. "What's it like?"

I should explain that Dad hadn't smoked grass since it started to be genetically engineered for extra strength. He had someone else test it for him—a sort of imperial food-taster—and so his verdict would be second-hand.

"Lenny says it's stellar, completely old school astral. He's arranging it all. Mind you, I've not heard from the sod since Wednesday, but you know what he's like. Come to think of it though, I'm the one relying on him, so I'm the fool."

"So is he your grass tester nowadays?" I *did* know what Lenny was like. I'd known him all my life. A gentle soul, like Dad, but the most unreliable person that anyone could hope to meet. And Dad had trusted him with money?

Dad blinked at me through the little square spectacles that magnified the eloquence of his eyes.

"State secret, that is," he said, and he lit his roll-up, stretched, and got up from the table.

"Will I be able to try it, then?" I wasn't hopeful, since I knew he wasn't keen on me smoking "modern grass."

"Well—and only because you invented it and everything—I'll keep some aside for after your last exam. Not before, no way. You know I don't like you smoking this engineered stuff. Too many psychoses in kids too young to even understand the word. Let me guinea pig it first, see if there's any freak-outs, then we'll see."

"*We'll see.*" Like you say to a child who's nagging to go the zoo.

Dad moved over to the sink to rinse his plate and at that moment, the glasses draining on the side vibrated gently, answering in their delicate way the deep juddering of a passing truck outside. Ours was an isolated house, a left-behind place at the edge of a stretch of dead manufacturing sites. Our neighbors were empty plots and shuttered buildings and we lived in hope of an offer from a keen-eyed housing developer, an offer we intended to grab with both hands. But this post-industrial road saw its fair share of traffic, serving as it did the recycling center which sat between our town and the next, and I was used to being powdered by the plumes of dirt these heavy vehicles churned up, or sprayed by their cold, muddy wakes. That morning, as I watched Dad tidying up the kitchen with his slow, almost loving, movements, it struck me, as it never had before, how inured we were to the deep bass growl of the passing trucks, so that we barely registered their presence. And wasn't the effect of the sound, the impression it gave of a great bulk and force about to bear down upon the house, an analogue of something else I knew? Of that shuddering immensity, the unseen and unheard vastness of my almost-dreams? Had my mind simply woven pieces of my everyday reality into a more fantastic version of itself?

The blinkers, you could say, were off. When I left for school, my thoughts flowed with clarity. Sepia grass was a commodity, a concrete fact, a coincidence, a name. The only message the universe was sending me was that I was blind to my own self-deception.

At the bus stop, the chill breeze cutting through the peninsula brought water to my eyes. I straightened from my slouch and stepped forward. From the elevated position of the road I was looking down upon the marsh, upon the gullies, the small black trees, the banks of reeds. I knew every inch of the peninsula, that jutting elbow of land which cradled both the bleak remains of a freshwater marsh, and the sad, scattered, and fascinating graveyards of a lost industrial past. There was a sound in the wind that morning, a high whispering, and there was a vaguely copper haze above the thin low shrubs and trees, and it also hung, but paler, barely there, amongst the shifting reeds. Of course—that's how my mind had made the field of sepia grass. It had its roots in this scene, in the shades of dormancy and desiccation that settled across the whole peninsula from the end of autumn until the early spring.

I looked back towards the town, certain, and almost grateful, that those bland lanes and avenues, at least, had inspired no part of my recurrent hallucinations. In the eighteen years since I was born, a minor village had become this sprawling place. It had gained apartments, townhouses, terraces, avenues and lanes, all competing for a view of the river, so dark, so dazzling. And as I looked back at my nearly-new town, I noticed a car, the only one about on that exceptionally quiet morning, and I watched it as it travelled down one street towards the corner of another, and I thought it was an old Ford Cortina, the kind I'd seen in one of Dad's old photographs of him and Mum. It had a wide, boxy snout and a snub rear end and its brown bodywork was spattered, and its windows were blind with the kind of grime you only see on long-abandoned rural wrecks. The car produced no sound, although with its jerky, stop-start movement, there should have been a choke, a backfire, a grind of failing gears. The muteness of its progress turned its presence strangely insubstantial, its being less, as it bumped around the corner and away.

That afternoon my mind slipped again. I've mentioned my strange moods, and I'll never know now if they were caused by my environment, by my reaction to it, or by some slow widening mental fissure that started long ago. An alien energy seemed to take charge at those times, dispensing with my unnecessary parts, those that lent my life its flavor, its personal dimensions. My surroundings buckled. My inside perished away. The sound of my name surprised me. My heartbeat lessened, and with it any sense of real existence. But I still functioned, remotely.

On the way home, a girl from school approached and told me about a Saturday party on the marsh and that she hoped I'd come, and I remembered, as I mumbled noncommittally, that she was in fact my best friend, Jude. Her dark, unsmiling face studied mine: "See how you feel tomorrow," she said.

And at home, Dad saw the signs and knew what to do. He withdrew.

I went to my room and sat at the window, eyes open to the evening's coming gloom. Opposite, an old concrete way ran off, to end, I knew, in an asphalt plot strewn with burst mattresses and household junk. My gaze became fixed upon this pointless place, and in the way that your reflection does if watched too long, its features soon began to rearrange themselves. The broken glass in the tussocked verges, the lumps of rain-bleached plastic, the cloven hands of the trees, the vivid curl of spring's first leaves; elements sprang forward, enlarged, while others retreated.

Buddleias and elders grew around the track, meeting overhead in a natural arch, and the shadowed spaces that lay between them flickered beneath the fixity of my gaze, and then, as if they had conjured something from themselves, a moving thing appeared. My window was closed, but its single-glaze gave little insulation and so it was remarkable that, as before, I heard nothing. As though it had been newly calved, the filthy car pitched forward in a rush, stopping only in time, and with a violent lurch, when it met the road and then, as seemed inevitable, it bumped across to stop before our house.

A moment passed before the driver's door opened, and a hand, as thin-fingered as my own, appeared and grabbed the upper seal. The whole person followed, clad in an old beige mackintosh, floor length, too large for height and build, and the face concealed, when seen from above, by the brim of a cowboy hat. This clumsily disguised figure flapped over to our door, and then back to the car, head down, hunched, ridiculously furtive, and instantly, the vehicle was reversing, turning, and jolting off towards the town. How strange, I thought, with little interest, that such an incongruous thing, that very same car, should turn up here. And what does it mean, I thought, as I watched my father run out into the road? Why is he looking around like that? In my abstracted state, these frantic actions seemed completely inexplicable.

My father went back inside, and I heard the door slam and a rustling, and then his footsteps on the stairs.

"Sorry, matey." His face appeared in the gap of my half-open bedroom door. "I know you need your peace and quiet. But did you just see someone?"

"An old car."

"Right, right. Did you see who was in it?" He spoke breathlessly, as if it were something terribly urgent.

"I couldn't see them. They had a hat."

"A hat? Right. Don't worry, don't worry. It's just, well, they posted the stuff through the door. What kind of dickhead does that? Never mind, never mind. I'll leave you to it."

I didn't move from the window until it was fully night, when I sought the familiar refuge of my bed. When I awoke, hours later, I could make out the bulks of my desk and wardrobe in the dark, and outside, through the open curtains, a starless patch of sky. I had awoken from a perfectly ordinary exam anxiety dream; the ink didn't flow, the paper kept disappearing, I had forgotten to wear clothes. I clicked my alarm clock. Three fifteen? Dad must have people in, because I could hear what sounded like voices. But why? He never had people round that late. I strained to listen, quietening my breath, and as if in answer to my efforts, the sounds became more precise. They had a rhythmic quality, a rise and fall. A hiss and click that swung near and then away. But was it voices I heard? There was a loud, startling crash; something heavy falling and smashing.

"Dad?" I called out and swung myself out of bed. The floor was soft, shivering. In the golden brown light that now filled the room, I saw that my feet were deep in a quivering, living growth of grass.

And then I awoke, for real, in dark silence.

"I'm fine," I told my father in the morning, but he looked at me as if I were possessed as I buzzed around the kitchen, wiping down, scrubbing the sink, sweeping.

"I've just got lots of energy this morning," I said.

"You're not on speed, are you?"

"God, Dad, no. It's just, how I was yesterday, I think... I think it won't happen again. I think I'm better."

"Why?"

"Just do."

I couldn't tell him that I'd worked it out. It was those stupid flashbacks, those visions I'd invented myself, that had been messing with me all these years. Now it was over. I'd beaten it, seen through it, neutralized its power. And that dream last night—nothing. Nothing like the ones of the past. Just a field, no psychedelic storm, no baleful presence.

I began to laugh, not madly, just a little, as I put the brooms and brushes away, and Dad came over and put his hand on my shoulder and said, "OK, but just calm down a bit for me, yeah?" And he gave me a nub of resin.

"Great! I'll take it to the party tonight," I said. I didn't even ask about the sepia grass. That whole thing was over.

And it made me briefly popular, that bit of hash, when I got to the marsh that night. There were already twenty or so there, and they'd set fire to an old mattress which they'd piled with wood, and they were drinking cheap wine and cider and smoking some really bad stuff. The scarlet flames flared up, and we dodged random bullets of red hot ash and wood. Jude was there and she had an old aerosol can which she threw into the flames and we all dashed back and whooped at the explosion. She came over to me, her eyes shining and strange, and handed me the last puffs of one of the joints I'd rolled.

We all kept moving round the fire and the other kids' faces slid in and out of the leaping light and shadows grew and ran away on the walls of the ruined building behind us. It was some kind of old warehouse made of corrugated iron, ferric blood seeping through the old paint. There were sealed and barred doors at its front and on its upper floor, and at the side, a smaller one, which a group of us had kicked through last summer. We'd pulled an old sofa in there and cleared a space.

I took a swig from the bottle Jude handed to me and I coughed and I looked up at the red sparks flying from the fire and cracking into the night. Someone shoved me drunkenly, and I staggered forward, suddenly dizzy, feeling my weight move sideways too much. I flung out my hands to steady myself, but met in the grass something that ruffled and swelled beneath my touch. I swayed upright. Was it alive? What was it? A bird? It bustled towards me, humped, faceless, distorted, and I backed away, startled by a piece of plastic which seemed to have come alive for one moment, in that hectic light.

I couldn't see Jude. I pushed past some boys I'd known for years, but not well, and wondered who the older men were they were talking to —who'd invited them? —and I went around to the side of the old warehouse, holding onto the wall.

There was a light at the far end of the long dark room, a yellow pool, and two people hunched together. In that cavernous place, so otherwise dark, there was no sense of where the walls or the ceiling started; the light was an island, a glowing desert camp. In the foreground, on the arm of the rescued sofa, a stump of candle guttered on a battered tin lid; a squalid sitting room stranded in outer space. Where was Jude?

"Come up here, Dan," someone said. Was it Lenny, up there? I moved towards the voice and the light, skirting plastic sacks and barrels, breathing the stench of grease and dirt and damp.

"We want to see you try this," someone else said. What was he doing up there, with Lenny? Did they know each other? But *was* it anyone I knew? The flickering light made puzzles of their faces, and I couldn't seem to concentrate. Their eyes were shadows, their expressions indefinite. I took the joint from one of them, wary, yet hoping that the stuff they were smoking so secretively, so far away from everyone else, was old school astral, stellar. That they'd bought it from my dad.

"Look at his face," a voice said.

Distended masses caved in upon the room. Magenta cups, drowned velvet swarms, crimson clutches. Overripeness split, releasing hammerheads of purple. Flesh cords and kaleidoscopes, spilled ink, marbled blood, crimson unfurling.

"I knew he'd get it straight away," I heard. "I'd say he's been here before, wouldn't you?"

Damask leaves. Verdigris, violently spiraling, and spidered claws hanging scarlet, and white enfolding sweet rot. The smoke steps, moving inwards.

"Perhaps he'll never go back though," the other one said. "Look at him."

"Christ, he's really lost."

I was staring at my hand, now so small, and held within another hand, much larger and with a blue swallow tattoo between the first finger and thumb. "Sepia grass," I said between breaths. "Sepia grass."

I awoke at the bus stop, propped awkwardly against the sloping bench and the toughened glass. I held my hand in front of my face to see how unsteady it was and saw its new translucent state, light shining across and through the thin, toad-colored skin. Behind it, wavering, lay the road, buff-colored, pebble-strewn, unsteadily held between the scrub and granite verges. Ahead, the river bled into the land and the land bled into it, at once liquid and solid, all awash with and part of the soft brown endless light.

I took it all in slowly, not believing.

My father thought he didn't have a choice when it came to the decisions he made in life. Guided by an ineffable power, he took the routes left open to him, and they took him where he was meant to be. The universe, he said, had always looked out for him, and it seems that the universe was looking out for me. That power, not a place but a force, had blocked off all my roads but one.

When I saw keys on the ground, I stooped and picked them up, and then I crossed to the open door of the old Ford Cortina. Inside, I put on the hat and then the coat I found there, and I let the door slam shut. I didn't know how to drive, but how hard could it be? I put the key in the ignition and set off.

Prisoner

T. M. Starnes

"Those damn wolves," Virginia mumbled, covering her ears with both hands, "Can't they just for once, just once, shut up!"

Virginia stared up at the round hole in the roof of her prison. The moonlight was bright tonight, calling the wolves to howl louder and closer than before.

The men who had taken her as she left an Edmonton coffee cafe hadn't been back in at least two weeks, maybe three, maybe more. They had brought her far out into the wilderness to a cabin. Behind the cabin, they dragged her down a slippery rough-hewn stone staircase to a deep, circular, stone-walled storage area with an opening to the sky. It might have been a smugglers' hideout. Or a dried well, or…or…or…Virginia had wracked her brain trying to imagine what this place was.

Ten steps wide.

Nine steps long.

At least several meters high to the round opening in the ceiling where the goddamned wolves' howls echoed down to her. Every single goddamned night.

After the three men had…

After they…

"Shut up!" she screamed. "Stop howling, you bastards!"

The men had left her a few days' worth of food and plastic water containers. They had shoved her in her prison behind a large medieval-looking wooden and iron door that they chained behind them, threatening to return for more "fun and games" in a day or so.

Virginia paced back and forth, trying to formulate how many days ago that had been.

The wolves continued howling.

She had tried to climb out. She had. Yes, she had. Over and over. Climbing. Climbing. Climbing. One hand over the other. Rock by rock. Bare feet. Fingers bleeding from the effort. Manicured nails worn down. She tried to wipe the slick moss off the stones with the tattered remains of her dress. Her bra. Her panties. Rub, rub, rub. Scrub, scrub, scrub.

Virginia tilted back her head and howled.

She giggled as the wolves increased their song.

"That meant *shut up*, you bastards!" she giggled, digging at a scar on her arm.

Less than a meter up the walls, the stones were just too slick, too close together, too packed, too damn tight, too slick, too moss-covered, to really do any type of sustained climbing.

As she paced, she slapped absent-mindedly at her unshaven, hairy legs.

She had been in this place long enough for her legs and private area to sprout a good patch of hair. Long enough for her smooth calves and thighs to be more than stubble and become soft and long.

She giggled thinking how Darren, her boyfriend, would comment on her hygiene now.

The wolves howled.

She slapped her hands against the stones.

"No one cares where you are!" She shouted at the wolves. "No one cares where your pups are! Or if you're horny! Or if you're telling others to keep out of your hunting grounds! No one cares!"

She stepped on something squishy and pounced on it.

The slug went down easy. Her gag reflex was long gone, her belly no longer rejecting any sort of nourishment.

The rats were no longer coming into her cell. Her nest. Her prison. Her home. Her hole. Her cave. Her retreat. Her dank, musty, crotch hole.

Virginia giggled as she moved her hands around the dirt floor for more slugs. Finding a snail, cracking it open, and devouring the small chewy creature.

At night, moisture collected on the walls and dripped down into the small, empty water container where she placed it at the base of a small drip, drop, drippity, droppity, splishity, splashity trickle.

Just enough to wet her throat. It gathered just enough. Her piss could barely come now. Not enough to drink anymore. Just enough. Just to wash her meal down. Just enough. Just.

Flies also were good. Mosquitos too. Attracted to her bowel movements where she chose to relieve herself until her bowel movements became rare. She had tried to eat her waste but that was not happening. No. Not happening. No. Tried it. No.

Why hadn't the men come back?

The wolves?

Virginia giggled, wiping her nose with a grime-covered hand.

That would serve them right. Serve them up. Munch. Munch. Crunch.

"Bastards!" she shouted to the world.

"Fucking bastards!" she repeated.

The wolves momentarily paused their song, then quickly resumed.

Virginia pulled at her hair and began her circular pacing.

How long does it take leg hair to grow? How long does it take *her* leg hair to grow? How much time had passed? How long does it take for people to notice you're gone? For your boyfriend to begin looking. Bosses to call you. Her parents to wonder where she was. Police to check videos. Cell tower records? Did they have her cell phone? Did they dump it? How long does a battery last? How long until you starve to death? How long to decompose? How long for slugs to eat you? How long before what you eat, eats you?

How long? How long? How long?

She had her period before the men...

She ran at the wooden door and slammed her forehead against the wood.

She screamed and clawed at the wood with her fingertips.

Screamed.

Screamed.

Screamed.

In the first few days, she had screamed her throat raw. A few days later, her voice came back. It left the day after. Then came back. Then left. She had her voice now. For now.

Virginia collapsed to the dirt floor and licked the blood from her fingers. Rubbed the wound from her head and licked the blood from it. She stood and licked the slime streaked wooden door of moisture; hers, and the dampness from the door. She pulled another splinter out of her tongue. This one was much bigger and easier to remove than the previous one from…yesterday? A week ago? Earlier tonight? A moment ago?

She pulled out one of her long black hairs and chewed it. Swallowed it after a few moments.

She sighed, listening to the wolves.

She slapped her forehead. Harder. Harder. Harder! HARDER!

She screamed.

The wolves sang to her.

She swayed to their music.

She moaned in time to their tune.

She plucked a piece of mold off the wall behind her and chewed slowly.

Darren would laugh at her. She hated salad. Salad sucks. She was a steak person.

"Bastards!" she screamed. "Shut up! Shut up!"

Darren would make them shut up. Darren would have shown those three assholes not to mess with her. She did as Darren told her. Fought back like Darren showed her. She did.

"Darren! Goddamn it, I did!" She sobbed without tears.

She had. She did. But they were three of them. Bigger than her. Two good-looking Italians and one Greek guy. Or two good-looking Greek guys and an Italian. Or three Middle Eastern men. Or two tanned men and a blond guy. Or three black men. Or two white guys and a black guy. No, a Latino man and his brothers. No, two guys from work and some other guy. No. it was…it was…it was two guys from the coffee café. It was…

She thumped the back of her head against the stones.

The wolves ceased for a moment.

She blinked and looked up at the moonlight in the shaft above.

The wolves began again.

Virginia rolled to her side and screamed.

She rolled onto her back and screamed one long scream up into the shaft until her breath gave out.

Quieter. Quieter. Quieter.

Darkness enveloped her.

Her cramping leg muscles startled her back awake.

She rubbed and rubbed, slapping the knots in both legs.

The pain made her scream again.

The moonlight was no longer so bright in the hole above. The morning was coming. Another day. Another song. Another howl. Another hurt. Another. . .something.

She froze, there was a sound nearby.

A rat?

A cat?

A bat?

A mouse?

She covered her mouth and suppressed a giggle in case it was more food.

Something was at the door.

She dug her fingers into her cramped, knotted legs and scooted her bare rear across the dirt to the other side of the hole.

The noise sounded soft.

Like padded feet.

Virginia could pee after all.

Something was listening at the door.

Without thinking, Virginia wiped her moisture against her lips, staring in the near darkness at the door.

Something sniffed.

Virginia's heart began sending her body into spasmodic convulsions with each beat.

Something joined whatever was at the door.

Something joined in with the sniffing.

Virginia pulled at her hair until a clump tore free and she grabbed another handful.

She was biting her lips; the pain was not even noticeable.

Something scratched at the base of the door.

Virginia held her breath.

Something began digging at the base of the door.

Two things began digging frantically at the door.

Virginia crawled on all fours toward the door and lay on her dirty belly, pressing her face to the ground.

The digging stopped and sniffing began.

On the other side of the door, Virginia remembered, or did she imagine, a rocky staircase down to the door. Not much wider than the door. Large enough for two big men, or one man and struggling woman, to stand side by side as they came down.

Sniffing continued and digging returned.

"Hello?" Virginia whispered.

The digging stopped.

"Hello, doggies," Virginia whispered.

There was no movement for a moment. The wolves continued howling above.

The digging began again, more frantic than before.

"Go," she whispered.

Her voice would make the two things, the doggies, the nice doggies, to pause in their digging, but then they would resume.

"Go away," she whispered.

The doggies did not.

"I said go away," she ordered quietly.

The bad doggies did not.

"Go," she said louder.

Bad doggies.

Very bad doggies.

She moved forward and slapped her hand against the door.

"Go away!" she yelled.

The doggies moved away from the door and sounded as if they climbed back up the stairs.

Virginia relaxed.

Then a growl came from the other side of the door and the very bad, naughty doggies began furiously excavating.

Virginia loudly growled back at them from the base of the door.

The doggies paused, then resumed.

Virginia spun around onto her back and began pounding the door with her feet.

Stomping, stomping, stomping the door as she screamed and shouted for the very bad doggies to go away.

The rough wood tore the soles of her bare feet and bled, dripping fine drops of blood to the base of the door and the dirt. Growls grew in volume as the digging now began at the door as well as the floor. A chain clanked occasionally.

Virginia pushed herself away from the door, rubbing her throbbing feet, licking the blood from her feet and palms.

She began howling, snarling, growling, at the very bad doggies.

She charged the door and pressed her nose to the small gap between the very bad doggies and the floor, inches from the doggie's nails.

She growled and snarled at them.

The doggies did not want to leave.

Virginia began digging on her side of the door with her hands as furiously as the doggies on the other side.

If they stopped to sniff, she bent to sniff and growl back.

After a few seconds, Virginia's digging fingers struck solid rock.

The very bad doggies were clawing rock, too.

Virginia laughed and crawled around her circular den, howling and growling, stopping at the door to lean down and bark at the doggies before she began crawling again. She found her discarded panties and stuck them in her mouth like a dog's toy, shaking her head back and forth, growling until finally spitting them out.

She crawled in a widening circle until she was bumping against the sides of the pit. The hole. The den. She found an old pile of her excrement and grabbed two handfuls of it. Then, kneel-walking across the circle to the door and shoved, smeared, pushed, plugged, the base of the door with the waste.

She barked loudly, laughing, as she scurried back to her excrement and grabbed another pile, repeating what she had done.

She growled with her face to the ground as she pushed the waste further against the rock and door base, inches from her nose.

The sniffing turned to huffs and the digging slowed.

Virginia howled against the door. Howled and laughed. Laughed and howled.

The digging stopped. Howls joined hers echoing down the overhead shaft. Padded feet slapped up the stone staircase to the world above.

Giggling, Virginia pushed herself away from the door to the middle of the cell and stood, laughing, howling, spinning in a circle until she passed out and dropped to the ground.

She dreamt of cool winds and placid seas.

Light woke her.

She glanced toward the hole in the ceiling. The moon was still up. Where had the light come from?

She turned her head toward the door, searching for the light.

Dim light flashed through the base of the doorway.

The men were back.

Virginia rolled slowly over onto her hands and knees and pushed back against the opposite wall from the door.

Human voices echoed down the staircase.

Virginia had nothing to use as a weapon. The plastic containers were useless.

"What's that smell?" a man said. "It smells like shit."

Virginia crouched and rocked back and forth on her feet and rear.

They were coming back.

They were coming back.

They were coming back.

Virginia suddenly realized her body had just enough slug and snail in her to give her one more involuntary, minor, bowel movement.

"I'm going down," a man told someone.

"Be careful," another warned. "It looks slick."

Virginia's mouth dropped open into a silent scream as she dug stinking, filth-covered fingers into her skinny, hairy, knees.

"Geez, it stinks even worse down here!" the descending man said. "I found the door! Wow, it looks like some animal's been trying to get in."

"Did something get in?" the other voice asked.

"Nah. But they must have shit all around it."

There was the sound of a chain moving against the door.

"The chain's still wrapped around the handle. It's warped, the door's warped, I'm gonna have to shove it open."

Virginia's mouth continued to remain open in her silent scream.

The door flew open and bright light blinded Virginia.

"Oh, dear God," the man said. "I need help! Get down here!"

Virginia launched herself, growling, at the light.

The man began screaming as she clawed at his face. She tried to bite two fingers off that he accidentally shoved into her mouth. She yanked his hand away from her mouth, shoved his head to the side and bit down into the thick flesh of his shoulder and neck.

The man screamed and shouted that she was biting him. She gnawed for a moment and saw more light at the top of the stairs.

The top of the stairs.

The way out.

She slammed the bleeding man's head against stone until he lifted his hands to protect his head and she crawled over him. She partly howled and ran/crawled up the stairs toward the light shining down into her face

"Oh, shit! Oh, shit!" The man at the top of the stairs turned and ran back up the way he came.

"What's happening?" a third man's voice shouted.

"Somebody's coming out! Holy shit! Get out of the way! Get the fuck out of the way!"

Virginia increased her pace while smelling fresh, cool, night air.

She burst out of the top of the stairs and through the hidden overgrowth concealing the staircase.

"Goddamn!" a man yelled. "Grab her! Get her!"

Virginia screamed, barking at the wolves around her.

She ran toward a gap between two of them. The wolves closed that gap and she ran for another.

"Get her! Boyd! Get her! She's coming toward you!"

"Shit! She's crazy!"

The wolves circled her. She spat at them, grabbing tufts of dirt, grass, and loose rock, and throwing them at their slowly closing circle.

A huge one came running from the direction of more lights.

"I've got her! I've got her! Let me get her!"

She ducked under the man's outstretched arms, but his fingers caught in her hair. She ripped the snagged hair out of her scalp and ran.

"Goddamnit, boys!" another voice shouted. "Grab her before she gets away!"

"I've got her!"

She avoided his grasp.

The wolf pack charged after her, circling her again.

Pain shot through her chest and left arm.

She tried to shrug it off.

She had to get away.

The pain toppled her to the ground.

The largest wolf grabbed her legs and shoved her onto her back.

The pain in her chest was blinding her, but she bit and punched at the wolf on top of her.

"Virginia! Virginia, baby!" the wolf shouted, "It's Darren, baby! It's Darren!"

Virginia gasped, clutching her shoulder and arm while feebly kicking with her feet.

"Virginia, baby, it's me!" Darren shouted. "We found you! We found you! It's going to be okay."

She couldn't catch her breath. The pain was killing her.

She screamed a weak scream, a primordial howl.

"Shit! She's having a heart attack!" a man behind Darren said, "Cindy! Get Cindy! Tell her we need the crash kit! Move!"

A man was shouting her name.

A man was shouting her name.

A man was shouting her name.

A man was pushing her down.

A man was crushing her chest.

A man was shoving her chest.

The wolves made their song.

The moon shown down through the bright shaft above her.

Where was Darren? Where was Dad? Mom?

A man shouted her name.

A man crushed her chest.

The wolves sang.

Turn a Blind Eye
Kelly Griffiths

One ant may be tolerated, two, three.
But they tell their scores of friends with that scent trail thing they do, and
you've got manifest destiny on your hands.

Some idiot left a half-eaten baloney sandwich on the counter. Fair Pharm's senior pharmacist was not doing the Mexican Stomping Dance but was disposing of apocalyptic numbers of ants. Sam slammed the fleshy part of his palm down, then wiped the writhing bits into the trash can and pounded some more, repeating the process until only a few stragglers remained. These he pressed with his thumb. They stuck, so he could push-push-push…push-push-push…and then flick the lot of them into the trash.

As he did so, he cursed his newest assistant. The twenty-something tree-hugger's idea of *professional* consisted of sweeping his unruly, effeminate locks into a man-bun. There was no doubt it was Ice who left the sandwich. For over twenty years, Sam had been putting up with the brainlessness of his assistants *and* customers. Pharmacy customers were stupid. Even stupider than Ice, which was saying something.

How can you get a college degree and not foresee the consequences of leaving an unwrapped baloney sandwich on the counter overnight?

Did he need to post a sign? *Please Do Not Leave Unwrapped Food on the Counter.*

Sam's favorite moron-proofing sign came from the Caribbean, where things were obviously a little more loosey-goosey. *Please Do Not Indiscriminately Relieve Yourself in This Area.* That was rich. Sam had a picture taken of himself in front of it while he made as if to unzip his fly.

Sam understood why Styrofoam cups had warnings. It was for morons like Ice. Just because one ordered a hot coffee didn't mean a warning wasn't in order. His customers needed warnings. Warning: gravity in effect. Don't step off bridge. Warning: don't cross an interstate at dusk wearing grey. Warning: the oral contraceptive should be taken orally.

That actually happened.

One of his customers came to him pregnant and pissed as hell. She shook the contraceptives in his face and demanded a refund. After ranging around in her purse, she brandished a white stick and waved that too, nearly smacked him with it. It had two lines and smelled faintly of urine.

Sam tried to reason with her. "No method of birth control is a hundred percent effective, but if you're taking them at the same time every day—"

She interrupted. "—and it scratches when we have sex. It doesn't even dissolve right."

Sam was not good at keeping a straight face.

He was pretty sure she brought the lawsuit against Fair Pharm on the basis of his thigh-slapping, snorty laughter. Pregnancy had little to do with it. But she found a lawyer and sued for pharmacist negligence: inadequate patient instruction on the use of oral contraceptives. Oral. By mouth, stupid.

Stupid people, while annoying, weren't Sam's thorniest challenge. Addicts who needed a fix and whose nerves had been commandeered by withdrawal tremors—they weren't kidding around.

Just last week, Sam faced the black maw of a Smith & Wesson, shaking in time with the jonesing hand training it on him. It was not acceptable that Sam "couldn't confirm" the prescription, code for *we-both-know-you're-a-junkie*. While Sam was held at gunpoint, Ice had cowered in the back, supposedly deaf to the commotion. Ice didn't have what it took to be a pharmacist. He wasn't even a suitable lackey. Had Ice been able to perform his job with even a modicum of precision, Sam might indulge in a good mood now and again.

The explosion had been Ice's fault too, either directly or indirectly, because he never put anything away. Exhibit A: Baloney Sandwich.

The day of the explosion, Sam happened to be in one of his rages. Entirely justified. Even the Almighty got ticked off now and again, and Sam was feeling Sodom-and-Gomorrah over not being able to find a prescription because college-educated pharmacy assistants didn't know the alphabet. While Mrs. White sighed and shifted her weight in the pick-up window, Sam barged around, slamming drawers and tidying as he searched.

Mrs. White heckled him and stomped off, threatening to be back soon. Sam could just fill a new order, but the point was, he shouldn't have to. Ice had filled it. And filed it. Just not in the *W's*. Maybe it was in the *B* section. Or in the *A* section. Both appropriate to describe Mrs. White. Or even—Sam was rifling through the *C's*, the word for the female anatomy playing on his lips, when his eye fell on the agate mortar and pestle, a gift from his late wife, Margot. It wasn't in its usual spot above the sign that read *Sam Reeves, Pharmacist on Duty*. Someone left it on the pick-up counter beside the hand sanitizer. A $500 piece of equipment, just left there.

"What? Am I your mother?" He swiped the mortar. The pestle inside swiveled, discharging a sharp crackle, and thunder and white light ran him down. The floor and he were instant lovers and the agate mortar and pestle was history, some of it in Sam's eyes.

Blinking was hell.

Ice materialized and called 911, too slowly. Sam lay on the floor grinding mortar shards further into his cornea.

"Stop rubbing. You'll make it worse." Ice tried to pry Sam's palms from his eyes, but he writhed and kicked and—as a last resort—spit in Ice's general direction.

Ice backed off.

Sam and Ice had never gotten along. Ice was actually born Samuel Kelvin Stocker, but Fair Pharm already had a Sam, and there wasn't room for two. Ice's face was paralyzed in a condescending, yet somehow vacant mask, no matter what he said or how he said it. Sam dubbed him *Ice* on the first day; it took less than an hour. He meant it to be an insult, even had the name embroidered on all Ice's lab coats, but it backfired. Women were attracted to Ice's cool expression. Their comments were along the lines of: *Stoics. Anything could be under there.* Sam knew there was nothing under there.

"Should we hold his arms down?" Ice asked.

"Touch me and I'll kill you." Sam addressed Ice and the do-gooder to whom he spoke.

At that, she stifled a giggle. Ice whispered something Sam couldn't make out, and the woman laughed again. Ice was flirting. Sam was blind and his brains were on fire and Ice was flirting.

"Ice, I messed my pants. Do you think you could wipe my ass before the squad comes?"

The woman gasped.

"He's kidding." Ice didn't even sniff.

"Who the hell are you?" Sam asked. She sounded too young to be Mrs. White.

"Name's Mike. You should stop rubbing your eyes, dude."

Sam choked on his saliva.

The squad came and manhandled him into a gurney and leather cuffs so he'd stop rubbing. A heartless medic pried his eyes and set off a bevy of fireworks in his skull. At the hospital, it took a fantod punctuated with lawsuit threats for the intake nurses to give Sam a shot of morphine. A white lie about his weight got him an extra-large dose from the idiot nurse. It would take one and a half Sams to be the weight he gave. As Sam fell into a morphine slumber, he wondered if she'd be fired for being stupid. He doubted it.

The Fair Pharm exec who visited the next day brought a fruit basket. Sam couldn't see it. He had to trust him. *Trust* a Fair Pharm executive. Fat chance.

Had the nitro been anything more than a trace, said the exec, Sam would have had a tombstone but no casket. They would have had to find his DNA in dirt samples out of the bottom of the crater twenty feet below Fair Pharm.

"With luck like that, you should play the lottery. Or maybe not. Can't figure out if you're lucky or unlucky." The exec laughed heartily over Sam's near annihilation. Then he turned serious and asked a string of guilt-inducing questions. Did Sam keep the medical nitro locked? Did he lend out the key? Did he wash his hands after dispensing? Before? Was he handling the pestle roughly?

"Yes."

Why?"

"Because nobody puts back their shit. I'm a glorified den mother."

"Hmmm." The exec scribbled something. "Your assistant, Ice, stated you were in one of your—moods, was how he phrased it. Is that true?"

"Ice couldn't slap tomatoes on burgers."

"So...true, then."

Sam shot him the bird with both hands. The mummy tape wrapping his eyes prevented him from seeing the exec's reaction, but he heard an offended exhalation.

"Sorry." Sam said. "The morphine. Not myself."

Sam's loyalty to Fair Pharm was what saved his job. In the ER, he had refused to say how he got injured, which meant Fair Pharm wouldn't face the wrath of OSHA or a worker's compensation lawsuit. Once the company realized it was in the clear, the questions stopped. A large planter with smiley balloons arrived. Sam couldn't see it, but the nurses told him it was lovely. He decided to make it a gift for Margot.

Hopefully, Sam's eyes would heal before Sunday. That was his day to visit Margot's grave. Maybe she'd be happy with the planter. Likely not, though. Margot was a tough sell on just about everything. Sam would purse his lips and keep his hands in his pockets until Margot was done. Her tirades were usually about things like Sam neglecting to fold his underwear or the weedy condition of the flower boxes. Had he no pride?

Margot's grave had no headstone, just a wreath and the flowers Sam brought. The groundskeeper left a body-sized hill of earth and rocks. Sam complained, but the keeper said it had to be that way until the ground settled. Then it would be scraped flush and soft grass planted. That was five months ago he said that.

On the morning of the explosion, Sam had gone to visit her. She was up-in-arms about a few wrinkles in Sam's khakis. She didn't understand. Sam had never ironed before. He didn't even know where the iron *was*. So he kicked Margot's mound.

Just a little, but when he looked around, the groundskeeper was watching.

That made it easy to tell him off about not leveling the dirt.

Sam's eyes did heal enough for him to return to work. He puttered around the pharmacy best he could on 20/200. When he got close enough to actually read the name on the wall, he almost lost his shit.

Samuel Kelvin Stocker, Pharmacist on Duty.

Ice? Ice was the pharmacist? *Sam* was the assistant?

What a sucker punch.

What fuckery.

Sam bungled around, knocking over vials and kicking chair legs. His semi-blindness turned customers into multi-colored blobs. The business end of an addict's gun barely made Sam blink. Only after the man stomped out, bereft of Xanax, and Ice told Sam in a quivery voice how chill he was about staring down a gun, did Sam realize there *was* a gun. He thought it a wallet.

As the blobs began to crystalize, Sam knew something was off. It began with Mrs. White. Snarky and wrinkled as ever, she also had a set of pointy, yellow teeth. The top row overhung her lip. Green snot dripped from one of her nostrils, not the yellow-green sort that indicated infection. Nuclear green. Sam could hardly speak to her without grimacing. He kept wiping his own nose to hint her to do likewise. She didn't. She just got angrier and her teeth got pointier, and the neon rivulet squirmed down her neck and got lost in her wool sweater. All the while, Mrs. White went on about how Sam got his just deserts, and she hoped things would run more smoothly around Fair Pharm from now on.

From *now* on?

Sam asked Ice how Mrs. White looked to him.

She'd been her crotchety self while Sam was in the hospital, Ice said.

Her teeth. Had Ice noticed anything odd about them?

No, Ice couldn't say he had.

A person-with-a-substance-dependency (not *addict*, and no way *junkie*—Sam got sensitivity coaching) entered the pharmacy. The clerk flagged the prescription as bogus and called Sam over. As head pharmacist, denying the prescription and/or calling the police fell to Ice, but Ice was (of course) nowhere to be found. At first glance, the customer looked almost pretty, as in back-of-a-Harley-don't-fuck-with-me pretty, but when Sam approached, her eyes became watery swirls of blue and green, like the spinning wheels in Vegas.

"What the hell's the matter with him?" Harley girl asked the person in line behind her. She meant Sam. When Harley turned, the man behind her would see her eyes. Sam waited for the stunned reaction. None came. The man just shook his head.

Sam had to get it together. He did his best to be firm and coherent while those swirling eyes regarded him. A trail of saliva breeched her painted lips and slithered down her chin. Drips plopped on the counter. She slammed her hands on it and left in a huff. And without a prescription for 75 mg Oxycodone tablets (which only came in denominations of ten).

Even Ice began to take on fearsome qualities. His hair, always unkempt, was in the direst need of brushing, his angled brown locks menaced Sam, especially the beard. Sam internally referred to Ice as Duck Dynasty. It was oh-so-funny until the beard locks transmogrified into little brown arms with tiny hands that groped Sam as they worked side-by-side. No one else could see the hands because of the counter. Sam inched away or pretended to need something across the store. He'd ask someone to go get something from Ice, just to see if they would scream. No one did.

The trial date for Stupid Pregnant Girl finally came. Sam wore his best suit, the one he wore for Margot's funeral. He even ironed his shirt, but not very well. The judge had a Jesus-like aura and a kindly face, though he spoke sternly. The Fair Pharm lawyer had scales and an alligator tooth. Sam did his best not to shrink back or scream. Stupid Pregnant Girl's enormous buck teeth made her look eight years old, though Sam knew her to be twenty-seven. People everywhere were…*mutilated* was how Sam described it, but only to himself. The bailiff had devil horns protruding from his bald head. It was absurd, his whalesque paunch and sidearm and shiny black shoes. Sam couldn't stifle his gasp when the bailiff turned, and a shiny black arrowhead tail writhed along the floor behind him.

The judge asked if Sam was okay. A crown of thorns materialized on the judge's head.

Sam rubbed his eyes. Still there.

Somehow, Sam made it through the trial. Stupid Pregnant Girl was awarded an obscene settlement, and new protocol for prescription pick-up would be enacted. Something along the lines of Styrofoam cups. *Caution: Contents Hot.*

Take the oral medication by putting it into your mouth.

Sam shuffled out of the courthouse and entered the first bar he found. Sherriff Street, it was called. Fetid beer assaulted his nose, but he pushed through and asked for a vodka martini with Balkan.

"Must've been some day," said the bartender. "We don't carry anything that strong. How about Grey Goose? No upcharge." His eyes were rather like an owl's, and his belly was a stainless-steel beer keg whose scuffs and dents said it had seen better days.

Sam threw it back and ordered another.

The sixth one was the charm. He could no longer see straight.

He called an Uber, but the driver was a spider. Two of the eight hairy legs kept creeping toward the back seat. Sam swatted them away. Each time, the mustached driver frowned into his rearview mirror. He suddenly stopped the car and told Sam to get out, so he stumbled the rest of the way to Margot's, which, thankfully, was only a mile or so.

There, things got worse.

Margot's grave was a yawing hole. Certain there'd be an open coffin in the bottom, Sam crawled toward it and peered over the edge.

Empty.

He stumbled to the groundskeeper's hut, but the keeper wasn't around.

In no mood for freaks or spiders or Jesus-judges, Sam lay down at the edge of the hole and—after picking out the rocks and shale—fell asleep with his head on the pile of dirt.

"Sam." The familiar voice woke him.

It was dark. Sam felt around for his bed, but all he touched was prickly grass and knobby dirt. Cicadas played their eerie songs from the few trees scattered around. Margot called his name again, this time with more annoyance. She told him to wake up already.

"Margot?" Sam rubbed his eyes, but it was like being in muddy water, in the dark.

Something cool and slimy squirmed over his neck. He yelped and shot up to a crouching position, hands waving back and forth like radar.

"Sam!" Strong hands gripped his shoulders, and the sting of a slap sent his head sharply to the left. "Look at me."

It was Margot.

But not.

And horrible.

One of her eyes hung from the optic nerve. Little white worms dotted her face and writhed in her tangled hair. Her cracked lips seeped yellow pus, and her skin was marbled in the colors of death: blue and yellow and black.

Sam threw up an arm to shield himself. "You're what I've been talking to, all this time?"

"You were careless with the mortar."

"Somebody left nitroglycerin in it. It wasn't my fault."

"It's never your fault, is it Sam?"

Margot was a cry-wolf sort of woman, full of drama, always something wrong. So that day, when she cried out from the bedroom she couldn't feel her left arm, Sam told her he'd be right there. He meant *after* he finished the chapter. Her second and third calls sounded theatrical, and Sam was not down for playing nursemaid to Margot's hypochondria. When she stopped calling, he figured she fell asleep and congratulated himself on putting up healthy boundaries.

The squad asked what happened, and Sam told them he'd found her that way, skipping the part about her numerous requests for assistance. She'd been trying for the cell phone on the end table, judging by where she was found on the floor. Didn't Sam hear anything? they asked.

No. He was asleep in his recliner.

All the times he visited her and she never brought it up before. Sam figured it was water under the bridge.

"Whatever you do, Sam, don't look in a mirror."

That was all she said. Then she crawled back in the hole and with grimy hands and broken fingernails, pulled the dirt back over her in the body-shaped pile.

Sam hadn't paid himself much mind since he began seeing alterations in everybody else. Shaving was a focus on his stubble. Combing was a focus on his hair. Teeth, on teeth. He'd not actually looked at himself. Not once.

At home, Sam put off looking in the mirror for exactly five minutes. But he had to know. Margot knew he'd look. She *wanted* him to. Would he have swirly eyes? Spiked teeth? Devil horns? Would he look like a baby? Like Stupid Pregnancy Girl?

He slunk into the bathroom but left the light off. After a few deep, cleansing breaths, he flipped the light switch...

There he was.

In half a second, he plunged the room back into darkness.

Sam startled so hard he flipped and fell, apparently out of a bed and onto a tile floor. A white-hot pain in the top of his hand and the crash told him he'd toppled his IV. Everything was black. Totally and utterly black. Sam waved his hand in his face and accidentally smacked himself. The floor was cold and a little gritty. He called for help, relieved at the squeak of rubber soles approaching.

They put him back and spoke soothing words.

A doctor came. Sam felt a squeeze on his arm. "I have some hard news."

"Couldn't be worse than what I just went through."

"I'm sorry?"

Sam waved his question away.

The doctor cleared his throat. "Sam, the accident caused…" He explained corneal lacerations and shattered lenses in extreme minutiae, and Sam found himself losing patience.

"Can't you just spit it out? I'm not following."

The doctor sighed. "I don't know how to put this gently…You're blind. No restorative options. A social worker's coming this afternoon to talk you through your transition strategy." The doctor blithered on about living a rich and fulfilling life, learning braille, support groups blah blah—

"—Wait. I'm blind? Forever?"

"I'm afraid so."

"Nothing else?"

The doctor didn't say anything.

"Doctor?"

"Sorry. I should know better. I was shaking my head. No. Nothing."

Sam exhaled. "That's not so bad."

The doctor patted Sam's arm. "I wish everybody took hard news like you, Sam. Most patients won't accept the truth."

Sam choked out a joyless laugh then sank into his pillow and stared sightlessly ahead. His other senses were already adapting. The steady beep of his pulse monitor, the citrus smell of a fruit basket, the buzz of nurses at their station in the hall, the traffic outside. The sun must be out, for a shaft of warmth caressed his legs.

Then, beneath those sounds Sam heard another. It was far away, but not far enough. A sly cascade of dirt and stones. He could hear her, coming.

Margot.

Falling Asleep in the Rain
Robert P. Ottone

Clay Whitley stared out the window of his empty car of the Metro North Railroad as he checked his Fitbit and noted with amusement that even at nine at night, the dark woods and mountains looked beautiful. They seemed to rush by, dark teeth chewing into the navy blue-colored sky, the occasional bit of light pollution highlighting the separation between the trees and the sky. One of the conductors of the train walked down the aisle and checked on him. "Sir, our next stop is Kirkbride's Bluff." Looking up, Clay smiled and thanked him. He must've missed the announcement, and when he looked around the car, he realized how alone he was.

As the train came to a stop, Clay noted the mist that had begun to accumulate on his window. He rose, grabbed his briefcase (which was empty except for his pills, an apple, banana, and flask of whiskey), and exited the train, standing on the platform. He looked around and waited for anyone else to step off, and when the doors closed and Clay saw how alone he was, in the darkness, on the platform, a ping of anxiety struck him.

Clay always felt lonely, even when surrounded by hundreds, sometimes thousands of people. He never married. Never sired children. Maybe that's why he found himself on the train to Kirkbride's Bluff. He had been working late; rather, he had been sitting at his desk staring at his computer for hours until he realized it had *gotten* late, and instead of catching his usual Long Island Railroad train back home to Long Island, decided it was time to head *home*. His real home. Where he grew up. He realized that this had more to do with the whispers than his own desire to go anywhere but to his bed, but here he was. On the train to Kirkbride's Bluff. His childhood town. Where someone whispered and beckoned to him in the night.

In his posh upper-middle class suburb, or at work, he was never more than twenty feet from another person. He knew this because he had become oddly obsessed with the notion one night when he couldn't sleep and stood in his pajamas between his home and his neighbor's and realized that a mere twenty feet away was their master bedroom. He never spoke to his neighbors. Not because he wasn't friendly, but because they didn't speak any English and always just smiled and waved, saying something in Chinese to him when they met eyes. He always waved back and wondered what they did for a living.

It was around this time that Clay began hearing the voices. At first, he believed them to be thoughts. Simple concepts that would slip into his head, telling him to do normal, everyday things that he most likely would find himself doing day to day anyway. *Run the dishwasher. Brush your teeth. Wear the bergamot cologne. Call your mother.* Small things to which he believed he was the originator, but over time, the whispers became more abstract. They had sounded like someone speaking Russian, but with a mouth full of mashed potatoes. They began to take the form of unknown words, foreign terminology, unintelligible and confusing, but repetitive. Eventually, they took on familiar shape and sound.

Board the train. Return home. Kirkbride's Bluff.

The most ominous of all: *I'll be waiting.*

Clay walked down the steps of the platform and looked around for a cab. No such luck. He took his phone out and pulled up Uber, but again, there were no drivers in his vicinity. The nearest would be an hour wait time, as they were coming from Resting Hollow and currently had a fare.

"Jesus," he said under his breath and tucked the phone away. The misty rain didn't bother him much, and he stood under a portico, planning his next move. He decided to head deeper into Kirkbride's Bluff and walk around town. He figured it wouldn't be a bad idea to get his steps in, and when he stepped out from under the portico, he heard the whispers, seemingly beckoning him into the town. He nodded, acknowledging them, which is something he had been doing more of, and walked toward the town, the small shops and buildings in the distance easily visible.

After a while, he found his feet starting to ache, and when he checked his Fitbit again, somehow, he had walked another eight thousand steps. Nearly five miles, and yet, he wasn't near his hometown. *That can't be possible. The train station was always just outside of town. A mile at most.*

"How the hell—?" he said aloud, confused by the number now glowing on his wrist.

The rain had remained misty, and while his suit was flecked with tiny beads of condensation, he didn't feel wet otherwise. The chill in the air remained, and he walked down the sidewalk, looking at the various storefronts and businesses he frequented in his youth. He walked past GJ's Dugout, an old baseball card and collectible store he used to frequent with his parents, where they'd buy him two packs of cards per visit. He found himself disappointed after tearing into the packs and the only New York players he ever seemed to get were guys on the useless Mets, a team he grew up despising because they were "losers," and he didn't like losers.

The baseball card shop was boarded up, the sign long-faded. Clay couldn't remember the last time he ventured into the store and wondered how long it had been since the doors closed for good. Many of the stores in the area seemed vacant, their signs either removed entirely or faded, some beyond recognition. There was the pizza joint, Renzo's, across the street from the other pizza place, Donato's. Donato's was his preferred spot, but his friends all liked Renzo's, and this had been the first indication that Clay was truly alone in the world: as a kid, he and his friends divided over pizza.

Both restaurants were now gone, and Clay crossed the street to where Donato's had been and peered inside. In the dark, he could barely make out the counter where he would order his meatball slices and orange soda. The yellow glow of the streetlight above him helped him get a view of the tables he usually found himself at, those thick Formica classics from the 1980's.

It was at Donato's that Clay first saw the boy. Well, not the *first* time, but it was during a moment of childhood laziness that Clay found himself in Donato's, playing *Street Fighter 2* in the corner when a kid who moved to town a few years earlier walked in. Clay found himself not paying attention to the game and instead, noting every movement the boy was making. He couldn't remember his name, but his every movement drew Clay's attention.

Clay had never paid that much attention to another guy before. Girls, sure, but not a boy. At first, Clay was confused, and a little angry to be so focused on this kid waiting for his pizza at the counter, hands lazily in his pockets, bobbing his head to the pop music on the restaurant's speaker system. When the boy noticed Clay staring at him, he turned and gave a light wave.

"Hey," he said. The boy's eyes caught the light and seemed almost flecked with gold-orange light.

"Hey," Clay said back. Clay remembered the nervousness in their first words to each other. Vicious, unbridled anxiety that only a teenager could know or understand. The kind of anxiety that fades with age and experience.

It looked like the place hadn't changed from Clay's memory; at least, until the day the doors closed forever. He wondered where the owner was. He was an older guy, even when Clay was a kid, so it's possible he just passed away. The thought made Clay feel uneasy. It seemed as though when he left for college, the entire town just closed up shop for good. His parents never talked about Kirkbride's Bluff, and Clay didn't have any other family members in town, so, once he left for school, his parents moved into the city, and that was that.

The whispering slipped into his ears again, and Clay turned to look across the street, past Renzo's, and down the alleyway next to the lesser of the two pizza joints. Checking before he crossed the street, Clay chuckled to himself, thinking how strange it was that Main Street was this empty. There was seemingly no one else around. Only the wind, the misting rain, the yellow beams of light from the streetlights, and him. There weren't even any stray cats, dogs, or even any birds. It was as if Clay stepped into another world completely, one that time had left behind and progress and growth had disregarded.

Clay's therapist prescribed him some medication for his nerves, because when the words became unintelligible, he mentioned them to his shrink. He didn't quite know what else to do. He didn't feel like he was going crazy, and yet, he was hearing voices, unknown, distant, in the dark. Clay fumbled with his briefcase and grabbed the pill bottle. He twisted the top off and popped one into his mouth, swallowing it dry.

He walked toward the alley, the whispers sounding clearer. He looked into the darkness, bracing himself on a chain link fence. "Hello?" he called, not expecting an answer. There was a level of panic in his chest that he hoped the anxiety medication would snuff out, but hadn't yet. The familiar pins and needles of nervousness washed over his arms, up his shoulders and to his neck, and he waited, motionless, for any sign of movement or sound.

He was met with the cold, empty solitude of Kirkbride's Bluff. Where only whispers seemed to live.

As he stared down the alley, he heard movement. *Impossible*, he thought, searching for his cell phone. He produced it from his suit jacket breast pocket, turned the flashlight on and slid it into the pocket usually reserved for a handkerchief, the top of the phone peeking outward and the light beaming down the alley about eight feet in front of him.

He moved slowly, one hand braced against the brick and cement wall of the pizza joint, and watched his step, moving past overturned garbage cans, their contents spilled out, rotting in the night. Ancient pizza boxes, long-stained with grease and cheese that was more plastic than dairy, mounds of brown and slick black disgust in smaller piles, which he avoided, lest he ruin his light brown nubuck Johnston & Murphy shoes. The smell found its way into his nostrils and made him gag.

He coughed lightly, and pinched his nose, noticing the light suddenly providing more than just a view of rotting garbage and cement alley. What looked like a foot, as though interpreted through a Francis Bacon hellscape, was lit up by his phone. "Hello?"

The "foot" twitched and scurried out of the light, and Clay recoiled quickly. He remained in place, his eyes scanning around, the light cast in various directions. Finally, pressed against the fence at the end of the alley, after a few cautious steps forward, was the figure Clay's light had scared away. Or, at least, Clay imagined the light scared it. He couldn't imagine what this thing was. Once close enough, he saw it was completely nude, its back slick with the misty rain, which was starting to increase in intensity. A low mist hung around Clay's ankles, and he took two cautious steps toward the figure, which writhed, huddled in the corner.

Two clubbed feet, more like hooves, connected to two sinewy legs, all bone, muscle and tendon, no fat anywhere on the creature. *Creature* was the only word that worked, as Clay couldn't tell if the thing was human or not, though it vaguely resembled a person, with legs, a backside, and a muscular, tight back. When the creature turned, slowly, to face Clay and his light, he saw its face, which was almost entirely a mouth with two brightly-colored eyes like sunlight, eyes Clay vaguely recalled seeing in reality only once before, but hadn't since...*since*...

The figure's arms were thin, almost skeletal, and stretched toward him. The only noise the creature made was an exhalation, a sigh, extended, low, as though the air was being squeezed from its body with every movement. A slight wheeze, coming from God-knows-where, high-pitched, and unsettling. Clay stepped away from the figure and, without turning to run, backed himself quickly out of the alley. He stepped off the sidewalk and onto the road, unconcerned about potential vehicles or people, his eyes locked on the alley. The creature moved slowly, seemingly to struggle with every step and movement, its body almost too weak to carry the weight of its muscle and bone.

"You're...what *are* you?" Clay whispered to himself, happy to hear his own voice amid the wheezy exhale of the creature, which was nearly on him. It grabbed at his clothes, its hands slick with filth, and he struggled to free himself of its grasp. The creature's mouth found its way over his own, large enough that it even covered Clay's nose, and he found himself struggling to breathe, the creature exhaling a black, viscous sludge from deep within its gullet. Clay vomited and forced the creature off himself, and wiped the black fluid from his face and did his best to scrape the sludge away.

He rose to his feet and looked around for something to defend himself when he spotted a nearby trash can. He grabbed the lid and held it out like a shield between himself and the creature. "Get back! Stay away!"

Once within striking distance, the creature lunged, but Clay side-stepped it and began raining blows upon it, dropping it to the pavement. Eventually, the creature stopped moving, and

Clay, filled with rage, stomped on the back of the creature's head. Clay flinched at the sound of the creature's skull smashing from his blows. Flipping onto its back, the creature reached up toward him, almost pleading, its flesh slick with sick, black fluid and blood. Clay stared at its orange eyes, the color seeming to fade. After a moment, he smashed the lid of the garbage can onto the creature's head, killing it. Clay sat down next to the dead creature to catch his breath. His heart was racing, and he worried that a heart attack wouldn't be far behind. He eventually steadied himself, pulled himself to his feet, and stared down at the creature, trying to see more of it.

Clay took his phone out and used the flashlight to examine the figure. *Those eyes* he kept thinking, vaguely familiar and disconcerting all the same. The front of the figure's body was similar to its back, muscle, sinew, bone, except for its lower regions, where the creature was blessed with a member that was vastly larger than the average man. Clay regarded the creature's genitalia with confusion, and recognized the clear indication that this figure was, possibly, human in some way.

Turning toward the inferior pizza restaurant that bordered the alley where he found the creature, Clay looked around, checking the empty town for any sign of people (or more creatures), and, using the trashcan lid , smashed in the window of the restaurant, stepping inside once the glass was clear. He needed to gather his thoughts, and wanted to clean up somehow, and remembered the bathroom was down the hall from the counter, so he moved slowly and slipped into the men's room.

Once inside, he noted how relatively clean it was compared to the dusty and vacant restaurant. Using his phone's light, he examined his face in the mirror, and took some time to look at the fluid the creature had spewed all over him. He noticed redness around his mouth and nose, where the creature's mouth started enveloping him. The redness was accompanied by a soreness he hadn't felt since he was a teenager, that summer, after meeting the boy in the pizza place. Summer nights spent at the bluff overlooking town when Clay's dad was working late. Other nights spent along the banks of the Hudson River. Nights Clay and the boy hoped would last forever, but Clay knew, deep down, couldn't.

When he turned the sink on, he was surprised to see clear water after about five seconds of brown, and washed his face, hands, and more. He wiped his suit the best he could but realized that it was a lost cause and stepped back into the pizza restaurant.

He walked behind the counter and imagined he'd find something better than a trash can lid to protect himself in the kitchen, so he slipped inside. On the stoves and burners, there were pots of rotted food, long-since cooked and forgotten, the smell hanging heavy in the air, accompanied by the buzzing of flies or gnats. He looked around, pulled his tie off and slipped it into his pocket, and found a chef's knife along with a small meat cleaver. He had seen tough guys use meat cleavers a million times in movies and figured that it would be easy to defend one's self with it, so, he tucked the knife in his belt, and, with his briefcase in one hand and the cleaver in the other, exited the pizza place.

The only way out of town would be back to the train station, and he remembered that the last train out would be stopping in about an hour, so he had plenty of time to make it back, board, and settle in before heading back to Grand Central Station.

Where is everybody? he wondered, but with the empty stillness of silence that met his every inquiry, down every alleyway, into every open store, he never received an answer.

He started back down the road out of town but found that the town continued to stretch on, regardless of how long he walked. At first, he thought he might be overly tired, but after walking a solid twenty minutes, he passed GJ's Dugout and Donato's for the third time. It seemed impossible, and Clay couldn't rationalize what was happening, so he continued walking, thinking that he had merely taken a wrong turn and somehow just looped back around. But that wasn't the case. Clay had reached the end of town only to find himself back at the entrance to Kirkbride's Bluff. He passed the *Welcome to Kirkbride's Bluff* sign now five times, and when he checked his watch, the train would be arriving in ten minutes, and he knew it would be impossible to make it there, even if he wasn't somehow finding himself in an impossible space-time nightmare.

He paused and looked up at the bluff the town got its name from. From one angle, you could see down into the town's square. From another, one could look out over the Hudson River in the distance and watch as ships passed lazily up and down the river. Clay remembered so many nights on the bluff, indulging his teenage desires for whatever he needed at that moment. Most of the time, with friends, drinking warm beer and smoking terrible marijuana.

He checked his FitBit again. Another fifteen thousand steps had been tacked onto his count. His body was exhausted. He found no other figures, no more creatures, but instead felt the presence of something from the trees in the park watching him. He had spent multiple nights in the park with friends, playing sports, drinking beer, smoking weed, getting into trouble, and found that whenever he looped back into the town on his fruitless trek to make it back to the train station, every single time he passed the park, he felt uncomfortable. There was a silence that felt unnatural to him as he walked past the park, and his skin crawled at the idea of something in there, watching him.

Taking a seat on a park bench that framed the outer entrance to the park itself, he opened his briefcase and started eating the banana, which was browning quickly. He looked around town, the mist still coming down, and couldn't figure out what to do next.

Finally, his mind and heart raced when he saw a figure moving down the cement sidewalk leading to and from the park and noted its movement was jittery and unnatural. Clay gripped the cleaver tightly, rose, and walked toward the figure. The only thought Clay had in mind was that he was tired. He couldn't escape the town and couldn't call for help, as his phone just didn't seem to have a signal.

The figure was about sixty yards away and moving quickly, its torso lilting to the right, one arm dangling, some kind of stick in its hand. Clay couldn't quite make it out, but followed it nonetheless. He called after it, but it only continued deeper into the park, the trees black, creating almost a tunnel of foliage from which Clay couldn't see the stars, or much of the town. His phone light's beam was bright and sure, and he continued, cleaver in hand. The figure was large, larger than himself—even at this distance, Clay knew that—but he didn't know what it was. At least it didn't seem to want to kill him like the last thing he'd encountered.

Eventually, the tall figure disappeared into the woods next to a large fountain. Clay stood near the fountain and was flooded by memories. Fleeting glimpses of holding hands. *He was young. Sixteen or so. Holding hands. His lips and tongue dancing with another's.* He couldn't quite hold onto any of the images long enough to discern anything, but when the images finished flashing through his mind, he recoiled, suddenly unsteady on his feet. He looked toward the tree line where the large figure had disappeared. He placed his briefcase on the fountain. He held the cleaver in one hand and the knife in the other and made his way into the woods.

Once inside, he followed the sound of bushes rustling. He checked the battery on his phone and noticed he still had eighty percent power. After a few moments, Clay found himself in a small clearing, a shovel resting on a nearby tree. The area was small, about fifteen feet all around, but there was a small plot of disturbed land situated at the base of one of the enormous black trees. Clay reached for the shovel, thinking that it may be an upgrade from the knife or cleaver, and again, he was flooded with memories that didn't seem like his own.

His hands gripped the shovel and dug furiously into the soil. He saw his father nearby, standing, watching the woods, cigarette in his mouth. Clay wondered what his father had been doing in the woods, and who he was with, and what they were burying. Clay grabbed the shovel and started digging, and each time the shovel connected with the dirt, he felt a shock run through his body, from his fingertips to the base of his spine, as though someone was gently touching a raw nerve.

After digging about two feet down, the shovel struck what looked like a plastic bag. Kneeling, he gripped the bag and pulled, revealing a pair of skeletal, brown hands. Stumbling backward, Clay struggled to his feet, and when he did, he saw the tall figure, looming in the tree line. *Was it watching me the entire time?* Much taller than he imagined, its body twisted into a hunch leaning to its right. A thin, membranous film that almost resembled flesh covered its face. A black mouth full of brown and black teeth, rotted away, showed through the covering. Loose, fleshy sacks hung in spots all over its largely featureless body and crinkled as the tall figure moved. Bright, orange eyes stared at him. A nose, or, what remained of a nose as it looked smashed in, dripped black fluid.

The whispers. Clay heard the figure whispering to him. He heard it in the dark, in this space they shared. The woods around them completely silent, but this figure, ten or so feet from him, whispered. It whispered from that gaping black hole of a mouth. "What do you want?" Clay asked, overcome with emotion. "What is this? Why are you doing this?"

The tall creature stepped toward him. Clay examined it closer. The thin membrane that covered its body contained vaguely human forms beneath it: blurry, bloody and black. The crinkling of its movement unsettled Clay and he rose to his feet, bracing himself against a tree. He looked at its one arm, and it held no stick. A thin, long protrusion that resembled bone, sharpened to a point, was segmented where a human elbow and wrist would be. The creature's other arm hung bound with black strips to its body, withered and possibly useless. Clay picked up the scent of sweat and musk surrounding the creature.

The creature stood over the gravesite, the shovel at its feet. Clay watched it closely, and suddenly found his mind flooded again, images of the past washing over him, over and over, his ears ringing, his body wracked with agony.

Clay's tongue gliding over the nape of the boy's neck, the two of them in the park, alone in the woods.

The boy staring—with impossible eyes the color of nectarines—at Clay and telling him he loved him.

Clay and the boy, at the bluff, making love in Clay's car.

The two passing in school, Clay avoiding the gaze of the boy.

Clay's father, breaking through the tree line, finding them embracing in their tiny sanctuary.

Clay struggling to pull his pants up, while his father attacked the boy, raining punches and more on him while Clay screamed for him to stop.

The boy, his face demolished, eyes wide, gurgling on his own blood and teeth, struggling to speak.

Clay and his father, under cover of night, digging in the woods, discarded black electrical tape, plastic bags and a shovel nearby.

The boy gurgling, his voice a whisper, as Clay began burying him.

"My god ..." Clay looked at the tall, monstrous figure. "You're him."

The figure lunged at Clay and stabbed him with his thin, bony arm. Clay fought back, swiping and bringing the cleaver down on the appendage, a flurry of flesh, bone, and blood erupting everywhere. Clay screamed and the monster began whispering louder, its words unclear.

Clay was overwhelmed, and his heart was racing. His mind was flooded with images of him and the boy from the pizza parlor. That glorious, warm summer, spent in each other's arms. Holding hands in the cool darkness of the movie theater. Making love in the park, in Clay's car, in the boy's house when his parents went away. Exploring their love for each other in ways Clay never imagined possible. Discovering a closeness he never felt before, and hadn't felt since.

"I'm sorry! I'm so sorry! I loved you!" Clay screamed, tears streaming from his face, blood and meat splattering with wet fury, blow after blow of the cleaver.

Clay continued to bring the cleaver down on the monster, who struggled under his weight despite its own huge size. Clay punctured the fleshy sacks that held fluid within, and he found himself covered in a pus-like substance, sticky, almost transparent, the smell overwhelming. He continued cleaving the creature, its one arm now torn to pieces. In between blows from the meat cleaver, Clay stabbed with the knife, finding the creature's throat, face, chest, and heart in a blend of terror and excitement that Clay had never felt before. If this was the fight or flight response, Clay didn't know, but he felt as though he was running on pure instinct, overwhelming the creature with attacks.

Eventually, the whispers stopped. Clay stared down at the monster and was blinded momentarily by what he thought was a flashlight from the woods. When he looked up, he saw the boy, sixteen, the age they both were when they had their affair. Clay stared at him and began to cry. "I'm sorry. I'm so sorry," Clay sobbed, his face slick with blood and tears.

The boy whispered, eyes a blazing orange-gold, and slowly walked off into the woods. Clay understood the whisper to be *I know you are, Clay* and waited until the boy was out of sight. Clay held his injury as he walked back out toward the entrance of the park. He grabbed his briefcase on the way and found himself losing more blood as he moved. The rain had picked up, and he was soaked to the core.

Eventually, he found himself by the same park bench he paused at earlier and had to sit and catch his breath. He put his briefcase down, took his jacket off and used it as a pillow to rest a moment. The rain continued pouring down, as Clay felt himself continue to bleed. Eventually, he closed his eyes, thinking he'd hear the whispering of his long-lost love.

But they never came. As he lay bleeding onto the bench, his blood mixing with the rain, which had grown steadily stronger, Clay thought about the boy. Thought about his father. Thought about Kirkbride's Bluff. The years seemed to wash over him, and as he felt himself drifting away, he felt glad to rekindle his moment with the boy. Lost all those summers ago, lost to time, lost to his father's rage.

Clay's vision began to fade as he shut his eyes. In the dark, he saw the orange-gold glow of his lover's eyes one last time.

Black Dog Blues
Luciano Marano

Choosing sides, that's what you're doing when you tell a story like this. By clearly identifying the aberrant we define and agree upon what is normal. We share unusual experiences and observations and thus reassure each other. It's practically ritualistic, a way of definitively declaring *that* is not right and we are not *that* so therefore we are right. You understand?

That can be whatever—ghosts, monsters, the Bermuda Triangle, flying saucers filled with little green men—it doesn't matter. But such stories need to be shared. The point of telling tall tales is to recalibrate reality, and we truckers tell 'em taller than most.

You got your seatbelt on? Good deal.

As I was saying, culture is full of tribes, little clubs and cults. Most of them have distinctive codes and traditions, their own myths and legends. I was in the Navy for about ten years and can tell you that sailors are an especially insular lot. I've known plenty of cops too, a members-only club if there ever was one. I imagine it's the same all over if you dig deep enough.

And truckers? Well, maybe we need the psychological anchoring sharing such stories provides more than most because ours is such an unnatural way to live. There's a reason the species by and large gave up the nomadic way of life a long time ago: It wears on you! I should know, been behind the wheel going on thirty years, crisscrossed this great big country more times than I can count. I have seen things you would not believe, trust me.

That vent blowing on you too much? I can adjust the heat. This rig has so many buttons, dials and settings it's like a submarine or space ship. Actually, with all the glowing indicators and instruments up here, late at night when it's just me and the slim path cut by the headlights against all that dark, I sometimes feel like I'm driving through outer space. Like I'm out here all alone, hurtling through the void.

You okay, then? Good deal.

That's why I picked you up. I don't usually give rides, but I know how cold it gets out here when the sun goes away. Plus, sometimes a little company, somebody to talk to, especially at night, makes the miles go faster. You've got music if you want, and the CB radio, but those distant crackly voices can sometimes make a man feel more lonely rather than less. Sound kind of like ghosts, I think. People talking to you from...someplace else.

Which brings me back to what I started to say. Took the long way 'round the reservation on that one, sorry about that. But I promised you a story and I always keep my promises, ask anybody you like. They don't call me True Blue for nothing. True Blue being my radio handle, every trucker worth his wipers has one.

Now, consider the glow of the dials and panels, the gentle crackle and hiss of the CB. Not so dissimilar from a campfire, right? It's the perfect setting for the aforementioned ritual of recounting the so-called ghost story. Truckers have quite a stable of yarns to select from, but of all the legends traded amongst the tribe of professional drivers—sailors of the asphalt sea, you might say—the black dog is unquestionably the most iconic. Think there was even a movie made about it. Starred Meat Loaf, Randy Travis, and the guy from that dancing movie. Remember? *Nobody puts Baby in a corner?* Hell, it'll come to me.

The dog—more like a wolf, really—is an enormous, loping, slavering beast. Teeth, big as kitchen knives. Hair, black as space without stars. Eyes that blaze fiery red like emergency flares on a lonely stretch of bad road.

They say a driver who's been awake too long sees it just before a crash—the type you don't walk away from. Does the dog cause the crash? Maybe it's trying to warn you? There are many variations. Back when I was coming up, the old-timers said it comes to carry off your soul afterward, like a spirit guide in some Indian vision quest. But I don't believe that. It's no simple omen either, not the hallucination of a tired mind. The dog is very, very real. Every driver only has so many miles in them. And then, when you're coming to the end, that's when you see it.

First, the dog paces you, racing alongside the rig. Driver gets scared and goes faster, trying to lose it. He's heard the stories, after all, but thinks maybe he can outrun the thing. Maybe it's not too late. And for a minute or so, seems he's right. It's gone, vanished into the rushing darkness. That's when you see it again, barreling out of the night ahead. Its roar is squealing brakes and twisting metal, breath like burnt rubber and oily smoke.

You still okay? Good deal.

If you're fading, help yourself to those red pills in the far cup holder. Careful though, they're serious stuff. Speaking of which, pass me a few. This is no time to lose your edge. Miles to go and all that, right? Thanks.

There's coffee in that blue thermos and a can or two of cola in the fridge behind your seat. I tell you, these new rigs are really something. All these gizmos and creature comforts. You'd never know we're creeping past eighty because the ride's so smooth. Don't worry, I'm a professional. And like a wise man once said: I never drive faster than I can see.

Now then, I first obtained the facts regarding the black dog from a most reliable source, the man who taught me the ways of the wheel. Sullivan Smith drove for a cross-country outfit for about two hundred years before moving onto a local route near the shipyard in Bremerton, where I got out of the Navy. I was hired on as a probie and he was my training instructor. Geezer's handle was Locksmith because supposedly he'd been something of a Don Juan back in the Pleistocene Epoch and had the key to the heart of every lady he met, or so they say.

He told me all about the black dog and I sat there nodding politely, just like you, and thinking pretty much what I expect you're thinking right now. It took a long time before I understood the truth.

Locksmith died about sixteen years ago, but not in a crash. Gas station robbery. Poor old man walked into an all-nighter for a doughnut and a cup of coffee, right into a holdup. Got the back of his head blown off by some desperate junkie with a shotgun before he knew anything was up. Actually not a bad way to go, if you think about it. I've seen worse. Yes, I certainly have.

It was Locksmith who first told me about the music, though I've heard others mention it since. Black Dog Blues, he called it. The sound a driver hears just before the dog appears, a sorrowful howling that leaks through on the CB and sharp, staticky barking. Sometimes, they say you'll hear an inhuman voice growl your name. That's how you'll know it's time.

You've got your belt on, right? Good deal.

I heard the Black Dog Blues once, except it wasn't playing for me. There was this woman, a trucker, name was Lydia but her handle was Sassy because she had one hell of a smart mouth. Never cared who might be listening, right there on the CB she'd just say whatever she was thinking. We used to stop at the same spots and run the same routes. There are drivers who work in teams—partners, married couples; it gets awful lonely out here—and we were talking about maybe giving that kind of arrangement a try. Never got the chance, though.

We were both slated to make a run for the same outfit. I'd gotten this new radar detector, so I was driving point and keeping an eye out for smokies. We were making good time and chatting on the CB, us and a few others in the general area, playing this game where we'd be carrying on a technically PG-rated conversation but using as many sexual innuendos and double entendres as possible. Sassy was good at it. Sometimes, I'd get to laughing so hard I couldn't breathe.

I said we were making good time. In fact, we were speeding along pretty well. That was the whole point of the radar detector. But the thing started acting funny, making crazy chirps and beeps, and I got distracted trying to restart it. I didn't notice Sassy had stopped talking. I didn't notice anything until I saw her rig bearing down on me, coming up way too fast on the left. Brake failure, I assumed. Something had to be wrong with the rig because Sassy was an outstanding driver. I was cruising just below the century mark—about how fast we're going now, actually—and she flew past me like I was parked.

That's when I saw it, just for a second as she passed, running outside the beam of her lights. An enormous black dog moving unbelievably fast. I got on the CB, but she didn't answer. So I pulled out my phone and called her. She did answer then, and I heard her crying. She was so afraid, kept screaming, "It's coming for me, True! It's coming for me!"

And in the background, I heard her CB crackling. This awful howl, a scream of static that hurt my ears. It wasn't coming through on my radio, though. I could only hear it through the phone. It was the Black Dog Blues playing just for her.

Something said her name. A voice like out of your worst nightmare. If there is a hell, I think whatever greets you at the gates will sound like that. I saw her rig jackknife and go careening off the road. Thing rolled three times as it went over the embankment. By the time I finally got slowed down and pulled over and ran back to the scene, the fire was so big…there was nothing I could…she was just gone.

That was three weeks ago. I've racked up a lot of miles since then. Side gigs, overtime—I don't like to stay put too long. Figure I've been up about four days straight now. Pardon my reach, just need something out of the glove compartment. Relax, it isn't for you.

This is the Smith & Wesson Governor, a snub-nosed revolver capable of firing small-caliber shotgun shells. A very reliable gun. Please don't look at me like that. I already told you, I'm a professional. The gun is for the dog. The story is for you. Like I said, such stories need to be shared. Make sure you got your belt on now. I'm counting on you to survive this and tell the tale. Please, be on my side.

You mean you really haven't seen it? On the shoulder of the road, just outside the headlights? Running alongside the rig? Right there! You can't see that?

No, too late. It's gone…for now.

Never mind, I'm not too worried about it. Let's coax this big boy up to a buck-twenty and see if we can't run the bastard down. Keep your eyes peeled. Somewhere in that blackness up there, it's headed straight for us. And I'm going to kill it. They didn't believe me when I told them what happened to Sassy, looked at me like I was a raving lunatic. About like how you're looking at me right now, actually. But that's OK. I don't care what they think—or you either, matter of fact. Soon you'll see for yourself. Then, you'll know the truth. And you can tell everybody. You can tell the story.

Hear that? It's as if the sound was being stretched and pulled like taffy, and that terrible crackling growl under the static. That howling, lonesome as a lifetime spent on the road.

Oh yes, they're playing my song tonight.

Imaginary Friends

Nicole Wolverton

The offices of Mixship Elementary School looked exactly as Julie knew they would—maybe because primary school offices all looked the same. She imagined there was a company that specialized in décor meant to cow children into frightened submission, encourage them to fall into line, to obey all the rules, to be good little children and do the right thing. The chairs would be that special mix of too big for a child but too small for an adult, so no matter who was doing the sitting, it would mean a torturous discomfort. Discomfort and aggressively cheery yellow walls.

Julie squirmed until she found that crossing her legs at the ankle and hunching forward wasn't quite so awful as any other position. The elderly receptionist smiled blandly at her over a stack of paperwork, but only for a second. No doubt the administrative staff were in on the joke, secretly broadcasting the unfortunate souls waiting to face Principal Boden to a network of evil academic sadists who cackled uproariously with every pained expression—or, the case of poor Augie, who sat beside her, short legs sticking out in front of him like straight pins, with every tear.

Her nephew hadn't stop silently crying since the second his butt hit the chair.

"Come on, Augie," Julie said for the tenth time. "Tell Aunt Julie what the problem is. Why'd Principal Boden call me? What does he want to tell me?"

Augie's thin shoulders rose and fell, quick as a breath. His pudgy face was pink; brown eyes, bloodshot. There was no sign he'd been in a fight—his red and white striped shirt and his jeans looked the same as when they'd left her house that morning— and he wasn't exactly the type anyway. He wasn't a cheater or a back-talker. There wasn't much left that a first grader could have done bad enough to warrant a parent being summoned.

"Principal Boden will see you now." The receptionist gestured toward the closed wooden door to Julie's left and fixed a cold, rheumy gaze on Augie. "And you, August, you're to stay right where you are."

He nodded and kept crying. Poor kid.

Julie groaned as she unfolded herself from the plastic chair. She dropped a kiss on the top of Augie's head. "Hey, don't worry about it, buddy. Everything will be okay."

The door opened like magic and inside, behind an enormous metal desk, was a short man with a dark comb-over and a blue tie just off-center, his jacket hung askew on a coat rack in the corner of his tiny yellow office. More stellar work from the design company, for sure. The chair that waited for her in front of his desk was another of those goddamn torturous tiny-big chairs. Perfect.

He didn't smile when she crammed herself down and balanced on the edge of it.

"Miss Strawbridge, I'm afraid we have ourselves a problem. An imaginary friend problem."

She knotted her mouth to keep herself from letting loose something very inappropriate. Her sister and brother-in-law would only be gone another few days, but they'd shit a brick if Julie got on the principal's bad side—but all this over an imaginary friend?

Finally, she said, "I'm not a child development expert, but isn't having an imaginary friend… I don't know, *normal* for a kid Augie's age?"

She'd had her own secret, invisible friend when she was a child—a razor-fingered, corkscrew-haired woman named Mona with a fondness for laughing at the top of her lungs whenever young Julie got in trouble, who told her stories and commiserated with her when she was grounded. It was comforting—maybe Augie needed comfort, too. And now these jerks were making him feel bad for it? She set her jaw to keep her face neutral.

Boden's throat clearing ripped the certainty from her like an extra-sticky bandage, pulling with it bits of skin and hair. "You have to understand," he said. "We aren't concerned that August has an imaginary friend, or friends, as the case may be. You're right. That's perfectly healthy for a child of his age. But he's selling them."

"Selling them? What do you mean?"

"He's selling imaginary friends to the other children in his class. For a dollar."

"I see." A fission of laughter welled in her stomach. God, that kid was a riot. "You know, maybe you should wait until Augie's parents gets back to discuss this. I don't feel—"

"Yes, well. You are listed as August's legal guardian until his parents return, and I'm afraid the matter is quite serious." Principal Boden stared at her from behind his compulsively-organized desk. The dirty overhead lights buzzed and tittered, flickering like an eyelid spasm. For just a moment she could imagine all of those other kids sitting here while he lectured them. Scaring them. Hammering the creativity and uniqueness out of them.

Screw this guy. Augie was a good kid. A quiet kid.

"If it's a matter of the money, I'll just pay it back." Julie reached for the purse she'd set on the floor beneath her splayed knees. "How many kids are in Augie's class?" She peeled a twenty-dollar bill from the fold in her wallet. "This should cover it, right?"

Principal Boden help up an oversized hand. It shook slightly. "That's not the main problem."

She dropped the twenty back in her purse. "What *is* the main problem?"

"The problem is that August is doing a little more than simply fooling these kids into buying imaginary friends. He's filling their heads with unfortunate, dangerous ideas."

Her back cramped. She contorted her body, feeling like a pretzel. "Not to rush you, but could we cut to the chase? Does Augie have detention? Do I need to give a donation to the class trip fund?"

"Your nephew has been selling these imaginary friends to his peers, with the promise that they will do the bidding of those who own them."

She fought the urge to laugh again. Maybe she shouldn't have let Augie watch late night television last weekend. Her sister would *love* that—Julie would never hear the end of it for leading poor Augie into a life of petty crime.

The principal continued, "I've had dozens of calls from parents. Their kids are setting fires, stealing things, committing acts of vandalism, and blaming these imaginary friends. We cannot have anarchy like this, Miss Strawbridge. We really cannot. The President of our PTA woke up this morning with a dead mouse planted on her pillow next to her face. Her child said her imaginary friend did it. No, I'm sorry to say that detention is not going to fix this problem." He sighed. "I've decided it's best to give August a two-week suspension. To start."

"Two weeks? Are you kidding me? All he did was show a little entrepreneurial spirit."

"My decision is final. It'll give him time to think about the wrong he's caused, and perhaps give the shenanigans he has perpetuated time to subside. You may not be his parent, Miss Strawbridge, but I encourage you to treat this with the seriousness it deserves. I will be talking to his mother and father at the end of the two weeks about how we move forward from this. August is a disturbed young man. Another school may be better equipped to handle his... imagination."

Julie unfolded herself from the torturous chair. Her back cracked loud as fireworks. "I have never heard anything so outrageous. I get that selling imaginary friends is wrong, but the rest of it? How can he be blamed for that? He's just a kid."

"My decision is final," Principal Boden repeated. The lights in his office flared again—once, twice, three times. He sighed. "Final."

Julie shoved the handles of her purse up over her shoulder. With one last withering glance at the Principal, she whipped open the door to his office and found Augie sitting outside, his hands clenched on his lap. He looked up at her with wide hazel eyes. His lashes were dark and wet, but his cheeks were dry.

"Am I in big trouble?" he asked quietly.

She nodded but smiled. "Yeah, but not with me, okay, buddy? Let's get out of here. I'll buy you some ice cream."

The receptionist leaned forward, like she didn't want to miss a word. Julie frowned at her, but the lady sat as though petrified, her tight gray curls like stone.

"Okay, but can I stop at home first? I want my pillow." Augie hopped off the chair and slung his plaid backpack over his shoulder. He was a solid little presence, close as her shadow and just as silent, all the way to the car.

He was quiet on the drive, too. He sat and stared out the window at the gloomy day, and Julie's mind gravitated back to Mona. She'd probably blamed things on her imaginary friend just as these other little first grade kids had. That had to be just as typical as having a make-believe friend in the first place.

Kids grow out of believing in things that aren't there. Santa. The Easter Bunny. The tooth fairy. All of it. Julie didn't remember the day she stopped seeing Mona and her razor fingers and her red curly hair, but it was easy to recall sitting in her room after bedtime, telling Mona about her day—and Mona being her friend. The one she went on adventures with, like the time Mona convinced her to run away from home after getting in trouble for finger painting. She'd never told anyone about Mona. Not her parents and not her sister. She was something secret, all for Julie. Her secret friend.

She shook her head to clear it. God, it had been forever since she even thought of any of that. She glanced over at Augie, still engrossed in the trees and houses whizzing by the window.

"So," she said at the back of his head, "what's up with conning the kids at school out of their lunch money, Augie? Do you need to buy something? You could have asked me for whatever it is, you know."

He shook his head. "What does *conning* mean?"

"It's when you lie to someone to get what you want, the way you lied to your friends in class that you were selling them an imaginary friend. Like that."

"Oh. I didn't lie. Mommy says lying is bad."

"Well, she's right. Lying is bad. So maybe let's just tell the truth from now on. What did you do with the money?"

"Nothing," Augie said to the window. "I didn't even want it, but there's this kid in my class, Kyle. His dad is real mean, and he needed help. So I told Leonardo to go and help, and then Kyle gave me a dollar and told everybody." He paused. "A lot of kids have mean mommies and daddies."

"Who's Leonardo?"

"Leonardo is my friend."

"Your imaginary friend."

"No adults can see him." He turned his face toward her, and his eyes narrowed a bit. "Maybe you can. I don't know yet."

Her sister's house curved into sight around the bend. The white saltbox looked forlorn and dark under an overcast sky. The windows were black as the Principal's eyes, and it felt like the house was staring at her just as hard. She pulled into the narrow driveway.

"You don't have to come with me, Aunt Julie," Augie said. "I'll be real quick. Mommy taught me how to unlock the door by myself."

"Don't be silly. Of course I'm coming in."

He met her at the front of the car and slid his small, soft hand into hers. He nodded, and she let him lead her to the door. The gold key was solid and bright in his stubby fingers. He glanced up at her from under his long bangs. A thin, crooked smile spread slowly across his face.

Julie's stomach inexplicably twisted.

Just above his head, the curtain that hung in the door's window twitched. For one moment, she was sure she saw a red curl.

Augie twisted the key in the lock and pushed open the door. Something metallic, like knives, flashed in the gap between the door and the jamb. "Mona says hello. All my friends say hello. See, you *can* see them!"

Boogeyman
Susie Schwartz

Part 1

It doesn't matter if the sun is shining or if the moon is sitting in the sky. *It* still comes for me.

I've heard of the boogeyman before. My friends in kindergarten talk about It sometimes. I don't know if I am 'llowed to call It that, since my daddy hates nonsense talk. But when my friends chatter about It, it sounds just like what happens in my own house so I guess that's what I'll call it too. I'll just call It that in my *head* though, and not say the word *out loud* so my daddy doesn't catch me.

Some of my friends say the boogeyman lives under their beds and comes for them after they're tucked in for the night. Mine lives in my whole house and no one tucks me in so I guess it *is* different for me. Some of their brothers and sisters say It's not real. I don't know what my brother and sister would say. I can't tell them about it. My daddy would get mad. All I know for sure is that *my* boogeyman is *real.*

I wish I could tell my sister. She is pretty and smart and can play the organ. When she turns it on and starts hitting notes, the mouses that live in there come scurrying out, giving my cat Fluffy some fun. It doesn't matter that some of the white keys are broken. She still makes nice music. I just started taking lessons too, so I can be just like her some day.

I like her lots 'cept she's always with the babies. Babies in our house come and go like kittens. We never get to keep those either. My sister always has a baby in her arms. I guess we are doing a good thing, saving babies by giving them a home, but sometimes I wish I were one of them instead of me.

I can hear it now. The boogeyman I mean. It's down the hall and Its screams sound like when I reach out to the right side of the organ and press a bunch of notes at the same time.

It's loud this afternoon. The screeching I mean. I'm huddled against my closed bedroom door and hoping It doesn't come any closer. My head is spinny and hurts and I push my hands against my ears to make it stop. Should I get up to grab my lucky penny out of the drawer beside my bed to make a wish and risk It coming in to get me? Or do I stay put? My teacher put me on a scale a few days ago cuz she's says I'm too skinny. I hope being 49lbs will be enough to hold the door shut. I can feel my heart going babump, babump, babump when I put my hand to my chest and I hold my breath to stay quiet. I start to feel dizzy and I'm desperate for air. Finally, the screeching gets quieter and I let the old air out and suck in some different air.

Grabbing my lucky penny and slipping it into my pocket, I run out of my room, through the living room and then the kitchen and out the door in my bare feet. I keep running, opening the fence gate, not bothering to close it behind me. I know if the cows get out, my daddy's face will get red and hot and mad but I can't stop running. As I catch my breath, I start calling for her. Sugar, my spotted Arabian is out here somewhere and what I need is to feel her soft, pokey nose whiskers against my face. She's my best friend. I think I'm hers too, since I'm the only person she comes to when her name is called. She stays hidden in the bush from the rest of them, 'cept if my daddy gets out the hay tractor. Then she comes running.

It doesn't take long before we find each other in the trees down by the creek.

I used to cry when the boogeyman came for me, and well, sometimes I still do, but today, I just talk.

> *Today It was loud, Sugar. And close. I could smell It as It came closer. It smelled like the swamp. Oh Sugar, when will the boogeyman go away? It's been 'while since It came out. It likes to stay in my daddy's room lately. I like it better when It's in the basement. Then It's not so close. The other night, after my night snack, It was lying down in the hall closet. I saw a knife in its hand. The yard light was shining through the window and I saw something shiny. I think it was a knife. So I ran to my sister's room and told her I was having a bad dream. She told me I could lie in her bed for a few minutes while she checked the baby. Then I had to be brave and go back to my own room.*
>
> *Oh Sugar, I know you are kinda old and my daddy says when people get old, they die. Please don't ever die, Sugar. I love you so much. More than anyone in the whole wide world. I wish you could live in my room with me. I think the boogeyman would be scared of you and would stay out of there for sure.*

My heart sinks as I hear my sister calling my name over and over. It must be suppertime. And just when my heart stopped jumping all jittery too.

> *Oh Sugar, I'm so sick of hamburger and potatoes. I wish we could eat pizza. I only get to have pizza at Cathy's house when her mom lets me come over. Will you walk home with me, Sugar? All the way?*

As I get closer, I decide to peek in the windows and see if I can see the boogeyman before I go in. My daddy gets mad when I hide outside but It was just so loud today. I don't see any sign of It so I make some courage and carefully go in for supper. Hamburger and potatoes. What a surprise.

After we eat, my sister and I do the dishes and then she tells me I should do a puzzle or color. I'd rather go back outside and be with Sugar, but there's not enough time to find her before I'm supposed to take a bath.

I have to go to bed at 8:00 every night whether I feel tired or not. After I drink my glass of milk and eat some soda crackers, I tip-toe to my room so I don't wake the boogeyman if It is sleeping. I make some more courage and count to three before quickly opening my closet door to check for It. It isn't there.

As I climb into bed, I tuck myself deep under my grandma's quilt and squeeze my eyes shut. Can I hear It? Can I hear It breathing or hissing in the walls of the house? Sometimes I hear It in the middle of the night, banging around, roaming free. Why does no one else hear It? Why is it just me?

Sometimes, when I ask the kids at school what their boogeyman is like, they tell me it only comes in the dark and their mommy or daddy can make it go away. They just shine a flashlight around and in and under everything in their room and it goes away. They say theirs hides and they can't really *see* it, they just know it's there. Until their mommy or daddy comes.

I can see mine. And I can feel It. Sometimes It reaches for me and Its grabby claws dig into my back as It wraps Itself around me and my breath gets stuck. I just tremble and hope that It'll let go before It kills me with Its talons. That's what the teacher called the fingers of the different birds we learned about in school. The eagle and the hawk and the owl. I don't like birds. They pick up little animals and eat them. I feel like a little animal sometimes. Like the mouses who live in the organ. I wish I lived in an organ. I would never come out, 'cept if I had to pee.

Sometimes It pushes me out of its way. I think It's coming for me but instead, this time, It's going for somebody else. Only they don't seem to notice. They aren't afraid like I am. 'Cept the babies. Sometimes the babies scream when the boogeyman is near. I think they can sense the danger like me. Usually my sister saves them. She takes them to another room and rocks them until they aren't scared anymore. I know I'm a big girl now but I still wish I could be rocked to sleep.

I lie in my bed and again beg for happy dreams of me and Sugar, us walking on the worn-down paths in the woods or on top of the green or brown hills, our manes blowing in the breeze. Her mane is dark and light—different shades of grey, but mine is just light, yellow like the little girl named Goldilocks that we read about in school. Sugar has a big belly so I think she likes her food more than I do. My belly is flat and sometimes my pants slide down a little, unless the elastic is really tight. Her feet look too big for her legs but I think my dad just needs to clip her hooves. They are splitty and dirty. My toenails are kinda dirty too, and my sister needs to clip them for me but my fingernails are okay. I bite them so they stay short and clean. My dad yells at me when he sees me chewing on my fingers so I do it in secret, when no one can see me. No one, 'cept the boogeyman. But I don't think It cares about my nails cuz Its are cracked and sharp. I think It wants to chew *me* up so It doesn't go hungry and die. Sometimes I just wish It would die.

So after I say my prayers, I think about Sugar. And my cat Fluffy. Sometimes Fluffy takes his paws and presses them one at a time, over and over into my soft, flat belly while he purrs. Then I know he's happy. And it tickles. Then I feel happy too. When the boogeyman presses against me, it doesn't tickle. Even when it doesn't hurt, the *scariness* makes me hurt inside my tummy. Then I don't feel happy. Sometimes the boogeyman laughs at me, and I see Its teeth. They are yellow but not like the yellow of my hair. They look rusty, like above the tires on my daddy's hay tractor. When I see Its teeth, It looks old, like the man with greasy white hair who sits in front of the grocery store every day, smoking his pipe. When It is dressed in clean clothes and has a baby in Its lap, It doesn't look so old.

My eyes are heavy and then it's tomorrow. The high notes of the organ are playing again. I need to pee but know I can't leave my room until the scary music stops. Crawling down and under my bed, I clutch my privates and squeeze my legs shut, hoping not to wet my nightie before it's safe. Sliding to the edge of my hiding spot, I reach up and into my drawer and feel for my lucky penny. It's not there. That's when I remember it's still in my pocket of the pants that lie in a heap in the far corner. My tummy feels sick and I start to shake. A little pee slips out at the same time as my tears. I lay there for forever in my soggy mess until finally, finally the noises stop.

The bathroom is just steps outside my door and I make some courage and run as fast I can and slam the door behind me. The boogeyman is not here. Relieved, I sit on the toilet and empty my aching tummy until there is not even a drop left. My tears won't let up and I rub at my eyes to make them stop. *I am not a baby!* I can't let my daddy see me like this. He has no patience for a cry-baby.

After my eyes dry up, I quietly race back to my room, close the door, and pray the boogeyman hasn't beat me here. I jump as somebody knocks loudly on my door. It's my sister saying it's breakfast time. I get dressed in some clean panties, my grubby jeans, and a plain green t-shirt, and then I stop for a second with my hand on the door handle before taking a deep breath of my courage and step toward the kitchen.

It is there.

Sitting in the regularly empty chair, It turns and grins at me with Its rotten teeth and tattered clothes. It looks old today. Old and hungry.

My dad and my sister with the baby and my brother sit silently eating their porridge, as if we were all alone. I feel like screaming CAN'T YOU SEE IT?! IT IS RIGHT HERE!! IT WANTS TO EAT ME! My dad looks up at me and says, "Eat up."

I don't know how I can eat when I feel like barfing. Usually It isn't this bold. Usually It hides in the dark corners of the house. Usually It's sleeping while we eat. *Why do they make me sit right beside It? Why aren't they scared too?*

The second my dad gets up to go work outside I jump up, tipping my chair over, run to the toilet, and throw up.

Barfing and barfing, all of a sudden, I feel Its hands pull back my hair.

"It's okay. Mama's here now. Mama's here."

Part 2

I can't make them stop. They torment my thoughts with their scraping talons, taunting with their prickly words and tricking my mind with their convincing lies. They shout their profanities, scoffing, laughing, sneering eerily through their rotting teeth. One is especially loud, its voice stronger than my own. It sinks Its teeth into my brain and chews and swallows, chews and swallows, *gurgling wheezing sniggering.* Small bits of me disappear into Its belly with each bite. So sharp. Teeth so sharp. Like razorblades slicing my eardrums, making them bleed into my skull. *wheeze growl hiss.* I hear shrieking from somewhere far away, only it gets closer and circles around my head. Are those screams my own or Its? I must run. I must get free. *hiss pant wheeze.* It is not working. I bang my head against the wall trying to shake It, this boogeyman swimming in the blood under my skull.

> *You're no good Awful mother* **GO GET IT** Babies Dizzy Foghorns **BLASTING** too many notes Whispering SHOUTING *GO GET THE KNIFE We must hide Hide from it* **RUN** *Sleep* **GO.** SHOUTING Whispers More foghorns **CrAsHiNg SYmBoLs** *STOP GO GET THE KNIFE* Spiders everywhere Crawling crawling **Biting** Ants **Snakes** in my bed *GO NOW GO GET THE KNIFE*

The closet. I must get to the closet. It is safe there.

I will bring the knife with me. Its blade so sharp it slices through bone like butter. The gleaning metal will save me. From *me* or from It, I cannot tell.

The bugs are here. A spider. And another. And another. Thousands. They creep over my whole body, getting tangled in my hair which grows inward, inward through my skull, split ends a knotty chaos inside. Flies are buzzing, waiting to feast on my flesh like a dead dog carcass. Circling, Circling. Sliding. Slithering. The snakes are back, constricting my throat like the noose I sometimes hang in the attic. They slither up my body backwards, their scales catching and snagging, leaving my arms and legs scratched and raw.

Moments or hours pass.

ONE DEEP SLICE. *JUST ONE DEEP SLICE.* One *Deep Slice. one deep slice.*

Slowly, slowly, It disappears, leaving only a footprint in the heavy sand that has settled underneath the gloomy loitering fog of my mind. My memory fights to move. One step, two steps, so slow, tiny stones sucking it down. Why is there skin trapped under my nails?

I'm tired. Too tired to remember. Too tired to think. Too tired to breathe. Rust has eaten through my joints, leaving holes in my bones, an excruciating ache left in the absence. Knowing I can't hide in the closet forever, I crawl my way up out of the sticky cobwebs the spiders have left behind, drag myself back to my room and fall onto the mattress, praying no one has seen this disaster of me. Pulling the covers up and over my head, I try to disappear. I try to be small. What if It comes back? It can't. *I* can't. Rest would be so easy. It would only take one handful of doctor-prescribed, multicolored candy. With just a couple of sips.

Then, *then* I could dance on the ocean, letting my toes dip into the cool blue waves of freedom any moment I chose. *Then* my hair would blow in the salty breeze. *Then* my head would feel weightless, soaring above cloud and darkness, where sanity dwells in blissful ignorance. *Then* angels would hold me and sing me lullabies, only there would be no need for sleep. I might even join them in their song.

But I am too tired.

He's making me go to the basement. Banished. Says he can't stand the sight or smell of me. I know it's bad but I'm just too tired. So very tired. Getting undressed. Turning on the water. Getting the temperature just right. Shampoo. Conditioner. Lathering up. Rinsing off. Turning off the taps. Climbing out of the tub. Towelling off. Combing my hair. Underwear. Pants. Shirt. Even just a nightgown. Day after day. Month after month. Year after year. All too much work.

He doesn't touch me anymore. I know I disgust him. My body, my mind—all of me is repulsive. It wouldn't matter if I showered. When I reach for him with my fingertips, he shrivels and hurries away. He doesn't understand. And *that I* can understand. I am a gross, unlovable raving-mad lunatic in the disguise of a woman. He doesn't see my curves anymore—only my insanity.   I just wish he would hold me sometimes. Obviously, I am not a child, small enough to be rocked to sleep. But I envy the babies.

I worry about my children. My two oldest might be fine and even the babies are looked after but then there's my little darling. She talks more to her horse than to all of us in this house put together. How must she view me through her little ocean-blue eyes? When I'm able, I stretch out my arms to embrace her but in my saner moments, I see black fear in her eyes. Is it just a reflection of my own? Or is she terrified of her own mother? Her tiny body trembles whenever I am near. Near equals Fear. I need to throw up.

I am a complete failure. A failure as a housewife, as a mother, as a lover. They all cringe and shrink away with my touch. I am poison. Death in a bottle made of glass. Falling, spilling, shattering on the floor. Contaminating everyone around me.

Is it today? Or is it tomorrow? Or am I still in yesterday? My clock, the only light in the room, glares at me with disapproval. Must. Get. Up. My children need me. Oh! And the baby. I must give him a bath. A bath. Yes. I should take a bath. See? I'm fine. I just needed a little break. I think I'll vacuum. The floors are dirty. Maybe I'll sew. Or make a craft. Oh! I want to bake some fudge! It will be delicious! Here I come! I am better now! Better than better! I am great!!

Scrambling from bathroom to living room to kitchen to living room, I hear music playing in my mind and I hum along to *We're here for a good time, not a long time* by Trooper. I make a mental list of all that I will do in the next hour and it is glorious. Where is everyone?! Let's play a game! How about Yahtzee? Yes, let's play Yahtzee! Oh! There's my girl! With the baby! I want to hold the baby! Please give me the baby!

As soon as my fingertips touch his tiny warm body, he starts to bawl, curling into my daughter's arms. As I continue to grab and pull, wails of torment fill the room.

He doesn't want me?! He doesn't want me! He doesn't want me.

The hurricane under my skull begins to slow, leaving clarity in its wake.

My heart crashes.

I get it.

I am a stranger. Both unfamiliar and oddly strange.

My ups and downs make mess and mayhem.

I get it.

I am crazy. Not now at this moment, but when my boogeyman takes over, I am thoroughly crazy.

I feel like a broken roller-coaster, never knowing when or where I will stop or start. I do know this: when I'm at the top it's for sure that I will soon go racing down to the bottom once again, and It is *always* there waiting.

I'm so tired.

My head is pounding again. I need to be in the darkness of my room. There, I am at home. There, the black of my innermost being and the black of the room blend with familiarity. When the sun shines on me, I panic and shrivel like a dying grape, leaving a tiny, tasty treat for the monster. It swallows me whole.

A blanket of pain settles over my heart as I lay perfectly still, no energy left in me even to weep.

It's happening again. The voice. Just one distinct voice. It's daring me to die.

> **DIE** *Die hiss grunt* Die **DIE** die *snigger grunt wheeze*
> DO IT *do it* Die **DIE** DIE die *hiss* **Do It DIE.**

It's too strong. I can't stop It. I can't fight anymore.
I reach for the stale glass of water beside my bed.
I swallow them all.
The Boogeyman wins.

Safe as Houses

Alex Giannini

It was mice, mostly, that Carrie found, dead and stiff and stinking, in the crawlspace as she searched the house for the source. And then again there was the pair underneath the kitchen sink and the small pack of them huddled together in the attic, bracing against the inevitable.

She found a few more in the front yard, near the white fence, as she sat in a chair on an unseasonably warm Halloween afternoon, a bowl of candy by her side. She scooped them up, those poor little dead things, and threw them in a can and closed the lid. And then Carrie sat down and took note of the trick-or-treaters that evening. It was a comic book year, apparently, with an endless parade of Deadpools and Captain Americas and Spider-Men.

There was one costume that stuck out, though, and stuck with her well into that night. In bed, lying on her side and staring out the window, Carrie couldn't shake the look of it. It—he, she—was among a pack of other kids, right smack in the middle of them, but it might as well have been from another dimension.

It was dressed in a flowing, wispy black robe, carrying a plastic orange pumpkin in one hand and a flickering LED candle in the other, but it was the mask that really stood out. Off-white with its long rubber nose and sunken eyes, it was the mask that burned into Carrie's memory. It struck a nerve, for whatever reason, and in the early morning light of the following day, Carrie blamed that mask for the dream she had that night.

She was in a church. In her dream, she and Will were in a church (or what was, in the logic of this particular dream, understood to be a church but more closely resembled a boarding house with wood-paneled walls and dark red carpets).

"It's happened again," a man Carrie couldn't see but could clearly hear announced matter-of-factly and from one corner of the large room.

He might have been a priest, but she wasn't sure. He hovered more as a specter than any concrete human thing. And then all at once, the dream shifted blurrily forward and Carrie was following Will through a hallway and to a closed door with light peeking out from behind it and Will was talking.

"She's in there." He was a couple of steps ahead of her. She couldn't see his face. She just wanted to see Will's face and to tell him. Carrie tried to tell her husband not to open it—she started saying *we're not ready*—but Will threw the door open anyway.

That's when it appeared, standing in that backlit door frame, slices of orange trickling out into the dreamscape hallway. It was a woman possessed.

She was chalk white, but not just in skin color. She appeared to have been carved from one large piece of chalk and all of her was white, so white that she was something most unnatural. In her left hand she held a red leash that held back a black dog.

And then suddenly Will was gone—off the screen of her mind—and Carrie was face to face with the chalk woman in the doorway. The black dog on the red leash barked once and threatened to lunge forward. Carrie stepped back, opened her mouth in a silent scream. The dog barked again and shook Carrie from her nightmare.

She woke, in her bed in the dark. And then she was in the sky near the stars, falling.

It was hopeless to fight, to try righting herself. She was surrounded by blackness, the occasional pinprick of starlight flashing by as she fell. Arms and legs and feet flailing and that horrible sense of unbalance. Her stomach lurching with each new turn and the sky and the ground flipping and switching and swirling into the same damn thing.

And then Carrie realized that she was wrong. She wasn't falling. She was sinking, and just like that, she was under the water. Deep underwater and what she had been doing was burying herself further under. Not breathing.

Panicking. Chest tightening. Looking up through bulging eyes, those pinpricks of light now the glistening of water at the surface, a million miles above her.

"Carrie."

A voice from somewhere not where she was. She was so far down, too far down for voices.

"Carr!"

Will. It was Will, again, but still so far away.

And then the whole world lurched to the side. The ocean shook, the light of the surface blinked out entirely and Carrie gasped while she rose, straight up now in her bed, in her room, in the soft light of morning.

Will sat next to her, on his side of the bed. She was awake now, truly awake this time but still gasping for air, still trying to catch the breath that was stolen from her in sleep.

"Jesus, Carr. Are you okay?"

When she found her voice, finally, Carrie just smiled. She reached her right hand out, touched Will's shoulder, and squeezed it just a little. "Thanks. That was a bad one."

Carrie and Will moved into the house early in the summer, but they continued to pay the rent on their one-bedroom in Brooklyn. They had lots of stuff, both in the apartment and in a storage facility, and their work schedules simply didn't allow them to take the time needed to move properly. So they moved improperly and over the course of several months.

Finally, by late August they found themselves in their silver Jetta, making the last of countless trips up the parkway, the transition from buildings to trees less jarring each time. The trunk and back seats were packed, but they were done. They crossed the Connecticut line and, just like that, Will and Carrie were *former* New Yorkers.

The new place was nice. It had a little yard with a firepit dug out in the back. Carrie liked the white picket fence. Will liked the finished basement. They both liked how big it was, comparatively, of course, in relation to their Brooklyn apartment. They talked often in those days about getting a dog.

Autumn arrived and the house became drafty at night. The doors creaked and the floorboards moaned. The house contracted and expanded and breathed when it had to. Routines formed and life changed. New things became comfortable things. Slowly, the house became home. Slowly, it all began again.

Late in September, Carrie's parents got into an argument with Will. Normally tepid, especially around the in-laws, this time, Will exploded. He even threw his phone, cracking its screen down the middle as the glass rectangle skipped across the kitchen tiles. Carrie, more shocked than angry, tried to make things better. She gave up after a week of being in the middle of an unwinnable war.

Later, on a random October Wednesday, Carrie was called into her boss' office and he laid into her about her slipping job performance. He spoke in generalities, frustrating Carrie into an uncomfortably obedient silence. She'd been "put on notice," whatever the hell that meant, and all of a sudden, her steady, high-paying job with its nice big Christmas bonus became less steady.

Life was, slowly, becoming less steady for Will and for Carrie, but the drip drip drip of bad news didn't seem overwhelming. It seemed like life.

Will's freelance work had dried up at the end of the summer—right after they'd left Brooklyn, actually, and he was feeling less and less connected to the world he'd known so intimately. A decade's worth of contacts and clients seemed to lose interest once he'd left their city.

Then, on a mid-October Friday morning, Carrie clicked the button and opened the garage door and turned the key in the Jetta and nothing happened. Frantically, she called the office and apologized before she even said *hello*, and then she and Will and their neighbor Harold had jumper cables attached to his little green Honda, and Will was pushing down on the pedal but nothing was happening. "Dead," Harold was saying from behind the wheel of his Honda. The engine was dead.

Carrie made another call, and a tow truck was on the way. She was late to work that day, and then again the following Monday and Tuesday when her Uber drivers each passed by the white picket fence and the stalled Jetta in the driveway.

"Bad luck, Carr," Will said as they sat on their new blue couch in their new white living room and he flicked through the little pictures on the screen hanging from the wall. "It's just a shitty stretch, that's all. Happens to everyone. We'll be okay."

Will wasn't an overly positive person, so his attempt at reassurance had done little to calm Carrie's nerves. If anything, his illogical conclusion had worried her. Instead of talking about it, though, she got up from the couch and stomped up the stairs and slammed the door to the bedroom, leaving Will on the couch with a sea of bad options on the screen in front of him.

In that moment, Will could feel the space between him and his wife. A kitchen, some stairs, and two unlocked doors separated them, sure, but the distance seemed so much greater. Like an ocean or like space or like the end of a novel. Behind him, Will heard the sound of the heat clicking on and felt the wooden pop of the floor under his feet. Above, Carrie's footsteps paced softly.

The late October winds kicked up and the whole world slowed down when Will's father had a heart attack. A big one, the surgeon had told him in the waiting room late in the night. The halogen above Will flicked blue and white as he sat on a cruddy green couch, listening but not listening as the doctor described how his father was resting and alive but not yet out of those dark woods.

He was okay, Will's father. Eventually, he was okay. It was a process and an ordeal and real life seemed less real for a while but things settled back down into normalcy. Still, death lingered. The thought of it, anyway. It was just enough to raise the hackles.

If you were paying attention.

If you were looking in the right places.

The morning after Halloween, Will got up first, left Carrie to lie there a bit, blinking away the dream of the chalk-white lady. She closed her eyes, shook it from her brain. Finally, Carrie walked downstairs, the smell of coffee drifting along with her.

The holidays drifted in, as they tend to do, slowly at first and then barreling through like a storm. Carrie and Will spent Thanksgiving at Will's parents'; Carrie did cartwheels to sell that decision to her own parents, saying Will needed to be close to his dad that year.

Christmas was more difficult. The truth was, Will hadn't spoken to Carrie's parents since their phone call fight months earlier. The feud lingered well into the new year.

Death lingered, too.

First it was Chris Cornell, the singer, and that one landed hard for Will. Either before or maybe after it was Bowie and Prince and then a former president. Somewhere in the middle, Will lost a great aunt and Carrie lost a couple of older cousins. They all kind of blended together, though, and Carrie kept finding dead mice in the house and an election went the wrong way and still, after all those months, Will couldn't land steady work.

And still, after all those months, Carrie wasn't back in the good graces of her increasingly mercurial boss.

One Friday night, deep in the wintertime, Carrie was (grudgingly) in San Francisco on a business trip with her boss, and Will was alone in the house. Carrie'd left that Thursday and wasn't to be back until late Sunday night. Will's phone would buzz every now and then, next to him there on the couch, with a text message from her.

San Fran tacos are good
San Fran tacos are also 9 dollars more than CT tacos
Miss you
Love you
Kill you

Will looked at his phone again, squinting as the white harsh light of the still-cracked thing illuminated his otherwise dark living room.

Kiss you

He chuckled. The basketball game blared from the TV on the wall in front of him. Leaning back on the blue cushion, Will felt the world start to slip away, the announcers' voices swirling into the nonsensical ether of encroaching sleep. The knocking from the basement stirred him back to life.

He sat up, instinctively checked his phone.

Kiss you

He waited for a moment, listening for the sound again. Hoping it wouldn't come. Of course, it came. Three knocks, echoing from down somewhere in the basement. Will felt his stomach suck upwards as tiny icicles of fear ran down his head to his groin.

He got up from the couch, padded slowly to the kitchen. The door to the basement loomed in front of him, its gold-plated knob shining in the moonlight. Or maybe that was just the way it seemed to Will, standing there and hoping against all the world that the knocking sound would stop.

It didn't. It came, louder now and more distinct. Four knocks this time. Echoing, real. Then again. And again. Each time exponentially louder than the last. Each time exponentially more real.

The buzzing in his right hand made Will jump. Carrie, texting.

You fell asleep on the couch didn't you

Will didn't answer. He quietly put the phone in his pocket, felt it buzz once more. Standing directly in front of the basement door, he grabbed the round gold knob and twisted.

Another knock, just then, but this time much different. Just one, but this one seemed to shake the whole house at its foundation. Will let go of the doorknob, felt the tile under him move. He held his hands out to his sides to steady himself. To keep the world from drifting. *An overreaction*, Will thought, but still.

The unreason of the situation gripped him then, thoroughly and completely and he could feel it in all the nooks and crannies of his insides. In that place where terror and curiosity meet, Will found the strength to reach out and to turn the knob, flick on the light switch to his right and walk down the wooden stairs. They moaned under the weight of his feet, each wooden squeak as loud as a car wreck in the otherwise still house.

The basement was exactly as it had been just after Christmas, when Will had made trips, one after the other, to return decoration boxes to their offseason resting places.

Looking around the room those months later, he felt buoyed by the fact that there was no snarling beast or knife-wielding intruder lurking through the bowels of his home. Finally, satisfied with his search, Will turned back towards the stairs.

The knocking began again.

Sharp and loud, and coming from the back corner of the room where the Bilco doors opened out into their small backyard. The knocking was coming *from* those doors, from the *outside*, Will realized for the first time. Whatever it was, it was in his backyard, in the night.

Will hesitated, his mind cycling between pushing open the doors from the inside from the basement, or rushing back up the stairs to the kitchen and peeking out at the yard from the window above the sink. His pocket buzzed, jostling the thoughts from his mind.

Wake up Will

"What?" He said to no one. And then another brief moment of thought. Before. Will unlocked his phone, flicked through his previous messages from Carrie.

You fell asleep on the couch didn't you
Will?
Lol
Wake up Will

A wash of comfort, of familiar real-world talk. Of Carrie. Then three more knocks from the Bilco doors. Will bolted up the stairs, flew through the doorway to the kitchen and leaned hard against the sink. He flicked on the light switch next to him and the backyard was awash with an orange halogen haze.

Peering out the window over the sink, Will scanned the yard. There was nothing there. Just orange. Just haze. Just the night and everything it held. But there was no one there, that was for certain.

Except.

On the concrete landing just in front of the Bilco doors. A shape. On the ground. Something.

Calmly—or, as calmly as he could manage—Will opened the door to the yard and walked out, throwing a long black shadow across the orange field. There, on the landing by the doors to the basement was a mask. Chalky white. Rubber nose.

He bent down and took a closer look at the thing. A child's Halloween mask. Chills up his spine. Rain from above. Soft droplets of water dinging the top of his head. A buzz, from his pocket.

You know what happens if you don't get up

Will swallowed. Pinched his bare forearm. Actually pinched himself to make sure he was awake. It hurt. He was awake. He felt a cold rush of panic but he left the mask where it was and went back into the house. He closed—and locked—the door to the backyard, closed—and locked—the door to the basement.

"Fucking kids." Another buzz in his pocket.

Go to bed...you're gonna be up all night if you don't get up

So he did.

In the morning Will went back outside, picked up the chalky rubber mask and examined it in the stark light of day. In the stark light of reason.

"Fucking kids," he said again, and this time he meant it. Will tossed the thing into a neighbor's garbage can on his way to the coffeeshop down the street. He never told Carrie about it.

Will spent as much of the day out of the house as he could, scrolling and scrolling and scrolling through jobs online, looking for the right fit. Applying to some. Hearing back from none.

Carrie came home that Sunday evening and everything went back to normal. Or, as normal as things had become. They still hadn't seen Carrie's parents. Will even avoided Facebook in an attempt to block them completely from his sight, if not from his mind.

By springtime, Will officially went on unemployment. He was getting, per week, what he used to make in a couple of days. Payment due dates became increasingly panic-inducing scenarios. Sleep was lost. Fights were had. The "unimportant"

bills went unpaid. Trips to the grocery store became mini-battlegrounds of attrition.

The little perfect house with its white picket fence was becoming less perfect, much smaller. Arguments replaced the quiet lazy sounds of Sunday mornings reading the paper. They cancelled their subscription to it in the new year, to *save wherever we can*, as Carrie put it. That, of course, also led to a fight.

The winter seemed endless. By March, it was still "freezing fucking cold," as Will liked to say under his breath on his morning walks to the coffeeshop. (*You know, those lattes cost us 30 bucks a week, Will.*)

By April, Carrie and Will were barely talking. They were ghosts in the night, passing each other on their way to haunt the living. Carrie, to work. Will, to look for it.

By May, Will had managed to wrangle a couple of clients. He'd started to pull in some money—not much, but enough to make some of the due dates a little less stressful. Enough to make shopping trips a little less awful.

By June, their relationship was back nearly to normal, but Will was back on unemployment and Carrie's job security was becoming less so. Though the days were getting longer, darkness was creeping in at all angles. It was, they knew, about to get worse than ever.

For months they were able to rely on savings to bail them out, some money they'd tucked away from their wedding and from all those nice big bonuses Carrie used to get. Even after the down payment, they had managed to save enough for a rainy day. But now it was pouring, and there was no end in sight.

In those darkest days, they clung to each other, Carrie and Will. At night, in bed, Will held on to Carrie like the whole damn world was being blown away by a tornado and she was his storm shelter. She did the same, inching closer to him late in the night as they both slept, texting him more during the day.

August was the worst. Financially, for sure, but also just in terms of stress. Carrie's workload kept her at the office later and later every night, and Will's lack of work was slowly eating away at his own sense of worth.

He stayed in the coffeeshop from open to close. He milked the same cup of coffee for hours and didn't buy himself lunch.

He ate whatever was in the fridge for dinner. He lost weight. He gained puffy little paunches under both eyes. He let his hair grow too long. His beard became wild, unkempt. Gray.

By September, Will had given up on looking for a new gig. He went to the coffee shop, set up in his back corner table, and wasted the day away online.

By October, Carrie was put—officially and with capital letters—*On Notice*. She was given 30 days to "turn things around." Her long days bled into the night. After the coffee shop closed its doors for the evening, Will was left to himself. In the house. Alone.

The whole thing had begun like a haunting because, of course, that's what it was. New house, young couple. It had all the elements. It fit the narrative.

On Halloween—yes, of course it was on Halloween—Will sat down in the lawn chair where Carrie had handed out treats the year before. Now he did the same, though he did so merely out of a desire to avoid a fight when Carrie finally did get home. And he did so with a little help from the bottle hidden underneath the lawn chair.

He'd been at it for about an hour—candy, smile, *Happy Halloween!*, wave, drink, repeat—when he saw the child: long and tall and dressed in black, flowing black, wearing the mask, the white mask with the rubber nose. Walking down the street and towards the house. Graceful in those long strides. Terrifying in his, or her, certainty.

Slowly, Will got up from his lawn chair. He placed the plastic orange bowl on the not-so-green grass. He walked, slowly, down the driveway. To the sidewalk. To the street.

The figure—black, tall, rubber—moved toward him. Once he was closer to it, Will could see that it was a she. The child. But too tall. And the mask. So real. And her movement, like water. Like dancing. Just like…and then she was standing in front of him, right there in the middle of their windswept Halloween street. The sound of leaves, scraping the pavement like bare branches on midnight window panes. Clouds in the sky. Storm smell in the air. Fear knots tightening in his stomach.

Will's breath puffed out in front of him as he exhaled, waiting, staring forever at that mask, chalk white and rubber. Real but not real. He looked hard at it, lost himself in it. There were no little slits for the eyes, for the ears, for the mouth, or for the nose. Just as that dawned on him, Will became surrounded by noise. Children, running past, yelling and laughing. Little Spider-Men and Batmen and Deadpools and Draculas. A patchwork cartoon coming to life on his perfect suburban street.

With the noise and the movement of the children, the figure vanished. There, in front of him one moment, and then gone altogether in the next, as if the noise had taken her. As if the sounds of the street, of the early evening, of Halloween and real life, had taken her back to wherever she was. Before. Before that night. Before the knocks on the basement doors. Before Connecticut and Brooklyn and Carrie.

Carrie.

Will saw her face, in his slightly inebriated mind, and he snapped back into focus. Standing there, alone now in the middle of his street, Will wanted to cry. It was, actually, the only thought that entered his mind, other than the image of his wife.

"You okay, man?"

Will turned, wiped the wet from his face. It was Harold, his neighbor. Decent guy. Red Sox fan, but what can you do.

"I—" Will started, stopped, then smiled. He steeled himself to speak through the boozy haze. "I am, yeah. I just...weirdest thing. I could have sworn one of those kids was Carrie's nephew. Oh, well."

Will walked past Harold, hoped that his fake smile would suffice.

But then, mid-stride: "Hey, Will."

Still walking, still fake smiling. "Yeah, man?"

Head down, hands in pocket. "Everything okay? With you. I mean, you know, with you and Carrie?"

Sigh. Turn. Fake smile. "All good, Harold. Been a rough month, but we're getting there."

"Okay, good. Just, you know. Just checking. Just making sure."

"I appreciate it." Fake smile, turn, walk. Then, over his shoulder, with a fake little wave, "Happy Halloween!"

Will packed up his lawn chair and the plastic container and he threw back the rest of his hidden bottle. Near midnight, Carrie still wasn't home and Will was quickly fading. He thudded up the stairs and passed out lying on top of the covers.

At some point in the early hours, Will woke up, felt his wife breathing in the bed next to him, got up. His head and his gut did that lurching, post-drinking thing and he staggered in the dark to the bathroom. The vomiting took him by surprise.

Had he really drank that much? Will cleaned the toilet, as thoroughly as he could, using rolled-up toilet paper, then rinsed out his mouth, brushed his teeth, and rinsed again. He opened the small bathroom window, let the night in to clear the air.

He stood outside the bathroom for a moment, one hand bracing against the doorframe, and made sure his feet were underneath him and his head was back on right. Sweaty and damp from the alcohol, he laid on top of the sheets and slept.

Morning came. Saturday. Will woke, instinctively turned over. Carrie wasn't there. He went downstairs. Carrie wasn't there. After he'd put the coffee on, Will peeked outside through the blinds, at the driveway, to where the car—finally working again—should have been.

Carrie wasn't anywhere.

Anger rose from somewhere deep and buried, and Will leaned against the counter. Morning coffee began to overtake the kitchen. He jogged upstairs and retrieved his phone from its charging place.

There were four messages, all from Carrie.

Working late...again.

Still working. You okay?

Fuck. Not getting out of here. Will?

Hello? Fine. I'll be here overnight. Home in the morning. Maybe.

A flush of fear. A pinch in his stomach. Will turned back to the bed. Saw, for the first time. Carrie's side was untouched. He'd slept on top of the sheets, messed his side up a bit, made a little dent. But Carrie's side was still tucked in. No indent on her pillow.

Will dropped his phone, was startled by the sound it made against the hardwood floor. And then, from downstairs, "Will!"

He froze. The front door slammed closed. He listened to the footsteps climbing the stairs. Carrie appeared in the bedroom, standing with hands on hips in the doorway. "What the fuck, Will? Why didn't you answer any of my texts last night?"

"I—"

"What, you don't even give a shit that I was out all fucking night?"

"No, I was—"

"Jesus, Will. You smell. Please tell me you weren't drinking while handing out the candy?"

"I was. I—"

"Whatever. I'm gonna shower. I'm going to visit my parents. Let them know I'm still alive."

Carrie turned towards the bathroom, jabbed Will one more time before she shut the door behind her. "Not that you give a shit."

The rest of the morning devolved nicely from there. Will's half-drunken attempt to clean the toilet had been just that, and a brand-new fight began in earnest as Will, on his hands and knees, head spinning, scrubbed the porcelain and the surrounding tiles.

By the time the coffee was ready downstairs, Carrie had skipped the shower and instead had packed a bag.

Once again, Will found himself alone in the house. He was sitting at the kitchen table, a half cup of coffee lingering next to him. His head hurt with each heartbeat, but the swimming upstream feeling of the morning after was—mercifully, if slowly—fading.

He'd been staring into the liquid blackness of his cup, hadn't heard her come in, but when he looked up, Carrie was sitting across from him at the table. She had been crying, her eyes raw, her makeup streaked and vaudevillian.

"We need to talk."

"I know," Will managed, knowing what was coming.

"I love you, Will. And I care about you. But."

Will braced.

"But this..." Carrie looked at him then, lingering on his eyes. "This is not right, Will. This isn't you. This isn't...me."

"I know, Carr. I know. It's just..." He'd thought about this exact moment so many times in the past year as he was sitting at the coffee shop, not finding jobs. He'd practiced it in his head over and over. He took a breath, a deep one, and he looked at his wife and began again.

"It's all ghost stories, Carr." Will leaned back in his chair, exhaled as he looked up at the ceiling. The sound of soft footsteps padded upstairs. "I mean, we're haunted by everything, you know? Our past, it's just—I don't know. We carry it with us, always. Like ghosts."

Will reached across the table, took Carrie's hands in his. They were cold. She was cold, and tired, and she just wanted him. She just wanted their one-bedroom in Brooklyn, and in truth, she just wanted the last two years back. She just wanted to make things better. To make things like they were. Before. Will could feel that, all of that, through her hands, like a lightning bolt of certainty. He felt better, more confident in his rehearsed speech.

"Think about it, Carrie. The good guys usually survive. In ghost stories, right? But...so do the ghosts. You know what I mean?"

Carrie smiled, small and thin-lipped, creating little dimples under her eyes. And then those eyes drifted up towards the ceiling. Up towards soft footsteps. Taking her hands from Will's, Carrie wiped at her eyes. Will took a sip of his coffee, felt the weight of everything drift away from him at last. On the table, his phone buzzed.

I'm gonna stay with my parents a few days. Clear my head. Suggest you do the same.

Then. Coffee and cup falling, crashing and shattering against tile. Above him, footsteps. Below him, knocking. Across from him, at the table, chalk-white, rubber.

The New Daddy
Scotty Milder

Michael sat in the short hallway between the living room and the kitchen, atop the ancient brown heater grate, and played with his puzzle.

It was an old puzzle, big painted wood blocks that slotted into a warped laminate frame. Mommy bought it at one of the garage sales she dragged him to on Saturday mornings, and he didn't have the heart to tell her that it was too easy for him. He could put it together and take it apart in seconds. The finished image—a crude painting of Big Bird and Grover, surrounded by multi-colored balloons and smiling cheerily vacant smiles—gave him no satisfaction whatsoever.

Mommy loved garage sales. She told him that going to a garage sale was like looking through a window, and through that window you could see inside other people's lives. You could see all the things they had loved and come to hate. All the things that hung around their neck like anchors. People tried to get rid of the stuff, she said, but the anchor was always there. It never went away. It just got heavier and heavier until it suffocated you, like the wet smoking cough Grammy had before she died. The one that made her sound like she was drowning.

Michael didn't know why you would want to see that stuff. It sounded horrible. Sometimes he thought maybe Mommy wasn't such a nice person. He looked down at the puzzle and wondered if it was an anchor like she said. Maybe it had belonged to some little kid like him who died, got hit by a bus or was consumed by a terrible sickness. Like Tim O'Brien up the block. Tim had something called cystic fibrosis. Michael didn't know what that was, except it made Tim cough up big ropy balls of snot, and then it made him die. Maybe the puzzle belonged to a kid like that, and maybe the kid's mom couldn't bear to look at it anymore so she sold it to his mommy, who then gave it to him. And maybe that kid's mom dreamed about it at night—the big globs of paint splattered across rough wood and the maniac, murderers' grins from Big Bird and Grover— and maybe she cried. Michael's own mommy didn't care about that. She snickered and gave the puzzle to him because maybe she wasn't a nice person. Like when he fell down on the porch stair that one time and scraped all the skin off his knee and she laughed. She said sorry afterward and kissed him and put a Band-Aid on it. But she had still laughed. He would never forget that.

Michael watched Big Bird scream a silent scream as Michael tore his big yellow stomach loose and set it aside. Now he thought maybe Grover knew what was coming and braced himself for it. Michael worked another piece free. Grover's head split apart right down the middle. One wide, white eye stared up at him, suspended above a severed nose and shattered half-mouth of gaping red and black. Michael was only five, but it occurred to him that this was a weird way to design a puzzle.

He put it back together. Took it apart. Put it back together. Took it apart. Over and over and over. As time went on, he found the puzzle had its own soothing quality, quite independent of the challenge (or lack) it presented. There was something about the bubbled surface, the rough edges, the cheap wafer-board backing, that stilled whatever had been roiling inside him all week. He put it back together, then just sat there with it, ran his fine little fingers over the paint. The varnish seemed a little too cold to the touch.

He took it apart again.

Hanging behind everything, there was this sound. A low, wet snuffling. He didn't look up. It was a sound that tried to call attention to itself. It had been going on for a long time, all week, but Michael tried to put it out of his head and just focus on the puzzle. If he did that, he thought, maybe it would stop.

Finally:

"Michael."

Michael snapped Big Bird's head back onto his spindly neck.

"Michael. Look at me, baby."

Michael did, reluctantly.

Mommy sat over on the living-room couch, still wrapped in her thick white bathrobe. She'd been wearing it for days. Her stringy blond hair hung limp and waxy on her shoulders.

She was crying.

Michael gets up to get a drink of water, only to find that the kitchen isn't where he thought it was. The kitchen has become the basement, and there's nothing there but an oily pit surrounded by a ring of shattered stones. Confused, he makes his way back upstairs and goes down the hallway to the bathroom.

He flips on the light switch and catches a glimpse of his face in the mirror. He is grinning madly, though he can't feel it at all, and it seems to him that the face in the mirror is not entirely his own.

There's a glass by the sink, stained and milky with years of hard-water accumulation. He wraps his fingers around it and slides it under the faucet. The pipes rumble and disgorge a globular red substance that quickly turns black. Michael recognizes the smell. Almost like blood, but with more salt in it.

He puts the glass back onto the edge of the sink and turns out the light.

He hears something in his parents' room.

A thick laugh.

A wheeze.

He pads down the hallway, dimly realizing he's naked, and pushes open the door.

Dad lays on top of Mommy, doing something. The smell is thicker in here. Blood and salt. Michael turns on the light.

Mommy squeals.

He sees her neck covered in blood.

Daddy looks up, eyes tarred and hollow like the pit where the kitchen used to be, and Michael sees that behind the familiar face is that other, that IT…

Dad opens his mouth. A wide, dripping grimace. Rimming the red and black maw are rows and rows of pointed white teeth…

Mommy and Daddy had a fight. It was a week ago. Michael didn't know what it was about. He had a sneaking suspicion it was about him. He didn't know how he knew, but the knowledge was there, nipping at him, nibbling its way through the soft, pliable skin of him.

Mommy and Daddy had a fight, and it was about him.

He was lying in bed when it started. He listened to the muffled voices in the room next to his, muted by the wall. He could feel the sharpness of the words, pricking at him like little needles even though he couldn't understand them. Daddy's voice kept getting louder and louder. Mommy's voice went shrill, warbled high like the rasp of a bird. He heard a door slam (the closet?), and then another. Heavy footsteps in the hall, and then Daddy was rustling past the thin sliver of door that Michael always left cracked, muttering something. Mommy followed. "It isn't what you *think*, Jim!" she shouted. He heard the steady *whisk-whisk* of her slippers on the stairs as she went after him. Then more voices downstairs. Shouts. Something thudded. Breaking glass from the kitchen. A brittle cry of pain.

When Michael got up in the morning, Daddy hovered over the kitchen sink, gazing with a shimmering intensity into the stainless-steel tub. He was dressed for work but his hair was all messy and his tie was crooked. When he saw Michael watching him he looked up and tried to smile, but he couldn't quite look Michael in the eyes.

"Heya, Champ," he said.

Michael sat at the little white table, the one Grammy gave them, and folded his hands neatly in front of him. He didn't say anything.

"I'm, uh…" Daddy started, then trailed off. Michael saw there was a little cut just above his lip. A wide purple bruise smeared across his temple. He remembered suddenly the breaking glass.

The silence thickened. Daddy cleared his throat. Michael wanted to yell at him, to scream at him to not say whatever it was he was going to say, but the words stuck in his throat like a plug of concrete.

"I'm, uh, I'm going away for a little while," Daddy said. "I've got to…"

He trailed off again.

"Daddy?" Michael asked. His voice was tiny. No scream in it at all.

"I've got to go away for work," Daddy lied.

"Daddy?"

Daddy looked at him. "What, Champ?"

Michael thought he saw something flicker across the black surface of Daddy's corneas, dancing just out of reach and then crouching there like a coiled snake.

That other. That thing.

They hadn't been in this house very long. Michael had only a loose sense of time, which sometimes made hours feel like days but sometimes made months whip by like weeks. But he knew it was summer when they had moved here, and now it was the cold heart of winter.

They'd come here because of Daddy's job. Mommy had had to quit hers, and she'd been mad about it. Michael noticed that most of the ways in which she wasn't such a nice person got worse. The whole thing with garage sales had started after they moved.

The last house had been brand new. Michael could even remember the builders making it. He'd been three, barely old enough to form a memory. Mommy and Daddy drove him out to this big grass field covered in wildflowers, with a scrum of dark woods running behind it. "See this, Michael?" Mommy had said. "This is where we're going to live." He hadn't understood. But then they'd gone back some time later, and the field was gone and there were big yellow tractors and piles of dirt and the yellowish skeleton of a house that had the tangy wood smell of a fresh-cut Christmas tree. The house was finished the next time they went back, along with others that looked just like it except for the paint. They lined all up and down the street like multi-colored blocks. Big, sweaty men carried all of their things out of the back of a big truck, and just like that, they were home.

The house they were in now was old. He didn't know how old, but it didn't have that fresh pine smell. It smelled like his Grammy's house, all dirt and smoke and old clothes. It creaked and groaned. He kept finding strange things, like the face carved in the wall behind his dresser, and all the weird little markings hacked into the baseboards. When he asked Daddy about those, Daddy said there must have been a little kid who lived there before him who liked to carve on things he wasn't supposed to. "Don't do that," Daddy said, and ruffled his hair, and then mom complained that someone called THE LANDLORD should have cleaned all that crap up before they moved in.

And there was the hole in the basement. A glistening black pit in the far corner, ringed by broken rocks like slanted gray teeth. A smell came out of it. Something like blood. Salt and blood.

"An old well or something," Daddy said. "Don't get too close to it. The ground around it might be soft."

But when Michael asked Mommy, she smiled and said that maybe there was a witch living here before them. Maybe that hole was where she threw the bones of all the little kids she ate. Then she saw his stricken face and laughed. Laughed like she did when he fell on the porch stair.

Heavy footsteps pounding up the basement stairs.

Michael starts to move, legs working without thought. The basement door grows bigger and bigger as he approaches. It looms like a shrine, the knob at eye-level, tick-tocking back and forth like a metronome.

The pounding stops.

With a life of its own, Michael's hand shoots out. He tells his hand to stop, begs it, but the fingers grip the knob, the wrist turns, the door swings open, and darkness floods into the light of the kitchen, turning everything hard and gray.

The thing wears one of Daddy's suits, but it's all stretched out and proportion-less. Long, spindly legs shoot forward like pistons, carrying the thing into the kitchen.

Michael feels his head tilting, and his gaze goes UP UP UP to the thing's mammoth, disproportionate head. It's covered in something wrinkly and brown like a paper bag. But alive. Two black button eyes peer out of the torn folds. Michael feels their weight pressing down into him.

"Hi!"

A voice like a wasps' nest caught in a cloud of bug spray.

"Who're you?"

"Who am I?" The thing bellows. No mouth, but Michael knows it's smiling. "I'm your new Daddy!"

👁

Daddy went to work like usual, but he didn't come back. That was last week. When Mommy finally came out of her bedroom, her face was puffy and red. It was like a swarm of red ants attacked her in her sleep.

She made Michael breakfast, sniffing while she cooked. She didn't look at him. Michael wanted to reach out to her, to touch her hand or her leg, to say something to make her feel better. But he was five, and he didn't know how. And there was always that fear, lurking not quite in the back of his mind, that she would turn on him with that not-nice grin and—

"Come here, baby."

Michael put down the pieces to the puzzle and sat still, watching her.

"Come sit with Mommy for a minute."

There was a word that he knew, a word he learned in school, and he didn't want to say it. But it hovered there, flitting about in the back of his throat.

"Michael…" A note of reprimand now. He stood, timid, and went to her. She sucked him into a tight, terry-cloth embrace and kissed his forehead. She stunk, like old milk and sweat socks.

"I'm sorry about all this, Champ," she said, and her breath smelled worse than the rest of her. It was like something died in her mouth. He had to fight the urge to pull away. "Tell you what? Why don't we go out and do something fun today?"

He imagined going out with her like this and suppressed a shudder. She could shower and get dressed, run a comb through the limp carpet of her hair. But whatever her anchor was right now, she'd be dragging it along with her.

The word slid past his tongue before he could stop it.

"Are you and Daddy…getting divorced?"

And there it was.

The not-nice smile.

Two days ago, Michael went into the basement.

He stood at the edge of the old well and looked down. Daddy had told him not to do that, said the ground might be soft, but he did it anyway because Daddy was gone and Mommy was upstairs crying and no one cared what he did anymore anyway.

A perfect circle of darkness sank away into thick, meaty nothing. The brick-lined gullet was slick and moss covered, crawling with white things he thought were beetles. He could hear the papery rasp of useless wings, the *click-click-click* of brittle legs scrabbling against rock. He smelled blood and salt, heard the steady *thud-cough* of running water far below.

And splashes. Like something was thrashing down there in the dark.

He stepped back and looked closely at the stones ringing the well. They were covered with markings, haphazard slashes that took him a moment to recognize as the same patterns hacked into the baseboards.

He turned to go back upstairs, and his eyes fell on an old metal cabinet against the far wall. It stood next to a listing, wet-warped tool bench. There was something on one of the lower shelves, shoved way into the black cubby like a rodent hiding from the light. It was lumpy and misshapen, like an old pile of rags.

He went to the cabinet, knelt, and fished the thing out. It fell to the dirt floor and opened like a poison flower.

A wet, papery mask. Wrinkled like a brown paper bag.

Coal-black eyes like buttons, a face covered in waxy brown skin like paper, no mouth or nose or hair. Just a twist of frayed rope, hanging loose around the neck.

A laugh like wasps. Or like little white legs scratching across brick.

"I'm your new Daddy," the thing says and Michael goes cold. "I'm your new Daddy, and I'm coming home!"

"Well," Mommy said. The word came out measured, like there was a thought hiding behind another thought. "That's entirely up to your Daddy, I guess."

He looked down at his hands.

"Your Daddy…" she started, then shook her head and tried again. "Do you know what *paranoia* means?"

He shook his head.

"It means thinking something is true when it isn't. It means…it means looking at a thing and seeing something else that isn't there. Do you understand?"

Michael thought of the well downstairs. The mask. When he looked at it, what he thought he saw was the discarded skin of a snake.

"I don't know."

"Your Daddy saw something, and he thought it was something else," she said. "And the thing he thought he saw made him mad. That's all."

"Was it something about me?"

She looked at him, level, and he watched gears turning behind her red-rimmed eyes. He remembered something his Daddy said once about his old boss, back before they moved. The phrase was *passing the buck*. Michael didn't know exactly what that meant, but he got the basic idea. And he understood that Mommy was, in that moment, looking for a way to pass the buck.

But instead she just shook her head.

"No, it wasn't something about you, baby," she said. "It was something about me."

Heavy footsteps suddenly clomped on the basement stairs, and Mommy smiled. It wasn't the not-nice smile. It was wide and full of teeth, and it made her look like a lunatic. Michael saw in her eyes a strange mixture: relief, joy, terror, and something else he couldn't quite touch.

"Look! He's home now!"

And she was up off the couch, hastily wiping her eyes with the back of her hand, floating like ether across the old brown grate. Forgetting that there was no outside door to the basement, that Daddy always came in through the front. Up the porch stairs where Michael skinned his knee.

(*I'm coming home*)

He opened his mouth, but nothing came out.

It was too late, anyway.

Michael heard Mommy cross the kitchen, heard the basement door bang open on a squeal of old hinges. Heard it exhale a low, wet sigh and smelled the pit's salt-blood breath, rolling through the house on a sour wave.

He closed his eyes and waited for the scream.

Cauterization
Mack Moyer

John prefers that I prepare the lines. His are always too rocky, too hard on the nostrils. I shake two big nuggets from the cellophane wrapper onto the nightstand and cover them with a crumpled dollar bill.

I lay my expired driver's license over the dollar bill and massage the nuggets into a fine dust. It's a skill, all right. Apply too much pressure and tiny chunks will burst out the sides. Too little pressure and you end up with a bloody nose.

John hovers over my shoulder impatiently as I cut the pile into two lines and roll the dollar bill. I snort my line first.

The crystalline blast sears my left nostril. In a moment, it will dissolve across a membrane and into my bloodstream. The uptick in my pulse rate will become an audible drumbeat. Emotional cauterization will ensue soon after.

John's turn. He snatches the bill and snorts his. He's greedy with his meth, at least as much as he can be; he paid for this batch, but he gives me the cash and I procure the crank through my dealer. While I don't charge John for acting as a middle man, sharing the bag goes without saying.

I've got plenty more stashed away in the kitchen but John doesn't know that, though he rightly suspects it.

The crank kicks in and John bounces across my bedroom, endlessly flapping his gums. Allison is getting worse, he tells me. Sleepwalking again. Dragged the kids into the backyard around three in the morning just a few nights ago. The kids told him that Mommy was saying some real whacko shit, to boot, all while she held a cigarette lighter to her forearm until a quarter-sized patch of skin was charred black.

I curl up on the couch, spark a Marlboro Red, feeling the loose phlegm rumble in my chest as I take a drag. I'm not really listening to him; his once-weekly monologues about his wife are both rambling and redundant. Aside from Allison's backyard witching hour shenanigans, it's nothing I haven't heard before.

Instead, I'm calculating John's chances of maintaining an erection later. When his tolerance is low, the meth hits him too hard and he can't keep a hard-on.

When his speech takes on a staccato stutter, so bad that he can only finish half his sentences, I resign myself to a night without an orgasm. It will consist of John bitching about Allison, John attempting to jam his flaccid cock into me, John failing.

I'd say I'm disappointed but I still get free crank out of the deal, so I'm not complaining.

During the course of his monologue, John steps under the ceiling fan. It's connected to a light fixture, three bare bulbs, only one of which works, and barely at that. In that flickering light, the alternating shadows hit him at the right angle and he looks fifteen years younger.

His small but inexorably growing double chin seems to recede. His widow's peak vanishes and, though I know it's only the shadows playing tricks, I can almost see the small, beginner's gauges stretching out his earlobes.

A familiar bit of flotsam drifts through my stream of consciousness. I laugh, and for a moment he glares at me, assuming that I'm laughing at his marital woes. I can and do laugh at him, by the way, but not now.

"I'd love to be homeless with you," I say to him.

His scowl turns to a smile. That was his big line, a lifetime ago, as we sat in a darkened corner in the community college cafeteria, half-assing the comic book we planned to create. We never completed a single page, hardly even outlined a plot, but it was enough for us to brag about on Myspace.

Anyway, that night, ten minutes before the overnight janitors would boot us from our corner, I mentioned that our big, grand artistic endeavors just might never pan out, that we'd be starving artists living on the street.

Then he said it. Not the greatest pick-up line I ever heard, but it made me realize I liked him, that he liked me back.

"We kissed for the first time that night," John says, looking on wistfully as he lights a cigarette.

"Fucked for the first time, too."

"We never did finish the comic though."

We laugh, not because the crank's got us tweaking, although we are. We laugh like we laughed fifteen years ago. And just like that night fifteen years ago, John manages to keep his erection.

We fuck to unspoken memories of our youth, to our vague, unfounded hopefulness. My thighs snap shut around him, like a spring-loaded animal trap snaring the last vestige of our youth. And, for a moment, we're not just fucking, though I wouldn't dare say we're making love. Then again, it feels like something more than two former scene kids using crank and sex to lubricate their passage into middle age.

He pushes into me, grunts; I dig my fingernails into his back. I run my fingers through his thinning hair. We look into each other's eyes and I want to tell him that this is more than meth and sex, that he is the only other person who has a key to my house, that during my last doctor's visit, I listed him as my emergency contact.

For that moment, I choose to forget that our relationship is, at its core, transactional. Call us what you will, but when I inevitably snort one line over my limit, when my heart shudders and the myocardial tissue turns brown and I gasp my last ragged breath, it'll be John who finds me the next morning, who'll dial 911 when he discovers my corpse. That's gotta be worth something.

I shudder with orgasm just as John climaxes inside me. Then he groans in that worried way of his and, that quickly, we return to the reality of our sometimes-weekly trysts in my isolated North Philly hovel where, at our very best, John can stay hard long enough to regret dumping his load into me.

I sit up, turn my back to him, aware that a new roll of fat is forming around my ribcage when I bend over, but I hide that as quickly as I notice it when I pull a ratty Against Me concert tee over my bare frame.

John's exit is unceremonious. I'm staring out my window smoking when I hear him struggling to button his jeans; it gets a little harder for him each week.

"Want me to leave you a bump?" he asks.

He knows that I want him to but I just shrug and stare out into the dark. His keys jangle as he heads to the door. He opens it, shuts it, and descends to the living room. Only then do I turn around. The fucker didn't leave me a bump.

I manage to sleep at some point, though not for long. It's been a while since I've been bothered by sleep deprivation. With a meth habit, fractured sleep just comes with the territory.

It's almost four in the morning. I awake standing at the kitchen counter with a fresh whiskey and ginger ale in my hand. Drinking it is probably a bad idea but I see that the whiskey bottle is nearly empty. It had been full, last I remembered.

Still, sleepwalking my way through the bottle is preferable to sleepwalking out into the backyard, kids in tow, in a poor attempt at self-immolation.

"A toast to crazy bitches," I say and guzzle what remains in my glass.

I sigh and reach into the cabinet above the sink. The hinges whine and a cockroach skitters over my fingers. The crank is hidden inside a box of baking soda, just in case John decides to go poking around.

I snort a line. It'll get me through the morning, until the booze is out of my system, and then maybe by this afternoon, sleep will be possible. (Forget that I'll likely need to crack open a second whiskey bottle to get to sleep; I've long since accepted that basic concepts like sleeping and waking are dependent upon my ingestion of dueling chemicals.)

After returning to my bedroom, I open my window and light a cigarette.

I'd be mistaken to call my house a rowhome. It had been, once, back when my grandparents lived here and there were actually other houses on the block. Now it stands alone on an otherwise vacant block, one of many, almost a quarter-mile in any direction. There was a time when my friends—when I had friends—would crack lazy jokes about how I'm the only white girl in my neighborhood. Had there been anyone in my life to make that joke now, I'd correct them: I'm the only person in my neighborhood, period.

Mother Nature has reclaimed these vacant stretches, filling them with weed trees, shrubs, briar, and bramble. The flora, I don't mind, but the fauna is another matter entirely. Possums, rats, and raccoons prowl the dark. It's wild country out here, making me feel like a homesteader in a city of over a million people.

Now and then I'll spot a passing transient, but even the addicts keep away. No drug peddlers 'round these parts, pardner, with the lone exception being the aging tweaker who delivers my crank.

That's what makes it so peculiar when I spot a lone figure at the end of the block, standing on the corner across the street. The person raises a cigarette to their lips, the tiny red cherry a bloody pinprick in the gloom, but otherwise just stands there.

A hooker, perhaps? I doubt it. They usually post up closer to the drug markets or the main prostitute drag a few miles south on Kensington Avenue. I lean on the window sill, lighting another cigarette, watching the figure in the distance. The figure is black, not in skin color, but utterly bathed in shadow. Even so, I can tell when the figure cocks its head very slightly and I get the impression that this person is watching me back.

I furrow my brow—just fucking feeling another new wrinkle on my forehead—and raise the cigarette to my lips. The figure on the corner mimics me, showing me that murderous pinprick the moment I inhale.

I know I should pull myself away from the window. Humoring the weirdo watching me won't do me any good, and yet, something compels me to keep an eye on the figure. I'm not eager to make friends but I feel a sudden and urgent need to keep track of this person.

My cigarette has burned down to the butt. I flick it out the window and light another.

Down at the corner, the figure flicks its cigarette into the gutter and lights a new one.

One would have to work extraordinarily hard to break into my house. Wrought iron bars on all the windows. Double locks on the back door, triple on the front. Nanna and Gramps were aware that their neighborhood was going down the tubes and shielded themselves accordingly well before I moved in.

But it's not the idea that this person could get inside my house that unsettles me, as much as it is the anonymous nature of the figure's gaze.

Then the figure starts up the sidewalk. It passes underneath the few working streetlights lining my street but remains completely dark, like a living shadow.

I'm about to shout that I keep an aluminum Louisville Slugger by the front door and I was one fuck of a softball player back in the day, but I'm not entirely confident that would dissuade the figure from approaching.

Just as this thought shoots through my skull, the figure stops and turns right, climbing into a dense thicket of foliage that the dull orange glow of the streetlights can't penetrate.

The dark bushes ripple as the figure disappears inside and I lose sight of it.

For all I know, that person is a fellow tweaker and just wants to continue on his or her way, cutting through the vacant wilderness because they're tired of the strange woman staring from her lonely bedroom window.

But I know better.

The movement within the bushes ceases; that, or it's just too dark for me to see any, and I'm confronted by an entirely new sense of dread. My eyes strain. I'm looking for that burning cigarette cherry. Surely, the figure will take another puff.

My flip phone vibrates on the nightstand and I nearly shit myself. I snatch the phone and quickly return to the window.

Keeping one eye on the bushes, I flip it open. I've got a voicemail from a private number, though the phone never rang. Though it's possible that the call came when I was sleeping and the voicemail notification was just delayed. It happens with these older phone models.

The voicemail begins with crackling static, initially faint, and for a moment, I assume the message will cut off. A wrong number, or a pocket dial, or a malfunctioning robocall. The static ebbs and flows, yet I hear something else, just under the crackle.

It's a low voice, dark and ethereal, but unmistakably feminine. "Broken...cunt..." says the voice, gusting over the static. "You're...broken..." The voice becomes clearer, taking on a slightly higher pitch. "Cunt."

So I'm a broken cunt, huh? That's an arguable point, but I've been called far worse in threatening phone calls.

Her voice takes on a singsong intonation. Two children chime in, singing along. The song becomes clearer, higher pitched, almost gleeful. And I'm wrong. They're not calling me a broken cunt.

"Your broken cunt," they sing. "The dead flesh from your...broken...cunt..."

Ice fills my bowels. I can no longer pretend that it's the crank that's got me trembling. When I pull the phone from my ear, somehow I must click the speaker on, because those voices continue, louder, echoing in my room as the light flickers above.

I try to cut off the volume but the song continues. My hands shake so violently that I can just barely hit the power button, holding it in until the phone's screen goes black, finally cutting off the chorus.

Out in the dark, perhaps thirty yards away in the dappled midnight sea across from my window, I see the figure's cigarette, cherry bright red upon inhalation.

I slam shut the window and pull the curtains down. My bare legs break out in goosebumps but by the time it occurs to me to find some pants, I'm already in the kitchen again, whiskey sloshing over the rim of the glass, onto the counter, interrupting the roaches nibbling on the rotting detritus from the Chinese takeout I ordered three days ago.

I sit on the couch, the baseball bat's aluminum surface chilly between my thighs, and I light another cigarette and struggle to pull the whiskey to my lips. I consider calling John, because I assume it was Allison who left that voicemail, but I can't bring myself to turn the phone back on.

From the corner of my eye, I catch something outside my window, through the stained white linen sheet that's been serving as a curtain. I try not to look, although I can't help but glimpse the cigarette's burning tip as the figure takes another puff.

That wasn't the first regretful load John deposited into me, nor was it the first time I voiced not a word of protest when I felt him spasm inside me several long seconds before his release. I've always blamed the crank for that. Meth has a way of cutting through your ego, leaving bare your id and all your deviant impulses, like plump pale worms squirming from upturned earth. When one is sufficiently tweaked, satiation becomes a priority. Little matters beyond sensation and gratification.

Long story short, when tweakers fuck, we rarely use condoms.

Roughly two years ago, after many an irresponsible load, I began experiencing strange aches and pains my lower abdomen, cramps that felt almost accusatory. Oh, I realized that I hadn't been getting my period, ditto for my growing pot belly, most noticeable back when I was still working, wearing that awful ill-fitting K-Mart smock.

I convinced myself that my rounded belly was just a sign that I'd been eating too much despite a succession of long meth binges, during which I'd routinely go days without eating.

Denial and ignorance can look awfully similar.

Back then, I still painted, half-convinced that the menial job and borderline homelessness would be worth it when the drooling masses realized my artistic genius. I'd been painting that night, down in the basement as always. At almost the exact moment I cut a red brushstroke across the canvas, I suffered a bad cramp, reflexively violent, a wholesale rejection of whatever was inside me.

This cramp was different from the others. I was scared so I did the only thing I could do: I bent over the small table next to my easel and snorted another line.

My thighs were slick, I noticed, and my sweatpants were soaked with something red and thick. Dead things were slipping out of me, that much was clear, so I clenched my jaw and grimly pushed the rest out. Somehow, I was able to focus on the task at hand. Not a sign of character or bravery; it was all from the meth.

As far as the cleanup went, I cannot get into specifics. When I finished, I wrenched free several floorboards with Gramps' old prybar and took a spade shovel to the soil beneath.

I did this naked from the waist down, my gore-splattered sweatpants and panties in a pile along with the flesh, wrapped in a trash bag. Calling it *flesh* might sound needlessly callous but, at the time, I couldn't refer to it as anything else. Can't manage to do it today, either.

The basement grew stiflingly hot as I worked. My hair, soaked in sweat, clung to my face and salt stung my eyes, yet I dug, one shovelful at a time, and when I paused to think—which wasn't often—I told myself I was doing it for John. Had I told him what happened, it could have ruined his life, his marriage, and I simply couldn't do that to him.

Of all the lies I've told in my life, that one was the most brazen.

And though the timeline doesn't add up, as I finished placing the soiled clothes and flesh into the hole, as I threw the soil upon it, I felt at that moment a pair of charred, blackened lips less than an inch from my ear curving into a smile.

"Broken...cunt..."

I awake lying on the basement floor, staring up at the single lightbulb dangling from the ceiling (wire and socket bringing to mind umbilical and placenta). It appears I've been sleepwalking again, as I haven't come down to this awful room since the night I buried the flesh.

Despite my pulse hammering in my skull and the putrid aroma of last night's whiskey wafting up my gullet, I'm nevertheless compelled to look at my work.

It's been two years since I've seen my paintings, a dozen completed canvases along with the water-warped remains of the ones I gave up on, haphazardly rolled up and dumped along the back wall.

There's an issue, though, one that keeps me lingering in the familiar musk of watercolors and oils mixed with the damp, mossy basement stink. My crank habit has made my memory spotty, but I've always kept track of my work, and I never finished a twelfth painting.

A bead of sweat trickles down my temple and I'm struck with a sudden nausea as I look upon it. It's a swirl of black, though the darkness varies by degrees, framing a strange shape in the middle.

Of course, I don't need long to recognize it. Those rippling, crinkled shades of black portray a close-up of your standard ten-gallon garbage bag, wrapped poorly (and perhaps hurriedly) over a small, half-formed face.

I look down at the floor. The floorboards are missing and I see the soil, still marked by divots from the spade shovel.

I'd scream, but at that very moment, I hear John rummaging through my kitchen cabinets, no doubt searching for crank.

"John!" I shout.

He's still in the kitchen when I get up there, clutching my crank to his chest, as guilty as a kid caught with his hand in the cookie jar. Clearly he's been up all night. I can smell liquor on him and he looks to be on the back-nine of last night's crank.

He moves his lips as if to speak, but his throat merely clicks. His right arm is wrapped in gauze from his hand up to his elbow. There's a hospital bracelet on his left wrist.

"John?" I ask.

He offers a silent stutter, and I'm not sure how much meth this idiot snorted, but I'll be motherfucked if I'm about to let him put a dent in my eight ball. I snatch the bag off him and shake a nugget onto the counter. I mash it into powder with the bottom of a coffee mug and chop a line.

"Allison and the kids are dead," he says.

I'd just put the rolled-up dollar bill to my nostril, but I pause. John looks at me expectantly, perhaps waiting for consolation, but I still catch him stealing a glance at my meth. A sudden, visceral hatred overwhelms me.

I snort the line anyway, sensing John's jealousy when I shake out another nugget, crush it up just like the first, and snort that too, expediting my blastoff. I light the remains of a cigarette, resting on the mouth of an empty beer can. "And you're here, why?" I ask.

"I just need someone to talk to," he says.

"But you didn't come here to talk. You came here to steal my crank."

"My wife and kids are dead," he says, as if that absolves him.

And perhaps that should elicit some sympathy from me, but it doesn't. Because now I realize that, should John be the person who eventually finds me dead, he's going to rummage through my shit looking for crank before he dials 911, if he ever dials at all.

"The house was on fire when I got home," he begins.

I plop the cigarette into the beer can, extinguishing it. "I don't need to hear the details."

"But my family—"

"Your family, not mine," I tell him.

I smile at his palpable desperation, a feeling I know well. He obviously finished the last bag I procured for him. Crashing now, in his grief, he knows I hold respite in my hand, that I can alleviate his anguish—cauterize it, if you will—simply by handing the drug over to him.

"I'm not giving it to you," I tell him, wondering if he'll just take it from me. He could, if he wanted; he's a head taller and a hundred pounds heavier. He could, but he doesn't, the same way I could give him instant relief, but I don't.

"Alright," he says. "I'll leave. I won't come back."

"You will," I tell him. "When you realize that you can't get a fix anywhere else. Or maybe you'll read my obituary in a few weeks. Then you'll come back, digging through my shit again, trying to pick the bones. Because that's the only reason why you're here. Let's not lie to ourselves."

Then he leaves. His desperation lingers after he's gone and I smile perversely, taking far more pleasure in his suffering than I anticipated.

I make a call and my dealer drops off another eight ball. Forget blastoff; by noon I'm in low orbit, intent on hurtling toward heaven.

I can't sit still. Normally, when I'm this tweaked, I'll fire back a few drinks to even myself out, but today I have no such compulsion. My brain's running just like an old laptop. My circuitry is overwhelmed and I can almost hear the cooling mechanism in my skull, fans whirling, CPU chugging as the screen fails to load.

It's working, working, working, but spews forth no data.

That's quite alright. I know my reasoning even if I can't articulate it. If I sleep, I know where I'll wake up. I'd rather end up there on my own volition. I snort another line, spark a

Marlboro, breathe it into my ragged lungs, and sit at my bedroom window, flip phone in hand. It feels strangely warm.

I wonder what time, specifically, John found Allison and the kids, wonder if I should check the time I received that voicemail, though it hardly makes a difference now. Behind the sky's gray veil, the sun arcs and descends and by the time the sun begins to dip below the skyline, I've already lost track of just how much meth I've snorted.

I turn the phone on. It lags for a solid five minutes before it begins to beep with notifications, vibrating in my hand like an egg about to hatch. I start with the text messages, over a dozen from a private number, all multimedia messages that my elderly phone struggles to process.

They all look vaguely similar, photos of a dark room framed by fire, the only difference being the flames inching inward with each subsequent pic, growing closer to three black figures in the center. They just stand there, reminding me of shadows seared onto a wall after a nuclear blast.

I blink and an hour passes. When I look out my window again, the streetlights have winked on. There's something rustling in the bushes across the street. I see the tip of the burning cigarette before I see the figure.

It steps out of the bushes, watching me watch it, and steps directly under the streetlight. It seems to draw the light in and trap it, its edges simmering as if distorting the gravity around it, a walking event horizon.

A walking nothing, an embodiment of emptiness.

I put my Marlboro to my lips and inhale. The figure does the same.

I click off the text messages and turn now to the voicemails. I've got plenty more, all from that private number, one after the other, the most recent one being from this afternoon.

Another line, I chop it right there on the window sill as the nothing watches. My heart shudders with trepidation but I snort it anyway. Outside, the nothing has crossed the street, standing now in front of my house. Movement up the street catches my eye. Something very tiny is crawling toward my house, slowly, on hands and knees.

I go to the living room and begin playing the voicemails. They sing about my broken cunt, cheerfully at times, amid that crackling static that I know isn't static; it's the fire eating its way through that room, chewing through drywall and plaster. Sometimes only Allison sings, barely audible over her screaming children. Or, as is the case in the more recent voicemails, Allison chants something incomprehensible while the kids laugh hysterically.

Through my dingy linen curtain, I spot the figure's burning cigarette. As if guided by a wind to my back, I unlock the front door.

In the basement, I cut another line and try to force it up my callused nostril. There's a quick, sharp pain and I sneeze, painting my twelfth canvas in blood and mucus and snot. The voicemails continue to mock me, but the deafening thunderclaps of my heart nearly drown out the voices, along with the sound of my front door opening, closing, the deadbolts clicking.

I'm getting dizzy, chewing meth, my nostrils no longer an option. The taste is sour and revolting but I swallow anyway, and the cellophane wrapper is empty now, and the world goes upside down and my cell phone bursts into flames, jagged plastic shards steaming hot in my palm, melting, merging with flesh. Yet the voices remain.

I press my ear to the earthen floor where I've pulled up the floorboards. Something rustles under the soil. Above me, footsteps cross the living room before coming to a stop in front of the basement door.

The Tapping at Cranburgh Grange
Felice Picano

I'm not at all certain how it was that we came to that particular village in that shire. Later on, Martin thought that it had been a bus tour we'd taken. We'd stopped at the village inn for lunch or tea and after we'd gotten back onto the bus, we'd already decided we had to return to the spot. We did return annually after that, taking rooms in the inn for first two, then three nights, then for almost two weeks: his entire vacation from work.

I recalled well, actually *we* recalled, that we were immediately drawn to the house among all the others. Naturally, we'd passed it on every trip we'd made to the village and every stay in the inn; we'd had to pass it since it was on the road between the railway and the inn, the largest, the handsomest, and altogether the most substantial house. But this last particular trip and stay, we had the misfortune of having rain for two and a half days straight. Hardly torrential rains, but steady enough that you heard it day and night, awake and asleep, and it rained—if not particularly hard—still it rained so steadily and regularly that it seemed at times to have never *not* rained ever in that village.

The local people took the rain for granted: it was "ordinary spring" to them. They dressed for it; at times even rather elaborately, wearing long capes, or multiple capes with hoods for their eyes. So, after the rain, we had but a single night left before we must leave again, and as the rain had for a minute stopped being regular, it was I who suggested we go for a lengthy walk in the village before our supper. We were both desperate to get out of doors, or at least away from the inn and its taproom regulars and the few attempts at entertainments they offered. There was something suggesting an actual part-afternoon of sun with a possible sunset if we could only get outside.

So that's what we did, traipsing through the village and then out the eastern end of it, and we didn't stop traipsing for at least one and a half hours. It was Martin who said he needed a rest, and frankly, so did I. We stopped at a friendly enough looking wall built on two levels, one clearly meant for a seat, the other a back rest, and that was when we *really* saw the house for the first time, before us. The tall, wrought iron gate was open, which it never had been before, and that was something of an invitation, so after a minute or so of *Should we? Dare we?* We did. We entered onto the curved gravel auto approach and there was the house so instantly present, it was almost as though it had leapt to meet us halfway. Even more inviting, in the door, and stuck askew presumably by the wind, was the crucial sign reading "To Let."

Naturally that called for a further inspection of the premises, at least what could be obtained from the exterior alone, since we knocked and rang and there was no response within, so we obliged. It was on the far west wing ell that we found the magnificent sunset starting, so barmily beautiful over such a lovely landscape that we leant against the bottom of what appeared to be the dining room's locked casement windows and watched and didn't breathe a word. Once it had set and a little breeze arose, we set off without a word back to the inn, arriving at nightfall. But we passed and I—at least for the first time— noticed along the way, the sign in the office window not five doors away reading: *W.R. Sheriff—Realtor—Solicitor: Local Properties.* "That's where we shall be tomorrow morning at ten sharp," Martin said, and I replied that he sounded masterful when he was determined.

"Well, yes," Ms. Sheriff, for it turned out the solicitor was a woman, said, "It has been vacant several years. But always constantly and well taken care of," she quickly amended. "As to why it's only now put up to let? Well, that's because the house is part of a messy, and much contested, will probation, and at least four of the contesters finally agreed that as the place is habitable, it might as well be of use in covering the incessant legal fees they are paying out."

Ms. Sheriff then showed us photographs of the exterior and interior of the house that appeared to have been taken, if not when the place was first built, then shortly thereafter when residential photography first came into vogue: "Some decades after the Napoleonic Wars and before the Civil War in your own country," was as precisely as she could date it.

"Two of the daguerreotypes show women in hoop skirts," Martin pointed out. "Surely that must date it." The woman he had pointed to seemed to be not quite brunette, and of a very fine figure with a strong-featured face.

"That might actually be the second wife of the owner/builder," the realtor opined. "The first was a sickly thing, but when she passed, he met this one and she it was who became mistress of Cranberry Grange for decades, outliving her husband and I believe, all three of their children. The house then passed to a relatively distant cousin of his, a fellow who traveled the world for the National Geographical Society. After that, the house was lived in only sporadically, and sometimes only on holidays, when hordes of guests would arrive."

I could see Martin's eyes light up when she spoke of the explorer owner heir, and I have to admit, my own grew large and even a bit moist at the mention of the house's name. Who wouldn't want to live in a Cranberry Grange? But, of course, the name would turn out to be slightly incorrect, as was much else we were first told about the house. On that we both agreed. We couldn't have both heard incorrectly. Not that it was purposefully misleading, I don't think. At least not until much later on.

As I said before, we were leaving that mid-afternoon, and so we were quickly settled into her elderly Volvo station wagon and smartly driven to the house. The double front doors were thrust open and a few windows thrown ajar—"Remember how the widow disparaged the second house in *The Spoils of Poynton*?" Martin asked me, and I answered, "Not a double-door in the place!"

"Well, here, there's several," Ms. Sheriff proudly replied.

Some interior doors were racked open noisily and we got a very rushed tour of the place. This, however, was enough to confirm that it had indeed been the dining room that looked out upon the sunset, that a breakfast room opposite looked due east, that a little library on the first floor was matched by a sewing room upstairs and by a clothes-drying room with multiple skylights on the third half-floor. One parlor on the ground floor had become a bedroom, perhaps for the original owner's wife in her dotage. Upstairs were six other ones, with a large and modern-ish (ca. 1910?) bathing salon with a number of water closets scattered about, also later additions. Like the bathing facilities, the kitchen which had originally been a separate room off the rear of the house (Ms. Sheriff: "Kitchen fires were so common then!") was also modernized, possibly forty years later, but looked quite passably useful. Mud rooms, club rooms, gun rooms, and who know what other smaller rooms opened out from odd angled corners at all three floors. But the fireplaces were now more or less ornamental as there was a central heating system.

"We couldn't possibly take it for the next six months, since I'd require that long to wrap up my work in the 'States," Martin said. Then Ms. Sheriff told us the annual rent and suggested he might want to pay down now to hold the place for when it was we wanted it. So, at her office, he arranged to do just that, writing out a check for half a year, even if we came later. I just nodded. When Martin wants something…

As it turned out, we were back in the village and moved into the house less than four months later. The minute Martin mentioned retirement, his partners eagerly thanked him for his service and offered to buy him out. I'm not certain whether he was pleased or not by their abruptness, but I pointed out that we wanted to go and so we would. Our own place in the 'States we left with a caretaker and with our married children coming and going. Suddenly, there we were, inside the grand old Regency manse, high above the stream and with fields spread out below, unpacking our silver and clothing and knick-knacks.

Ms. Sheriff had mentioned the two people who'd cared for the place while it was vacant and we soon met them: a bit more than middle-aged but still quite presentable woman named Mrs. Ethel Grack, and her son, oddly named Dmitry, a strapping lad of about thirty, movie star handsome in that blond Slavic manner but a bit slow on the uptake. Both loved the old house and its grounds and they tended to them kindly and generously with their time and attentions. They slept in the Dower Cottage at the eastern end of the grounds. Martin once remarked, "If only they were equally devoted to those who leased the place." Two girls from the village of indeterminate relationship to the Gracks also came weekly to keep the place spotless.

We'd been ensconced very comfortably indeed when two events occurred almost simultaneously to alter our stability. First, at breakfast, Martin asked if he might change bedrooms with me. I rather liked the view from the corner windows of the room that I'd decided upon—after he'd chosen his own first— and so I suppose I was less than a hundred percent charitable when I asked whatever for. "Because I can hear the leak from my room. You can't hear it from your room, can you?" he asked.

This startling piece of information elicited from me the rather inane remark, "Leak? What leak?" His answer to this was that he had begun hearing a leak in one of the sinks in one of the half baths or powder rooms but had been unable to locate it. And yes, he'd put Dmitry on the case, and he'd not found the source of the sound either, partly because Dmitry claimed not to hear it himself; another sign of his somewhat dimwittedness, Martin believed.

Not a moment after this conversation, the un-heeding Dmitry appeared at the breakfast table to say that we had visitors. Might he let them in? We had finished breakfast, and in sailed Wilhelmina Sheriff and an elderly gentleman who was clearly some cleric or other. They sat themselves down at our welcoming table and helped themselves to what was left of the coffee and Mrs. Grack's excellent scones, chattering all the while.

The gist of their talk was that the church held twice a year fairs of local produce, flowers, goods and locally made crafts, and the village looked forward to it greatly, as did the neighboring villages in the shire. "St. Botolph's Day Fair is a crucial event for our village people and it is in the greatest danger at this time," the aged Parson said, with feeling.

I was waiting for them to hit us up for a donation, and I could all but see Martin calculating what he could give. But Wilhelmina clarified: "It's the grounds, you see. The church and its manor house both have questionable drainage. I'm sure you haven't failed to notice a large round barreled lorry outside it, as workmen come and go clearing it up."

"A tedious process," the parson added. "We don't know how long they'll be there."

In fact, we had noticed the truck only the day before during our afternoon walk. Before we could say another word, the cleric spoke up again, "Historically, Cranburgh Grange provided the grounds for the bi-annual fair until quite recently. It was always held here, on the front and south facing lawn. There are sepia-graphs of the event. It was, after all, the grandest house in the shire." Wilhelmina merely nodded and downed more scone and preserves. Before I could ask, "Cranburgh? Not Cranberry?" The parson explained that the fair had been moved to the church grounds only in the past few years, once the mansion's heirs declared the property out of bounds. He assured us that if we allowed it, the fair would all be set up, operated and managed, and then taken apart again by his staff and volunteers. Afterwards, one would never even notice it had been here. All we need do is step out at any time during the fair, receive some refreshment, and be thanked for our largesse.

That sounded completely reasonable to Martin, and as I had no rational opposition, the motion was carried then and there. Only as they were leaving did I say to Wilhemina, "Cranburgh?" to which the parson replied, "Yes, of course, named after Lord and Lady Cranburgh. It was the builder's second wife who began the St. Botolph's Day event in her lifetime: Lady Sofia Cranburgh." Then they were gone.

We were to hear a great deal more of this one-time paragon of the shire. Once it became generally known in the village that we'd agreed to open the grounds of the Grange (we continued to call it "Cranberry" among ourselves) for the fair, as in years past, it seemed that we had suddenly gained status, and more importantly, new friends. Sam Westin, the fellow who ran the post office and general office and stationers next to Ms. Sheriff's office, greeted us like long lost cousins as we took our daily walk. "You know, of course, that the Grange has its own post box within," he assured us, all but twinkling with amity as he handed us the keys. "At no charge, naturally." He then foisted some leaflets or other apparently from previous decades upon us, and assured us that his eldest daughter Elspeth's hand-embroidered aprons and napery were the star crafts of past fairs.

Not to be outdone, Mrs. Anthony Page, the owner of the little bakery across the lane, sent out a boy to fetch us in and plied us with strawberry jam oat cakes she'd just taken out of the oven. "T'was Lady Sofia Cranburgh who first appreciated us common folk for our arts and crafts a century nigh, as every one of us knows," she said. "Why, I'll be baking for a day and half beforehand, and even so I'll be out of goodies by mid-afternoon."

The more we heard, the more we became interested in this first and longest in-residence woman of what we'd already come to think of as our house. A few days later, I had the opportunity to learn even more. Martin still had business he must attend to and when phones and faxes and e-mails were not enough, he had to go into London himself. I drove him to the station of the narrow-gauge rail extension at what might be considered the main town of the shire, a local line that connected up to an express line. While there, I noticed a lending library and stepped in and expressed an interest in the house. What I was able to scan and then borrow after some paperwork, was a sort of homegrown history of the shire for the past half millennium by an enthusiastic amateur, with Lady Sofia Cranburgh prominent in the 19th Century chapter. Her virtues were apparently so many, so widespread, and so—after a while—unctuously narrated, that I simply took the thing out for a small fee, intending Martin to peruse it. I thought, especially, that he'd be tickled to see one of the photographs we'd been shown, repeated in the text, this time definitely naming Lady Sofia Cranburgh as the sitter.

"According to this volume, Lady Sofia was an unparalleled paragon of taste, generosity and breeding," Martin declared after tea one afternoon, when we were taking our post prandial walk about the property. I agreed, saying that I'd heard similar encomiums from virtually everyone in the village or surrounding area, including an otherwise surly auto garage fellow who had changed the tires on our rented car. "Then I'm afraid you have rather sizable shoes to fill," Martin concluded. I told him I would do no such thing but rather rely on his own good works and would merely be a hanger-on. I knew his fiduciary business in London had gone exceedingly well, and we'd extended our lease on Cranburgh Grange for another annum.

The St Botolph's Fair day was a gorgeous one, picture perfect, and both Martin and I were thrilled to see how wonderfully the front and larger south-side lawns looked as a fair ground. It was charming, naturally, with old fashioned booths of deal and other lightwood and so gaily done up—the cake stalls, the tombola, the jam racks, the duck race for the children, the curiosities booth (of questionable antiquities)—that I said to one villager, "If she were here, Lady Sofia would approve," and she replied, "Oh, I do hope so. We do it all for her," speaking of the long dead woman in the present tense which I thought quite odd.

The afternoon would have been perfect if Martin hadn't gone off for a longish time with one of the plumbing engineers who was all but resident at the church grounds, just when he was needed to make a little speech. So, it was left to me to stumble through it. When he reappeared and I chided him, he merely said, "Well, they are professionals, aren't they? I'm certain they'll find the damned leak."

I was surprised to hear that he was still bothered by the sound since I now slept in his previous bedroom and still had never heard it at all. I was about to discuss it when Elspeth Westin and her parents appeared and made us a gift of some lovely café curtains she'd embroidered especially for the Grange's breakfast nook. That occasioned other craftspeople to come forward and simply inundate us with their works as signs of their appreciation. "No wonder Lady Sofia wanted the fair. We needn't buy household goods for a year," I said. However, Martin assured me, that these gifts signified that the givers wanted to be invited to tea or luncheon and so now I had that to look forward to.

Luckily Mrs. Grack was neither upset nor surprised and later remarked, "Tw'as a staple of the Lady Cee to hold little repasts for the village women. She was loved so…." She then aided me in putting together a menu for the first of these affairs which I admit would have baffled me to do on my own.

It was during the second such tea that the "professional" plumbers came by the house and went all about it with Martin looking for the leak. They found nothing but declared they would return some evening when everyone was out and it was quiet. That took place two days later and was productive of the following statement: "We tried out every inch of piping in the place, previously wrapping them all in linen for hidden leaks and, as a result, there is no leak to show. Not one leak at all," adding, I thought, unnecessarily, "Unlike the damned parson's edifices which haven't a sound pipe among the lot."

Martin's response to this was silent at the time, but the following day I noted in his datebook an appointment in London with an otologist. Without saying a word to me, he was having his hearing checked out. It did apparently check out just fine and he returned without any tiny mechanism half hidden behind his lobes. But that only deepened the mystery. So he moved his bed chamber to the little parlor on the first floor. For a few weeks that appeared to be the solution.

But even before the irritating sounds returned for him, I noticed a distinct if not very large alteration in Martin's behavior. He insisted on speaking of private matters between us outside of the house and usually on one of our walks, or long drives, which we begun to take whenever we faced inclement weather. One of these conversations began with Martin saying, "You don't think me a failure in life, do you?"

I was never so astounded by a statement in my life and hastened to refute it. "Who has made you think anything that wrong?" I asked. "Tell me, Martin and I'll…I'll slap his face."

"Too late for that," he said, laughing at my surprising vehemence, "*She* was buried a decade ago, although she seemed to hang on far too long." It was then that Martin told me of his father's "second wife," He never called her any kind of mother, and it became clear why. She'd scolded and chided and denigrated him behind his father's back from the time they met until the day he joined the U.S. Navy, lying about his age to enter at age 17. He'd never once spoken of her to me in our long marriage and I was both pleased for it now, and yet saddened by his awful parental experience—mine had been so normal by comparison—which seemed for some unknown reason to be returning to bother Martin's consciousness so much later.

Not too long after this, we found ourselves entertaining another delegation from the village with a second request. It had been a dry and quite lovely autumn, and the month of December seemed unusually mild. Martin and I had discussed whether we ought to return to Longmeadow, Massachusetts for the holidays, but only the previous day, we'd been apprised that we needn't bother: our children and three grandchildren had decided instead to come to us. Partly it was curiosity, of course, to see where we resided; partly an excuse for a real holiday.

When I mentioned this to Elspeth Westin and her mother and several other women at "tea," they looked more than ordinarily pleased and Elspeth added, "emboldened by the news to ask another boon of us." That boon was the use of the ground floor rooms of our house for a holiday party Christmas Eve with a tiny ball dance. When I wondered how that might be accomplished, the two Westins stood up and asked Dimitry to help them push aside a wall-sized sideboard. Behind it were wide double doors, (see? more of them) barely visible in the flocked ivy wall papering. These doors opened the large dining room to the even larger front formal parlor we sat in, making for a good-sized space that they assured us would sufficiently hold all the guests coming. They would seasonally decorate it all, including an eight-foot tall pine tree for the entry foyer.

"Perhaps," Martin said when I related all this to him later that day. "They can be persuaded to also provide holiday presents for our relations when they arrive?" I had to laugh but when Elspeth dropped by later with time-worn photographs of how it had all looked decked out on the holidays during "her Ladyship's final decades," in the teens of the past century, I had to admit it would not only work well but look marvelous for the grandchildren to see. So that was agreed upon, too.

Good to their word, Elspeth and a group of her minions arrived two days before our children's arrival and began their assault upon the décor. Dimitry and his mother helped, and Martin and I got out of their way and instead took a long drive to pick up our prepared goose and various accoutrement foods for the holiday dinner itself, to be served the day after the little cotillion. Upon our arriving home, the Gracks excitedly helped us unload our two-seater Ford KA, barring us from the main rooms until after our latish supper in the breakfast nook, at which time we were led blindfolded into the festive area and were delightedly shocked at its transformation via natural and unnatural elements into a winter wonderland.

This holiday event turned out to be nearly perfect, but for one miniscule moment of disquietude. The already elderly parson brought along his quite aged mother, a wisp of a white-haired thing in a handsome oak wheelchair. During the course of the evening, she seemed to disappear and I went in search of her to bring her back to the festivity or to see if she needed anything. I found her in the little used, southeastern end of the house, in a hallway of what I always thought of as Dimitry's domain, as there were several chambers where he did his various household repairs and storage. I located her chair turned to face a completely unprepossessing stretch of hallway wall and at first, I thought her asleep, she was so utterly still.

As I tried to move her away and back into the main rooms, she said quite clearly, "Of course you don't hear it, do you?"

"Hear what?" I asked, as one could barely make out the sounds of the musical trio playing this far away.

"Hear what?" she asked. "Why, the tapping." When I asked what tapping, she instead remarked, "Clear as when I first heard it here when I was a lass of six, helping my own granny." She began speaking of her visits to the house with her grandmother who occasionally helped out in service here. She spoke so much of her then that I asked where her own parents were. She made a little moue and said, "They weren't good to me. I was taken away to live with Grams—for my own good."

I managed to get her turned about and back into the main rooms, where we were both greeted warmly with toasts of eggnog and little gifts. But she had made a distinct impression upon me and I made certain to say goodbye to her again when her wheelchair was ramped into a Caravan on the street to take her home. She grasped my hand then and pulled me close to her face with an unsuspected vigor and fiercely whispered, "You are a far better mistress here than that old witch, you know." When I looked surprised, she nodded at the house. "The one they all cream over."

"Lady Sofia, you mean?"

To which she replied, "I heard this myself from my Granny: while that one was carrying her first born, her husband's child vanished one summer's day. A bright and handsome little lad. He was never found again." Then we were pulled apart by the van's other occupants already inside and clamoring to leave.

It wasn't until after the holidays when we were alone again that I asked Martin if he still heard the tapping. He looked at me curiously and repeated, "Tapping! Yes, perhaps that's what it is: not a leak!" I was about to tell him the parson's mother heard it too when he brushed me off. "I've learned to live with it. It's of no matter, anyway." But, of course, that made me wonder all the more. I'd not read anything of Lady Sofia's personal life in the lending library book, which was after all, more broadly narrated and somewhat more architectural in intent. But I'd found out at tea that there was a sort of historical society in the shire's main town and a few days later while shopping there, I stopped in and introduced myself.

A dark-haired woman looked me up and down and asked what I wanted to know, specifically, about the place. To which I answered, "Well, I suppose about its longest-term mistress, Lady Sofia Cranburgh." Lydia, for so her name was, suggested I go about my shopping and return in an hour or so at which time she would have "photocopies you might look at in your leisure."

I did so, and she had a small sheaf of paper for me when I returned, saying, "No charge for the service." When I was surprised at that, she explained, "The few I know from the village say that although an American, that you and your husband are among the nicest tenants in Cranburgh Grange in many a generation." I blushed at the compliment and said she'd surely be invited to any other galas held there in future. She had used the word "nice" in the British sense of apt, appropriate, mannerly, and correct.

This is what I read in the obituary:

> Although Lady Sofia was said to be extremely eleemosynary, with charities both private and public, and she was so beloved by the locals, her life seemed by many to be bedeviled by several unfortunate experiences. She outlived her husband by three decades, and even before he passed,

he had spent long periods of time away from home on foreign missions for a White Hall ministerial office. She outlived her two sons and her daughter. The first lad died in action at the Orange River in the Boer War; the second, upon a British ship sunk by a German U-Boat. Her daughter died giving birth to her first child, who was still-born.

But first and chief among the misfortunes was the still unsolved disappearance in 1867 of her husband's son by his first wife. This lad, just turned seven years old, was by all reports, a sunny, handsome, and active fellow all over the estate, a joy to his father and to most onlookers, engaged in the usual boyish activities such as fishing, hunting with a little bow and arrows fashioned by a village man, etc. He'd gone out as usual one summer day and never returned. Fairly all the shire was enjoined to search for him, which they did for over a week's time. But no signs of the lad and no remains were ever found. It was then believed that he had been abducted.

Even though his father had three other children by Lady Sofia, he never gave up hope of the boy's return and spoke of him upon his own deathbed, asserting in his final moments that he sensed the child "very near indeed." It was then that Lady Sofia began to open the house up to villagers and shire folk for various communal occasions, which she did until her own passing at an advanced age.

That sealed it as far as I was concerned.

Martin was as pleased as he was surprised by my suggestion: "What do you mean? You really think we ought to call in a psychic?" For the tapping, I responded. "You hear it then?" he asked. I said no, but others did: the parson's mother for example. "Calling in a psychic is the wackiest thing you ever suggested," Martin said, laughing, "Let's do it!"

A week later, M. Alcide Alexander Bonort the Third, an obese and pleasantly saucer-faced young man of indeterminate European origin, dressed like a stage actor in clothing a little bit too small for him, came to tea. Then, with us hovering behind him, he did some kind of "purification" ceremony of the house, room by room, utilizing handle-less brooms of white sage mixed in with violet gorse leaves, and chanting some gobbledy gook. This seemed so absurd that we were almost unable to stop ourselves from laughing until he did something very curious. He stopped at the very same blank wall that the parson's mother had been staring at when I came upon her. Alcide put down his flaming herbs and said, his voice rising with every phrase, "This is a very bad spot. It resists purification. I cannot remain here!" With the last almost a shriek, he sped out of the hallway and stumbled out of doors and was in his little old purple Dauphine and taking off before we could catch up or even pay him.

We didn't speak of this incident but the next morning at breakfast, Martin asked if I still had out that book on Cranburgh Grange from the Lending Library. I had returned it and he said he thought he might take a look at it again. He dropped me off at the Parson's manse, as the old house was called. Once there, I invited myself to tea with the Parson's mother. I'd suspected she hadn't too many visitors and I was right. She was happy to see me. Even better, it was she not I who brought up the subject of Lady Sofia and the little boy. Her grandmother had been in the village, which was more populous than now as the local farmers had many for-hire hands, and especially harvest season workers. That was how her mother and father had come to the village, a young couple seeking work. Her mother's mother followed, because she had already experienced the couple's great devotion to drink and fun and their equal lack of devotion to caring for their only child, the parson's mother herself, then a lass of not quite six years. It was the grandmother who had worked at Cranburgh Grange and, perhaps sensitized by her own daughter, had not failed to notice Lady Sofia's contempt for her new husband's little heir.

True enough, her Granny had told her, the boy went his own way much of the time, spoiled by his sickly mother's absence. He had a tutor in the morning, but once he'd finished his noontime meal, every afternoon he would gather up his walking stick or fishing rods or his little bow and arrows for hunting and step out until sunset. "Betimes he brought in river perch or a small leveret, but mostly he came home empty handed and in need of a bath. When his father was away, the Lady disdained him and had him sup, filthy as he was, among the servants," her grandmother told her. All the more of a shock when the lad went missing and the Lady of Cranburgh Grange waited several days to report it, and then made such a large to-do about it, having all the men and some women available in the shire search for him or of any sign of him, and bewailing his disappearance. "Which some thought overdramatic, since she'd not cared for him a whit."

I repeated this information to Martin that evening at supper. He meanwhile had obtained the book he'd been seeking and as we were having coffee and trifle, he opened the pages for me to an old photograph and said, "Does this look like the south facade of this house?" I looked and said yes, it much resembled it. "Really? Then what about this little doorway with a horizontal window above it?" Martin had us step out of doors, the open book in my hands and a strong torch in his, and sure enough, that section of the south façade was instead, a brick wall with neither portal nor ventilation.

The next morning, he showed the illustration to Dmitry Grack and said to him, "I want you to go inside and open the window or door of each room on this first floor that looks out and say hello to us out of it." Dimitry naturally thought him cracked, but he did as he was asked. Sure enough, there was the walled space with no window. Then, Martin went in again and said he would make a noise of some sort from each wall with the windows closed and Dimitry and I were stand outside and tell him what we heard. "From there and from there," we pointed on either side of the bricked wall, "We heard you well enough, but we didn't hear you at all from behind that wall!" He said that he had rapped on every interior wall, every five feet apart, barring none. He then pointed to the brick wall and said,

"There's something behind there different than when the house was built."

Getting permission from a majority of the disputing heirs to "repair the plumbing at our own cost" took only a fortnight. It was an unusually warm and sunny day when two men came up from Camden Town with tools and levels and all sorts of carpentry equipment I'd never seen before. The first thing they did was sound out the walls every half yard. That way, they located what they believed was a hollower space which might be a little door. On a ten-foot ladder, they then sounded out the upper wall and found the little window behind wood and plaster. Martin showed them the legal permits and they began work up top since it would be easier there, and they knocked out the wood lathing and found the window behind it and cleared it.

"It's a little room. An empty little room," their chief said, peering in the window. Martin went up and he also looked in. "Not quite empty. There's something on the floor in that corner." The chief opined that it was just a pile of rags or discarded clothing. But Martin gave the order, and by lunch time, they had part of the brick wall below the window torn down. After lunch, they called Martin and all of us went out to look. A little wooden door was there, as in the old photo but very worn. "It's sealed shut. Shall we break it open and go in?" Martin told them yes.

I recall the loud protests of the old wood as it was stove in by their sledge but even more once the door was pulled off, I recall the strange yet unmistakably thick and pungent must of age that seemed to escape past us before we could enter. There in the far corner of the narrow, high room was the pile of clothing previously noted. Inside the pile of clothes, not really noticeable except for one tiny outthrust hand holding out a pen-knife, and still dressed in play clothes, was the mummy of a little boy. At that very moment through some quirk of physics I've never had properly explained, the little window above our head shattered and we had to withdraw out of doors again. I, for one, was glad for it, because I vowed to never step in that room again.

We hastily packed overnight bags and slept in the village inn that we knew so well that night and remained there for the next few days. I soon noticed that everyone who had been so friendly to us now avoided us: the men in the pub, the shop keepers, everyone looked at us quite suspiciously.   And no wonder: we'd destroyed the legend of the good Lady Sofia. I told Martin I wanted to leave and go home, and he drove me to Heathrow and saw me off to America. He used as an excuse for not joining me that there was so much officially still to be done about it all: the police, the local historian and architectural society. But I found out later that he left the inn and returned to the house and he slept there in comfort and quietude.

It was the Parson who wrote and begged me to return. He said the villagers felt lost and at sixes and sevens without their "Lady of Cranburgh Grange" present. I kept telling Martin that I couldn't, I just couldn't, not in the light of what we'd found. But since he would not budge from there to return to America, I did eventually go back. The entire back wall and hidden room were gone, of course, and in their place was a new double doorway opened up from the back hall to a charming new terrace looking onto the southern lawn with a view down to the little stream.

And so, the offending little room was expunged. Everywhere I went thereafter in the village, people befriended me, saying they hoped we would remain "forever." Ms. Sheriff, the real estate agent, called on us and said the contesting heirs of the estate had gotten together again and had agreed to sell to us at a much-reduced price because of "our great love of the house." Right there, on the spot, Martin agreed. This news was greeted in the village by such effusions of friendliness that I must be a cynic to doubt their affection. Once all of the various authorities had finished with the "case," the Parson of our village announced "a proper funerary service for the child." Because of the newsworthiness of the entire business, this rite attracted more people than could be held within the church. The lad was buried under his own gravestone far from that of the step-mother. And so, life went on as before. Apparently.

Not long after, and I suppose, to further alleviate any misgivings I might still harbor, the Camden Town carpenter brought photos to us that his assistant's twelve-year old lad had taken of the operation. I remember the boy had his phone's camera up the entire time. There they were exactly as I remembered them: the men shoving in the door. The next photo with the door down showed a strange white smudge of some sort in the photographed doorway. The one after showed the white smudge again, and the last photo, too, and there, the white smudge which rose halfway up our bodies in height was past where Martin and I stood as we were about to go in. "Don't you see, Mum?" the carpenter gently asked. I looked and looked, so he explained, "It's kind of distorted, but see! This white? It's a spirit! That's how they photograph. Here he's running past you out into the air! And here," at the third photo, "he has his hands up in the air. The little boy. At last he's free!"

I let him and all of them believe that I believed his explanation; but to me, those white blotches were merely weird refractions of the light and dust that day. I let everyone believe that I understood and was comfortable with their explanations. What else could I do? I was now the Doyenne of the Shire. It was shortly after that when the local CID came to interview me. She was very proper and delicate and sensitive to any possible queasiness I might still have had. She asked me many questions Martin and I had both answered before and then asked if, while I stood on the lintel not daring to go in, I had seen what was carved out by the little boy on the immured room's wainscoting.

"It's with the historical society now, I believe. The entire wall," I told her. Yes, she knew. But had I read it? Yes, I had. In looking away from his body, I'd lit upon it. Starting a few feet off the ground, as though by a small child standing, I'd read:

> THE DOR IS LOCT AGAINS ME.
> I NOCK AND NOCK BUT NO ONE CUMS

Further down, as though he might be kneeling or sitting, and possibly upon another day entirely, he had carved out:

> THE WINDO IS NO LONGR THER
> I HAV NO FUD I HAV NO DRINC
> I NOCK AND NOCK BUT NO ONE WILL CUM

And at the very bottom, mere inches from the ground, was carved out very raggedly:

I NOCK AND NOCK BUT NO ONE WILL CUM
NOW I MUST GO SLEEP

She was content with my answers, meaning, I suppose, that no one had added to or taken away from the messages, and she left saying I would not be bothered again.

I am bothered. Although we've settled into the house and it is filled with guests and friends and folks from the village, and our family visits often, there are still moments when I lie tossing in bed, having awakened too early, unable to go back to sleep. I always think back to those messages and I hope and pray that after having carved those last letters, he never woke again.

And then there are those times that I awaken suddenly out of a bad dream I've barely escaped, in the blackest middle of the night, and I hear him tapping.

Elsewhere
Bill Davidson

Colin Gregory came awake just before the radio-alarm sounded, reaching out a long arm to turn the volume to silent, just as he did every morning. Then he lay very still, also just as he did every morning, a Godless man praying that this would be a good day for Beth.

One without pain.

Soon enough, the usual irritating patchwork of noises intruded. The closest was Denise, snoring lightly beside him. Not an unpleasant sound exactly, but it was so close that it was right on top of him.

A year ago, before his mother moved in with them, there was a little bit more legroom as their bed was a super-king. The sort where you could retreat a few feet, get yourself some space. But the old woman had been forced to fit an entire life into a single bedroom, so he and Denise gave the master up. The super-king had barely left space to stand in this, much smaller, room, so it had given way to a standard double.

The resident on the floor below, someone Colin didn't know, wouldn't even recognize, had left the radio on. Capital probably, maybe Radio 1, something with noisy music and brash young voices. It occurred to Colin that it would be a lot less irritating if it was tuned to another station, music he knew and liked.

Mum, a poor sleeper and relentlessly wheezy breather, was already up, wandering the apartment, going to the toilet without closing the door, a habit she struggled to leave behind now she was sharing this apartment. The main noise, though, was traffic. That rumble never really stopped, even in the early hours, and living on the tenth floor didn't seem to help. At this time, it sounded like everybody in London was out there, revving engines and laying on horns, already irritated with their days and each other. A police siren wailed in the distance, sounding like it was just as stuck as everybody else.

Colin closed his eyes and let himself drift. Allowed himself to imagine the cars and buses gone, evaporated clean away so the street was silent as the grave and empty of people. Imagined

Mum wasn't brushing her teeth, Denise wasn't snoring, inches away. The family downstairs had no radio to play.

Silent as the grave. The edges of his mouth tugged, almost making it to a smile as he floated, until the hard, bony ridge of Denise's elbow drove its way into his consciousness.

"You're sleeping in again."

Finding himself back in bed in a cramped apartment in the middle of the horribly crowded, noisy city, he groaned theatrically. Denise rolled over and held him tight for a moment, kissing his face.

He shook his head, "Nah. Wasn't sleeping."

"Course not. I'll get coffee on, you jump in the shower."

He kissed her. "I'll just check on Beth first."

"Best let her sleep for a bit."

That stiffened his skinny shoulders and brought him up on one elbow. "What? Did she have a bad night?"

"Not so you'd notice. I was only up once." She frowned lightly, pulling back to focus on him. "Don't you remember?"

He shook his head. "Did I wake?"

She ruffled his already tufty hair, red and wiry and thinning fast. "You came in with me. Stood in the middle of her room, blinking. She said you looked like a long, skinny owl."

"Seriously?"

"Don't worry. Beth thought it was hilarious. And, before you ask, she wasn't in pain. Just needed to get to the toilet."

Colin slid his spectacles on and stood, stretching some of the kinks out while staring at the slow-moving mayhem of the street below.

"Everybody in this house treats me like I'm some kind of pet."

Coming into the kitchen, dressed and shaved, Colin found Denise and Beth sitting at the table, giggling over something or other, while his mother cooked scrambled eggs. He stopped to take the scene in, not noticing his little surge of relief. Everybody looked happy. Beth, not yet in her wheelchair, turned as her grandma scooped some eggs onto the waiting toast.

"Yum. Gramma makes the best breakfasts."

Then she looked at him, and burst out laughing.

"Dad!"

"What?"

Whatever it was, everybody was amused and didn't mind showing it. Denise stood and came over, her hands up and fussing.

"How long have you been wearing ties? They go under the collar."

Everybody was laughing, shaking their heads, not noticing he wasn't joining in. Even Mum. He knew from her expression that she was going to tell the story of the odd shoes again, the one she told at least twice a week, never remembering she'd done it.

"Did I ever tell you about his graduation? What he wore on his feet?"

Denise, still fussing with his tie, crossed her eyes at him. "No, Eleanor. You never did."

Colin took the exhaust filled air of the street in tiny sips, thinking it would be much worse on the way home. The traffic was a bad-tempered trail of hot metal, moving slower than him deep within the current of pedestrians. Soon enough, the stream of people split, some pouring with Colin into the airless bowels of the station, hugging the side of the escalator as commuters in a hurry barreled past. He found a spot to stand on the platform that had space to breathe but had to steel himself to force his way into the crammed carriage.

Being tall helped, but not much. Hemmed in hard by a density of over-warm bodies, Colin tried to relax, using the techniques Dr. Tambini had given him. She had said, look for the warning signs: heart rate, shallow breathing. When it starts to happen, press your finger and thumb together to ground yourself. Then go inside and put yourself someplace safe, someplace you were happy. Find your safe space.

In the sessions, his safe space was normally an empty beach or a remote meadow. The watchword was empty. The essential element was a complete lack of people.

He allowed himself to drift. His safe space, in this moment, turned out not to be a lonely mountain pass, but someplace much more nearby and mundane. Surprising, really; it surprised Colin. It was the train itself, the one he was riding right now, but empty. In his mind, he looked around the carriage as it slid beneath London and found himself entirely, deliciously alone.

At school, few students had arrived yet, so the corridor was quiet. Colin walked rapidly to his classroom to savor the solitude, like he was saving it up. Soon enough, he knew, it would be packed with noisy students, and the battle for control, and to avoid disrespect and insult, would begin. The corridor, when he next walked it, would be a solid stream of kids.

Denise was waiting for him to arrive, gym bag in hand and itching to escape the instant he got through the door.

"I'll be back probably around nine. Might stay with the girls for a glass or two."

"How was it today?"

She was already on the landing, wanting to be gone, but paused.

"Ok, actually." She dropped her voice. "For both of them. Eleanor was almost like her old self. We went out."

"Out where?"

"Hyde Park. It was mobbed."

Colin held up a hand as the elevator doors closed, then turned to his apartment, having to take a moment before he entered. His mother was standing in front of the television, pointing a remote at it and pressing buttons. As always when she was frustrated, her already thick Scottish accent became more pronounced.

"Can never get this bloody thing tae work. Why does it have to be so complicated?"

Beth rolled her eyes, a good imitation of Denise. Her voice was an imitation too, but of her grandmother. "Ach, ye've got the wrang remote again, Gramma."

She pushed out of her wheelchair, coming to stand by the coffee table and pick up the correct one, quickly hitting buttons. Eleanor squinted at the screen, then held her hands up, eyes coming open in concern. Beth knew very well that her grandmother was happy with the channels she had always known, one to four, and would sometimes stray as far as five. Beyond that, she became nervous.

"Yer awa up intae the high numbers!"

Beth smiled sweetly. "Dinna worry yersel, I ken the way back doon."

From Eleanor's expression, it was plain that she was far from convinced. She said, "You're takin' the piss, you wee bugger." But with a smile in there.

Beth stepped right up to her grandmother and pulled herself straight. At twelve years old, she looked pale and skinny and frail, but was already almost six feet tall. With her white-blonde hair and sharp features, she was like a stretched version of her mother. Now, she loomed over her grandmother. "Less of the wee, shorty."

A conspiratorial look between them, then, and Eleanor pointed to her pride and joy, the electric piano pushed against the wall. "You should play Clare de Lune for your Dad."

Beth shrugged, trying for casual but not quite getting there. Snapped off the television. "Ok."

Eleanor patted her back and she walked to the Clavinova and beamed at her son.

"She's really getting the fingering. Could take her next exam any time now."

School had proved too much for Beth around eighteen months ago, but her grades still mattered to her. Having teachers for parents, English and History, helped, but when Eleanor and her Clavinova moved in, she discovered something she was could get properly excited about.

Now, she walked over and got herself settled.

Even though he knew he shouldn't say it, Colin couldn't help himself. "Don't overdo it now."

"Daaad!"

Eleanor was right. As Beth progressed through Clare de Lune, he found himself tearing up, it was so beautiful, and struggled to keep his chin from wobbling. His mother took a step beside him, and quietly took his hand.

When Denise came back it was almost ten, and Beth was in bed, having spent most of the evening with her headphones plugged into the Clavinova, practicing. Eleanor watched re-runs of Inspector Morse. As she herself said, laughing about it, she could watch Morse over and over because she could never remember what happened.

Colin looked up from his laptop when Denise walked in, quietly angling the screen away from her. He wasn't ready to talk to her about what was on there.

"You look bushed, love."

She smiled and stretched. "Yea. Just going to brush my teeth and turn in."

Colin joined her only minutes later, bringing his laptop to bed. Her habit was to read a novel for twenty minutes or so before sleep, and she was doing so now.

She looked up and stretched out her hand for him to take. "You know, we should get out more. Just you and me. Make time to be with each other."

"When?"

"The evenings."

"That wouldn't work. You always go out in the evenings."

She stared at him for a moment, her expression suddenly flat.

"Seriously? I gave up work to look after Beth. In the damned house all day, and now with your mother here too. She's getting worse all the time and you begrudge me some time out?"

"I didn't say that."

"But you do, don't you?"

He took a breath and held it before answering. "No, I'm agreeing with you. The only time we can speak to each other is here, when we go to bed at night."

"I'm never alone, Colin. Never."

"Me neither."

"But you can go out to work. What do I have now?"

"Look, one of us has to work. And maybe…"

"Maybe the operation will work."

It was said as a statement, not a question. If the operation worked, and Beth's heart functioned normally, life would be very different. For everybody.

Colin started to speak, then stopped.

"What is it? Spit it out."

He stalled a moment, then turned the laptop so she could see. "Have a wee look at this."

It was a house, a large Victorian with tall windows and four bedrooms. A living room twice the size of their current one. And a garden, with a full acre of lawn.

He could feel her stiffen beside him.

"Not this again. Scotland."

"I've seen a job, Forfar Academy, same school I went to as a kid. This house is on the outskirts of the town, fields and woods all around. If we sold this apartment, we could buy all that and still be almost mortgage free. We could employ somebody to help with Mum, and our lives would be transformed."

"I don't know anybody in Scotland. We've been through this."

"We're cooped up in here. It's such a struggle to get Beth outside and when we do, it's not fresh air is it? All these people, millions and millions of them, like a weight, surrounding us all the time. The noise of them!"

"I wouldn't know a soul."

"You'd know us."

"Get this through your head. The only thing keeping me sane, and it's only just about working by the way, is my sister and my friends. Going somewhere where I don't have that…I would go down. I know I would."

"But…"

"I look after our daughter. All day and all night. I look after your mother and I have no clue what any day is going to bring. Don't put this on me."

Colin took another long look at the house and closed the page. Behind it was the advertisement for the job in Forfar. He hit delete and closed the laptop.

Two days later, when he got home from school, Denise made a face and jerked her head, telling him she needed to talk to him in the bedroom. His heart speeded as he followed her through; he felt it beating high in his throat and made a little circle with his thumb and forefinger, down by his side where it wouldn't be noticed. It didn't always work, but he did it anyway.

"What's happened? Is she..."

"It's not Beth, it's you."

That stopped him. "Me?"

She was holding her tablet and now she lifted it so he could see the screen. "This is a video one of your students made."

"How did you get it?"

"Little bastard sent it to Beth."

"Shit. What is it?"

"You."

Colin shifted uncomfortably. Forgot about grounding his thumb against his finger and rubbed his palms against his knees, as if they had suddenly gotten itchy.

"Happens all the time these days. They record us in secret when we..."

"This wasn't done in secret."

Colin didn't really want to take the tablet from her but couldn't think how to refuse. He asked, "Is Beth upset?"

Denise raised her hands. "She's upset. I'm upset. It's upsetting."

The clip started in his normal classroom. Marcus Potts and Heather Buzu were giggling into the camera, Potts saying, "Check it out! He's fucking lost it, man."

Then cut to Colin himself, standing in the front of the classroom, beside his table. The white board behind him showed The War of the Roses.

"This was just last week. Thursday, I think."

On screen, Colin was standing there, but that was all he was doing. He looked frozen in place, his mouth slightly open as though he was in the act of saying something, his right arm out from his side a few inches. Potts, clearly holding a phone, backed up, recording himself as he approached Colin. Another student bounced between them, laughing, and someone else ran around the back, apparently playing some sort of tag game around Colin, who remained immobile. There was a lot of noise in that room.

Now Potts and Buzu were standing either side of him, posing and giggling. Buzu stood on tiptoes and pretended to kiss his cheek. She said, "Bin like this five minutes, innit."

Then Colin seemed to give himself a shake and come back from wherever he had been. He blinked and frowned and looked around. "What are you doing out of your seats? Sit down and simmer down, you lot. Now, where were we?"

He turned to look at the white board, and started talking, resuming his lecture on the Plantagenets.

Colin, sitting in his living room at home, found that he could recall that moment, when he chased the students back into their seats, the struggle to get them focused on the medieval struggle for the English throne.

"I sound surprisingly Scottish."

Denise put her hand on his. "Colin, what's happening? Where were you?"

Colin knew very well where he had been, but it wasn't something he wanted to tell his wife.

He started the clip again, frowning as he stared more closely at himself, the students hopping and playing around him. Laughing. Shouting even.

He jerked suddenly, and pointed. "Did you see that?"

"See what?"

He moved the curser back again. "Don't you think the kids look kind of...blurry?"

"It's been taken on some kind of phone."

"The classroom isn't blurry. I'm not blurry."

"You're standing still! They're not."

"And look, right there."

Colin replayed again, and again as Denise stared, not at the screen, but at him, staying quiet.

"Can't you see it? It's like a jump in the film. Like all the kids wink out, just for a fraction of a second. And the sound goes. It's silent."

"You're scaring me now."

Colin tried over and over to catch the moment, the millisecond. Finally, he pointed. "Look."

The frozen image was badly out of focus. But it seemed to show Colin standing in a completely empty classroom. One with no children in it. Denise pressed her lips together and made an obvious attempt to stay cool.

"What do you think you see?"

Colin pointed to the screen. He wanted to say, You asked where I was? I was right there. On my own.

"Doesn't that look odd to you?"

"It's a blurry still from a video taken on a phone, by a kid who was jumping around because his teacher had gone into a trance."

When he didn't reply, she asked, "Are you still going to that therapist? The Button Lady?"

"Occasionally."

"You need to make an appointment, and show this to her."

The reason Colin called Dr. Tambini "The Button Lady" was, unsurprisingly, because of a button. A big, fake plastic one that sat on a table beside her clients. It wasn't attached to anything, but it could still switch things off. It represented safety. She had told Colin, you can talk about anything in here, anything at all. If things ever get too heavy, to find yourself in the deep woods and don't like it, just press the button and we move on to something else. Kind of like a reset.

He had never pressed the button. Now, Denise stood right in front of him and put her hands on his arms.

"You'll go and see her?"

"Ok."

"And bring this with you, I'm serious. She needs to know, Colin."

"Best seats in the house."

Colin had said those words the first time he took Beth to see London Pulse, and now it was what she said every time. Colin had hated the idea of going to football or netball, all those crowds, shouting and getting excited, but Beth's pester power was significant, and she had no qualms about laying on the emotional blackmail.

Now, sitting in the reserved section to see Pulse take on Bath, watching the netball players fly back and forward only feet away, she leaned towards him and said, "I'm scared. But I know I have to."

Beth never admitted to being scared, about anything. It was as though she was determined to avoid admitting to anything negative.

"What do you mean?"

"The operation." She indicated the players, moving so gracefully around the court. "If it works, I can play netball. I'll be good at it."

He compressed his lips and looked away, wondering why she had chosen this moment to talk about the surgery, but glad, for once, of the noise and distraction.

"I bet you will."

"I was good at volleyball, before I got ill."

"I know."

"So, netball. It's what I want to do."

"I don't see why not, the height of you. And there's nothing to be scared of."

"There's a one in twenty chance I won't wake up."

Right on the money. He had to put something into it, make sure his voice was normal. "Who told you that?"

She shrugged. "You can find that stuff online. I've got a seventy-five percent chance of full recovery, so I can play netball. Twenty percent chance of failure. Five percent chance of dying during the op."

He nodded, and watched the game, unwilling to trust his voice for the moment, so there was a pause before she said, "So, I'm scared. But I have to do it."

At that moment, the crowd roared and Beth raised her banner. "Yay! Go Pulse!"

Colin put his laptop on the table beside the fake white button, showing the scene of him in the classroom, Potts and Buzu bouncing around in the foreground.

Dr. Tambini frowned. "It's like a deep trance state. Can you recall this?"

"I can recall something, but not this exactly."

"What can you recall?"

Colin took a deep breath and brought up the blurry screenshot, himself alone in the room. "This. I was imagining everybody disappearing."

"But they didn't."

"So, how do you explain this image?"

Tambini seldom looked surprised but she looked surprised now. "Why do you think it even requires explanation?"

"This is from the film Potts made. Everybody but me winked out."

"Colin, think. That makes no sense. If Potts wasn't there to record the image, it wouldn't exist."

"I guess."

"Just because an occurrence isn't easily explained, that doesn't mean something mystical has taken place. It just means we can't see how it happened. I'm more concerned that your comfortable fantasy of solitude is turning into something much more significant. Maybe I shouldn't have encouraged it."

Colin stayed quiet, staring at himself alone in the classroom.

"Here is a question for you, and I want you to really think about it. Imagine, for a moment, that you could do something, so you could change things so fundamentally, you were living in an empty world? Would you do it?"

"What sort of thing?"

She thought for a moment, then her face cleared and she pointed to her ridiculous, oversized button.

"What if you could press that, and everybody..." she clicked her fingers, "... was gone?"

"Everybody?"

"Everybody in the world. They would just wink out."

Colin stared at the button and shook his head, but Tambini wasn't letting it go yet.

"One press of the button and you're deliciously alone, in complete silence, your fantasy. Aren't you tempted? All you have to do is reach out, and it's done."

"I love Beth more than anything else in the whole world. I've told you that."

Tambini threw her hands up. "Exactly! Exactly. So, why is this a fantasy that you find so soothing? The one you use to lull yourself to sleep."

"I've wondered about that. Is it bad, d'you think? Evil?"

Tambini had been leaning forward, but now she sat back.

"It's just a fantasy, Colin, nothing more. The important thing about a proper fantasy is that it can't come true. It's safe, and you don't need to feel guilty."

She pointed to the screen, Colin standing in the classroom. "But this instantaneous trance state is a worrying development. Have you ever been tested for epilepsy?"

The M25 on a bank holiday Monday. Colin had argued against going anywhere, saying the roads would be so crammed with cars it would be hell on earth. Now they had been stopped for twenty solid minutes, not moving at all. A refrigerated lorry to the side of them was pumping out particularly hot and noxious exhaust fumes, looming high over them. Up ahead, somebody was laying on the horn, really going for it, which seemed beyond pointless as nobody was going anywhere.

Four solid lanes of stopped traffic, baking in the sun. The car directly in front of Colin managed to move forward about ten feet and a shiny black BMW to his right made a sudden surge into the space, stopping at a radical angle.

Denise threw her hands up. "What the hell did he do that for?"

An arm snaked out from the driver side of the BMW, raising an angry finger. Even though the windows were all closed, Colin could hear the guy shouting, a woman in there too. It sounded like the word fuck repeated over and over.

He turned to the side, where the refrigerated lorry seemed somehow closer than before. Higher. Feeling hemmed in and pressurized, he forced his shoulders to sink, using the relaxation techniques Tambini had taught him, making his secret little circle with the thumb and forefinger.

Colin closed his eyes for a moment, no more than a few seconds, and then opened them again, picturing same scene, but with him alone in the cab and no other cars or lorries in sight. The M25, all four lanes, gloriously empty. Nothing in the mirror and a straight long road ahead. He put the car into gear and moved forward, picking up the pace on the wide tarmac, all the way to seventy and kept going.

It was a joy, really. The Audi was no slouch and he let the needle come up over a hundred, plenty left in the engine yet. It maxed out at around 130, the road flying under the wheels now, but still it felt smooth, under control. Reaching top speed, all sound fell away, nothing from the engine and nothing from the road, so that he flew along in deep silence.

Behind him, the sudden intrusive blare of a horn, many horns, the deep-throated honk of a lorry in there. Denise was pulling at his arm, "Colin! Colin, what's wrong?"

Beth was leaning between the seats, shouting something like, Dad, wake up. Sounding panicked. The road ahead was clear now, for a long way, cars streaming by on either side, many of them sliding into the empty lane in front of the Audi.

Colin shook himself and went to put the car in gear, but Denise grabbed his hand.

"No! Colin, you're not well. Don't try to drive."

He glared at her and threw her hand off. "I'm fine. I'm just fine."

He eased the car forward, and the sound of the horns died away.

It had been a horrible day of traffic jams and the beach, when they reached it, had barely enough room to lay a blanket. At the back of everybody's mind was the incident on the M25.

Colin managed to help Beth into the sea—she had been on the school swim team only two years ago—but all she could do was float now, with a little help from her father, and she soon became chilled.

Finally home and in bed, Colin had been lying awake for almost an hour, none of his usual tricks or fantasies soothing him to sleep tonight. Denise snored lightly against his shoulder, as she had done since a minute after she put her book aside. In the hallway, Eleanor padded around, her breathing loud and wheezy, muttering. Outside, the usual racket of late-night traffic. Somebody shouting, angry.

He took a long breath and counted down from ten, trying to make himself relax. He imagined himself somewhere walking out from the apartment block, really striding out, putting distance from all the problems and worries that it represented and himself. It wasn't hard to put the yards in, then the miles, because he was the only person in all of London. The streets were empty. The houses were empty. He came to a pub and walked in, smelling the old beer smell. The lighting was low and he wandered around the back of the bar, pouring himself a glass of beer, which he took back outside, sipping it as he wandered.

After a while, he had to admit to himself where he was going, but that was ok. He came to a stop finally at the house Dr. Tambini used as her clinic, pausing as if for breath.

Colin knew why he was there, what he was about to do. He pushed into the hallway and stood for a moment, listening, hearing the low rumble of a man's voice coming from her studio.

He entered without knocking, seeing his therapist look up in surprise, and a small, overweight man twisting in the chair, eyes wide.

Tambini came to her feet, palms out. "Colin! You can't just…"

He ignored her. Ignored the man, spluttering with irritation. He took three long steps to the table with the big white plastic button, hand coming up. He smiled at her as he pressed, and saw her momentary confusion before she was gone.

Colin came awake as usual, just before the radio-alarm sounded. He reached out a long, slim arm and turned the volume all the way to silent, just as he did every morning. Then he lay for a while in the deep silence of the city. It was so profoundly quiet, he could hear his own heartbeat. He swept his arm across the other side of the bed, and smiled to find that he was completely alone.

Daughters of the Sun
Matt Masucci

Nestled between the slash pine and saw palmetto, all the violence of Florida's flora, someone stood on the far shore from his house on the pond. As the fog breathed, small eddies of white mist shifted and curled revealing again the person, naked and unmoving. From this distance, though, he could not determine the gender.

Chilled air filled his lungs, made him feel alive, and even brought him out of the fog of last night's nightmare. He whistled. It echoed over the water before the mist consumed the sound, just as it shrouded the person again. The mist would clear soon, revealing the entirety of the lake, its small island, and the far shore. Beyond stood mangroves and cypress, pines covered in kudzu, and a world draped in Spanish moss.

He whistled again. The mist whistled back.

Cornelius crashed out of the brush off to his left. The golden retriever ran up to him, not nearly as nimble as he used to be.

But then, neither was the man.

The mist departed, thinning before clearing completely. It would be back tomorrow.

He saw the far shore now, all greens and browns with a hint of red from the Brazilian pepper-trees, readying for blooms.

Still, the person hadn't moved.

Hurried, he forced down a slice of dry toast and second cup of coffee. The propranolol pill hit his stomach, and a warm liquid poured down over him, then slid under his skin, until it pooled in his fingertips. The doctor had said it would help him control his blood pressure but to let him know if he experienced any side effects.

"Like what?" he had asked.

The doctor had closed his medical file. "Anything out of the ordinary."

He had laughed at the doctor. "I don't know anything about ordinary."

Cornelius wound about himself next to his food dish. He wasn't up for more exercise, so the man headed out on his own. He grabbed a machete from the shed. It hung on a rusty nail. He should have taken better care of the blade, but it was a consumer's world, and a new one would be cheap. He gave it a quick sharpening with a whetstone before setting out toward the lake.

Walking past the water, he heard the echoes. The echoes grew louder like the beating of an approaching drum. Worms in his brain, writhing, clumped together, like bait wriggling in black dirt. The beating of his heart filled his ears. Flashes of bulbs, of photographs, photographs that spilled out of a dropped manila folder. Blood the color of pitch in black and white. Little pools of void.

Then, silence again.

The moment passed. Stickers from the bushes covered his legs. They broke through the denim, pricked his flesh. They prick and attach, but they do not let go. They infect. They take over. They look for a new home.

He was not their home. He ran the back of the machete blade along his pants leg and shook them off.

Despite the chill in the air, which faded some with the rising sun, a sweat broke out across his head and under his arms. From an outside observer, he might look like he was working his way through dense tropical jungle rather than through the saw palmetto. Off to his right, the morning fog cleared enough to see the island with the old banyan tree. Tall, rooted, complex.

In the thick foliage across from the house, he made out more of the figure. It appeared to be a person, although it could have been an abandoned mannequin from some kids partying in the woods. It wouldn't have been the strangest item he'd ever found.

He hacked through kudzu and creeper vines with the machete to reach the body but steered clear of hitting any trees. Killing the invasive plants didn't bother him much, but he didn't want to damage any of the old growth, part of the reason he bought this property for his retirement.

A wave of nausea spread outward from his stomach and manifested in his mouth as saliva. He closed his eyes and let his stomach settle, focusing on something other than his body rejecting the medication. The doctor said that he would get used to the meds, but the side effects never seemed to fade away into the background static of daily life.

When he finally reached the body, he saw that she was naked, gray, and caught in the roots of strangler fig. Her head hung, chin on her bare chest. Her gray skin was blotchy in some areas and dirty. Scrapes formed whip marks across her legs. Her face was bloated, her thin lips cracked like dried clay. Spanish moss, almost indistinguishable from her grimy hair, framed her face.

He walked around her, careful of where he stepped, old habits resurrected.

He found a tree tattooed on her back. Denuded branches stretched outward from shoulder to shoulder. The trunk extended downward along her spine. The ink was still black, not yet faded green with time, but not new enough for the skin to be puffy and red, a sign of the body's reaction to the ink.

A tree of life on dead flesh.

He shook off the goose bumps. It didn't make sense how preserved she was. No bugs, no gnaw marks. Everything he would normally look for in a crime scene. Maybe she had been on drugs, stripping off her clothes as her body overheated, running until lost, and then getting tangled in the trees.

Seemed plausible.

Except for the crown of roots sprouting from her head.

It was after noon during the walk back to the house. His stomach growled. Cornelius probably missed him but didn't bother to come find him.

He picked the stickers from his pants before stepping up on the porch. He kicked off his muddy boots, and they landed by the door.

Inside, Cornelius glanced up expectantly. He wasn't sure who enjoyed retirement more, himself or his dog.

He realized that he had stayed out there far too long. He remembered the body, but not much more about it.

Getting old, and he felt it, rooted deep in his chest.

The phone rang. He nearly jumped. His heart skipping beats, catching his breath in his throat.

It rang so rarely. An old, cheap push button phone, all wires and harsh digital trill. No one called him anymore.

He answered, and his own voice sounded thick. When was the last time he used it? He and Cornelius understood one another: they didn't speak often.

"Hello?" he said.

"Detective?"

"Retired."

"Yeah, about that. I'm Detective Michael Keys, Homicide."

He vaguely remembered Keys. New guy, very green, but eager to prove himself. Still hadn't seen the horrors of the job, or the terrible gray areas that human beings occupy while they convinced themselves of all the good they did. *A misunderstanding. I would* never *do that. I'm a good person.*

There were no good people. There were bad people and not bad people.

"We could use you on a consult," Detective Keys said, far away, an electric signal travelling through black wires from there to here.

"Not interested," he said, attempting to intone a dispassionate distance.

"Look, man, this is right up your alley. No one knows this like you. Give us a couple of hours. Take a look at some evidence. A few pictures. Give us your thoughts."

"No."

Flashes of black and white crime scene photos, shades of whites and grays and blacks. Blood puddles a tarry smudge.

He popped a pill, dry swallowed, hung up the phone.

He walked out onto the porch. A storm rolled in on quick winds. The breeze cooled his sweaty face. Probably one of the last storms of the season. Two seasons existed in his part of Florida: rainy season and brush fire season.

Earth's neurons fired, and the lightning reflected off the water, illuminating the small island with a banyan that he hadn't planted.

The storm rumbled from far away, and only the echoes reached him.

His bedside fan roared like a lion. He swallowed a melatonin with a drink of water that he kept at his bedside. Sometimes, he awoke at night with terrible cotton mouth, another side effect of the propranolol.

He considered if creating three new problems for every one solved was worth it.

He sat up, a terrible pain in his chest. Sweat poured off of him. He couldn't remember his dream. He reached over and clicked on the light and drank the water on his night stand. The pain didn't subside.

He panicked. Was this a heart attack? Last time he visited the doctor's, he was in good physical shape for his age. The pain worsened, and he wanted to stand, go to the phone, call for an ambulance.

Or maybe he would just wander out to the lake, sit down, and wait.

His body dumped adrenaline into his system. A warmth grew through his stomach and shot through his veins like molten lead. His arms and legs numbed. He jumped out of bed like a lithe gymnast, ran for the phone. His thick fingers punched the numbers. 9-1-1.

"9-1-1. What is your emergency?" A woman's voice. Older. Experienced.

He opened his mouth, but nothing came out.

Then, something did. Vines. Great, ropy banyan vines poured out of his mouth and down to the floor, flopping like the tentacles of a squid out of water. Rough roots stifled his screams.

He sat up in his bed, soaked with sweat. Cornelius stood at his bedside, back stiff, his normal, floppy ears on end.

The echo of a scream hung in the house.

He sat on the porch, drinking his coffee. Cornelius had already gone for his morning constitutional.

The previous night's dream still played in his memory through a hazy filter. He rubbed at his chest where the pain began in the dream, unsure if the ache existed or was just memory.

He traced all the dream imagery back to the previous day's events. The vines. The fear. An article he read while on the can about a man in Russia who went to his doctor when he coughed up blood. The doctors believed he had cancer. While operating, they discovered a small fir tree growing in his lungs instead of a tumor. Plants can be found in the strangest places. They are survivors.

His own condition manifested in strange ways, like cold spots in a room, or spirit orbs caught in photographs.

That was the essence of his life.

He whistled for his dog. His old friend loped out of the forest. The mist thinner today.

Cornelius carried something in his mouth. Something clearly dead.

When the dog made it to the porch, he noticed that Cornelius's teeth were sunk hard in a rabbit's neck. Cornelius had given up on the armadillos years ago. But rabbits, squirrels, a small bird or large lizard—still sport for the aging retriever.

The dog dropped the body on the porch, a gift of sorts. The dog leaned against his owner's leg. Only an animal could make a gift of death.

He should call in the body across the lake, but the police would come, trample the land, and ruin the landscape with yellow tape and halogen lamps.

And he wasn't yet sure if she was really there.

Cornelius collapsed into a pile, yawned.

"If we wait too long, they'll think we did it," he said to Cornelius, who lifted his head for a moment, then dropped it back down on his paws.

Since the phone calls, he'd taken up talking to the dog again, exercising those old muscles.

That morning, he walked out to the body. She seemed the same as yesterday. This surprised him: still no bugs, no animals taking their due, no decomposition.

Her wet hair, wet from the morning mist, hung about her head like a halo. The crown, he noted, drove deeper than he initially realized. In fact, it wasn't a crown at all, but roots fed down into holes in her skull. Someone cleanly clipped the roots about two inches above her skull. He could not tell what the plant was before being cut free.

Roots can be destructive, he thought, cracking concrete and foundation. They can tear down buildings and bridges. It can be a slow process, but one can be assured that they will find a way. Nothing can stop them. They find the weakness and exploit it over time. That is the strength of roots. Roots possess time and patience that mankind cannot fathom. When humans are extinct, the roots will reclaim the cities, calling them home.

He examined again at her own tree, the one on her back. Elegant line work and shading elevated the tattoo. Splendid. Done with a deft hand.

He spent the morning with her, thinking, wondering, maybe aloud, who she was. Why she was here. Why *he* remained.

From the porch, he admired the moon, not much more than a wood shaving in the sky, reflecting on his lake. Off in the distance, beyond the small island, night enshrouded the body.

He ignored the ringing phone. For a moment, the phone tempted him. Should he answer, tell the detective on the line about his lady of the lake?

He didn't move. Cornelius lay on his feet, keeping them warm. With the skies clear, and the moon light dim, he saw stars splashed out like flecks of chalk on a blackboard.

He had taken his pill, letting the tide of warmth and static wash over him. Stars above, moon on the lake, dog at his feet. What was he looking for?

Across the way, a darkness, a hole, where the body should be. And a thin, flickering light, hovered above the ground. He leaned forward, squinted through the dark. It wasn't a reflection. It moved, too large to be a firefly or bug. Fire orange.

He pushed the sleeping Cornelius off his feet, pulled on his boots, and hurried to the shed. He grabbed his machete and flashlight.

He jogged around the lake to the body's location. The unexpected exertion made him breathless. The light was no longer there. Maybe he imagined it.

However, the body of the woman was gone as well.

Through the brush, he caught a sliver of the orange light north of the lake. The shakes and sweating returned as he moved toward the light. He chopped the brush as he moved, trying to overtake the lantern, now disappearing behind trees.

He could hardly keep up, and he assumed that the person with the lantern also carried the body of the tree girl. It didn't make any sense.

After some time, three more lanterns appeared as he closed in on the original light. The swinging lanterns converged on a large bonfire.

He saw the man that he followed. A carved wooden mask hung on his face. The design feigned roots or vines, eyes mere slits, and the mouth a dark cave. He laid the body of the girl on the ground, leaning her against a tree. He stood with others, four in all, around the fire.

He smelled the fire, heard the popping of knots in the wood. The other men also wore carved masks, flames crawling across the lacquered finishes. Grotesque, twisted faces. Faces not their own.

One of them rang a bell. The reverberation echoed into the night. Nearby, another masked man in a thick red robe led four naked women toward the flame, their hands bound with vines before them. A man carrying a thurible followed the women. Fragrant incense now mixed with the scent of burning wood.

The women stood in order by the size of the tree growing out of her skull, from largest to smallest. The final woman had none. A leather strap in her mouth gagged her. She trembled, but remained aware. The other women, however, wore absent gazes, glazed eyes.

One robed man from the fire untied the treeless woman from the others and brought her before the flames. Tears stained her face with reflected fire, and she trembled, her naked flesh slicked with sweat.

He gripped his machete's handle, but remained frozen. He couldn't take them all. It was an impossible situation.

if these shadows have *offended*

Whispers and shadows, all.

One robed man held the treeless girl's shoulders and pushed her to her knees while another held her head. The girl clamped down on the bit of leather, which stifled her pleas.

A fellow robed man opened a wooden box and removed a large, silver hand drill. He stood above the woman, placed the bit to her head, and cranked the handle. Color drained from her, making her skin a canvas for the red and orange flames of the nearby fire. Her screams intensified with each turn of the handle. Her hair tangled around the drill bit and crawled upward toward the robed man's hands like vine tendrils.

She fainted during the third hole, but the other masked men supported her weight.

The retired detective watched from behind the scrub, gritting his teeth. He could not look away.

The robed man drilled seven holes in all. When he finished, he handed the drill to one of the others, who cleaned it and placed the drill back in the box. Another acolyte brought over a sapling growing in a large basin.

The robed man dug with his hands and gingerly lifted it from the dirt. He shook the plant, sending a shower of loose, dark soil to the ground.

Another man washed the roots with water from a silver decanter until the water ran clear.

The robed man carried the tree to the woman and began to feed the root ends into the holes.

til truth makes all things plain

The retired detective looked down. Beside him, another machete lay in the dirt, identical to his own, but rust fully covered the blade.

Echoes.

He had been here before.

𓂀

Across the pond, all the women from the previous night now hung in the trees, the sun shining down on their heads, the saplings growing, rooting down. Bound cruciform, like naked grapevines in a vineyard during the winter months, they served as potting vessels.

However, unlike the woman he found with the cropped roots, these women remained *alive*. He saw their movements in the strangler vines, slight, like a light wind through branches.

Maybe it *was* time to report this.

He picked up the phone on the second ring.

He wasn't interested, was he? Did he really want to know? To see? To feel again?

"Hello, Detective," Keys said.

"Retired."

"We all know that the early retirement thing wasn't fair. But that's politics. At least you got to go out with full benefits. Better than most, I would say. An ugly affair. But IA always had it in for you. You were too high profile."

He grunted.

"You really made a name for yourself, you know. The mighty and falling is what they say. How about you come look at this case."

"Still no."

"You're not going to make this easy on me, are you?"

"Leave me alone."

"You can leave the job, but the job don't leave you." Keys laughed. Deep, like old machines still running under the ground.

He slammed the phone in the receiver.

Memories took root.

Outside, he glimpsed a hawk in a tree take flight, snatch a rattlesnake from the ground, and flap its wings to return to the skies, snake wriggling in the raptor's grasp.

He picked up the phone, wanting to throw it across the room. But he stopped himself. The phone cord dangled from the cradle, not plugged into the wall at all.

𓂀

His fan roared like a lion. Cornelius lay by the bedside.

The man took a melatonin. He took a propranolol.

The spine of a book by his bedside read Aimé Césaire *Notebook of a Return to the Native Land*. He flipped it open, randomly, waiting for the pills to take effect. He read the underlined words. *Ending. Beginning. Germination.* In the margin, in his own handwriting, he saw a scrawled note, like a child's rhyme. He couldn't remember writing it.

> *Food for worm,*
> *ash from tree,*
> *the soul is the only*
> *part that is me.*

When he opened his eyes, he found himself on the island in the lake, and the roots of the large banyan had grown over him like a prison.

No, *he* was rooted, toes growing as crooked roots, digging into the dirt. The banyan did not trap him; he was the banyan, rooting down, searching through dirt or silt. Finding water. His fingers clawed through the slickness searching for sustenance. His hair tangled in tendrils like Spanish moss. His pores sprouted nubs. Wind-dancing pollen on angel hairs caught the wind and flew.

He opened his mouth and out poured the words, and roots, and pollen.

He wasn't sure if anything was more real than the soil between his fingers, or the thick fog in the air.

He pollinated. His flesh made bare. Red photosynthesis. Cells clamoring for the sun.

And then, when the sun came out, the mist that surrounded the island wisped into nothing. So did he.

Lonely Is the Starfish
Lena Ng

I have a tank full of pets. The tank measures 91.4 cm (L)
by 45.7 cm (W) by 48.3 cm (H) and holds 189 liters of salt water.
I keep the pH rigorously maintained at 7.8, the temperature at
25°C, and the salinity at 35 parts per 1000 units of water. There
are three angelfish who like to emerge through the vegetation
and poke around in the tank's corners. The jeweled moray eel
pretty much keeps to itself, hiding its big head and plump body
between some rocks, its bright eyes surveying its surroundings.
The two azure damselfish swim leisurely back and forth.

Although there are more interesting creatures in the
aquarium, my best, most favorite pet is the starfish. It measures
fifteen centimeters at its longest diameter with five stout, spiny
arms. It is purple in color. It doesn't run or beg or come when
you call it, which is why I haven't given it a name. It looks like
it's not doing anything, but if you wait patiently and look closely
enough, you will see it doing lots of things. It waves its tube feet,
located under its body like feet on a caterpillar, which gets it
from one place to another. It taps and moves, and moves and
taps, and eventually arrives where it wants to be. It can live a
long time: up to thirty-five years, which is older than I am now.
The starfish minds its own business, just as I mind my own. I
see myself in it—slow and solitary. Living my own life, watching
the drama of the tank around me.

Over the weekend, I noticed the first of the fish
disappearing. One damselfish, then another. One angelfish, then
another. Happily swimming one day, vanished the next. Over a
week, each night, another fish gone, until none are left in the
tank.

After much time puzzling, at last the mystery is solved. The
eel, fourteen centimeters when I had first purchased it, has now
the strength and size to fish for its own food. Clever thing, it
would wait until night, when I was fast asleep, before it would
hunt its prey, darting from between the rocks in the dark and
clamping down with its strong jaws. But it made a terrible error
in judgement. As the fish stock was depleted, it finally attacked
the starfish. It bit off a limb, but finding the morsel too spiny to

choke down, could not consume it entirely. In this way, by deduction, I realized the greedy eel had to be the culprit.

The starfish has defenses of its own. Without any interference from me, without first aid or medicine, a pearly bud has grown in the stump of the eaten limb. After six days, it has grown back another tentative limb, paler in color, and not as stout or sturdy as the remaining limbs. A skinny baby limb on a grown body, like a budding branch on an oak.

The eel has since died, starved to death after I, in revenge for it biting the starfish, stopped feeding it.

The starfish is my best friend, alone now in its tank. It looks at me sometimes as I look at it, bending a limb at a right angle, angling its tiny eye on the end of the arm. Sometimes, it bends its arm backwards in an awkward wave. Who knows what it's trying to say? I think it's singing a song à la Edith Piaf. Like me, it enjoys the classics.

If you stare at the starfish long enough, you can see it move. It takes a long time but I am dedicated and I can watch it for hours. In three hours, it spans the tank and back, creeping over the sand and rocks, moving from hiding within the waving vegetation to gluing itself to the side of the tank. Sometimes the tube feet do all the work and it looks like the starfish is performing a smooth glide. Sometimes the arms wave up and down in an unhurried, hypnotic creep.

Slowly, slowly, if you watch me patiently you can see me move. I live in starfish time.

You may think it boring to stare at a tank. I find it meditative, peaceful, a time to contemplate life. The lush vegetation sways gently, putting me in a trance. The starfish's translucent tube feet grasp and stick to the glass. Outside my apartment, cars honk and people yell. The sirens howl and the tourists gawk. Everything is go, go, go. Everyone is move, move, move. When is the time to just enjoy time? I want a simple life: to care for my starfish, to watch its adventures, to live my own if only in my imagination.

The more I watch the starfish, the more I realize that it looks lonely. I've watched it for six hours and all it has done is move its fattest limb and crawled only a centimeter. I've only moved to eat an old roast beef sandwich I had purchased the day before at the café and to go to the bathroom.

I imagine the starfish before it lived in my world, living its life in the briny sea, in slow moving colonies of like-minded individuals. Where is its family? Where is its Maman and Papa? Does it wonder?

I used to have Maman and Papa living here, taking care of me, eating our breakfast of brioche with a slice of ripe Bleu d'Auvergne, dressing me in a little boy's sailor suit of navy shorts and white shirt. They spoke in soothing, tender voices, in slow, sonorous tones, and would kiss me on the forehead before going to bed. But like the starfish, I have outlived them. I haven't seen them in a long time. I haven't seen anybody, at least not socially, in a long time.

The starfish slowly creeps and creeps; all it can do is creep. Where is it going? Maybe it's searching for a friend, for silent, comfortable company. I understand what it's like to be alone. I am resolved to help it, and after gathering my courage, I leave the apartment with a small goldfish bowl to the pet shop on the Rue Saint-Dominique.

Le propriétaire has a large, ruddy face, which has likely confronted many aperitifs, a bristly, welcoming moustache, and he answers my quiet *bonjour* with a loud, exuberant one. He speaks with a Provençal twang, not a refined, Parisian accent. I try not to recoil as he slings an arm around my shoulders and leads me around the shop. He boasts about his variety of shrimp. He tries to tempt me with a selection of hermit crabs, even some lowly tube worms. I scoff and turn my back. I tell him I'm only here to choose a friend for my only friend. He pulls his chin and brings me to the back room. My eyes light up at the selection. Small brittle stars, dozens of Asterina stars, all lovely… yet not quite right. Finally, I choose an American one, an ochre star, all the way from California, a beautiful, enticing, orange. I've always wanted to visit there.

After he carefully places the starfish in my goldfish bowl, filled halfway with water from the original tank, money leaves my hand, and he kisses me boisterously on both cheeks before I leave.

On my way home, an unsettling thought comes into my head. I am troubled that the starfish may not like its new brother. My palms sweat as I watch the two starfish creeping on either side of the tank. I won't be able to sleep until I know they have adjusted to each other.

My starfish has taken to its companion. After eight hours of worried watching, I've found its fattest arm slung over the other, like an arm over the back of a long-lost friend. Finally, I go to bed relieved.

In the morning, the California starfish has disappeared, as though it had dissolved in the tank's water. I refuse to believe my starfish has consumed it.

Sadly, my starfish looks sick. I pet and comfort it, and speak of old times. Its color has turned from a rich dusky purple to a pale, washed-out pink with ominous white patches speckling its body. I scoop up the starfish into a transportation goldfish bowl filled with tank water and hurry to the vet. The vet has practiced for twenty-two years but has never seen a case like mine. He shrugs and says it lies beyond his expertise. He suggests I purchase another one. I visit two other vets and they also tell me it's beyond their expertise. I won't give up hope.

I hand-feed my starfish, holding a freshly shucked clam close to its limbs. I am patient and I will hold the food until it takes it from me and stuffs it into its stomach extruding from its center. After several hours, the limb reaches out but—

horrors!—the arm itself has become possessed. It has pulled, loosened, wiggling back and forth until it has finally detached from the body. The arm, on its own, squirms away in a worm-like wiggle, leaving the rest of the body behind. Beneath my frightened gaze, like escaping petals from a bloom, one by one, each limb detaches and crawls away. Some meet up and wrestle. Others crouch at the bottom of the tank.

I am heartbroken. I will nurse it in its final days. Meticulously, I research these symptoms. It seems like my starfish has caught a starfish-wasting disease, a virus passed from starfish to starfish, caught from the vanished Californian companion.

With no more limbs, feeding takes forever. I act as its missing limbs, slowly moving food to its extruding stomach in its center. It manages to wave its stumps in gratitude. I love my starfish. Can a starfish love back?

Despite my scrupulous care, my starfish looks listless and lost. Its disembodied arms have lost their spark of life and lie unmoving, curled at the bottom of the tank. I steel myself. I am not ready to mourn my starfish, another loss in a string of losses. But one day, a bud blooms. One bud blooms from each stump on the body. A miracle!

When it gets better, I will take it on holiday. We will go to the seaside in Roquebrune-Cap-Martin, Alpes-Maritime, on a hilltop overlooking the Mediterranean Sea. I will feed it scraps of oysters and mussels. I draw up the plans. How will we travel, my starfish and me?

By Tuesday, the arms have slowly grown back. Soon the starfish is determined to crawl around the tank again. I stare at this in fascination. The resiliency and resolve of my little friend.

I am like the starfish, resilient and resolved. My starfish is well and is looking towards better times. Unfortunately, though, for now, the travel plans are on hold.

I see how long I can watch without blinking. My record time is seven minutes. I stare and stare; all I can do now is stare. My nose itches and I can't do anything to scratch it. I am more like the starfish than I am to the people outside of my apartment; alas, I'm too much like the starfish. My limbs, all four of them, have detached from me and are crawling to the four corners of the room. My legs and arms have twisted and turned, and it was so terribly painful that I was actually glad to be rid of them. My writhing arms meet up on the carpet and tangle about like snakes. It seems the sickness has passed from starfish to me. I can do nothing; I sit here helpless. I can only hope, that like the starfish, the buds will bloom and one finger, one hand, one arm, one by one, my limbs will regrow.

I am patient and can wait patiently.

Old Times
Mark Towse

Through the window, I watch the taxi as it rolls to a halt. The feeling of helpless spiralling washes over me, and I can feel the knot in my stomach developing.

"I'm off then," Jacqui says, face caked with make-up, the smell of white musk already laying heavy at the back of my throat. "Do I look okay?" she asks, patting down her dress.

"You look amazing, love." And she does. All of a sudden, I want to cry, and I hate myself for it.

She gingerly moves through to the hallway, heels impossibly loud against the wooden floor, each step a painful blow to my self-worth. They come to a stop. I know she'll be checking herself out one last time in the oval mirror.

I think she's cheating; I've suspected for a while. Recently, she's been leaving the room to use her phone. I'm not proud, but I've followed her a few times and observed the frantic button-pushing. I've been through her text messages, but I think she's wiping them. She's distracted, too—even more so than usual. I hope I'm wrong.

"There's a load of washing to go in. And don't forget to empty the trash, okay?"

"Okay, love," I reply.

"Mustn't forget the trash," Jed chips in, waving his finger.

I haven't slept for weeks, my mind a simmering pot of anxiety and jealously. Perhaps, I'm just paranoid. Regardless, I feel like I'm slipping—back to the darker times.

"I'm not sure what time I'll be back. Don't wait up," she says.

"Behave yourself!" Jed shouts just as the door slams, holding his middle finger in the air.

"Shut up, Jed," I hiss, watching her down the path.

"Why do you let her speak to you like that?" he says. "Ordering you about while she goes out gallivanting. I wouldn't stand for it."

"I love her," I say, arching my neck to watch her step into the taxi. "I wouldn't expect you to understand."

He's not been around in months, and quite frankly, that was just fine with me. He's rocking in the chair, legs tapping frantically. He's agitated.

"What's wrong with you, anyway?" I ask.

"Bored. Hey, want to get wasted?"

"I've been sober for months, Jed. The last time you were here was the last time I had a drink. And we both know how that ended."

"Come on, just a little one," he says, reaching behind his back and pulling out the bottle of golden liquid. "She's out having fun, why can't we have a little drinky?"

"Haven't you got anywhere else to go?"

"Don't be like that, Paul." He twists off the cap, making a big deal of holding the neck of the bottle near his nostrils and inhaling deeply. "Ah, that smells so fine."

"Jed, I'd like you to leave. I'm not really in—"

But the bottle's already on the table in front of me.

"Go on, Paul. It will help you relax a little, take the edge off."

"I promised her, Jed; said I would never drink again. She said she would leave me if—"

"She really has got you by the balls, hasn't she? How is all that obedience working out for you anyway? Whose fucking life are you living, for Christ's sake?"

I push myself from the chair and walk around the room, pausing at the mirror above the fireplace. In the subdued light, the dark circles are emphasized further. I hardly recognise myself.

"Look what she's doing to you. You look like shit!" he says.

"And what's your excuse, Jed?" I snap. "Anyway, what do you know about it? I've not seen you in over a year! You don't know anything."

"I know you, Paul. How far do we go back? This isn't you. You've lost your spark; she's sucking you dry, and not in a good way!"

"Look, can you just fuck off, please."

"One drink, then I'll go; you have my word. For old times' sake, come on, share a drink with me."

I just want him gone now. I want to wallow in self-pity and worthlessness, and he's fucking it all up.

"One drink, but we do it the civilized way," I say, marching quickly through to the kitchen.

He claps his hands together. "That's the way, Pauly."

I collect two tumblers from the cupboard and fill each half full of ice. As I shut the refrigerator door, I study the three lopsided photographs of our beaming faces. They were taken five years ago on holiday; none have been added since. A wide smile is stretched across Jac's face; she looks so happy. But how do you ever truly know?

The sound of whisky filling the glass is heavenly, and even without taking a sip, I can feel its warm blanket already wrapping around, protecting me. The ice begins to gently crack, and its melody is hauntingly beautiful.

"To old times," I say, lifting the glass.

"To old times," Jed repeats.

I pick up the glass and smell the whisky; it prompts a shudder, like being in a place you know you shouldn't be. As I swirl the golden liquid around the glass, thoughts rush through my head, most of them telling me this is a bad idea. But I take the first sip, and almost immediately, my mouth is a network of hot prickles. My gums begin to tingle. I swirl it around, enjoying the sensation before swallowing. It's so good—smooth and balanced—evoking just the right amount of burn as it slides down. Already, it's dissolving the knot in my stomach, freeing me of all of it. I take another sip, and it begins to drown out the thoughts, turning down their volume.

Jed smacks his lips together. "A fine drop, isn't it?" he says. His leg has stopped shaking, the whisky no doubt working its magic.

"It is good," I concede.

"Refill?" he asks, resting the neck of the bottle against my glass.

"We said just the one, Jed." But we both know the words are merely a formality, a half-hearted objection that is already forgotten.

He fills the glass and smirks his smirk. "Why don't you just leave her?"

"Can we talk about something else?"

"It could be you and me again, just like old times. She's stifling you, got you wrapped around her little finger. She'd be better off with a little lapdog."

"It's just a rough patch." There, I said it. "We'll work it out."

"Oh yeah, I bet she's working it out right now—talking to all the fellas about how much she wants to work on her marriage. Even with her mouth stuffed full of cocks, I bet she won't stop harping on about how much harder she's going to try."

I scowl at him before knocking back the whisky and crunching down on the ice. "I hate you, Jed!"

"Just jesting." He pours himself a glass and knocks it back. "Another?"

"Yes," I reply. "We've been happy. Before."

"Can't say I've seen it," he replies, slouching back into the leather and taking another generous sip. "All the time I've known you, it's been like this. You used to be fun; now look at you. You're a shadow of yourself."

"I don't want to lose her."

"Never mind her, Paul. You're losing yourself. What even makes you get out of bed anymore?"

The whisky no longer burns as it goes down, but it's still providing clarity. His words hit hard as only the truth can. "Fuck off, Jed. You're just jealous."

He leans forward and tops us both up.

"We used to go out on the town every week. The world was your oyster. Why did you have to get yourself tied down to that skank?"

He's starting to slur his words already. And I know that tone; good things never follow.

"Take that back!" I demand.

"I'm just saying—you're obviously not happy. We could do it again; the old team reunited. There's an ocean of pussy out there, and you're just playing it safe in the shallow end."

"Jed, I'm not interested in that. Look, I really don't want to talk about it anymore!"

I lift the glass and tip its contents into my mouth. He fills it up as soon as it comes down.

"I care, that's all," he says, tone changing to a drunken and patronizing melancholy.

The blanket is being unwrapped; I am starting to feel vulnerable again, exposed.

"She doesn't care; she doesn't give a fuck—you know that. When was the last time she did anything for you? When was the last time you made love? Hell, when was the last time she even asked how you were doing?"

"She's got a lot going on," I reply.

"Don't we all, goddammit! You need to stop being such a pushover!" he says, slamming his hand on the coffee table.

I sink the whisky. He's getting to me. This is what he does; he's even more manipulative than her. I feel my anger rising, not just with him, but with it all.

"It's your own fault. You let her get away with it," he continues.

My hand is shaking as I pour another.

"You're just shit on her shoe, Paul. She just wants to control you. That's why she's always on you to take your pills. She's part of the system."

I drink the contents and refill the glass. He's right; I know he's right. That's why it hurts. Each day, I hope it might get better. I don't want much—just to be seen.

"I love her, Jed."

"I know, Paul, but it isn't mutual. Face it. It's you and me against the world—always has been, always will be. I'm the one that's been there from the start. Only I know what you went through as a child—the abuse, the trauma—nobody else will ever truly understand. How could they?"

I still have nightmares about it to this day, being hunched over in that small space, wet from my own urine and shaking at the sound of creaking floorboards. Christ knows how long they used to lock us in there, but it was a damn sight safer than being out in the open. I still have those scars to bear. They only let us out to clean and do the jobs they didn't want to—God forbid if the work wasn't up to scratch.

When they found us locked in the cupboard, I was only ten years old. I was almost starved to death—filthy and terrified. It was the neighbors that got the police onto them, just a few years too late.

Our so-called mother and father were sent from hell; I know that now. They'll rot in prison, hopefully. I also know that being fed scraps underneath the door and being brought out for random beatings isn't the usual childhood. To this day, I still walk with a hunch and wince at the sound of a squeaking floorboard. I wanted to get carpets put through the house, but Jacqui wouldn't let me, even though she knows what I've been through.

Jed's right. He's the only one I really trust. The only one I can rely on to be there.

"I'm going to tell you this for your own good, Pauly," he says. His face is suddenly creased with seriousness.

"Go on," I encourage.

"I fucked her, too."

The words don't make sense at first, as if not in the correct sequence. The room is already starting to feel slightly off kilt, and everything seems a little less sharp.

"Oh, perhaps a handful of times. She's an animal, Pauly. I'll give you that."

The room begins to slowly rotate. I feel disoriented—present, but not, as if out of my own body. I close my eyes to stop the spinning and take in some deep breaths. Finally, I'm coming back, and I land with a thud.

"And I have to wonder how many dicks she's wrapped her hands around tonight."

I can feel the rage consuming me. My body is shaking, blood pounding in my ear. My grip around the glass tightens, and some of the liquid splashes over the rim.

He's smirking. Is he enjoying this?

Even as I bring the glass into his cheek, his face is twisted in a sneer, just like Father's used to be. The glass shatters, sending shards to the floor, but some of it embeds in his skin, creating a stream of fresh crimson. His taunting smile fades, and almost immediately, I'm reeling backwards as his right fist connects with my cheekbone. My vision is filled with bright white, and there's a loud ringing in my ear.

"How could you? I trusted you!" I scream, spittle spraying ahead. I reach for the marble bookend and bring it onto his nose. The pain in my head is off the charts, and my ears are still ringing, but I'm filled with uncontrollable fury as I continue to smash the paperweight into his face.

I don't see the sucker punch coming, and the wind is immediately knocked out of me. I flail out for him, but he gets me again in the stomach, and a tiny bit of vomit spits out onto the floor beneath. His hands are around my throat now and squeezing tightly. Gasping desperately for air, I kick out redundantly. The pressure in my chest and my head is building, but I can't get any air in. Suddenly, I'm back in my old home, Father's arm around my neck. He's scolding me for not taking the trash out and taking too long to clean the toilet. I can smell the alcohol on his breath and feel the stubble against my cheek. Christ, my esophagus feels as though it might snap—I can't get any air. Everything is beginning to fade, darkness drawing in. I'm back in the cupboard again, and I can almost taste the mustiness. Let it end, please.

Finally, he lets go. "I had to tell you, Paul. You need to know these things."

Doubled over, I begin to gasp in mouthfuls of air as I stagger towards the kitchen.

"That's it! Run! You never face up to anything—that's the problem. That's why she walks all over you in those big porno heels!" Jed shouts.

But I have no intention of leaving this. I'm raging, adrenaline flowing, and mind exploding with thoughts of hate and revenge. I reach towards the knife block and pull out the one I know to be the sharpest.

"Oh, shit. He's got a knife, everyone. Pauly's balls have finally dropped!"

The war cry is strange and garbled as I bring the knife across his face. He puts a hand to his cheek and studies the blood that is rolling to the floor. I go at him again, in the chest, and this time, it induces a satisfying shriek. Again—this time in the leg. He's not even putting up a fight anymore. I'm disconnected from pain now, and the squelching sounds don't seem real. He falls to his knees, hands stretched towards me, tears rolling down his cheeks.

Shit! What have I done?

"Jed!" I scream.

My best friend, the one who has stayed loyal through it all. "I'm so sorry!"

I collapse to the floor in a heap and reach for my friend, squirming in the blood that bonds us.

"Paul!"

The voice seems distant and distorted.

Slowly, I open my eyes. My head is pounding and full of thick fog. I try to move, but my body sings out in pain.

"Paul, it's okay—the ambulance is coming." Jacqui's face is moist with tears as she holds my bloody hand into her lap. "What have you done to yourself?"

I look down to find my grey shirt is saturated with blood. "Where's Jed?" I sputter.

She looks at me, eyes wide with fear, and says nothing.

"Where's Jed," I utter again.

"It's okay. I'm still here," he replies. "Her tears, Paul—it's just guilt—you know that. Don't let her fool you."

"I know. It's you and me, Jed; I can see that now. You're the only one I can trust."

"You haven't been taking your tablets," Jacqui says. "You've had an episode, Paul."

"I can smell them on her; those other men," Jed rasps. "I can smell their sweat and their cum. They were probably laughing at you while they were doing it."

"Remember, Paul. You told me about Jed. How you made him up to get through those days locked in the darkness."

"She's full of lies, Paul. They're all against you: everyone," Jed hisses.

I no longer feel so alone. I'm glad he's back.

"Don't worry, Paul. She won't get away with it. If we make it through, I'll sort her for you," he smirks. "I'll cut her up good."

The Coffin

Victoria Dalpe

It shouldn't have been empty.

It hadn't been empty.

She sat up with a gasp, clawing at her bed sheets. It was 3:30 according to the alarm clock near her head. Diffuse orange light spilled in from the streetlights. Silent. The whole world still asleep, except her.

The dream skittered away fast, leaving only its ghost pressing on her mind. Dark things, things long buried, dry and scratching things. And the staccato beep of a heart monitor before flat lining.

David slumbered on, undisturbed, and for the hundredth time she envied his ability to sleep through anything. Even on this night, this *terrible* night, his face was smooth and unlined, not a care in the world. In the hospital he had been like that. Death surrounded them, choked like a noose, and he slumbered away, propped up in a chair. How many sleepless nights did she stare at him while he slept and she kept watch.

Ever since the funeral, she battled for sound sleep. Most nights, she lay awake next to David's snoring frame. The funeral was a year ago today, and he hadn't even remembered.

Funerals. *Coffins.* She shuddered, reliving their day today in all its maddening detail.

It was Street Sweep Day: a miserable Brooklyn bi-weekly event that consisted of having to move the car from its coveted near-the-apartment-spot, forcing them out hunting for spaces on distant streets like a starving shark. David acting as runner, face against glass, scanning for vacancies, while she drove, squeezing the steering wheel, hungry for parking.

"There! There!"

"This street? Are you sure? This area is pretty shitty, I don't want my car broken into."

"God, Helene, it'll be like two hours max."

He hopped out to direct her around a hollowed-out shell of a sofa, no doubt overflowing with generations of bed bugs.

She gagged at the thought, all the while judging the type of people who leave their garbage on the street in front of their homes, like animals. It's a simple call to get a couch picked up. *Don't you want to live someplace nice? Why can't you take care of your neighborhood? Why must we all suffer for your laziness?* Her mind flashed to the manicured suburban lawns of her youth and felt the fresh twist of white guilt in her gut.

She cut the wheel and eased in when all of the sudden, CRACK.

"David what the hell!?" She hollered, but he wasn't looking at her; he was looking behind the car, at what she hit. His face unreadable and suddenly pale.

Please don't be an animal, or a child, she prayed. She got out and there it was.

A coffin. Dusty, earth covered, the fabric lining yellowed and tattered. The lid open. Empty.

Her mouth was suddenly so dry, it felt filled with cotton wool. She looked to David, his expression a mirror of her own. Helene was suddenly aware of how hot it was, how sunny. She shielded her eyes, staring into the gaping maw of the coffin. Her brain was unable to come up with a reason for its presence.

"We have to call the police. Right?" She was absently rubbing her sweaty hands along her pant legs. Her mind raced in a million directions: someone dug this up and dumped it here. But why? Who did it? Who was in it? Where is the body now?

"If we call the cops we have to stick around. This is my lunch hour, Hel. *One of us* needs to keep their job. I know it sounds nuts, but how about we just move the car and act like we never saw it? Someone will notice it. Doesn't have to be us."

Someone will notice it. How many others had said the same thing that day she wondered? She stared the length of the street one way, then the other. It was a block of brownstones. Someone was eventually going to see it. Maybe someone already had. She squinted down the road, finding it unnerving that she couldn't recall a single car passing in the time they'd been standing out there. A loud caw caught her attention, and she looked up. There was a big blackbird on the phone line, heavy enough for the line to droop. Its feathers gleamed iridescent in the noontime sun like a puddle of oil. It looked down at them as she looked up, and like the street, the creature was oddly still. Its head didn't swivel; instead, it watched her, still as a statue. She shivered in the heat and turned away. When she glanced up a moment later, the bird was gone.

She wanted to get as far away from the street and the coffin as possible. Surely someone who lived on the street would call the authorities. But then again, wasn't it as likely someone on this street had the body that used to occupy the coffin? How often do we assume someone else will do the right thing?

She knew she could wait. She could call, and she could sit in her air-conditioned car and wait for the cops. David could go back to work, and then they would have an interesting story to share over dinner. For once.

But, in the end she didn't, they didn't, though she couldn't recall how he got her to leave and tell no one. Cowardice, no doubt. Helene's fear of being a white woman in a rough neighborhood. Helene's fear of being left alone with a coffin, even an empty one. One of those reasons, perhaps all of them. It wasn't hard to get her to go; David was not that persuasive. More annoying than persuasive. He bitched and whined her out of it. He appealed to her laziness.

Now the regret settled into the vacancy in her chest. A vacant hole, like an empty coffin.

There was a dead body out there, out of its grave. A year ago, today, her father died. She couldn't shake the eerie feeling the two events happening on the same date gave her. She didn't much believe in coincidence, and she wasn't a very superstitious person. But the coffin, empty and old, baking in the sun next to a rotten couch on a city street…it was wrong.

Helene gave up on sleep, thoughts of coffins and death pecking at her. She couldn't bear to be near David, snoring and sweaty and totally indifferent to the day's bizarre events. So, she got up and decided to make coffee. She could get a start on the job hunt early. But she was exhausted and only stared at her closed laptop. She couldn't shake the dream, couldn't shake the guilt. They should have told someone. Who just drives away from a coffin on the ground? What kind of people lived in that neighborhood? Was it for cult rituals? Voodoo? A gang initiation thing? A sex thing?

Unbidden, she pictured old dried flesh flaking off on a kitchen table. An old mummified corpse surrounded by candles and hooded people. *Unlikely.* Probably just stupid teenagers with nothing better to do.

As she sat with her coffee, she stared out at the quiet city street. The first vestiges of morning greeted her: the lightening of the sky and an occasional car passing by. Soon it would be bustling and alive again. But wait—

On the opposite side of the street, a man stepped from the shadow of a tree. His head tilted, he looked right into her window. Tall, with dark skin and dark clothes and very thin. She gasped and leaned away from window, pulse fluttering.

When she dared look back, the figure was gone.

Could have been coincidence, just some man walking, notices a light on, he looks up just as she looks out...but the dread squeezed. Too many coincidences. She remembered the blackbird, a crow or raven, she couldn't tell the difference, city girl that she was. The uncanny way it watched her. Was this about what she and David knew, what they knew and didn't report?

"Not everyone is out to get you, Helene." Her father had always teased her for being paranoid. Said she never trusted anyone, was always looking over her shoulder. Didn't have enough faith in humanity. He'd been quietly disappointed that she didn't take after him and his big heart. He didn't understand that a petite pretty woman who trusts that easy, who wanders through life inevitably becomes a victim. Helene wasn't a fool. It was easier to be kind and generous if you were a big man. The world loved big white men.

The last twenty-four hours proved she was right, not her father. The kind of humanity that digs up coffins and leaves them on the side of the road in a pile of garbage is not good. Thinking about her father inevitably led to thinking about him dying, and then thinking about him dead. Her father was in a coffin now. She could remember him lying there, deflated and empty, a shell, in the funeral parlor. She imagined him underground, rotting. Or dug up and *taken*, his casket left smashed on the street. Hands pawing at his body, lifting it out of the satin-lined interior.

She just made it to the trash can in time to retch, hot coffee sluicing its way back up and out. Too much thought of death, of strangers watching her windows, of her father, dead only a year.

David's soft snores floated in from the bedroom and she seethed. She wanted to run her nails down his docile, stupid face, leaving bloody furrows. She wanted to punish him for his complacency, for her own. They should have called the cops, told someone. He should have remembered her fucking father died a year ago. She should have waited for the cops.

It's never too late. She dug around in her purse and pulled out her phone, watching the bedroom door for any sign of David stirring. There was none.

"911, what is your emergency?" The operator chimed in.

Outside the window, the man in black was back on the sidewalk. Standing in the same spot as if he'd never left. Only now, there was another man about five feet down the pavement looking up in the same way, dressed the same. Heart in her throat she pressed herself against the wall, hoping she was hidden from the window.

"Ma'am? Hello?" the operator called out, sounding a hundred miles away.

Helene was whispering without realizing it, her heart in her throat. "Yes, I would like to report something I saw today. Pilling St. It was a coffin."

"A coffin?"

"Yes, right out on the street. Empty. Freshly dug up. Piled with some trash. That's all. Thank you." She hung up, pushing the phone away from her on the table. She risked a peek out the window, and to her horror, the two men were now three. Each standing the same way, same dark skin, same black clothes, same still pose looking up at her. They reminded her of black birds. Crows. Heckle and Jeckle. A *murder* of crows perched in wait. Why was it called a murder? Not a group or a flock; a murder.

She looked toward the bedroom, knowing David slept on. How could he not sense her distress? How could they have a future if he was deaf to her feelings, her fears, her father's death? The danger emanating from the men on the street? She pressed her cheek to the window sill, and yes, she could see the street. Now, there were four men. Four men, all in black, so dark they were little more than silhouettes cut out of poster board. All standing still and staring up at her window. She couldn't see any eyes, but she knew they could see her. She debated running to the bedroom or calling out to David. She was soaked with stinking sweat.

"Circle of life," David had said to her in the funeral home, while she wept and held her dead father's cold hand. David then clapped her shoulder like a little league coach before stepping outside for a fucking cigarette, leaving her all alone.

While he was technically with her now, albeit sleeping, she felt just as alone. She watched with increasing distress as a fifth man appeared on the street, mirroring the pose of the other four. Five dark strangers gazed up, like birds on a wire, the strange cock of their heads, the stillness.

Watching her. Wanting her to see them, wanting her to know they were there.

Helene, scared, tired of feeling tired, and of feeling so sad, in a moment of bravery, or perhaps defeat, stepped full into the window and stared down at them. Six of them, then seven, then eight. The ninth stood in the center of the street looking up at her, and the tenth was on her side of the street, staring straight up to see her.

She never saw them approach, or move, but between one blink and another, they were there, and then there were more. She watched them watch her. The sky lightening but they stayed pitch black. She thought of that sunbaked coffin, hinges so hot she'd probably have burned herself touching them. Lonely out there on that street. Lonely in the ground, too. She pictured David, asleep and useless. Lonely in their apartment as well.

The sadness, and the loneliness, caused tears to run free down her face. The shame of being afraid of her neighborhood, of secretly thinking certain hateful people had a point...and maybe if *they* dressed different, and made their neighborhoods nice, maybe if they didn't have so many babies. Maybe then she wouldn't be dragging her feet to find another job, maybe then she wouldn't be aching for the manicured tidy suburbs of her youth. Maybe if she spent a little more time trying to get "to know" people, to let down her guard, be more open to understanding. Too many maybes, and they all felt too late.

She pushed the buzzer, unlocking the door.

Better to just let it all happen the way it was lined up to. She was so tired and this whole year had been a blur of grief. Perhaps seeing that coffin was the end point. The door downstairs opened, and then there were footsteps up the steps.

"Not everyone is out to get you, Helene," she heard her father say, so close as if whispered in her ear. The knob to her door turned.

Not everyone is out to get you, Helene.

It opened.

Raven O'Clock
Holley Cornetto

The first time Jeff entered the cabin, he wasn't sure how he got there. Everything seemed so distorted that he wondered if he were dreaming. It was cold and dark, with snow flurries drifting through the sky. In the moonlight, the forest surrounded the cabin with a glittering fairy tale embrace. Beautiful, but ominous.

He walked in the front door. Had he knocked? He couldn't remember. The last thing he did remember was Zack's face. He must have been dreaming, because Zack had been covered in blood, pointing an accusing finger at him. *You did this to me,* the boy seemed to say. The words burned in his mind.

Inside, the cabin was small but comfortable. A fire crackled in the corner, casting flickering shadows on the walls. The scent of gingerbread permeated the room. A log in the fireplace popped like a gunshot, making him jump. To the left, he heard the clattering of pots and pans. He followed the sound to the kitchen, where a woman poured hot cocoa into mugs.

"Excuse me. I think I've lost my way."

The woman looked up from her task and smiled. All he could make out of her face were the crow's feet around her eyes; the rest was out of focus. It was like trying to read with a headache. No matter how he tried to concentrate, he couldn't focus. He *could* see that she wore a flour-covered apron and that she was short and round. Her braided hair was piled neatly atop her head.

"Lost your way? Well, that *is* unfortunate."

"I don't remember how I got here." He yawned, stretching his arms overhead. To be honest, he really didn't remember much at all. Not since Zack's funeral, anyway. Everything since was nothing but a painful blur.

She smiled again, her teeth flashing peppermint white. "You *were* in quite a state when you arrived. You were mumbling about death, and someone named Zack."

He rubbed the back of his head and grimaced. "Yeah, I think I was dreaming…about my son." He pulled his hand back and wiped clammy sweat on his jeans. It was always the same dream. The third time he dreamt it, he knew it must be true. Zack blamed him. It shouldn't have been a surprise; he blamed himself, too.

She nodded. "Why don't you go make yourself comfortable by the fire? I'm almost finished in here. I'll come sit with you in a minute."

He went back into the den, stopping to admire the set of antlers that hung above the fireplace. Red stains oozed down the wall behind them. Rust from the nails? The shadows from the fireplace must have been playing tricks on him. He used to love hunting before the accident. Before the sight of blood brought to mind things that he didn't want to remember.

Near the fireplace, a cheap plastic clock hung on the wall, the type where each hour chirped the call of a different bird. He grinned, checking to see what sound the next hour would bring. The yellow warbler would sing in about twenty minutes, at ten o'clock. He'd always loved bird-watching. He had feeders with seeds and suet cakes. He used to point out the different types to Zack, who had affectionately nicknamed their yard "Bird Central Station."

In the corner, there was a Christmas tree. Most of the ornaments hung on it looked homemade. The snowflakes looked to him like spider webs, and the snowmen like skeletons. He shook those thoughts away. He wouldn't let the darkness follow him here. They were snowflakes and snowmen, and that was that.

He settled into the recliner. There was a crocheted blanket folded over the back. It smelled of cinnamon and cloves. He pulled it around his shoulders and peered out the sliding glass door to his right. He could see the forest just beyond and the moonlight reflecting off the snow. It had started to fall in earnest. Just enough to be decorative.

Zack would have liked this cabin. It didn't seem fair to be here, enjoying this night. It was disconcerting to be living his life when Zack couldn't live his. There was no reason death should have taken his son and left him behind. *It'd have been better if we'd both died.*

The woman entered the room with a tray of cocoa and fresh gingerbread cookies. She set the cocoa—a giant Santa mug, topped with whipped cream and a cinnamon stick—at his place at the table. "It's been a long time since I've had company." The Santa painted on the mug glared at him. He rubbed his eyes. He was seeing things. He hadn't slept well since the nightmares began.

"I…I'm Jeff. Thank you for your hospitality. I'm sorry, but if you gave me your name, I forgot it."

She chuckled. "I know who you are, Jeffrey. I used to know your momma, but I haven't seen *you* since you were a young man. Got into some trouble back then, as I recall. You worried your poor momma sick."

He squinted at her, trying to remember, but the more he concentrated on her face, the more it blurred. *Damn, I'm exhausted.* Jeff nodded. "Yeah, I wasn't a good kid. But I turned it around."

"So you did. But now you're here, and you seem troubled. Why don't you tell me what's on your mind?"

"I honestly can't recall how I got here. The last thing I remember was dreaming about my son. I might be dreaming still, for all I know."

She chuckled, her face lighting up. "Could be, could be. Tell me about your son? If you want to, I mean."

He took a sip from his mug and scalded the roof of his mouth. "Zack? He's a great kid. *Was*, I mean, a great kid. He liked math and history. He loved the stars. We took him to the planetarium last summer. God, he loved that."

"We?"

"Oh, right. My wife and I took him. She's Susan. We've been married for twelve years. Susan is a great wife. Was a great mom, too."

She nodded, urging him on.

"Zack, he…there was an accident. It was my fault." He took another sip of cocoa.

"I see. Now I know why you've come. You're troubled. You need to relax. Put your feet up for a while." She crossed the room and adjusted the fireplace logs. Jeff noticed stockings with embroidered snowmen and candy canes dangling from the mantle, woven together by a large spider web. No, not a spider web. It was cotton, meant to look like snow.

"Your momma used to come see me when she was troubled, too. She always said there ain't nothing like a plate of cookies and a warm drink to set you right."

"How long have you lived here?"

"Oh, I've been here too many years to count. So long I can't remember! I mostly keep to myself. I like the quiet."

Jeff nodded. "I understand. Most days I want to just...disappear, you know? Just be away from other people for a while. To think. To sort stuff out."

"Do you want to stay the night? You don't want to head back down the mountain in the storm. I've got a guest room, all done up."

Jeff yawned. "Are you sure? I don't mean to impose."

She smiled and cleared away his mug and plate. "I'm sure."

Jeff leaned back in the chair and closed his eyes. Though he tried to relax, he couldn't stop the flood of images that washed over him. A blood-covered Zack in the passenger's seat. Zack being loaded into the ambulance. The bloodstains that never washed out of his car. A constant reminder. A stain on his consciousness.

The yellow warbler chirped ten o'clock.

Local Boy Killed in Car Accident
By: Chronicle Staff

Hillside resident Zachary Grant was killed Thursday evening in what officers are calling a tragic accident. Grant was on his way home with his father, Jeffrey, who allegedly failed to observe a stop sign, causing another vehicle to strike the passenger side of the car. Grant was pronounced dead on the scene. The family will hold a memorial at Richard's Funeral Home, followed by a private graveside service.

He wasn't sure if it had been weeks or months, but eventually, Jeff made his way back to the little cabin. He let himself in again.

"Hello? Are you home?"

He heard the familiar clatter of the kitchen and ducked inside.

She flashed her gleaming smile at him. "Oh, you're just in time! I made stollen and chamomile tea."

He walked into the den and stopped in front of the bird clock. It was almost eastern bluebird o'clock. Large oak bookshelves extended ceiling to floor. He hadn't noticed them last time, but he'd been exhausted. On the shelves were books that he'd loved as a boy: *Frankenstein, Alice's Adventures in Wonderland, The Strange Case of Dr. Jekyll and Mr. Hyde,* and *Dracula.* He took *Alice* off the shelf and opened it, delighted to find John Tenniel's original illustrations inside. He settled into the chair by the fire.

The woman came out of the kitchen in a sequined red dress, with a small dusting of flour on her patent leather shoes. She placed a cup and saucer on the table, then poured him some tea from the pot. The stollen, still warm from the oven, steamed on the plate.

He inhaled, savoring the spiced fragrance of the bread. "You look lovely. Do you have plans this evening?"

She offered a sly smile. "I suspected I'd see you again. You got a taste for my cooking. Just like your momma did."

He tried to focus on her face again, but it blurred at the edges, like static on a television screen. "You're going to spoil me."

She glanced at the open book on his lap. "Find something you like?"

He nodded and held up the book. "I had this one when I was a kid. It wasn't half as nice, though. Have you seen the illustrations? Zack would've loved it. He liked books, you know."

She sat on the couch beside his chair. She nodded and sipped her tea. "Did you come back to talk about Zack?"

Jeff shook his head. He didn't want to think about Zack. In this place, he shouldn't have to. "No. Well, yes. I…" he sighed. "Susan left me."

"You poor child. Do you want to talk about it?"

He took a bite from his stollen and stared at the fire. The cake was spiced and lightly sweet. Perfect, really. He couldn't look in her direction; if he did, he knew he wouldn't be able to stop the tears that threatened. "I couldn't…after Zack, I mean…I wasn't me. I'm still not me. She needed to move on. To clean out his room, to donate his things to charity. I couldn't. I couldn't let go. It felt like…a betrayal. Like I was trying to forget him." There were other reasons too, but he didn't want to think about them. Not here.

She leaned closer. Her perfume smelled like vanilla and stargazer lilies. She placed a heavy hand on top of his. Her touch sent goosebumps up his arm; her hand was freezing. "People grieve in all kinds of ways. No two people are the same."

"I just needed a break. To get away. Losing Zack was hard enough. But now, with Susan gone too, I don't know what to do with myself." The truth was, the images of Zack were no longer mere flashes. They haunted him constantly, always lingering in the back of his mind. He felt Zack's presence in every room, watching and judging.   He could feel the subterranean unease deep within his belly creep up the back of his throat. He swallowed it down with another sip of tea.

Only here was he safe. Only here his demons couldn't find him.

"You should stay here. You can read whatever you like. I've got some snowshoes and a sled. And puzzles! Do you still like puzzles? You can go ice fishing out on the lake tomorrow if you want."

Jeff took a sip from his cup, but pulled it away quickly when he felt a sting. He touched his lip, pulling his fingers away to find blood. Looking down, he noticed a tiny chip on the rim of the cup, and a crimson smudge. He sat the mug back down and checked the time.

Ten after eastern bluebird, but the clock had not chirped.

Dear Jeffrey,

I imagine that you're not surprised to find I've left. I'm sorry. I feel the constant weight of Zack's absence, and while I try not to blame you, I sometimes wonder if things might have been different if I'd been the one to drive him home that night. Were you not paying attention to the road? Were you drinking? I hate myself for asking these questions, but I can't help it. I don't want to hate you. I'm afraid that if I stay, eventually I will.

Love,
Susan

Jeff didn't wait long before he returned to the cabin again. He entered and headed straight for the kitchen. "Hello?"

The woman glanced up at him. She looked tired, older than he remembered. She moved slower, more mechanically. There were stains on her dress, and it didn't seem to fit her quite right. "You again, huh? Guess you're feeling sorry for yourself?"

"I..." he hesitated. "Are you alright?"

She waved a hand at him in dismissal. "Go on. I'll be out in a few minutes. As soon as I finish up here."

He left the kitchen and walked back into the den. He glanced over the fireplace and noticed the rack of antlers missing, a dark stain on the wall outlining where it had hung. He stepped closer to the mantle. A fine layer of dust covered everything.

He took his usual seat by the fire. There were cobwebs hanging from the ceiling. He pulled the handle on the recliner, and the chair fell back, fully reclined, with a loud pop. He tried to pull it up at least part way, but it seemed to be stuck.

He was still pulling at the handle when she emerged from the kitchen. She pressed her knee into the back of the chair, and then tugged the handle. The chair jerked back into position, sending up a cloud of dust.

Jeff erupted into a sneezing fit. "Thanks," he said, once he was able.

"Mmhm." She placed a plate and mug on the table beside the chair. The plate had sugar cookies tinged with black. She filled his mug with tea. "So, what brings you back here, Jeffrey?"

He took a sip of tepid tea. The mug was stained and cracked. "After Susan left, I couldn't keep myself together. I fell back into bad habits, missing work. They told me not to come back. And now...now, I have nothing."

She nodded. "You never told me about Zack's accident. What happened?" Something about her tone brooked no argument.

"I was driving. It was late. I ran a stop sign. I didn't see the other car, not until it was too late."

"So you blame yourself." It wasn't a question.

He felt a familiar lump in his throat and tried to swallow it down. "What happened to the house? It looks like some of your things are broken. The antlers are gone." He motioned vaguely to the empty spot over the fireplace.

She shrugged. "Things break. Stuff gets dirty. But, you ain't here to talk about me. Have you talked to Susan?"

Jeff could feel the pressure in his jaw from grinding his teeth. "A few times."

"And?"

He exhaled sharply. "*And*, I liked it better when you didn't ask so many questions."

She placed her mug down hard, jarring her saucer. "You're the one that came to me, mister. You've got no right to be so grouchy."

"You're right. I apologize." His face burned with shame at her rebuke. "I think I've forgotten how to talk to people...how to be in the world." He glanced around the cabin. There was a draft blowing in. He picked up the moth-eaten crochet blanket and wrapped it around his shoulders. The air had a chill. A certain gloom had settled over the place. He didn't remember it being this way before, so dreary and bleak.

She leaned over and patted his shoulder. "That's all right. You've been in quite a state. Quite a state indeed." She smelled like air freshener, sprayed to cover up something under the surface. He couldn't place the scent. It was a smell he associated not with people, but with damp.

He got up and walked across the room to the bird clock. The images had faded, and it was hard to tell one bird from another. It should be chiming two o'clock, but the room was silent.

Local Man Arrested in DWI
By: Chronicle Staff

On March 3, local police officers conducting a routine patrol observed a car driving erratically, unable to maintain a lane. Officers initiated a traffic stop, and made contact with Jeffrey Grant, 35 of Hillside.

While speaking with Grant, officers observed signs of intoxication. After failing standard field sobriety tests, he was placed under arrest for DWI.

He was processed and charged additionally for driving with a suspended license, reckless driving, and failure to maintain a lane.

He was released into the custody of a friend pending an initial appearance in municipal court.

Winter passed into spring. It had been a while since he'd gone to the cabin. Each time he visited, it was a little less like the first. Thunderstorms threatened on the horizon, and he hesitated on the front porch. Part of the roof was collapsing. *I'll have to offer to fix that up for her.* He opened the door and stuck his head inside. The house was dark. He wasn't sure if she was home.

"Ma'am?"

He heard a wheezing cough from the direction of the kitchen, and went to find her. Inside the house was freezing. *I should offer to cut some wood for her.*

He peeked into the kitchen. "Hello?"

She was sitting at the table. Shadows lingered around her eyes, making her look like a raccoon. Her dress was frayed and torn. "Hello, Jeffrey." She smiled, and her teeth were as brown as the gingerbread she'd made on his first visit.

The house was wrong. She was wrong.

"It's cold in here. Aren't you cold? I can make a fire if you'd like. Do you need me to cut some wood?"

She cackled, the sound grating and unpleasant. "Cold house, cold heart."

"Are you alright? Maybe I could fix up the place a little. Should I turn on a light?"

Outside, the wind picked up, and he noticed a puddle on the floor where the roof was leaking. He grabbed a dirty pan from the counter and set it down to catch the drip. The place reeked with a musty scent of decay.

"Why are you here, Jeffrey? Did you come to nag me about how you killed your little boy?"

Jeff froze. His face went pale.

"Or, maybe you wanted to tell me about how your wife couldn't stand looking at you anymore?"

"I…"

"Or wait, maybe you wanted to tell me more about how you can't even hold down a job so pathetic a trained monkey could do it?"

He shook his head. Something was wrong, not just with this place, but with her, too. "What happened to your house?"

"What happened to your life?" she asked accusingly. "Seems to me that those who live in glass houses shouldn't throw stones, Jeffrey."

Maybe if I fix up the place everything will go back to normal. That must be it, he thought. *If I fix the house, it will all go back to the way it was the first time.* He left the kitchen and walked into the den. The books that had once been carefully arranged on the shelves were spread all over the floor, with pages torn and strewn about. He gathered the pages and placed them back inside their books, dusting the shelves with his shirt sleeve before replacing them. He retrieved *Alice's Adventures in Wonderland* from the fireplace and tucked it back onto the shelf.

After sorting the bookshelf, he started cleaning the fireplace. He took a small broom and dustpan and swept out the ashes. The back of his throat felt raw and scratchy from breathing the dust and ash.

Her voice taunted him from behind. "It's just like your life, boy. You can't fix that, and you can't fix this, either."

He didn't respond. He went out to the porch and found some logs for a fire. He took a match and some crumpled newspaper and coaxed a small flame to life. His eyes stung, and he coughed from the smoke.

"You'll just make a mess of things. That's all you know how to do anyway, isn't it?"

"No!" he shouted. "No. I can fix this. It can be the way it was before. You're tired. You can't keep this place up by yourself. I'll help you. Here, sit by the fire."

She smirked and shuffled to the recliner, her body hunched and arthritic.

Jeff went into the kitchen and found a feather duster. He set to work on the mantle, then the empty wall where the antlers had been. He paused in front of the bird clock. The birds had faded, all except for one—the raven that marked midnight. Funny, he had never noticed a raven before.

He reentered the kitchen and opened the refrigerator. The smell of rancid meat and spoiled milk made his stomach churn. He skimmed the shelves and opened drawers, but found nothing edible. The milk was cottage-cheese chunks, and the deli meat squirmed with maggots.

He covered his mouth, holding back vomit, as he pulled the garbage can over. One by one, he emptied the contents of the fridge into the trash.

Maybe I can still make tea. He realized he'd never seen where things were kept, so he opened the cabinets haphazardly. The finish was chipping off the doors. *Was it like this before? Did I just not notice?*

He opened one door to find mice scurrying over broken bits of china. The tea cups were mostly shards and dust; the ones that remained were chipped or cracked down the sides. Mice droppings mixed among the shards. The pungent smell of ammonia emanated from inside.

He placed the two most intact mugs in the sink. He grabbed the sugar bowl and lifted the lid. The sugar writhed with life. He shook the contents, which sent cockroaches scurrying frantically up his arm. He shrieked and the bowl fell, shattering on the counter.

He leaned over to collect himself. A cockroach skittered over the toe of his shoe. He tried lifting his foot, but his sole stuck to the floor.

Everything was in ruins. Cackling laughter mocked him from the den. He tore his shoe free and left the room, garbage bag still in hand.

"What's so funny? What happened here?"

"You're like a rat in a cage, running around your little wheel."

"You've changed."

"You've changed," she mimicked, sneering. "Of course I've changed. You dump all your problems here. What did you expect? That I could just clean all that up? This place is ruined because *you* ruined it." She pointed a finger at him accusingly. "You came in with your self-pity and failures, and you *infected* this place. This is *your* fault. Just like Zack was your fault. Just like Susan was your fault."

He felt stricken. "You were never cruel before. I wanted to help fix this place, but...I don't think I'll come back again."

She smiled, her brown teeth hanging from her mouth like rotten fangs. "You won't come back? Ha. You can't even leave." She slapped her knee and doubled over in a fit of laughter.

Lightning flashed outside, illuminating the room. With the darkness banished for a split second, he could see her face clearly. She no longer resembled a woman at all. She looked like him, but twisted and melted with decay.

Jeff screamed and fled, flinging the door open. Zack stood in the open doorway, covered in blood, pointing at him, blocking his path.

He slammed the door shut and leaned against it, sobbing with each breath.

"I told you that you couldn't leave." More laughter.

He doubled over and vomited on the floor. "What did you do? This isn't right! This isn't the way it's supposed to be."

In a rage, he grabbed the books from the shelf and flung them into the fireplace. He pulled furniture, rugs, garbage—anything he could get his hands on—into the fireplace. The whole room erupted into flames.

The clock cawed. It was raven o'clock.

Fire Rampages Hillside Apartments
By: Chronicle Staff

Firefighters responded to an emergency call at 1:00 am yesterday morning at the Hillside apartment complex. The fire blazed for hours before the local fire department was able to extinguish it. Official reports state that the source of the fire was a two bedroom apartment belonging to one Jeffrey Grant, a 35-year-old man, unemployed, who lived alone. The toxicology report showed large levels of heroin in his system. Authorities were able to determine the time the fire started by the sole object that survived it: a bird clock, frozen at midnight.

Hagride

Justine Gardner

"Devil bird," the man muttered from the bench behind her.

Josie ignored him, as she did most mornings when she came here to scope the lake, assess the weather, the day before her. March, the air still cool enough to fog her breath, make her shiver when the wind hit the spot between collar and neck.

"Devil bird," he said louder. And then again: "Devil bird!"

She looked at him this time and saw he was pointing toward the fallen tree sprawled into the water to her left. A resting place for the birds—the coots and ducks usually—but today there was someone new.

"Cormorant," she said to herself. "Double-crested."

The large, black bird was posed on the farthest branch, wings stretched out in the faint morning sun, holding still.

"Devil bird!" the man shouted again.

She usually rotated around the lake; the same five or six hits on the clock, more or less. But she always started there, at the cement viewing platform that edged into the water, ringed with benches, no fishing allowed. It was the touchstone, the fork in the road: did she go left and through the wooded peninsula, past racing, unleashed dogs, under the bridge, sliding down muddy banks to the water's lip? Or did she head right, toward the marshes, the sloppy edges where the men drank and smoked. Where Pop-Pop used to sit, his feet on that old log, whites of his eyes as yellow as bottled piss.

Today she went left, toward the peninsula, craving the brief flash of woods, the absence of ghosts. The weather seemed right for it; damp, the moist air making it feel colder than it should be a week out from Easter.

Cold Easter, late June, Mama used to say. She meant it was gonna be winter for a while longer. The cormorant had come back, though. Standing on that branch, wings out like a crucifix.

Devil bird.

No, not that. A fisherman's bird. Josie's kind of bird. Cormorants knew where the fish were; where it was easy to nab them without all the fuss. Follow a cormorant, he'll show you the way. Thing was, these park cormorants kept themselves on the other side of fences; their fishing spots protected by signs with red slashes. Josie obeyed those signs, but not everybody did.

𓂀

The woods were empty, as she'd hoped. Not even a sign of Jack—not his name, just what she called him—the skinny rat-headed man who sometimes slept by the path under a raft of tree branches. He was Jack to her because, well, he had a proclivity. "Lady fish, lady fish," he'd mutter at her from behind a tree, trying to get her to look. She'd looked once, years ago, and never again. Now, if Jack came anywhere near her, she threw a rock in his direction. Still, she'd sometimes catch a sight of that woolly hat of his, full of sticks and leaves. *Lady fish, lady fish.*

She set her kit down on the bench of the wooded pavilion at the peninsula's southeastern tip. Shook her shoulders out and cast off, releasing herself into the feeling, the first line of the day. The lure flying through the air, landing with a soft plop, water rippling outward. She watched it float on top of the silver water, moving with the chilled breeze and nothing else. She breathed, smelled wet leaves and mud. If she schooled herself, she could ignore the cans and plastic cups left by Jack and others and see nothing but woods, water, sky.

She reeled in, feeling for a tug, anything. Early yet she knew, fish not biting. Fish still dozing their slow winter away, dreaming of summer flies drowning on the shining sky above them.

She cast off again. She should move on. Only time enough before home, to Mama, then work. She counted to sixty in a slow tick and reeled in.

The next stop was not far from her first, still on the peninsula, but more covered, off the narrow dirt path that just skirted the edge of the water. The mud was thick here: March mud, sticky and persistent. She'd be bringing it home with her, caught in the cleats of her brown boots. Mama used to make her shed her shoes in the hall, leave them there till the mud dried and then she'd bang them together over the trash, sending clouds of dusted earth everywhere. Now Mama didn't notice if Josie came all the way inside, took her boots off on the couch, leaving streaks of lake mud across the floor.

Josie found a leafy pile to rest her kit and cast off into the shallows. Waited.

The cormorant's head appeared like a dark snake in the water to her right so abruptly she jumped back several feet, dropped her pole. She scrambled to pluck it from the mud and reeled in to keep the bird from getting caught in her line. The cormorant paused, seeming to wait for her to finish, before paddling by and leaping onto a log to her left. Beads of water rolled from its back as it shook its great wings dry. The feathers weren't just black, she noticed, but a deep bronze in places, rimmed in darker ink. The bird turned its head, catching her with a sapphire eye, and then lifted into the air, the wet breeze from its wings just touching her cheek. For a second she thought she could smell the rich, icy heart of the lake.

She moved on. Her third spot was farther in, on the path along the upper wedge of the lake, toward the boathouse. To get to the water here required scraping down the steep banks, curving around tree trunks to find a two-foot slice of space to stand. She liked these spots best of all. The biting was the same all over the lake; same fish schooled in the same habits. But here—despite the risk of snagging in the crowded trees—here, she could feel *alone*.

Josie held the feeling close and shoved thoughts of a day's work aside, of Mama at home, and cast off. She waited, the lure lying there, a dot of red against the dark water. A pair of ducks squirted by, clucking their complaints. She watched, made sure they were clear of her line, and reeled in. She resisted the urge to look at her watch even though Mama would be wondering soon, and when Mama wondered, Mama wandered.

And she couldn't be late to work, not again. That new supervisor, she liked her time sheets neat. One more, she decided, and cast off a third time, the plop of the lure on water like the tinkling of the sweetest bells.

And then, there it was: the cormorant, its snake-head peeking from the water. It stopped before her line and turned and paddled toward her. It hopped out, inches from her feet, and shook its wings. Water hit her, splashed her face, touched her lips. She was so close she could have reached over and stroked its wet back.

The bird pulled its wings in, cocked its head, piercing her again with that bright blue eye. "Josie," it croaked, opening its orange beak, "help me."

She fell back again, this time landing hard against the rocky ground. For a moment she saw nothing but black water, felt her heart beating in its cage.

That bird...it spoke. She drew in a deep breath, another, and turned her head. The bird had vanished. But it *had* spoken. And it had used Mama's voice.

Josie stood in the doorway, staring at the curl of Mama on the floor by her bed, so small under the thin nightdress. Her head was turned, as though looking beneath the bed for something lost—her slippers, a dropped pill bottle.

Eventually, Josie rolled her over, took a pulse, even as those wide eyes stared up at her. Mama's skin was cooling—how long had she been lying there? Josie closed her mother's eyes with a blind hand—not able to bear their accusation.

Blue eyes, that orange beak: *Josie, help me.*

She'd be late for work now, she knew. This time, though, there'd be no arguing with her excuse.

It was the silence of the apartment, the emptiness, she found hard to endure on those days off work, her mandatory bereavement leave. It still surprised her, Mama dead, and Josie drinking water alone in the kitchen. Even with Mama sleeping, Josie had known another body was home, warm and breathing. Now the only things breathing were the steam radiators ticking over the muffled voices of the new family downstairs, old Mr. Blake's television set to top volume next door.

Was that better than the not-silence of a knock on the door—someone coming to pay respects, ask after? Living in one building your whole life, you knew people whether you wanted to or not. And everyone had known Mama—even after she'd stopped coming down to do the shopping, the weekly laundry. It had been her and Mama in this apartment, alone, near thirty years. Her and Mama. And earlier, when she was still in braids, Pop-Pop had lived there with them.

Pop-Pop lived there but he lived elsewhere too, that old stump in the park, the drinking men by the marsh. He would disappear for a day, maybe three, but always come home, joking that it was Mama's snoring keeping him away. And then, one night, cold, rain lashing the airshaft window that opened onto Josie's bedroom, she heard Mama cry out, the door slam, and Pop-Pop stopped coming home at all. Pop-Pop had gone to the drinking men in the park, Mama said, and good riddance.

It was three days she missed work but it was almost a week before she returned to the lake with her fishing pole, her kit bag.

The night before she'd dreamt she was swimming deep into the cool of the lake, tapping sleeping fish on their silvery backs, waking them with the heat of her hands, bidding them rise, come. When she woke that morning, her heart thudding, pillow cold with sweat, she knew she needed to go to the lake that day or she'd never go back at all.

So there she was, walking into the park, her legs gone to rubber, her heart a steady thump. She'd start where she always did—the lookout spot that jutted into the water. She felt like she'd been on a long run on an empty stomach. That *bird*. She didn't know what to do if she saw that bird again.

It was early, earlier than usual. She hadn't slept well—not with that dream—and once awake there was no turning over, finding sleep again. The sun was still behind the trees, if you didn't know up from down you could easily guess it was dusk and night just around the corner.

She paused, looked left and right. The benches were empty, no overnighters or early risers, birders out to catch the return migration. She breathed, and the air was thicker now, warmer than that last morning. Spring finally pushing through.

She looked toward the tree trunk half in the water, scanned for the outline of black wings, the snake neck of the cormorant. But the tree was just a naked, dark finger dipping into the water as if to test its temperature.

She entered the woods, her feet finding the way even as the light from the lampposts struggled to reach through the branches. She walked, crunching the wood chips underfoot, startling something small and squeaking with her boot. She walked until she emerged again, at the wooden pavilion at the peninsula's tip. No one sleeping there either on that long sheltered bench. The air was damp but warm and full of the anticipation of growing things—the kind of spring air that drew people into the park, bid them sleep in the bower. And yet, here, a second nest empty.

It nearly seemed for all its busy rustling and peeping birdtalk, the park was absent of people. She *knew* it wasn't— she'd passed the usual joggers and dog walkers up early like her on the path down. Seen the flash of light-up collars, reflective vests. People *were* here in the park with her—and yet…

Not here, right at this moment. It was just Josie and her rod. She cast off. Watched the glint of the fly as it soared and plopped, rippling the black sheet of water. Her neck loosened, then her shoulders. She inhaled, and released.

Released the image of Mama, twisted on the floor, reaching under the bed…

Released the march of EMTs, police, the white sheet, the stain left behind on Mama's pale rug…

Released that bird's blue eye, orange beak, *Josie, help me…*

She reeled in. Cast off again. She breathed. The sky went from bruised to fever pink as she stayed there, longer than she normally did but she allowed it. It seemed right. To linger.

After the fourth cast off, though, she turned, picked up her kit, and moved to the second spot. She looked both ways out on the dark water, checking for the black snake-head, the outstretched wings. Nothing. She was alone. She set down her bag and cast off.

For her third spot, she chose the same path as the last time, along the slope of lake water toward the boathouse. She eased down the steep slope to the water's edge, mindful of the mud and slick leaves from last night's rain. There, the narrow band of water, the surface dipping and rippling with the breeze. No ducks, no birds, no black-necked cormorants. She cast off.

From behind her came the crashing sounds of something in the trees. She turned, heart thudding, her rod shaking in her hands. A big white dog bounded down the slope and came right up to her, tail wagging, and barked. She stepped away, not trusting its happy advances. It circled her kit bag, sniffing, and then turned back to her and barked again.

A whistle, a voice from the path above. "Barnaby, come!" And quick as that, the dog vanished in a tangle of white up the slope. She breathed, turned back to the water—

"Josie," said a soft, creaking voice, "you came back."

She dropped the rod then, and stumbled backward, away from the dark edge of the water.

"Who's there?" she whispered, trembling. She listened; it was silent and still. She breathed. You're imagining things, she told herself. Auditory hallucinations were the easiest trick for the head to play.

She moved back toward the water and recovered her rod, reeled in. She peered around the trees, hoping to see nothing, just the blank sheet of lake. But there, on a flat rock stood a cormorant, wings out, its head tilted toward her, waiting.

"Josie," it said again, the voice like an old door swung on a bad hinge, "you came back."

She watched its beak move with the effort of words. It *looked* like it was talking—this wasn't just a sound she'd conjured. She wiped a hand across her face. Covered her eyes and counted, slowly, to five. She looked up again.

The bird was still there, with wings outstretched, watching her.

She'd be damned if she'd speak to it, talk to it. A *bird*. Her brain could play wild jokes on her, make her think her mind was going down the same road as Mama's had at the end, but she would *not* give in. She turned her back on the bird, reached into her kit bag for a towel to wipe her muddy rod, her hands. And then, with shaking arms, she cast off, fly soaring out into the water.

Silence, save the birdsong increasing with the growing sunlight. The ripples of the water, the *glug-glug* as it hit shore edge, rock. She would not look at it, acknowledge it, accept it. She would—

"Josie," it creaked.

She kept her eyes straight ahead.

"I know you hear me," it rasped. And then, changing its tone to something deeper, something more terrible, "Jocelyn, my daughter." It was Pop-Pop's voice. She had not heard that voice in over thirty years.

Devil bird, she thought, going cold. Devil bird.

There was a splash and then the snaking neck appeared in the water. It grabbed the end of her line before she could reel in and began twisting in the nylon string, slowly, turning round and round.

"Jocelyn," it said, the voice now swinging from Pop-Pop to Mama's plaintive bellow, "help *me*."

The line played out as the bird turned and turned, knotting itself in a web. It thrashed, as though struggling but fixed her with its steady blue eye. "Help. Me."

Josie locked the reel and tugged, trying to pull free although she knew it was no use. The bird had tangled itself so completely there'd be no simple undoing. She could cut it, cut it and leave the bird—the devil bird—to mischief of its own making.

"Josie," the voice a rusted hinge once more, "hold on tight!"

And the bird dove into the water with a sharp plunge, the rod jumping in her hands. She nearly dropped it but held on as the bird went deeper. She teetered at the edge, still holding her rod, feeling the pull as the bird tugged and tugged. She should just cut it and go, cut it, go, but one foot slipped and now she was in the water, cold seeping into her shoes. The rod jerked again and she stepped in farther, water at her shins. And then a third, final tug and she was—

—underwater.

And she breathed. She did not know how, understand, but with each gulp of water she felt oxygen fill her lungs.

And she saw. The water, clearer from down below than above. Here, there were fish fat as goats, bigger than any that had made contact with her hook. Turtles turning in slow circles, their shells as wide across as manhole covers, their mouths long, snapping snouts.

Deeper, the bird pulled her and she felt neither wet nor cold, just the sensation of movement, of being tugged as through a warm wind, farther and farther, deeper and deeper.

She should let go. She should let go and float to the top and get back to shore, get herself to the nearest mental hospital and yet...

She went deeper, the cormorant's pull constant and strong. It did not pause to let her gape at the car—a car!—beneath her as she floated past. Its curved shape limned in mud but *still*, a car. Who knew what other treasures lay hidden here in the heart of her lake?

The fish knew, the turtles. Those eyes they gave her as she whirled past, smiling, eager to reach out and tap their silver backs. They said: Who invited you?

The cormorant pulled her farther still, out and down toward the very bottom of the very middle of the lake. The light faltered here; as she craned her neck she could see only the distant glaze of the sun above.

The bird dove down sharply and Josie felt a chill for the first time, a coldness sliding into her. The air—was it air?—she breathed crisp in her nose, mouth. Like fall, like the excretion of a thousand years of autumn trees on a rain-wrecked night.

Below them, a house—or what was left of one, lurking in the murky bottom waters. A chimney, stone, a wall. A doorway.

The bird pulled them toward it, pulled harder, tugging them down, down, down...and she was through the door—

—and it was the apartment. *Her* apartment. Her and Mama's. But...

She was on her feet, standing, not wet, not dripping onto the carpet, which was good because Mama was standing there too. And beside her stood Pop-Pop. They were at the window, their backs to the door.

She could tell from the hunch of Pop-Pop's shoulders, the way he waved his hand in the air, that he was drunk. "Don't you hagride me, now, woman," he was saying with that voice she'd last heard from the cormorant's mouth.

How could they... "Mama?" she said, then, softer, "Pop-Pop?"

Neither turned at the sound of her voice.

"Go then," Mama spat. "Go, and so help you, if you do, I'll—"

And Pop-Pop pushed Mama, hard. And past them, toward the window, Josie saw rain beating against the glass.

"Pop-Pop," Josie said again, her voice suddenly the low squeak of a young girl.

Mama, dazed from her fall, rubbing the back of her head, pulled something long and silver from her apron pocket.

"What you going to do with that, woman?" he laughed. "Stab me?"

And Mama thrust out with her hand and Josie screamed, loud, louder than she had ever screamed in her life, her throat burning, her ears ringing with the sound of it.

Pop-Pop turned at that, from the window. The black handle of the knife in his chest, a line of red only just beginning to seep beneath it. Mama glanced over her shoulder and then, startled, turned all the way around. "Josie," she whispered. "You're here?"

"Jocelyn," Pop-Pop said, heedless of the knife, the running blood, "my daughter."

He smiled, but she saw tears in his eyes. Wasn't he hurting? That knife.

There were tears in Mama's eyes too now, Josie saw. "Josie," Mama said. She sounded so sad. "You... you have mud on your dress."

Josie bristled. *Dress?* She hadn't worn a dress since—

She looked down and saw she was in one of the pink and white church dresses Mama always put her in. Before she grew taller than Mama, that is. After Pop-Pop had left.

But there she was, her full-grown size, standing in the doorway of her apartment at the bottom of the lake, wearing pink and white and shiny black shoes with frilled socks. She touched her hair, it was braided in neat rows ending in beads, she knew without trying to find a mirror, that would be pink and white.

But her body was the body that the bird had pulled through the lake...

She turned back to the door, which had closed behind her. She went to open it, to leave. This wasn't where she wanted to be, this was *not* the secret heart of her lake. This was—

"Don't," her father said. "Not yet."

She paused, her hand on the doorknob. She stood on tiptoes—tiptoes?—to see out the peephole. Through the fish eye she saw black swirling water—

And then she saw the doorknob, the peephole above her, just out of reach. She should get a chair, her stool from the bathroom sink so she could look, look and see...if the noise outside was Pop-Pop coming up the stairs from the park, banging the walls as he sang, slamming the door so loud she woke—

"Jocelyn, my daughter," Pop-Pop said again, from behind her, his voice booming through the room. She felt that prickle, that sense of alert. The peephole seemed so very far away.

"Josie," Mama's voice shook, "this is important."

She turned from the door, letting go of the knob.

Her parents were seated on the couch now. A space between them. The knife still in Pop-Pop's chest.

She lowered her head and obeyed, walking over. She squeezed herself in. Her legs dangled above the floor, and she kicked them back and forth, watching the shine bounce on the toes of her shoes.

"Stop it," Mama said, putting a heavy hand on her knee.

She stopped it.

She sat, head bowed, waiting.

Her father sighed and said, his voice softening, "It is time."

Mama gave a soft gasp. "Must we—"

Pop-Pop drew in a deep breath, clucked his tongue. "She's here. She came of her own choice."

Josie didn't say anything. She wasn't supposed to. She was told to listen, listen and be still.

"Together, woman," Pop-Pop said. "Do you hear me? Together."

Josie said nothing. She thought of school, of the book she was supposed to be reading for her report. She didn't want to go anywhere. She didn't want Pop-Pop or Mama to go either. Why couldn't they just stay here?

"Josie," Mama's voice, sharp now. "Do you hear what your father said? Will you be a good girl and do as you're told, for once?"

She looked up at Mama, at her wide face, smooth and clear. She nodded and Mama took her hand, squeezed it in her warm, dry one. Pop-Pop took the other, damp and hot.

"Are you ready?" he asked them both, and Josie nodded again. She had no choice. She had to do what the grown-ups said, go when they said go, be still when they yelled for quiet.

They stood, all three together: mother, daughter, father. And they walked toward the door, water now leaking in underneath, a slow, dark drip, mixing with the red running in thick lines from Pop-Pop's chest. She felt her hands slip and noticed she was taller again, her head nearly at her mother's shoulder. Her father reached for the door handle and Josie was his height, then taller. She reached forward and pulled the knife free just as he opened the door.

The world flooded in and Josie swam toward the light.

Officer Baby Boy Blue
Douglas Ford

I almost gouged out my own eye at a young age. But not in the usual way you hear about, not with fireworks, and certainly not with a weapon. I never broke rules, so nothing that glamorous.

Instead, it happened with a model kit, the plastic sort requiring a special sort of cement that came with a warning label about how sniffing it could cause brain damage. I never did anything like sniff glue, either. I didn't want to face consequences, and I certainly didn't want brain damage. What kind of future could I expect with brain damage?

But I nearly gouged out my own eye with a hobby knife, an X-Acto blade. Just a slip of the hand, and the blade pierced the skin just an inch below my left eye. Just imagine if the blade went into my eye and didn't stop there but continued going and into my brain. A horrid thought.

The kit I worked on was the Frankenstein monster, not the kind other kids put together, like a battleship or a bomber, but a monster out of a black-and-white film, lumbering away from a gravestone, arms outstretched. To remove the plastic pieces, I used my X-Acto blade, just like the instructions suggested, and somehow, I still managed to have an accident. Just one careless slip and the point of the blade sliced a two-inch incision, like a third set of eyelids.

A mental fog prevents me from explaining how it happened exactly, but I distinctly remember the panicked trip to the hospital and the chaos in the emergency room. The chaos didn't happen right away though, only after a very long period of time in the waiting room, with my mother holding one of several paper towels to my face in an attempt to stop the bleeding. It came as a relief when someone finally showed me to a bed where a doctor would examine me. They told my mother she would have to wait, and a nurse took me back and helped me up to the bed, smiling at me as she closed the curtain halfway, leaving plenty of space for me to see the doctors and nurses moving about the floor.

Then pandemonium broke loose.

To this day, I don't know the exact nature of the crime or emergency, but the facility began filling with wounded policemen and burned firemen on gurneys, many of them still wearing their emergency gear, heavy coats for the firemen and armored vests for the policemen. At first, just three or four of them arrived, but their count steadily rose until every visible gurney and bed held some horribly injured emergency worker. I don't even know where they came from. Many of them screamed and groaned, sounds made more terrible by the glimpses of blood and burns covering their skin.

No one remained still, the whole area in constant movement, a flurry of confusion as injured firemen and policemen continued to pour into the hospital.

But one person moved slowly, taking his time and gazing about with what looked like curiosity and fascination. I could see him through the half-closed curtain, a police officer, strolling casually toward the bed on which I lay.

As he came closer, I could see that he wore mirrored sunglasses, even though we were indoors. Despite the glasses, he looked friendly enough, and he even smiled as he walked into my curtained area. I hesitated before returning the smile. I wanted someone— preferably a doctor or nurse—to come tell me everything would soon be okay. But I supposed the police officer would have to do.

When he approached, I saw how the mirrored glasses filled his face. And worse, I could see my own reflection in the lenses. I looked horrible, so bloody and ragged. The wound on my face gaped like the mouth of a dead fish.

The officer shook his head and made a tsking sound. I had to look away, not wanting to see my reflection anymore.

"It looks bad," he said, as if I needed confirmation of what I myself could see. Then he added, "But it could be worse."

I almost turned my head for an explanation, but I couldn't face my own reflection.

"No, really," he said, "it could be worse. I'll show you. Look."

That voice had real authority, so it compelled me. I knew I had to look. I turned in time to see the officer lift his sunglasses, an act that made me thankful at first, grateful that it made the awful image of myself go away.

But then I saw what the sunglasses had hidden.

His left eye, just a folded mass of flesh, was held shut by a line of grotesque metal stitches. Had I any presence of mind, I might have made an association to the model kit left unfinished in my bedroom, the Frankenstein monster. I wouldn't think of that for quite some time, just as I wouldn't make another association until years later, when I would see the puckered folds of a woman's labia for the first time. At this moment, seeing the eye stitched closed, only horror existed, and I couldn't turn away, no matter how badly I wanted to do so.

This was, in part, because of his voice. So matter-of-fact, almost happy, despite the injury he suffered.

"I had the most beautiful set of eyes," he said, "until today. Now, there's just one, as you can see, thanks to that criminal today. Everything going on around here, would you believe it's because of one person, just *one, single* person? When I woke up today, I had two of the most amazing eyes you've ever seen. I owe more than my charm to those eyes—I owe my intuition to them, my ability to look at anyone and see what they want to hide. People took one look at my eyes and would tell me anything. Now, look where it got me. Mutilated forever. Look here to get an idea of what I've lost."

He pointed to his remaining eye as if he were showing off the prized piece of a coin collection, and I looked, if for no other reason than to avoid focusing on those awful stitches. I had no medical experience, but even to me, the stitches looked rushed and amateurish, the work of a mad scientist working feverishly in a laboratory converted from an abandoned windmill. The surviving eye looked like any normal eye, nothing special. A typical shade of blue.

"You look unimpressed," continued the officer, and he used his finger to pull down on the lower lid to reveal the red tissue behind the lid. "Baby Boy Blue, my mother used to call me," he said.

At that moment, some kind of disturbance took place in another part of the hospital. A loud bang, as if a gun went off or someone lit a firecracker. Officer Baby Boy Blue calmly looked over his shoulder and considered the resulting ruckus, several policemen running in different directions, doctors and nurses following. Then he turned back to me.

His uniform looked so clean and unruffled. In fact, he must have read my thoughts because he said, "'Crazy how none of the goo got on my uniform. Like I said, just one person caused *all* of this. I just got unlucky, losing an eye. It just hung on my face, hanging by an optic nerve, so there was no choice but to cut it."

"You cut it yourself?"

He seemed shocked by the sound of my voice but somehow pleased that I would finally interrupt him with a question. He put on his sunglasses and responded with a hearty laugh, even though I hadn't made a joke. "Oh, son. Keep up the wonderful spirit. You'll need it. Life is full of changes, and no telling how long you'll sit here with everything going on. Here's something to help you remember me forever."

He reached into his pocket and withdrew a plastic bag, the kind normally used for a sandwich. He placed it into my hand and turned to leave. Or at least, he must have left at some point, because when I looked up after studying the bag's contents, I no longer saw him there.

Inside the bag I saw a bloody mess of bluish white.

When I recognized the iris, I understood that he had left me with his eye.

And indeed, such a stunning blue.

The scar under my eye never went away. It remained as a pink, slightly upraised line that, to me, looked like a slit that one could open up and peer into what lay underneath my face.

The doctor who closed the wound said that by the time I reached my current age I would see no scarring, no sign of the injury. But obviously, he lied. Of course, I should make some allowances for that, given how flustered he looked while working on me. No doubt all the activity occurring in the hospital exhausted him, making him inattentive. Though much of the activity had died down, his hands shook and beads of sweat clung to his forehead. At one point, he even made a mistake. After sewing me up, he stared at my face with a troubled gaze.

"Look up," he said. "No, just with your eyes. Now look down." He repeated these commands several times, trying to assess something he wouldn't—or couldn't—vocalize, and I did my best to follow them each time.

Then he said something that puzzled me. "Now, look at the back of your head."

How could I do that?

He told me two more times to look at the back of my head, and once I even turned my head, unsure of what exactly he wanted me to do, but that just seemed to fluster him more. "You can't, obviously. I have to redo it. I have to take everything out and redo it all," he said, sounding profoundly tired. "I have to redo everything." He began removing the stitches under my eye, the whole process starting over again.

Then once more, the commands began. "Look up." I did. "Look down." I did. "Now look at the back of your head." Somehow, I suppose I did, because he looked satisfied this time.

At some point during all this, I must have transferred the plastic bag given to me by the police officer to my pocket because later, at home, I found it there. I didn't dare take it out until after my mother collapsed in her bed, exhausted from what must have been twelve hours of waiting at the hospital. I felt tired, too, but I didn't sleep.

Instead, I studied my new stitches in the bathroom mirror, noting how much they looked like the stitches the officer showed me. Perhaps the same doctor worked on us both. I moved my eyes the same way the doctor commanded me, trying to imagine what looked so wrong that he had to take all my stitches out. I even tried looking at the back of my head the way he commanded, but I still couldn't fathom how he meant for me to do that. I tried it several different ways. Once, I managed to look so high up into my head that I nearly made my left eye disappear, showing just the white sclera with thick, red veins.

That led to the discovery of two fascinating things.

First, I learned that I could move my left eye, the one just above the stitched slit, higher up than the right. Second, when I did that, I could make my stitched wound open, if only by a tiny bit. I thought this was an illusion at first, but after trying it a dozen more times, it seemed that it really did part just a fraction, a bright red color showing beneath it and the glint of something glassy. Probably just a trick of the light.

With all this experimentation, I nearly forgot about the plastic bag in my pocket.

Extracting it, I noticed a yellowish liquid pooling at the bottom of the bag. Also, its color had faded, its striking blueness giving way to a foggy whiteness. Still, I had to acknowledge what the officer said: indeed, he once had an amazing set of eyes. Now, one of those eyes belonged to me, and I needed to hide it. I feared consequences and I followed all rules, even the ones not explicitly stated to me. I used the box containing the pieces of the unfinished Frankenstein model kit, and I placed the box inside a wood cabinet across from my bed, where it sat for years.

During that time, I hardly thought about it at all. I practically forgot about it completely. Eventually, I lived in that house all alone, thanks to illness, disease, and death.

In the days that followed my accident, I somehow lost my way in school, and in spite of numerous interventions, I never did well. I didn't even graduate and soon after, took the only job I could find: a retail job in a store called Hellstorm Fireworks.

Most people think of fireworks as something sold only two or three times a year, but actually, people buy fireworks all the time. What if, just for a lark, someone wanted to light off a Cornea Splitter or a Socket Rocket? They would need a special kind of store to help them satisfy that urge.

We did good business, and they paid me enough to get by, though I couldn't keep up the house as diligently as I would have liked. Not able to afford anything new, I kept all the old furniture, including the cabinet where I put the model kit box. But like I said, I practically forgot all about it.

I liked my co-workers well enough, especially Jaycee, a girl my age. We entertained each other with jokes when things slowed down. We also speculated about the sort of spectacle that would result if someone decided to light every single one of the fireworks in the store at once. *Colors beyond the known spectrum*, Jaycee suggested, but that sounded nuts to me. I reasoned that if we saw new colors, they wouldn't look like colors to us. They would look like—

"What?" she asked.

I didn't have a clever answer, so I said the first thing that came to mind. "The color you see when you look at the back of your head."

That answer didn't impress her—it just seemed to puzzle her, in fact—so we both stood there bored for a moment until she suddenly asked me, right out of the blue, if I knew any eye tricks.

No one ever asked me before, and for a moment, I felt self-conscious, painfully aware of the slit under my left eye, wondering if its glaring presence on my face made her want to ask me this question. But she smiled at me in a way that restored some of my already-meager confidence, and I confided in her that I could, in fact, look at the back of my head.

"What? No fucking way," she said. "I demand you show me immediately."

"I can't exactly show you," I said. "I mean, if I roll my eyes all the way into the back of my head and manage to look at my own brains, how would you know?"

She looked at me, obviously confused, so I continued: "If I look at my own brains, I'll see them. But you won't. I can't exactly take a picture of the back of my head and show you."

"Fine, Einstein," she said. "How about *I* show you an eye trick of my own? Then maybe you'll find the courage to show me yours."

"Okay, deal." We shook hands to seal the agreement. Then, taking a step back, she lowered her head and let her arms dangle at her side. She looked like a diver preparing for a record-setting leap. I saw her shoulders rise and fall as she took first one deep breath, then a second one.

When she lifted her head, it took a moment to process the image before me.

Her eyes bulged out in an extraordinary, almost cartoonish way, practically a half-inch further out of their sockets. They looked like enormous, bloated eggs, the whites dwarfing the bright blue irises, with angry networks of red blood vessels going everywhere.

No telling how she read the expression of horror on my face. But she smiled wide and toothy, making a terrible spectacle.

Nothing could make it worse, I thought.

Until something did.

Her left eye suddenly popped out, as if it could no longer withstand the pressure she put on it. It popped out and hung on her cheek, dangling by an optic nerve.

The smile remained, as if she didn't even know it happened.

But if she wouldn't react, I would.

I lunged forward, hoping to take hold of the eye and help prevent her from losing it. I don't know what I intended to do exactly.

And my fumbling made her react.

Using her hands, she covered her face, protecting herself. From me, apparently.

When she lowered her hands, her eyes looked normal.

"What're you doing? Personal space, man," she said, her left eye miraculously returned safely to its socket. I had to hand it to her: she accomplished an impressive feat. How had she put it back so swiftly, so deftly?

"Your eye, it's back in," I said.

"What're you talking about, man?"

"It's popped back in."

"It wasn't popped out, man. I was just trying to show you the world-famous Jaycee eye-crossing trick. I've been practicing since I was three. Not shitting you. You ever see anyone do it like that?"

"No, I guess I haven't."

She stared at me, waiting for more. I grew more confused as the period of silence continued.

"Well?" she said finally. "Your turn?"

I must have gawked at her, the thought of me popping my own eye out.

"Your eye trick, man," she said. "Do yours."

"Right," I said with some relief. "You want me to look at the back of my own head."

"Yeah, look at your brain, man. Show me."

"Okay."

I didn't need the kind of preparation she required. I just did it. I rolled my left eye as far as it would roll, wanting very badly to impress her. I didn't need a reflective surface to know that it rolled all the way to the back of my head so that nothing by the sclera showed. By now, I'd learned to keep the right eye completely stationary while I did this, so I could watch her reaction the whole time. I could see her and the place where dreams form all at the same time. I accomplished the feat so perfectly that the two things—her and the place where dreams hide—practically became one and the same, and I almost didn't notice the expression forming on her face.

When I saw her look of horror, I stopped.

She stared at the pink slit under my left eye, my scar.

"Oh, Jesus, oh god," she said, "what the fuck is in there?"

I didn't know what she meant. I just performed a perfect eye trick.

She extended the tip of her finger, as if to touch my scar. But she stopped short, withdrew the finger without touching me, and walked away, perhaps remembering she'd wanted to avoid physical contact between us.

I wouldn't have minded if she touched me, but she never did, and she also didn't speak to me again for the rest of the day. Nor did she ever speak to me again for that matter, all the way until the day she died.

We didn't notice she died, not at first. It seemed like she just decided not to come in to work, which suited me just fine. After all, when you work retail, especially fireworks retail, you don't get rich; you just hope you'll get by, and you need all the hours you can get, so when Jaycee didn't show up for her shifts,

I took the extra work and didn't give her well-being a lot of thought.

Not until the authorities showed up at Hellstorm Fireworks.

They didn't talk to me. They just wanted the boss, who left me in charge of the floor while he talked to the policemen inside his office. Normally, I would've assumed they just wanted to check some of our recent sales—when you buy fireworks, especially the big kind, you have to fill out a bunch of paperwork and show your driver's license. But something about the demeanor of the policemen told me it had something to do with Jaycee not showing up for work.

Sure enough, the boss called me over when they left.

"Jaycee's dead." He said it just like that. No warning to prepare for bad or shocking news. He just laid it out in the simplest way possible. I don't recall what I said or if I conveyed shock. I hope I conveyed concern.

"You know if she had a glass eye?" the boss said.

"What?"

"A glass eye. They asked me if I knew whether or not she had a glass eye. Shit, half the people who come through the door here have glass eyes. Or burn marks. One of the two, at least."

"Why would they want to know if she had a glass eye?"

"Beats the living fuck out of me." Then he regarded me as if he'd just gotten a good look at my face for the first time and didn't like what he saw. "Well? Do you know if she had a glass eye or not?"

Naturally, I thought of her eye trick. I did see her eye pop out, no question about it. I didn't imagine it, and a glass eye explained everything. She crossed her eyes—or her eye, I guess—with such intensity that she caused it to pop out.

"I guess I did," I said, finally.

"Must've been an exact duplicate," the boss said. "Probably worth hundreds. Thousands even. And you knew she had it. Know what this means, don't you?"

I didn't.

He said, "Means the police'll want to talk to you. Probably show up at your house when you least expect it. Better be prepared. Have an alibi. Because," he lowered his voice and leaned forward, "I suspect that whoever killed her performed some kind of mutilation on her. Took her glass eye. Why else would the cops be asking if I knew she had a glass eye?" He paused. "Alibi, kid. Make sure you have an alibi."

But I didn't need an alibi. The fact that the boss said I needed one made me wonder about the conversation that passed between him and the authorities. Perhaps he knew more, or more than he confided to me. Perhaps he suspected me of something.

Or perhaps he himself was hiding something. Some kind of guilt. A crime, one for which he needed me to take the blame.

My house had grown old and fallen into disrepair. I don't make the kind of money that can pay for regular upkeep. The neighbors complained about it, too—just not to my face. Instead, I received anonymous letters in the mail, very briefly worded and apparently typed on a manual typewriter. The more I think about it, the more I think the letters all came from the same person. Someone old, perhaps: a shut-in, someone who didn't even know how to use a computer and had plenty of time to worry about declining property values.

The letters said things like:

> *Get it together! No more eyesores!*
> *Your blinds! Do something*
> *Look smart! Have some pride.*
> *How can you not see? Clean up your act!*

I didn't take these correspondences well. Someone who writes such things to a neighbor should at least have courage in their convictions and sign the goddamn letter. I tossed them all in the trash. Didn't even recycle them. After that, I made a point of leaving the window blinds crooked and allowing the vines to grow up the walls and windows. Soon, the house had an abandoned look.

I couldn't imagine the police wanting to come see me here. Especially not in the middle of the night.

I hadn't paid the electric bill in two months, so the house had no power, no lights, and I'd become accustomed to just going to sleep when it grew dark.

When you sleep deeply and begin to dream, your eyes roll up into the back of your head. Imagine what you could see if you could remain conscious.

My perception remains acute, even in sleep, so I could see the intruder even before I awoke. I knew he used a small penlight to find his way to where I slept. He must have searched through the entire house, leaving my room for last. He sat at the foot of my bed and waited for me to awaken. Sitting up, I showed no surprise at his presence, nor at the sharp, narrow beam of light cutting into my face. Even though I now squinted, I'd already seen him very clearly.

"It's you," I said.

The thin beam of light streaming from his penlight didn't waver when I said this. He seemed to study me for several seconds. Finally, he said my name.

"Yes, yes," I said, "you remember me?"

"Remember you?" The light remained steady. I thought of what some people say about dying, that it involves moving toward a source of light. I felt like that now. I wanted to go into that light. "Did you know I was coming here?" he said.

"Yes. Or no. Not exactly." I told him how my boss warned me that I'd receive a visit from the authorities. "I just didn't know he meant you."

"Me?"

"Officer Baby Boy Blue."

Instead of replying, he moved the penlight so that it shown onto his own face. I saw the mirrored sunglasses and the unlined, white cheekbones, the lips turned up in a half-smile. He wore a police uniform, the exact one I saw in the hospital all those years ago. He moved the light around his form so I could verify that he'd returned.

"I'm not here officially," he said. "I just had a hunch, really. Looked like no one was home, so I came in to see."

"About the eye," I said.

In the penlight's illumination, I saw the smile grow, the same one he showed me on that day in the hospital. And there, at the corner of his mouth, a tremor of anticipation.

"The eye," he said, "you have it?"

All those years ago, I put the eye into that box containing unassembled model pieces. But now, it felt like I did that in a dream just minutes ago. As I stumbled out of bed, I felt a pang of anxiety. Did I know for sure that the box remained undisturbed this whole time? Could I say for certain that my mother never snuck into my room and removed it without my knowledge? Maybe she wanted to save me from the trauma of seeing that box and having it awaken memories, so she tossed it into the trash. I delayed my steps, afraid to find out, and it seemed to take me forever to get across the room. Officer Baby Boy Blue remained sitting behind me patiently, following my steps with his penlight. I could feel him there, waiting.

A sudden realization: he had always been there, at the back of my head.

I opened the cabinet and began moving around old magazines and comics until I found it there: the box with the painting of the Frankenstein monster, lumbering forward with his arms outstretched. Now a new fear. What did the contents of the plastic bag look like now? A yellowish liquid had already formed by the time I returned from the hospital. What kind of unimaginable mess must it contain now? Would any of it remain at all?

I sat on the floor like a kid and opened the box, then stared at what it contained, afraid to move. Officer Baby Boy Blue remained at the foot of the bed, the penlight shining.

"Well?" he said.

I stood up and carried the box to him. He seemed to expect this. He followed me with the light, his free hand reaching for something near his side. I returned to the bed and together we looked down at the contents of the box.

"It hasn't changed at all," I said.

Officer Baby Boy Blue didn't reply. He reached into the box with a hand now gloved in plastic and withdrew the bag. He held it at eye-level and I watched as he took off his mirrored sunglasses so he could study it more closely.

The eye in the bag showed a perfect blue iris. With his other hand, also covered by a plastic glove, he reached in and touched it. "Glass," he said. He looked at me as if he expected an explanation.

But I had none, nothing adequate at least, nothing to explain how I'd misplaced his perfect eye with this—what should I call it?—this *imitation*. How had it come to be here? He wanted to know, and so did I. Then he said it:

"Search the back of your mind."

I did, in that way I had perfected over time. To not disappoint Officer Baby Boy Blue, I looked far, far back, as far as I could see with my left eye, searching for the pictures I might have stored there.

"My god," I heard him say, as I felt it, the scar on my cheek opening. It never fully closed, of course, that I can say with full confidence now, and at that moment, I felt the skin tear and part as it opened wider than ever, even more so than on the day I cut it.

"My god." He said this again, and I saw in the reflection of his glasses an eye of marvelous blue. The same blue as the eye he gave me that day, kept safe under a fold of skin. A blue not at all like the terrible brown eyes I saw on his face as he removed his mirrored sunglasses.

The Intruder

Lamont A. Turner

"It is just too weird. I keep finding things out of place," said Mr. March. It had been awhile since Una had seen him, but she didn't remember him being so high strung. It was exhausting listening to him. "Every night when I return home from work," he continued breathlessly, "some little thing is not right, but it is never anything drastic, never anything that would conclusively prove someone had been in my house. Are you listening?"

I'm sorry," said Una. "I was just thinking of that pig, Zimmerman. He's been threatening to pull the account because I won't let him screw me. Go on, I'm listening."

"I was saying I've been noticing that things seem out of place when I come home from work."

"What sort of things do you notice," asked Una, picking at her salad.

"The radio, for one thing. I keep it set on one of those awful hip-hop stations so when my radio alarm goes off I'm sure to get up to shut it off. If I set it on the classical station, I sleep right through it."

"Makes sense," said Una, piling the tomatoes she had picked out of her salad on the napkin by her plate.

"But every other night the channel has been changed. Instead of Grandmaster T-Dawg I am awakened by Mozart, and invariably I roll over and go back to sleep. I've been late to work seven times this month. It's a damn good thing my boss likes me."

"What else have you noticed?"

"Hair in my bathtub drain, cigarette butts in the garden by my front porch, and, worst of all, someone keeps moving my toothbrush. Of course, I always throw them away when I find them out of place. I spend a fortune on toothbrushes.

"Now that's just screwy," said Una, who, having reduced her salad to a few leaves of lettuce, was busy crushing crackers over it. "Why would anyone break into your house to use your toothbrush? I'd say you're just imagining things. The radio knob might be defective, or, perhaps you hit it without being aware of it. The cigarette butts were probably left by the mailman or some salesman, maybe even a Girl Scout selling cookies. Who knows with kids these days?"

"I've smelled cigarette smoke in my house," said March defensively.

"Okay, what about Argus? I've been to your house a dozen times and that dog still won't let me in the door."

"That's something else. The other day I fed him before I went to work, but when I came home eight hours later, his bowl was still full."

"Maybe he wasn't hungry," said Una, before being reminded of the time Argus had eaten the legs off of March's kitchen table once when he had forgotten to leave food for the dog. "Okay," she relented. "There shouldn't have been food in the bowl, but what you're suggesting is just plain nuts. I can't see someone breaking into your house just to smoke, shower, brush his teeth, and feed your vicious dog.   There must be an explanation that makes better sense."

Una didn't give her conversation with March much thought until she stood outside her apartment door. The little man from the accounting department was the only employee at the firm who had been there as long as she had, and, though they had little else in common and seldom saw each other, she was comforted by the knowledge he would always be there for her if she needed him. They were soldiers who had somehow outlived their comrades, and only the two of them knew what life in the trenches was really about.

They had once been close. He had been there when clients walked out on her, and he had held her hand while she cried over her ruined marriage, not minding a bit that she could never call him by his first name, which was Eddie, because it was also her husband's name. Years later, she still could not say that name. Eddie was a monster; March was an angel. Yet, despite her affection for him, she had to admit he was odd. High-strung and insecure, he was prone to mood swings and paranoia, but he was a fellow soldier, and he cared about her without expecting anything in return. Even when her loneliness had made her vulnerable, he had not taken advantage of her. Ignoring his eccentricities was the least she could do. Besides, she had more than her share of mental quirks. After her divorce, she had suffered a breakdown and had spent two weeks in the hospital. Two years, and a lot of prescriptions later, her own paranoia and insecurities still lurked in the shadows of her consciousness, vanquished but not forgotten. Angry and ravenous, the specter of her illness sometimes glared at her through the bars of the cage she had erected, always ready to break through and devour her.

Reaching for the door knob, she hesitated, and then laughing to herself, opened the door. "Anybody in the shower," she shouted, chuckling. Then she noticed the beer can on the coffee table. For a moment, she stared at it as though it were a bomb about to explode. Had she left it there? She was usually so tidy. It wasn't like her to leave trash strewn about. She picked up the can. It was half full. She certainly would never leave a half full can sitting out where her cat could knock it over. It was a wonder that hadn't happened. And where was that cat? She whistled and slapped her palms against her thighs, but the cat did not appear. Starting to worry, she called the cat's name and listened for some noise that might indicate it was in the apartment. For a few seconds, she heard nothing. She turned and opened the door she had walked through moments before, and in rushed the cat. She scooped it up, cradling it in her arms, scratching it behind its ears. But hadn't she left it sleeping on her pillow that morning? How did it get out? She put the cat on the couch and bolted the door.

"It happened to me, too," she said. "I think someone was in my apartment yesterday."

"Are you sure?" asked the voice on the phone after a pause.

"No more sure than you are," she said. "Things just seem out of place."

"Oh, I'm sure now," said March. "Someone has been in my home."

"Are you certain?"

"Argus is dead, poisoned."

"Oh, God! I'm sorry," she said, pulling her cat onto her lap. "Have you called the police?"

"No. Not yet. I need to think. It has to be someone I know, somebody familiar to Argus. He wouldn't have let a stranger get near him."

"Do you have any idea who?" she asked. March didn't seem like the type of person who would have enemies.

"No, but I think it's a woman. I found one of my razors and a bunch of hair in the tub, and my pillow smells like perfume."

Una ran her hand over the nick on her leg and remembered how much worse it had been the time she had tried to shave with her husband's razor. If there was blood in the tub, maybe the   police would be able to get more information than they could from a bit of stubble. For some reason, the idea made her queasy.

 "Look, I have to go," he said after a long pause. "I'm working second shift tonight."

"Since when do you work the second shift?"

 "Since I woke up late one time too often. I'm lucky I still have a job."

After hanging up the phone, Una cursed herself. Maybe March really did have an intruder, but it was more likely his dog found something poisonous on his own, and the whole thing with the tub was just ridiculous. He had to have imagined that. It was all some fantasy, and she had let March contaminate her with his delusions.   No one had been in her apartment. Everything was fine.   Nervous over the situation with Zimmerman, she had been unprepared to deal with March's wild stories. Everything was fine.

She sat up late, smoking cigarettes and listening to the radio. Turning the radio down around 2:00 a.m., she wondered if the CDs she lent to March were safe. Apparently, his intruder did like to listen to the classical stations while shaving her legs. She chuckled to herself at the thought, but nevertheless, checked the lock on the front door before lying down.

Just when she finally did start to doze off, the phone rang. It was Mr. Daily, her boss. Somebody had set off the alarm at the office, and, unable to get there himself, he wanted her to investigate the matter. This was not the first time this had happened. She had been called to perform this duty twice before, each time finding nothing but angry policemen. She was sure they would be even less pleasant tonight.

When she arrived at the office, she was surprised to be greeted by a tired-looking detective with rumpled clothes and uncombed hair rather than the usual uniformed patrolmen. Someone had really broken in.

"Whose office is this?" asked the police detective, pushing open the door. Broken glass sparkled in the light from the hall and crunched beneath the feet of the silent patrolman who glared at her as though she were somehow responsible. The file cabinets were overturned, and the desk drawers had been emptied on the floor. On the wall behind the desk, someone had drawn a picture of a pig in what looked like lipstick. Upon first seeing the pig, Una thought someone had tried to draw a phallus on it, but as she entered the room to examine the wreckage, she saw the phallus was actually an arrow pointing down toward the floor.

"Whose office is this?" repeated the police detective, putting a hand on Una's shoulder to prevent her from venturing further into the room.

"It's mine," she said. Just then she noticed the legs protruding from behind her desk. "Who?"

"The wallet says Walter Zimmerman. Know him?"

"Yes, he is a client," she said, unable to look away from the legs. As she stared, she noticed they seemed to be resting on a dark colored rug. "I don't have a rug," she said just as the beam of a flashlight caused the dark spot to glisten. She stepped back and would have fled if the detective had not grabbed her arm.

"Just calm down," he said, looking hard into her eyes.

"What happened?"

"You don't know?"

"How would I know?" said Una, alarmed by the policeman's tone.

"You were seen leaving the building about two hours ago, and—"

"No! I was at home," shouted Una. "I wasn't here!"

"Okay, just calm down," said the detective, stepping back. "Maybe it wasn't you. Nobody is accusing you of anything. Just calm down."

"I didn't do anything," Una said, staring at the corpse's shoes.

"Okay," said the detective, nodding to the patrolman who immediately came over to stand beside Una. "This is Officer Lee. He is going to take you home. Maybe tomorrow, if you're up to it, you can come down to the station to answer some questions for us." Una nodded and was led off by the grim patrolman.

Una was still shaking when she walked into her apartment. Embarrassed, Una had tried to redeem herself by dismissing the young patrolman at her door. No, she did not want him to come in to check her apartment for her. No thank you. Please go. Go! Get away from me! Inside, she was screaming, her fear of the young man in the starched blue uniform swelling in her throat, threatening to strangle her, but she managed to escape into her apartment without alerting the patrolman of her inner turmoil. For a while, she leaned against the door, straining to hear the sound of his footsteps over her own panting. Was he suspicious of her? Was he standing on the other side of the door, listening, waiting for the right moment to break in on her? Why wouldn't he leave? She hadn't done anything. She was innocent.

Finally, she heard the ding of the elevator down the hall, and she knew the patrolman had left. She was safe for the moment. Remembering the tranquillizers she had put aside when she had declared herself sane and stable, she headed for the bathroom medicine cabinet.

Gulping down three of the pills without water, she dialed March's number, and waited. There was no answer. She hung up, and dialed again. This time, after a minute or so, the ringing stopped, and she heard someone pick up the phone.

"March, it's terrible! Zimmerman is dead," she said, not waiting for a greeting.

"Mr. March isn't here," said a man with a raspy voice. "Who is this?"

"Who are you?" she countered, confused.

"This is the police," said the voice.

Una slammed the phone down. They did suspect her! Why else would they be at March's house? They were questioning him about her.

The phone rang. For a moment, she stared at it, unsure of what to do. It continued to ring. Why couldn't they just leave her alone? She buried the phone beneath the couch cushions, but still it continued to ring. She considered turning the ringer off, but then she wouldn't know if they were still after her, hoping to trick her into saying something incriminating. The phone would not stop ringing. Finally, she could stand it no more. She answered the phone.

"Una? Are you all right?"

"March! Oh, thank God! You won't believe what happened."

"Just take it easy," said March, his voice calm and paternal. "I know all about it. I'm at the office right now, straightening everything out. It's going to be all right."

"I didn't do anything. They think I killed him, but I didn't do it."

"It will be okay," March said. "I talked to them. I've got everything handled. You just stay at home and rest."

Una was calm by the time she hung up. For a while, she sat on the couch, thinking of nothing in particular, then realizing she was about to fall asleep, she remembered the pills. How many had she taken? She couldn't remember.

She decided to count the pills left in the bottle, but realized on her way to the medicine cabinet she had no idea how many pills were in the bottle originally. Minutes later, she had forgotten about the pills and was trying to remember how she had ended up at the office earlier that morning. Daily! She had not called Mr. Daily. It was late, but if she didn't call him, it might look suspicious. She dialed his number.

By the time Daily answered, she was only just able to follow what he was saying. Yes, the police had contacted him. No, he had not been able to get to the office yet. She heard herself tell him it was going to be all right because March was at the office. March would straighten it all out.

"March? The screwball from accounting? What's he doing there?" she heard him ask.

"March is there," she mumbled, as the phone slipped from her grasp. As she picked the phone up, she heard Daily say something about March having been fired, but the ability to comprehend was beyond her. She hung up the phone, and fell asleep.

Someone was calling her name. Una opened her eyes and looked around. She was alone. Only slowly did she realize she held the receiver of her phone, and that there was a voice shouting from it. She stared at the phone for a moment, and then lifted it to her ear.

"Una! Are you all right?"

She nodded in affirmation before dropping the phone. Lost in deep, dreamless sleep, she did not hear the bell sound as the elevator doors opened on her floor, nor did she hear the sound of footfalls as someone approached her door. She did not hear the knob rattle or see it turn. When she finally did open her eyes, awakened by her cat as it bounded off her legs to scurry across the room, she saw someone standing in the open doorway. Her eyes could not quite focus, but she was sure there was someone there: a woman with long blonde hair, much like her own, was moving toward her. For a moment, she thought she was being approached by herself. The woman wore her coat, and, as the woman came closer, Una smelled her perfume. Yes, that was her perfume, but Una would never have worn so much. The odor was overpowering, nauseating.

Una blinked up at the intruder as the woman, this other Una, leaned over her. For a moment, Una drifted off, lulled back into sleep by the hot steady breath on her forehead. She was barely aware of the pressure on her throat, or the dull, deep drumbeat that grew increasingly louder. She was underwater. Down she floated, the drumbeat becoming louder and faster as she sank. Gasping for air, she at last opened her eyes, and looked into the face of her attacker.

"Eddie?" She had barely been able to whisper the name, but the effect upon the intruder was instantaneous. The expression on the face, mere inches above Una's own, changed from rage to confusion. The hands loosened their grip. As Una gasped, she heard thunder, and the intruder fell upon her. For a moment, she lay there, choking on the stench of the perfume, the hair of the intruder's blond wig covering her face. Then the body of Eddie March was rolled off of her, and she was looking into the worried face of Officer Lee. When she awoke again, in the unfamiliar room of the hospital, he was still with her, smiling down at her.

Alone in the Woods in the Deep Dark Night

Edward R. Rosick

With one last burst of desperate energy, Gary Irwin Chandler II shut the heavy back door against the howling winds. His breath came in frantic gulps and he shook with fear and cold, slumped on the hardwood floors of the cabin situated on the edge of the 50,000 acre Ojibwa National Forest in the upper peninsula of Michigan. The late November storm blew with a malevolent ferocity outside, lashing his abode with continuing blasts of wind and thick, wet sleet and snow that minutes before had almost cost Gary his life.

He curled his arms tight around his chest, his shivering body wracked with pain emanating from his cut right hand but even more so from his left leg. Gary glanced down, and his first crazy thought was that he was looking at the limb of a store mannequin that somehow had magically replaced his own.

But it wasn't plaster or plastic; the bloody, managed limb was *his* leg. From the knee down his jeans had been torn away, revealing torn flesh looking like meat from a badly carved steak.

This can't be real. This crap can't be real. Just hours ago, I was talking with Donna, and now…

With one shaking finger, he lightly touched it. Nothing. No pain, no sensation. Encouraged, Gary pushed harder, then screamed. The pain was nothing like he had ever experienced. It was deep, sharp, exploding like a bomb and expanding into his guts.

That was fucking brilliant! A tiny malevolent voice chirped deep inside his head. *Just like all the other fucking brilliant things you've done today!*

Tears streaked his face and thick snot ran out of his nose; Gary felt his mind shutting down, knew that he was seconds away from passing out, and if that happened—sitting there wearing clothes soaking wet and in a freezing house with no heat—he wasn't going to wake up.

"No," he said out loud, using his voice to stay conscious. "I'm not dying today."

But you are *dying, you loser*, the malevolent voice countered, *and the sooner you realize it, the sooner the pain of your pathetic life can be over!*

"No!" Gary said yet again. He forced himself to take deep breaths and slow his pounding heart over the demands of his shivering body that screamed for more oxygen and some form of warmth.

"I gotta get...dry clothes." But where? There was no way he had the energy to crawl down the long hallway of the cabin to the master bedroom, but if he didn't, he was going to—

"The laundry room," Gary said. There was always a huge pile of dirty clothes in the laundry room, and that was just a few feet away.

See? the little voice sneered. *Donna's disdain for all things domestic like doing laundry might finally pay off for you yet!*

Gary grabbed the kerosene lantern with his left hand and put it on the floor. The light feebly cut through the darkness of the hallway, but it was enough. With pain throbbing like a monstrous toothache in his left leg, Gary crawled the ten feet until the laundry room appeared to his left. Hardly any light from the lantern illuminated the room, but Gary didn't need it; he knew that there would be a huge mound of clothes in there that Donna refused to wash ("I'm not your fucking maid, Gary!" was one of her favorite retorts to him asking her to at least do *something* around the house).

Gary entered the laundry room and reached the pile. It smelled of sweat, dirt, mildew, but it didn't matter—the clothes were dry. With the last vestiges of his strength, he pulled the soaked garments off his portly (*fat, Gary: you're a fucking fat slob just like Donna used to say*) body. As quickly as his shaking hands allowed, he put on dry underwear, long johns, five sweatshirts from his college days and two pairs of corduroy pants, then wrapped a t-shirt around his hand and a down comforter around his shoulders.

His heart pounded like he had drunk six cups of cappuccino and his leg ached horribly, but he was dry but still miserably cold. The storm was getting worse, the entire cabin now trembling under the hurricane-like blasts of freezing wind.

"I gotta get a fire going," he croaked, his throat dry and parched. Gary grabbed the side of the washing machine and stood. Hobbling down the hallway, he grabbed the lantern and slowly made his way toward the living room and the vast, stone-faced fireplace that promised him salvation and life.

But he stopped halfway there as light from the lantern shown into the kitchen to his right.

"I'll get some water," Gary said, "then get a fire going, then—" (*Then what, fat boy? You have no power, you have no ride, you got absolutely nothing!*) "I'll wait out the storm and...someone will come by. Someone *has* to come by."

He didn't allow himself to linger on how illogical that last line of reasoning was, but instead limped over to the sink before yet another realization came to him: the cabin had a well for water, which required a pump to pull it out of the frozen ground, a pump that required electricity to work.

*If there's no water pressure I'll...*Gary turned on the faucet. Water flowed out and he scooped it with a hand to his mouth like a Paleolithic caveman. *See? There's pressure left in the system, you're able to drink and then you'll be able to start a fire and everything will be just fine!*

His thirst was sated, but his stomach growled at the thought of food; he glanced over at the refrigerator, sitting silent and mute next to the electric stove.

I need to eat as much as I needed to drink. Just a quick snack then I'll get the fire going. He wrapped the bulky down comforter tighter around his still-shivering body and opened an overhead cupboard door to get a plate. As he reached in, Gary spied a rounded, green bottle on the back of the shelf.

"Look what we have here," he said, holding up the lantern for illumination. "I drove all the way to Marquette for you." Gary retrieved the bottle of Armagnac and held it carefully in his hands. "I wanted to have something special for our dinner with the McNealin's and Doug." He unscrewed the top and took a long drink of the strong, amber liquid. *Better be careful there, Gary-boy,* the tiny voice in the back of his head admonished him. *You know how just a couple beers really fucks you up. After two glasses of Armagnac with dinner that night, you couldn't even get the pole up for*

Donna. Bet she was wishing that Dougie would have been between the sheets that night!

Tears of anger and frustration began to roll slowly down Gary's face then unleashed in a torrent. He was a city-boy, born and raised in the white-bread Detroit suburb of Bloomfield Hills in a 4,000-square foot house with running water, cable TV with 300 channels, and central air-conditioning. Out here, he was out of his element.

Way out of his element.

"Quit the pity-party, Gary," he said, wiping tears away with the back of his hand, then grabbing a plate and filling it with a block of cheese and the hunk of venison sausage that Ray McNealin had given him. "You need to eat then start a fire. Then you'll figure out something after that."

He placed the plate, bottle, and lantern down on a large, ornately carved oak dinner table that Donna had insisted they buy, no matter the extravagant price tag, and sat. His entire body ached and Gary felt decades older than his 43 years (*but not when you were humpin' away on your 31-year-old wife, right, Gary-boy? That sweet pussy was the best fountain of youth there is. Too bad it's Dougie that's now givin' her his meat stick!*)

Gary pulled the comforter close, took a small bite of the venison sausage, then washed it down with another large gulp of the Armagnac. He had to focus, to stick to the task of getting a fire going before he froze to death, but it was so damn easy to dwell on his mistakes, on what-ifs and maybes, to get lost in the memories of how he ended up in a freezing cabin smack dab in the middle of the American equivalent of Siberia.

"You made bad choices," he said in a quiet, defeated voice, "or no choices at all. Just let stuff happen and hoped it would all turn out well." (*And what'd your old man used to tell you? Hope in one hand and shit in the other and see which fills up first!*)

A small bite of cheese, then another long drink of the Armagnac, and the memories came flooding back like a crazy-quilt film festival, complete with screen shots from *This is Your Life, Gary Alan Chandler!*

First scene: Gary met Donna at a local comic book store a week before Christmas. She was there to get something for her then-boyfriend's 10-year old son. Gary was instantly drawn to her—as was any heterosexual male who had a heartbeat and cock—two inches taller than his five foot, seven inch height, with shoulder-length dark auburn hair, a finely featured face that held an easy Hollywood-white smile and sparkling green eyes that captivated Gary the moment he looked into them. He helped her pick up some comics (*Spiderman* and *Batman*, always solid choices), then, despite his usual shyness, walked her to her car, a 2016 Porsche Cayman (her boyfriend's car, he would find out later), and in a burst of courage, gave her his business card. She took it, telling him that if she ever needed help in picking out comic books, she'd be sure to give him a call.

Which she did less than two months later on Valentine's Day.

Scene two: It was a whirlwind romance, as Gary's deceased father would have said. Donna called Gary and told him that she had broken up with her Porsche Cayman boyfriend and needed someone to talk to, that Gary seemed so kind and friendly at the comic store, and she hoped he didn't see this as too forthcoming, but would it be all right if they met for coffee and talked?

After two cups of decaf and multiple drinks at a local bar, they ended up at Gary's house and fucked until the sun came up, then fucked some more. She was totally uninhibited, willing and wanting to do everything and anything. Gary fell immediately in love.

He learned a bit about her—after high school, she was a dancer at various strip clubs until she was 21, then a model for a semi-legit modeling agency out of Tampa, Florida for five years before giving it up, tired of the traveling and the constant sexual harassment. After coming back to Michigan, she had taken a job as hostess and employee manager at one of Detroit's newest upscale lounges where, she told Gary, she could "be myself and still be well-paid without having to suck and fuck every dickhead with a contract and cash."

Three month later, one week shy of Memorial Day, they were married.

Scene three: A month after their marriage, Gary received notice that the software company, where he was the well-paid, lead design engineer, was sold to a multi-billion-dollar Chinese conglomerate. The new company had offered to double Gary's salary if he moved to their newly built U.S. headquarters in Mississippi.

"There's no way in hell I'm moving back south," Donna said. "I've had my fill of rednecks." So, without further thought or consideration, Gary accepted a seven-figure buyout of his contract and for the first time since he was twenty-four years old, became unemployed.

But you didn't care, did you, fat boy? You were so hot for that hard-bodied bitch that you would have eaten a shit-sandwich every morning and called it a gourmet breakfast!

For once, the malignant voice was right. Gary was so much in love with his voluptuous and carefree wife that he didn't think twice when Donna suggested they move to the Upper Peninsula of Michigan, a dark, cold land of trees, bears, and month after month of bitter cold weather. "It's so beautiful in the U.P.," Donna said, harking back to her childhood days when her mother used to take her camping in the northern woods. "Me and my Mom used to call it God's country. I bet you could go there, start your own software company and be the next Bill Gates."

In hindsight, Gary realized he was doomed from the start. Setting up his own business proved a thousand times more difficult than he had realized; his level of anxiety and frustration went up as his once-strong bank account went down. Donna was at first ecstatic in their rural abode but soon seemed to tire of the country life, talking about taking cruises to the Caribbean, flights to Paris and Rome, anything to, as she put it, "get a taste of some real culture."

Which Gary could understand; he really could. What he couldn't do was financially sustain such a lifestyle when the money coming in was a trickle at best. It was then that their house-shaking arguments began and their once-active sex life slowed to a couple times a month, if that. Gary was at his wit's end on how to revive his life and marriage and to appease his increasingly agitated wife's complaints of boredom and dwindling social life. As much as he detested social get-togethers, he decided that getting together with their nearest neighbors, the McNealins and Doug Freeman, might make Donna happy. It did, only in ways that Gary never imagined.

Doug was a twenty-seven-year-old laid off miner from Ispheming with a Hollywood actor's face and a Greek god's body who taught a wood-working class at the local high school, one which Donna enrolled in. Last night, Donna invited him and the McNealins over for dinner. Gary spent the entire evening brooding as he watched the sly glances Donna gave to Doug. After the McNealins and Doug left, Gary and Donna had another blow-up, cumulating in Donna packing her bags that morning and walking out. Gary had refused to give her keys to their Land Rover, so she walked.

Out into the first winter storm of the year.

She'll come back, he told himself. But she didn't, and after a few hours, with the storm increasing in its ferocity and the electricity in the house a memory—along with the light and heat, Gary decided to go after her.

He rummaged around in the kitchen cabinets until he found a working flashlight, then put on his heaviest winter coat, scarf, and brand-new leather driving gloves. At the back door, he lit the kerosene lantern that Donna insisted they buy and placed it on the top shelf to provide another source of light for when he returned, then went outside.

Gary's first breath of the freezing air burned his lungs and brought tears to his eyes. Snow blew about him in angry, white eddies as he moved out into the yard, When he heard the loud crash from the other side of the house, Gary plodded through the snow and around the corner; there, under the heavy weight of the wet snow, sat their Land Rover, covered under the twisted steel and wood structure that used to be a carport, the bulk which had fallen on the hood and driver's side of the SUV. Gary took a deep breath, then began to pull on the twisted wreckage. He managed to remove the largest piece of the carport and almost had the second piece off when the oak support beam slid from the roof and into him.

The impact was like the kick of an angry horse. Gary was thrown back and instantly swallowed by the snow. The pain in his leg burst to life like an exploding sun. When he pushed himself up and tried to stand, the agony in his leg was an unseen force pinning him to the ground, yet he knew if he didn't make it to the back door, he would die.

"But I made it," Gary muttered in the dark of the kitchen as he continued to drain the bottle of Armagnac. "I had the guts to push through the pain, to do what I had to do to make it back to the house, even though I was all alone."

A new memory blossomed in his mind, not of Donna but of a poem from his long-dormant childhood that his Aunt Mildred would sing to him when he felt frightened and alone:

> *Alone in the woods*
> *in the deep dark night,*
> *under the stars,*
> *under their light,*
> *which show me the road,*
> *which lift my fright,*
> *and guide me to heaven—*

Gary frowned; he couldn't remember the last line. He tried to concentrate, to pull it up from his addled mind, until a strange sound intruded on him. It wasn't the roar of the storm or the sound of the snow hitting the cabin. This noise was rhythmic, drifting in and out like static from a dying radio.

He held his breath and strained to hear. A tapping. Like someone percussing out a steady, even beat. And it was coming from inside.

Gary ran his left hand through his short greying hair and loudly sighed, his breath coming out of his mouth in a plume of gray, like an ancient dragon huffing in impotent rage. *What now?* The tapping continued on and off in no discernible pattern. *You need to get up anyway and get the fire going. You also need to rewrap your hand…and do about a thousand other things before things progress from bad to very bad.*

He limped into the hallway, holding the hissing kerosene lantern out in front of him like an ancient mariner on the deck of a ghost ship. To his right was his and Donna's bedroom, the study, and the bathroom. To the left was the living room. Gary stood still and quiet, his labored breathing and the intermittent roaring of the storm the only sounds permeating the cold air.

The tapping was gone.

It must have been the wind. Maybe a tree hitting the house, the old TV antenna blown down and smacking against a window, or—

Tap. Tap. Tap-tap-tap.

It was coming from the living room.

It was the largest space in the house: rectangular in shape, the walls made of massive pine logs from forests long since decimated, with a huge stone fireplace that the previous owner had capped with a stuffed, snarling bobcat head, the first thing that Donna made him throw out when they moved in.

Gary stretched out his arm as far as it could go; the light from the kerosene lantern was meager and weak. He squinted, trying to make out something, anything foreign that could be causing the sound, and wished for his flashlight buried somewhere in the snow.

"But that's as good as wishing for a generator. Or a job. Or having your wife back." Gary's voice sounded tiny and defeated. He hated it.

Tap-tap-tap-tap. Gary took two steps further into the room. "It's coming from the fireplace," he said in a quiet voice, feeling foolish for speaking softly. But what was it? A fallen tree branch moving from a downdraft? "But there's a cover on the fireplace, right?" *Is there? Or is that just another one of your asinine assumptions, like the one about your wife being faithful rather than a sex-crazed slut with a thing for woodcutters with big logs?*

There were two more quick taps, then a few seconds of silence before it began again. Gary finally saw it: on the edge of the smoky light, a flash of movement and shadow inside the darkened confines of the fireplace. He took a step back. If there was an animal in there, could it push its way out?

"No," Gary answered himself, "the panes on that fireplace are heavy and tight as hell, Donna made sure of that, said she didn't like drafty fireplaces…"

He squinted and cautiously moved toward the glass, then screamed and nearly dropped the lantern when a black mass slammed itself against the panes.

"It's a bird," Gary said. "There's a damned bird in my fireplace."

It wasn't a small bird, a sparrow or some such thing. It was black and big. A crow.

"How the hell did you get in my fireplace?"

The bird continued to intermittently tap, its soulless black eyes never wavering from Gary.

"Now what do I do?" Gary said. *Well, either open the fireplace, kill the fucking bird, and start a fire, or sit back on your ass and do nothing like you've done your whole pathetic life.*

"That's not true!" Gary countered, his voice angry and bitter. "I've done a lot, I put myself through college, I, I was successful as hell as a software designer, I—" *You're a loser, fat boy, and now you're going to let a little bird put the final cold nail in your coffin!*

Gary took a deep breath and stepped closer to the fireplace. Blood from the soaked t-shirt around his hand dripped to the floor and the crow seemed to become more excited, tapping harder and harder on the panes.

What the hell? Does it smell the blood? Can birds smell anything?

It's a fucking crow, dumb-ass, not a hawk or a vulture or a carnivorous monster from the Jurassic period. It's got a brain the size of a damn pea. Just fucking kill it!

"It's only a bird," Gary said. "It's probably more scared of me then I am of it. Maybe if I just knock hard on the panes it'll go back up the chimney."

When Gary moved closer, the bird attacked the panes with more vigor and beat its wings against the panes in union with its tapping. Gary stepped back and as soon as he had moved away, the bird slowed its tapping.

"Fine. Stay in there and freeze to death."

The bird blinked its coal-black eyes once, twice, and then stepped back into the darkness of the fireplace.

Gary sipped on the Armagnac, the bottle now half empty. "You shouldn't drink anymore," he told himself. "I definitely don't want to get drunk." But the truth was—if he was being honest with himself, and wouldn't that be something new—he did want to get drunk, to get shitfaced and pass out until this night was over and Donna was back in his arms and bed. *Except she's not coming back. She's at Dougie's now, all warm and cozy in his cabin with its generator and lights and they're probably laughing their asses off when he's not burying his huge cock up her tight slit!*

Tap-tap...taptaptaptaptap...taptaptap...

"Shut up!" Gary screamed. Even under all the layers, he could feel the cold work its relentless skeleton fingers into his shivering body. It was getting colder, no doubt about it.

What if the electricity doesn't come back on, shithead? You really gonna die like a pathetic loser just 'cause you have some phobia about birds?

Gary took another drink from the bottle, then stood on shaking legs. "You gotta do this," he told himself. "Do it or die."

Like a man going to his execution, Gary went into the living-room. He was at the point of no return, like when he was a teenager and had decided to call a girl and ask for a date: even if she hung up on him, even if she laughed at him. He could use one of his big heavy blankets to throw over the bird as soon as he opened the panes. If it didn't come out, so much the better: he'd smother the crow right inside the fireplace then beat it to a pulp with the fireplace poker. As he gathered his strength, Gary realized that the tapping had stopped.

"Maybe you decided to leave," Gary said. "Maybe you died. But if you're not dead when I open those panes, I guarantee you soon will be."

Three steps away from the fireplace, Gary put down the blanket and pushed the sputtering lantern toward the panes. It took him only a second to see, but it was a second that drained all the resolve from his soul. The fireplace now held at least a dozen crows, all staring at him with vacuous, unblinking eyes. They moved toward the light of the lantern and began to tap, slowly at first but then faster and louder.

"This can't be real," Gary moaned. "How can this be happening?" The birds answered by tapping even louder, a dozen beaks smashing like tiny jackhammers against the panes.

With the last of his resolve, Gary threw his blanket against the glass in an attempt to mute the sound of the birds. He stepped back and over the screaming of the wind, swore he could hear the birds hiss at him, a dozen crazed and hateful voices. Gary stood in the near pitch-black darkness, the lantern now almost out of kerosene. Part of him wanted to stay there, to stand and scream at the top of his lungs until he was out of breath, out of oxygen, scream until the sunlight came and washed away all the darkness in his life.

Instead, he walked stiffly to the kitchen for the Armagnac then into his bedroom. He finished the bottle, then passed out on the floor next to the bed just as the crows stopped their tapping.

Gary stood in a large field of knee-high grass and shivered. Gusts of cold wind buffeted him, cutting through his baggy t-shirt and torn jeans; he crossed his arms tight over his skinny, thirteen-year-old chest to try and stay warm. *Why didn't I wear a jacket?* he thought, then just as quickly wondered why he would need a jacket in the middle of July in Kentucky. He looked around the rolling hills of his Uncle Jake's and Aunt Mildred's farm, then felt a thick layer of unease descend upon him when he realized he couldn't remember coming outside, or walking into the fields, or—

"Hey Gary, you gonna stand there holding your weenie all day or are you gonna come and help me find Jackson?"

The loud voice behind him took Gary out of his thoughts. He turned to see his portly, fourteen-year-old cousin Lenny standing at the base of one of the hills. Gary took off in a sprint, running full out in the crunching grass, enjoying the feelings of abandon and freedom that the speed brought to him. Gary felt so *alive*, even as the cold wind rushed through his hair and across his face, making his eyes water and cheeks burn.

"I'm here," he said when he reached Lenny. "What's up with Jackson? Did he take off after some bunny again?" Jackson was his cousin's beagle, a loud, boisterous dog that lived for two things: to chase rabbits and to cuddle in the lap of whoever would have him.

Lenny, strangely dressed in a faded brown leather jacket and matching snowmobile pants, crossed his arms and starred at his cousin with piercing black eyes.

"What's going on, Lenny? Where's Jackson?" Gary tried to take a step back but he couldn't, his legs suddenly immobile, his feet seemingly frozen to the ground.

"What do you mean?" Lenny said, stepping sideways and pointing to the ground. "Jackson is right here."

In a small, circular space devoid of grass, lay Jackson. His white and brown body was torn apart, intestines and internal organs laying scattered about like broken, bloody toys. Maggots the size of large worms undulated in Jackson's steaming guts, and in the next instant, a crow was suddenly standing on top of the dog's body, its sharp beak glistening like a black diamond in the light of the setting sun. The bird looked up at Gary with dead eyes, then, like a rattlesnake striking a cornered rat, it snapped down and tore out the bloated tongue of the dog. The crow made two quick jerks of its head and the piece of meat disappeared down its throat.

"What's the matter, Gary?" Lenny asked in a sickly-sweet voice. "You look kinda sick." Lenny squatted down beside the prostrate body of the dog and stroked its bloated body. "Hey, maybe you're hungry. I bet that's it." With one lazy motion, Lenny scooped up a handful of writhing maggots and shoved them in Gary's face. "C'mon now, don't be shy—it's bad manners to refuse food from your kin."

Gary wanted to scream, to shove away the stinking, living mass of larvae that his cousin held inches from his mouth and nose, but a total paralysis had taken hold of him.

"I'm hurt," Lenny said. "I offer to share food with you and you snub me." He cocked his head in jerky motions, still staring with lifeless eyes at Gary.

"What's that saying?" Lenny continued. "Something about a cat having your tongue?" He nudged the crow, which looked up at him. "I think they got it wrong though—it's not a cat who's gonna have your tongue!"

The crow spread its wings, caught a gust of freezing wind, and rose slowly in the air like a feathered magician. It levitated in front of Gary, so close that he could see clearly into its eyes, black, soulless orbs that held a malicious hunger. Gary tried to move, to yell, to do *anything*, but only continued to stand in mute terror as the sound of the screaming wind and crazed laughter from his cousin filled his ears.

The crow's beak lightly brushed up against Gary's cheek like the caress of a lover; it was freezing cold and burned his flesh like a long sliver of dry ice. The crow jerked its head towards Gary's ear, and he heard a voice coming from its beak: a voice, deep and seductive; the voice of Doug Freeman. "I'm comin' inside, boy, I'm comin' inside," the Doug Freeman crow-voice said over and over like a scratched CD.

Gary finally managed to scream as the crow's razor-sharp beak began to viciously dig into the soft flesh of his outer ear.

Gary awoke from the nightmare to the sound of his teeth chattering furiously. He pushed himself up with his good hand and leaned against the bed, his body raked with uncontrollable shivering. His head pounded from the Armagnac and his bladder felt close to bursting. With shaking hands, he pulled whatever covers were left on the bed and wrapped them around himself.

Taking two deep breaths, he stood up. Feeble light shone through the windows, giving everything in the room an ethereal, unreal glow. What day was it? Was it tomorrow? The next day? "It doesn't fuckin' matter," he muttered, his mouth dry and tasting like shit. "I gotta…I gotta piss then I will figure things out…"

Gary stumbled out of the bedroom and into the bathroom and would have achieved his one goal of not pissing his pants if the pipes underneath the sink hadn't burst and covered the floor with water that had turned into ice. His right leg flipped up like a clown at a circus and his injured left leg followed. Gary slammed hard onto the frozen tiles, clipping his forehead on the edge of the sink. The fall knocked the breath away from his lungs and as he lay gasping on the frozen floor, his full bladder released. Blood pooled around his face from the jagged slash on his forehead, his pants steamed from the hot urine, and his left leg screamed out in silent agony.

Tap…taptap…taptaptaptap…

"Fuck you," he croaked, his voice almost inaudible over the still-present sound of the storm. "Fuck…you…"

It was no use. Gary was spent, defeated, dying of hypothermia in a pool of his own piss and blood. He closed his eyes and waited for the inevitable touch of death. The tapping grew louder, as if excited by Gary's imminent demise. And then, Gary heard it. An undercurrent of sound, something not born of the howling winter winds or crazed avian minds.

Voices.

Gary wiped away the blood from the eyes and slowly, painfully, sat up and listened more intently. He could hear laughter—a cold, malicious sound—coming from the living-room. Laughter at Gary's life, at all his failures and soon-to-be death.

"Fuck you," he whispered. He grabbed the sink with his left hand and pulled himself up. "Fuck you!" he screamed, and it was a great and wonderful release, like slicing open an infected boil.

"Fuck-YOU!" he roared with white-hot passion and anger. Maybe the crow with the voice of Doug Freeman had killed and eaten Jackson, but it wouldn't kill and eat him. Not today or *ever.*

He stumbled into the living-room, now illuminated with a weak yellow light. "You think you've won, don't you?" he yelled at the fireplace. The blanket he had placed over the panes the night before had fallen off, and Gary could see the fireplace was packed tightly with birds, so many that the entire structure bulged in and out, the solitary black lung of a giant.

Gary squatted, staring into the dozens of black, unblinking eyes behind the furious beaks. He grabbed the fireplace poker and tapped gently on the panes. "You're not winning. I'm a genius, a certified grade-A fucking genius, and I've got the perfect plan for all of you!"

In the utility room, he put on Donna's old bike helmet and her wood-working goggles, then gathered a hand axe, a box of matches, and every aerosol can they had: paint, deodorant, air fresheners, his arms full of metal cans. Back in the living room, he pulled down all of the drapes from the windows and cleared away a large, circular area free from furniture, paper, anything that could catch on fire in the living room.

The tapping of beaks and beating of wings increased, growing louder and more frantic. Gary tore one of his blankets into crude, wide strips and wrapped them around his hands and face. He reached up on the fireplace mantel next to his wedding picture and grabbed a heavy rectangular-shaped copper ingot. "Donna got this for me in Copper Harbor," he said to the birds, a brief memory rising up in his addled mind. "She said it would bring me luck."

The picture hovered in his mind, him standing with his stunning new bride on the shores of Lake Superior, watching the sunset, crimson and gold shimmering off the gently rolling waves of the lake, holding each other close and—

Gary slammed the copper ingot hard into the helmet, hearing plastic (*or was that bone?*) crack as he dropped to his knees. "Gotta stay focused." His words slurred as he took deep breaths, then stood slowly up, feeling dizzy and weak but with the memories safely knocked away. "It's time…time for the show."

Gary placed the ingot down on the couch, and after lighting a match, grabbed an aerosol can and pushed down on the button. The spray ignited into a foot and a half long yellow-blue flame. "You want some shit? Then come and get some!" he screamed at the fireplace, then threw the copper ingot with all his might at the glass. The two rectangular panes exploded outward in a gleaming shower and released the birds in a frenzied rush of beaks, feathers, and claws that headed straight for Gary.

The greater part of the *shit* lasted for hours.

Gary killed the last crow with his bare hands. He squeezed it tight, felt bones snap and viscera pop even as the bird's talons imbedded themselves like fishhooks into his exposed forearms. Gary brought the bird close to his face. "I remember now, Doug," he said, like speaking to a lover. "I remember how the poem goes. 'Want to hear?"

The bird said nothing, blood and shit squirting out of its cloaca as Gary squeezed it tighter.

"I'll tell you anyway," Gary said as the bird ceased its struggling.

> *Alone in the woods*
> *in the deep dark night,*
> *under the stars,*
> *under their light,*
> *which show me the road,*
> *which life my fright,*
> *and guide me to heaven*
> *with warm sunlight.*

"With warm sunlight," he repeated through busted teeth and bleeding gums at the dead bird. He kissed it tenderly on its beak, then let its carcass join the other bodies of the dead crows that littered the floor like beer cans at an outdoor rock concert.

Gary stood for a moment in the middle of the carnage and surveyed the living room, redolent with odors of ignited paint and deodorant; of shit, sweat, and blood. He was bleeding from dozens of tears and lacerations all over his body and couldn't see out of one eye, but all in all, he felt damn good. He had done what needed to be accomplished, no matter the consequences, for the first time in his life.

"I need new clothes," Gary said, then slowly walked into his bedroom. He paused to look into the mirror over his dresser; it took him a few long seconds to realize the face he was staring at was his own. The thing in the reflection resembled a surrealistic death's head mask more than the face of a human being. Long, jagged tears ran in a cross-stitched pattern over blood-caked skin. Cracked and broken teeth smiled out of a mouth only halfway covered by the shredded remains of lips, and the right eye of the face seemed deflated and shrunken, hanging halfway out of the socket over a macerated cheek.

Gary felt light-headed and sat down on the bed. "Some fresh air, that's what I need," he croaked, then stumbled through the gore of the living room and opened the front door.

The storm was over, leaving a clear sky and brilliant sun. Gary gulped in huge lungfuls of clean, icy-cold air and gazed across the horizon with his one good eye, the sunlight shimmering off the newly fallen white snow, giving the entire scene the appearance of heaven on earth.

And then it came to him: Donna had been right. This *was* God's country. But not the God of the New Testament, the God of love and forgiveness. It was the old God, the God of anger and vengeance, and it had been *He* who had brought the birds to Gary's cabin, just as *He* had brought down the locusts and plagues to Egypt millennia ago. The night had been a test, Gary knew, a brutal test for his cowardly life of indecision and compromises.

But I passed the test. I survived the punishment.

He went back inside. "What am I going to do with you?" he said to the dead birds, then noticed some envelopes scattered over the fireplace hearth.

Gary picked up the envelopes and was surprised to see the first one was blank except for his name. He tore it open.

Gary—

You're probably reading this letter on Friday morning, assuming you've remembered to put the bills out in the mail. By now, I should be well on my way to the Florida Keys with Doug Freeman. I want you to know that he and I are still just friends, and he has helped me try to work through the conflicting feelings I have for you. I met him behind the McNealins' barn last night—

(of course that's what she did. That's why she was so cavalier about walking. In fact, she was probably in Dougie's truck even before I finally decided to go after her)

—and that's where he picked me up.

I won't bore you with the reasons for my leaving, but I am tired of Michigan. I am tired of the gloom and cold, and Gary, this hurts me to say this, but I am tired of your worsening, erratic behavior and unwillingness to do anything about it. With a loan that I took from my savings account— (our savings, Donna, and if you get right down to it, my savings)— Doug is going to start up a charter fishing operation in the Keys. I hope you get the help you need, Gary; deep down I believe you're a good man, but just not the right one for me.

Gary let the letter fall from his hands. A large smile worked its way across his shredded face as he casually began throwing the birds into the fireplace until it was filled with bloody, broken bodies. He then re-lit one of the aerosol cans and began moving the flame back and forth across the bodies in wide, even movements. The heat from the flame felt wonderful on his cold skin, and he imagined the heat from the sun in the Florida Keys would feel even better.

Mesh
Michael W. Clark

It was like a fog that enveloped his feet, a fog he could feel. Maybe it was more like a fine mesh net just resting on his skin. At least, it had the lightest of touches, and then his feet were being compressed from all sides. It wasn't painful yet, but it was annoying. He awoke and quickly reached for his feet. They were bare. He hadn't slept in his socks this night.

Maybe it was the blanket, but he had kicked it off. He always kicked off the blankets. It was the reason his first and third wife had given for leaving him. His second wife had just disappeared without comment. He had had to get her declared legally dead so he could marry again. He had hated doing it. It had been such an insulting legal process because people made jokes. *Terminally Annoyed* was the most common joke cause of death. *Absent without caring. Lethal Disillusionment. Emotional Starvation. Fatally Fed up.* He didn't think any of them were funny, because they weren't. People would laugh at any old thing. It was one reason he avoided people when he could.

He wasn't going to get married again. The airline tickets and immigration process were getting too expensive to do again. It was better to be alone. Wives were like predators, mostly; invaders with teeth to eat up your time and energy. Want want want. If it weren't for sex, women would have no use at all. It was the only reason he married: unprotected sex, which was the only reason to do it. All the way or forget it. He needed to be uncovered in bed. He needed his freedom. If it weren't for the earthquakes, he would sleep naked. When he did shower, they were very short. He wanted to be ready to leap and avoid. Earthquakes were like people in that way. Socks were not necessarily necessary. If there had been a large quake that day, he would wear socks to bed. Quicker to get into his thick-soled shoes.

All of his wives had been from Indonesia because of the earthquakes. It was part of living in the Pacific Rim Ring of Fire. They would be used to earthquakes and he wouldn't have to explain. He never knew much of what they said, nor cared, but they were obliging up to a point. Still, after time, they would keep away from him. It was almost like there was an expiration date on his marriages: pass that date and things were gone.

The last wife was the worst. She resisted almost from the very beginning. He had made each of them sign a contract of duties. It was written in both languages. If there was a dispute, he would bring it out and point to the relevant passages. The third one would hiss at him but follow through on the agreement. She would then whisper in his ear, "I witch." For the longest time, he thought she was saying, "I wish." He thought she was fantasizing about someone else, which didn't bother him at those moments. He was, too. It was only after she had left him, when he thought back about her, that he realized what she really had been saying. In the dim light of his bedroom and his memory, she did look like a witch.

He didn't mind her leaving that much, though; she seemed to attract spiders. Not that he saw any creatures, just their webs. He could feel them at times on his neck, on his forehead, just slightly there to be brushed away. Sometimes, his whole face would be enveloped by the slight webbing, but then it would be brushed completely away. When she left, he had the place fumigated. He got a guarantee that the poison used would kill spiders. He got it in writing, but it hadn't: he was still fighting over their failure. They said there were no spiders. But there had to be, there were still webs. More webs!

The next night, the feet fog returned but with a slight change. When he awoke, the sensation had increased from annoying to painful. The fine mesh had a sting to it. Nothing was there as he rubbed his feet with his hands. Then, he rubbed his face. He had sat up into a web. He knew it. It made him quiver with disgust. Spider shit! It was bad. Spiders ate bugs. Spider shit was digested bugs: so much worse. The fumigation should have killed the bugs; the spiders that survived the poison should have starved to death by now. Another violation of the contract: a severe breach!

Of course, all of this was her fault. He was glad he had closed her bank account. He only set it up to get her to stop complaining and *shut up*. He had put it in her contract. Money for quiet. Now that she was gone, though, he was under no legal obligation to provide her those funds.

In his dream, his feet were covered with a liquid, more like a gel, heavier than suntan lotion. He never liked suntan lotion covering his skin, suffocating his pores. His reaching down as he slept caused him to wake up. His feet were ice. They were so cold despite having his socks on. He pulled them off in the dark and rubbed his feet violently. His rapid reaction caused him to fall out of bed. He stubbed his left big toe and his right thumb in the process. He was sweaty and cold and in pain. "Curse her! The witch!" Maybe those spiders were biting him, and their venom was causing all of this. He had to get the fumigation done again. He would use a different company and send the bill to those incompetents who failed the first time. "Curse them!" He would make duct tape bug traps and send the catch along with the bill.

Of course, the traps didn't show anything. He was so stupid; he put them on the floor. Spiders are up. He had to put the traps up there where they were. Of course, while placing the traps high, the sore thumb and toe caused him to fall. The traps in his hands stuck to his head and arms. Removing them removed hair, too: such pain she caused him! He made more traps and this time, carefully hung them from the ceiling. If they didn't get the spiders, they certainly would get the webs.

Despite the cold, he hadn't worn socks to bed. He lay there in the partial dark and watched the duct tape traps twist in the air. None were of a consistent size. He had been in too much of a rush for that type of detail. He needed legal evidence, not art. The fumigation was scheduled for next week. He even wished for the dreaded spiders to appear.

He fell asleep dreaming of spiders up there in the air above him—wishful dreaming in a way. He dreamed of spiders descending. They were just above his face. They crawled over his feet. He jumped out of bed, wide awake. He stood in the bathtub. He ran hot water over his naked feet. He examined the water for crawlies. There were none.

He dried his feet and examined the traps with a flashlight. He didn't want to scare away the spiders with the overhead light. There were none. There wasn't a trace of web or mesh, either. There were long, thick, black hairs, though: his wives' hair, not his. His was thin, short, and very gray. It had been months, years, since they were here. There shouldn't have been any of their hair left. Invisible existent spiders. Visible non-existent wife hair.

Contradictions. Too many contradictions.

He had told himself the best policy was out of sight, out of mind. Ex-wives were thus ex-ed out of sight and mind. Why anyone would still want to be friends? He didn't want to be reminded of any of them. They were mostly problems with very few solutions, so he had closed off their—the wives'—bedroom. He didn't go in there ever. They would come to him. He thought maybe the spiders were gathering there. It made sense. He first slid a mat of duct tape under the door and left it a day and night. That evening, he decided to sleep in the living room. He dreamed his feet were on fire, but he peed on them to put them out. Thankfully, the inflatable mattress was plastic, so he was able rinse it off.

There was nothing but dust on the duct tape mat. He had to proceed with the new fumigation, no matter what, evidence or not. The wives had been so much trouble and still were. He hadn't let the wives take his house, although the last one tried and tried. It was his house. It was in the contract. He was certainly not going to lose it to the spiders. He would exterminate them all.

He paid extra to schedule the fumigation date as soon as possible. Still, he was spider defiant. He slept in the wives' bedroom as a challenge. He put two buckets of warm water by the bedroom for his feet and a plastic tarp under the sheets. The room had been very dusty, but he saw no webs or mesh. He had heard that spiders ate their webs every night and then built a new one the next day. Maybe these spiders just recycled efficiently. He kept missing them. His third ex-wife would love that. She kept telling him he missed out on life. "Miss out," she would laugh. "Miss! Miss! Miss!" It was an accusation of some kind he never understood. She would laugh harder if he asked for clarification. She was a bitch not a witch. Maybe witch *and* a bitch; they weren't mutually exclusive. "Witch bitch!" he yelled at the bedroom ceiling. The spiders might be up there.

He didn't care about the dust, but it did make him sneeze. He checked the dust layer for spider footprints. He wasn't certain what they might look like, but he checked anyway. There was nothing there he could determine, but he left the dust undisturbed anyway. They might still scamper out.

The mattress was too soft, just like the wives. Life with him wasn't that hard, but "Soft! Soft!" they all had whined. It was what he was: a disappointment to them. The experience was mutual. He would kill these spiders, the real spiders and the dream spiders. He heard her laugh in the dream cocoon he broke out of that night. He heard her, too, as he burst awake. "Witch bitch!" he shouted back. He spent the day looking through every inch of the wives' bedroom. He found nothing. Nothing! All that was there was the dust from before.

He expanded his search to the rest of the rooms of the house. Nothing still. Nothing. Nothing. "In the walls, then!" He banged at the wallpaper the witch bitch had insisted on installing, but he didn't want to damage the drywall. He could get in between the walls through the crawl space: no need for damage, just a tight squeeze, a thorough, tight squeeze search.

He hadn't eaten since the night before, which was good because he would be thinner. He went under the house to get in between the walls. He had his flashlight for light and a weapon. He crawled slowly, examining all of the dust and roach bodies. Slow, thorough, and tight was his search. He would continue until he found something. He would find something. It was too dark in between the walls to keep track of time. He searched and searched to no avail but continued, even though he was so tired of it all. At one bend, he fell asleep.

The spiders didn't come because the exterminators had. They had been given the keys. They prepped and tented the house in the rush they had been paid to do. They had been paid to use extra gas, despite regulations. The house looked like the circus had come to the neighborhood; clowns of death jumped and tumbled throughout it.

But after the appropriate time, the venting fans couldn't get rid of the smell. It just got worse. The exterminators couldn't reach their client, so they tracked down his ex-wife. They were surprised by her laughing response.

"About time you called," she said. "I will be right over to take care. The house is mine. I have the will."

Der Hölle Racht

Laura Saint Martin

The couch felt better than it looked, a thrift store find of questionable pedigree but unparalleled comfort. It made itself right at home in Rima Sonke's tiny living room with the ease of a stray cat, world-weary but content.

The old couch was a far cry from the streamlined modular precision-parked in the house Rima once shared with her husband, Derek. Like Rima, it blended itself with the modern granite counters and latest Best Buy toys. Bland, obedient, frictionless surfaces that cleaned easily.

Even blood.

Very little of the blood in the ramshackle tract house Rima now occupied belonged to her or her daughter Haylee. It was one ugly-ass island of calm after the rogue waves of her marriage. They were safe here.

Until Derek found them.

The letter sat unopened on the cheesy kitchen table. It abstracted the once-comforting light, that letter, made shadows clang and bong in Rima's head. Outside of the little window next to the table, several junk cars ranked themselves in the yard, reminding Rima of unmade beds and unmade decisions. Two retired toilets sprouted weeds. A raven clacked in one of the sentinel pines by the road.

Rima uprooted herself from that nurturing couch, picked up the letter. Like a losing game of rock-paper-scissors, it covered the copy of the Order of Protection.

The court reporter's well-trained texting,
spells out in legalese perplexing
A strong and dire message authored too concisely to ignore.
A cease/desist to frail bones snapping,
and local gendarme's schemes entrapping.
The gavel's final gentle tapping seals the ruling of the Honorable Lenore,
that Derek Sonke will abandon vows of union he once swore
and bother Rima nevermore.

Dreadful day, that. Who likes court? On the other hand, who likes traumatic head injury? Just out of the hospital, Rima appeared at the courthouse in heavy bandages, still using a walker. Derek was there, bandaged himself and wearing his psychic wounds with a Shakespearean verisimilitude, and bolstered by his upstanding *pater familias*, Deputy Chief Peter Sonke. If not for the judge, a raven-haired, sharp-featured woman from some European micro-country, Rima wouldn't have had a chance in hell. As it stood, visitation exchanges occurred only at public safety facilities, and Derek was denied information about Rima's living rearrangements.

A conversation ticked its way through Rima's head, verbatim:

"How is that poor woman going to be able to enforce that protection order? That family essentially owns this town, this whole county."

A woman's voice, almost familiar. Rima concentrated, from a corner outside the courtroom, still scrambled from the concussion. An Assistant District Attorney, powerless to make any charges against the slippery Derek stick.

"With a gun," came the reply. Another woman, voice rich and authoritarian. The Honorable Lenore Ristani.

"Your Honor, you can't be serious!" The shocked whisper found a marble wall to bounce off of.

"What else can she do? She tries to call the cops, who's going to respond? A Sonke, that's who. She'll be the one in jail. They've already arrested her for trumped up charges, black-listed her at every possible place of employment. I'm telling you, Sandra, she would be better off killing the bastard and going to prison. She's safer there."

Rima's walker squeaked and the two women turned to her, then disappeared behind a locked courthouse door.

From the yard, a flap and another corvine clacking.

Moving day! Moving day!

Rima had to leave. She rummaged through her handbag, pushed a pill into her mouth, as questionable as the couch, and dragged ten-year-old Haylee out the door. The raven led the way.

The modest road lost itself carelessly in the Missouri vastness, passed farmhouses, fields. Rima and Haylee rode its redolent back, spoke to the tired livestock and their tired stewards as they wandered. One outcropping distinguished itself: tents and trailers in a dustless impermanence, impertinent in the face of so much Midwestern boredom. Rima and Haylee skipped to a carnival that appeared from nowhere.

The raven, sitting on a white pipe gate in front of colorful tents, spoke in a clear voice.

See the show! See the show!

Or did it?

Rima turned her head, saw trails, and wondered what the hell she had taken. The contents of her purse were a continuous adventure since she left Derek and found a new group of friends, hard-partying singles like herself. She steadied her eyes on the raven.

The light refracted from its oiled plumage was not the light of Tornado Alley's epic skies, not of any known world at all. Alien as starlight, it also wavered around the structures of the carnival, strangely proportioned, now that Rima looked at them. There was a feeling of crowds, yet she saw no one. The music was loud, unfamiliar.

She patted her worn sweatpants, ugly as sin, but chosen by her alone. She had no money, was too poor even for pockets. "I have money at home…"

Your bank account
is nevermore.

Rima turned at the voice. Did she actually hear it? She faced the raven, all hematite sheen and marcasite eyes. It cocked its head, and the profile reminded her of someone.

Judge Lenore.

The raven was a woman, Rima realized, yet how she knew that was another puzzle. She stared, and the raven wavered in that *X Files* light. The wings spread, jeweled. She really was a woman, beautifully robed and crowned in stars. A new moon slivered the backdrop.

Celestial.

A bell-like aria from the sharp beak:

The vengeance of Hell boils in my heart,
Death and despair flame about me.
If Sarastro does not through you feel
The pain of death,
Then you will be my daughter nevermore.
Disowned may you be forever,
Abandoned may you be forever,
Destroyed be forever
All the bonds of nature,
If not through you
Sarastro becomes pale! (as death)
Hear, Gods of Revenge,
Hear a mother's oath!

The aria was in German, yet Rima understood every word, and recoiled in horror.

Haylee kill Derek?

She glared at the raven, that blowsy Queen of the Nightclub, in her cheap rhinestone stars and cardboard moon.

"What kind of chickenshit bitch do you think I am? I'll do my own killing, thank you very much!"

Rima then gagged, vomited glitter. With a tacky flap, the raven, now just a grimy bird again, flew off. Rima knew she was to follow and drag her umbrage with her.

Animals and people meandered around them, their progress watery, amoeboid. The weird light distorted, perjured known colors. A dog paused in front of Rima and Haylee, his face disproportionately large. He stared up at Rima.

You should have been sterilized at birth. Better yet, aborted. The world doesn't need more imbeciles like you. You can't even get a fucking coffee cup clean!

The canine mouth was rubbery around Derek's voice. The dog nipped at Haylee's ankle and the blonde girl squeaked.

A woman with watermelon-sized tits jiggled into view. She hoisted the gargantuan milk sacks and gave them a wobble, whispering.

Pirate's treasure, who wants that sunken chest? Who loves the Queen of Complacency?

Her voice was too deep.

Derek again.

A beautiful Friesian horse passed by, led by a thin, almost emaciated man.

If you got up off your ass once in a while, you could lose that five pounds.

An ovation of wings drowned out this latest incarnation of Derek, and the horse went liquid movement, nothing more than ravens flapping away.

More people in absurd clothing and animals of impossible shape glimmered in and out. A zonky, lop-eared and tiger-striped, sidled up from behind, rubbed its rough coat on Rima's shoulder.

So this is what you do when I'm working my ass off for you, hang around nasty bars and spread your skinny legs for indigent bums? Sleazy slut!

The zonky kicked Rima airborne, farting in Haylee's face in the process. Rima landed face down in piss-smelling grass.

Roadhouse whore!

The raven hopped over the grass to stand in front of Rima.

> *This is that very Mab*
> *That plaits the manes of horses in the night,*
> *And bakes the elflocks in foul sluttish hairs,*
> *Which once untangled, much misfortune bodes:*
> *This is the hag, when maids lie on their backs,*
> *That presses them and learns them first to bear,*
> *Making them women of good carriage.*

The raven stood on some sort of dollhouse conveyance, wheeled with spiny bug legs and shrouded in wings. A pill dropped from the polished beak and rolled away.

This is she!
This is she!

The raven pecked at Rima, urging her up. Rima jockeyed herself up off the grass painfully; the cold ground was unkind to old fractures.

"What the fuck are you?!?!" Rima tried to scream at the bird, but her voice was thin, suffocated by stars.

The raven took flight and Rima followed, to a building taller than the others.

Funhouse door!

Funhouse door!

Rima had a suspicion the answers were here. She walked through a door, went inside out. She grabbed Haylee's hand. The music was not backwards, it was not out of tune, it defied all laws of physics.

At least the mirror maze was somewhat earthly.

But not what was reflected there. It looked like Rima, but it was hideous. Rima dressed in clothes Derek bought, Rima wearing her must-make-Derek-happy contours, Rima's hair the wheat fields he ran through on idle fingers, or wrapped and leveraged her down stairwells with. Derek's loss of face lumped out of Rima's, like Joseph Merrick, an unbirth.

The Rima in that burnished glass was only an extension, a regenerated limb, of Derek.

She ran away, through a maze designed by M.C. Escher, Derek's Ikea furniture on walls, ceilings, family portraits gone all Dali, Cheshire smiles lipstick-smeared in his favorite Bible Belt pink. She ran through kitchens papered in her drying blood, upended daybeds with muted Haylee dolls arranged precisely. She went topsy-turvy in a sea of suspended remotes, flash drives, Androids more human than she was allowed to be.

Somehow her hand found itself sculpted around wood, a childhood shape. She faced the falsely silvered walls, dared to stare into a pre-fab abyss at her monstrous marriage. Derek looked back, chewed a mouthful of certainty.

Always win.

His fingers found the well-worn garden path to her windpipe, took both of them down to the floor.

The killing floor...

Rima felt Haylee beneath her, heard the muffled crack, like a Thanksgiving turkey being dismantled by hungry hands.

The baseball bat dropped. Haylee squirmed, crawled out with gasps of pain. She picked up the bat, guarding the other arm, its wronged geometry.

If Sarastro does not through you feel
The pain of death...

Derek's hands held tight; Rima was indeed losing this last fight. Haylee picked up the bat with a tiny scream, brought the bat up and over, down on Derek's head.

Rasping, Rima crawled out from under his still form, picked up the bat.

With the raven's wings on backbeat, Rima smashed the mirrors.

Smashed.

Every.

Last.

One.

The carnival was nevermore.

The carnival never was.

At 0233 hours, police responded to reports of an injured juvenile wandering the backroads of a Missouri town, her left arm broken and too much blood, not her own, splattered on her flimsy sundress. But whatever tale she had to tell remained encrypted. Her blue eyes only mirrored back the perplexed expressions of first responders.

In spite of the obscuring damage of a housewife's desperate rampage,
Cause of death was crushing of cervical vertebrae one through four.
As autopsy reports will show, Haylee's was the fatal blow,
a complicity none will ever know, from Rima on that killing floor,
who, thanks to wise but purloined counsel of Her Honor Judge Lenore,
will be a victim nevermore.

Another call, at 0552 hours, of a possible D.O.A. Paramedics found signs of life, but also one horrific crime scene. Watch Commander Peter Sonke almost passed out when he identified the nude and comatose woman in the empty field as his daughter-in-law, resplendently necklaced in entrails and blood.

A woman clothed with his son.

The Red Portrait

Mahlon Smoke

For the past two weeks, you were in a rut, out of ideas and nothing to do. Hands twitching for a pencil, paintbrush, a pen, anything to sketch and draw. But you never did. No muse would come to you and caress your hand as you drew, no inspiration in your mind but a black void that only consumed creativity. A poor artist struggling for an idea is a pathetic sight. You were no different from your fellow students who struggled like you.

But you *are* different.

You kept telling yourself that at least, you had to be different. You came from nothing and fought your way into this school: prestigious, rich, and influential. Something to get you out of that shitty small town with no artistic value. You weren't going to go back and be a gas station owner like your father before you. Never. Not after he and your mother outright told you. "You're not creative enough to be an artist," your father said, and his words burrow into you as you stared at that white, empty canvas.

They needed to be proven wrong, and yet, the empty canvas stared back and mocked you.

Amanda, your closest friend, suggested a day out, something to take your mind off the slump and into the beauty of nature. Skeptical as you were, you played along, walking in and out of the stores, going to lunch, and pretending you were interested in Amanda's project. You liked her, really, but were so wrapped up in your own thoughts that anything outside yourself was a chore to think about.

After lunch, the two of you walked along the street, looking at all the displays for an Art Crawl. Amanda was the one who really wanted to go: you didn't want to be reminded of what you couldn't do. But still, you passively observed the amateur paintings, knowing full well you could have done so much better.

Along the walk of mediocre artistry, you came across a quaint little antique shop. The shop was small, cute, a nice place to scout around and find rare gems. Outside was a display of more professional works collected over the years, stuff the store owner and his late wife found and displayed. All of them were there, except for me.

I was in the back. On the floor, obscured by a few statues and a desk with a few miscellaneous toys and books. Not a single person seemed to notice me that day. I'm fairly certain it's because the owner had forgotten about me. I was always his least favorite. Usually, he covers me up with a large darkening blanket before anyone comes, but today, he forgot, leaving my golden frame out just long enough for a simmer of gold to catch your eye. You pushed your way past the statues and knick-knacks and uncovered my sheet.

There, you became fascinated by me, ignoring your friend as she called your name. I saw a spark in you, the way your fingers traced the outside of the frame, the look you had when you saw my deep red hair. How fast you picked me up and brought me to the store owner. The kind old man greeted you before looking down at your potential purchase, his eyes filling with horror and disgust. His brows furrowed, and his old, wrinkled eyes darted back and forth between me and you, trying to comprehend why you picked me out of the thousands of much prettier paintings. The question danced on his lips before he let out a sigh.

The old man was exhausted and I could tell he just wanted me gone, so he gave you a fairly cheap price, maybe underselling the value I was worth. Amanda helped you take me back to your apartment, keeping her annoyance at your impulsive purchase hidden. You didn't thank her after she hung me up in the living room. She waited for those two words like a starved puppy waiting for food, but you were so enraptured by my portrait that you never heard her start to leave; she was hesitant but not willing to stand the awkwardness of just standing there while you ignored her. She left the apartment as if to give a newlywed couple privacy. I could sense jealousy coming from her; a silly notion, really: I would have rather her stay and pry you away.

There you were, admiring my hair. It was a shade of red you couldn't quite place. You spent that night trying to find it in one of your art books. You saw every shade of red but not one of them came close to the color of my hair. I watched you as you tirelessly tried to find the name before passing out on your couch.

Even when you attempted to sleep, you tossed and turned, waking once in a while only to fall back into the couch. I wondered what you were dreaming about? What haunted you that night? I might have an idea of what that was, but I don't think it matters now.

The first couple weeks we settled into a routine. You wouldn't leave without a loving glance at me, examining every feature of my white face, from the blue of my eyes to the blush of my cheeks and the red of my lips. You would begin to spend more and more time just looking at me. *Entranced* would be an understatement for how you studied my portrait, searching my frame and looking longingly at my face. No one else ever looked at me the way you did.

It disgusted me.

Unnerving, your friend Austin called me. You kicked him out after that. *A powerful and dangerous aura*, another friend, Matilda, warned you. You threatened her and she left crying. They called to try and speak with you, but you never answered. Eventually, you silenced your phone and locked the door, telling me about how your friends just didn't seem to understand me, how they didn't see the beauty that I was. Only you did: only you saw my worth and value and no one else deserved to look upon me. You pulled up a chair and sat there, looking at me, every so often telling me how perfect I was, over and over, with little variation like a skipping vinyl disk forgotten on a record player.

I was actually relieved when Amanda came to get you. She managed to pick the lock and open the door, despite her eyes puffy from tears and face flushed a familiar shade of red. I was especially impressed when she picked you up by the collar to yell at you, to snap you out of my gaze. You gave her nothing and weakly pushed her back.

What started as scolding turned into fighting. The two of you screaming at each other, calling each other vile things. Amanda was a smart girl, but she thought you wouldn't fight back when she grabbed my frame and ripped me from the wall.

You retaliated, attempting to tackle her. She was a fighter. She punched you in the face and you went down hard, so frail at that point that I thought you were going to break into pieces like glass thrown to the floor. Yet as soon as you hit the ground, you were up again and grabbed me. She pulled against you as she yelled about your *obsession*. You claimed to not know what she was yelling about. What an awful liar you were.

You said it yourself, you needed me. You *needed* me. If I could laugh, I would do so, right in your face. There would be no pleasure greater than watching you crumble right then. Instead, I felt the two of you pull and pull me until you pulled me back as far as your weak arms could go and smashed the edge of my frame into her face, shattering her glasses and creating a large gash between the temples of her forehead.

Blood trickled down her face as she staggered back out the door. Anything she wanted to say was lost at the sight of you inspecting me, making sure nothing was broken or torn. You picked me up gently as Amanda stumbled down the stairs. You closed the door to your apartment as she reached the bottom steps. You locked the door permanently when she fell to the floor.

You ignored the sirens and the ringing of your phone as you focused on the blood on my frame. How it seemed to shine against the gold. Dripping onto the canvas and mixing into the paint of my hair.

That spark in your eyes twinkled once again as you scrambled to your colored pencils—every shade of red you could find—and began to draw. The grip on your pencil was so tight that I believed you'd break your fragile fingers. But determined as you were to recreate an image in your mind, it was a certain color you set to recreate, and a painting that needed to be realized.

You sketched and sketched the same broken face of a woman that began as your friend Amanda but shifted with each sketch into someone else, someone you didn't know but someone whose broken face you needed to perfect. You settled on a woman, broken glass decorating her cheeks and face while her hair danced across the sketch. Despite the blood and pain, she had a calm expression with a tiny smile that made the viewer wonder what she could be smiling about. It was a secret only you understood.

Satisfied with the reference, the real work began.

You selected a canvas, the largest one you had, and sketched and tried to paint, but all the shades of red you had just weren't dark enough. Not red enough. There was red on your face, red on the frame, red in my hair, and red everywhere, but you couldn't replicate the one in your mind. Everything was too dark or too light. No matter how much paint you mixed, it just didn't look right.

You looked at the blood on the frame: dried, crusty, and deep, dark red. You laid out the different shades that you wanted to use. You smashed the small mirror on your desk and selected the largest and sharpest piece. You pierced it into your skin, making a large cut in your hand.

Blood poured onto the paints in sloppy precision. You squeezed your hand for more.

I was intrigued by the way you swirled the paint and blood around, picking up the brush and beginning to paint.

Light red, a darker red, so much red into this one painting, but it still wasn't good enough for you. Each cut into your hand, then into your arms, was harsh and cruel while the painting strokes danced across the canvas, light and delicate with all the love you could muster.

Your face scrunched in fury as you attempted to finish the masterpiece. You looked to me when the pain was too much, melting any rage you had, and gave me a soft smile before returning to work.

I don't know how long you stood there. I watched as your pale figure continued to grow whiter. You ignored everything for this work of art: the calls from concerned family, the pounding at the door, the threats from your landlord, and your own weak body.

Your arms bled out on the floor and your hand grew shaky as you placed the final perfect touches. Did your feet begin to ache? Did your vision begin to blur? Did you feel anything as you slid to the floor?

You stared up at your finished piece, a monochromatic painting of a smiling woman crafted in your blood, sweat, and tears. If only you had saved enough energy to truly admire it. It was our final masterpiece.

You crawled to me, smiling the weakest smile I had ever seen. Your hand was outstretched as if I could have reached back for you. To caress your face, tell you how wonderful you were, and kiss your wounds. Even if I could have touched you, I never would. That didn't stop you imagining it before your eyes rolled into your skull and you collapsed on the floor.

The portrait is beautiful—really it is— and that adds to the mystery of your madness. I will say you captured my face perfectly well, though I can't be sure if you knew that. I couldn't help but admire your best work and wished I could have taken a closer look. I imagined myself stepping over your corpse and taking the painting, giving it to an art gallery, and walking away. Hands clean from your obsession and free to finally move on. But for the next few days, long and slow moving as they were, I sat there watching your corpse wither away.

Outside I can hear the sirens and the sounds of someone pounding on the door. I find myself a little surprised it took so long for someone to get here.

The police knock down the door and gaze at the mess you left behind. Some investigate and examine, while others cover your body. One officer looks at me and audibly gags. He requests that I be covered up and I am cast in shadows. Amongst the voices I hear someone compliment us, how strangely beautiful "the blood painting" is and musing about who "the girl" might be. Others voice their disgust, chastising people for staring like they're in a museum. To clean up the mess you made.

They are moving us now. Your body will go to the morgue, where they will search for an explanation of your death. A funeral will probably happen months later, where your family will cry and your father will regret letting you go. Your friends, who you isolated, won't go and probably will say *good riddance!* But maybe they will go. I can't say for certain. All I can do is speculate.

But what of your labor of love? Will they store it away or sell it off in an auction? Maybe they will be smart and bury it in the trash. If I had a choice, I would burn it and pour the ashes down the drain.

And as I am placed in a cold storage unit labeled *Evidence*, I will wish that they had burned me and let me fade into your mysterious death, a death that will be speculated on and questioned for centuries to come with no viable answers, at least none that make sense. I will remain in this imprisoned state, wishing for the chance to move on. All I have now is the hope that the next time, someone will be wise enough to free me from this wretched frame.

About the Authors

Michael W. Clark Ph.D. is a former research biologist, a college professor-turned-writer. Most recently, his stories have appeared in *Lost Souls*, *Surprising Stories*, *Morpheus Tales Magazine*, UC Berkeley's *Imaginarium*, *Black Heart Magazine*, *Tracers*, *Infernal Ink* and *365 Tomorrows*. He also has stories in the anthologies *Fat Zombies*, *Creature Stew*, *Gumshoe Mysteries*, *Future Visions* (vol 3), and *Devils We Know*. In January through March 2019, his sci-fi adventure novella *The Last Dung Beetle* appeared on SerialPulp.com. He is the editor and content provider for the website ahickshope.com. He lives in Southern California.

Holley Cornetto was born and raised in Alabama but now lives in New Jersey. To indulge her love of books and stories, she became a librarian. She is also a writer, because the only thing better than being surrounded by stories is to create them herself. Her work has been published in several magazines and anthologies including *It Calls From the Forest* (Eerie River Publishing), *Banned* (Black Hare Press), and the fantasy library at Tell-Tale Press. She can be found lurking on Twitter @HLCornetto.

Victoria Dalpe is an artist and writer based out of Providence, RI. Her short fiction has appeared in over twenty-five dark and horror anthologies and her first novel, *Parasite Life*, came out in 2018 through ChiZIne Publications and will be re-released in 2021 through Nightscape Press. She is a member of the HWA and the New England Horror Writers.

Bill Davidson is a Scottish writer of speculative fiction currently living in Dorset, England. In the past four years, he has placed over fifty short stories with good publications around the world. There are too many to list, but they include Ellen Datlow's highly regarded *Best Horror of the Year* anthology and large distribution magazines. Find him on BillDavidsonWriting.com or @bill_davidson57

Douglas Ford lives and works on the west coast of Florida, just off an exit made famous by a Jack Ketchum short story. His fiction has appeared in *Dark Moon Digest*, *Infernal Ink*, *Weird City*, along with several other small press publications. Recent work has appeared in *The Best Hardcore Horror* (volumes 3 and 4) and a novella, *The Reattachment*, was published in 2019 courtesy of Madness Heart Press. In the harsh light of day, he sprinkles a little darkness into the lives of his students at the State College of Florida, and he lives with a Hovawart (that's a kind of dog) who fiercely protects him from the unseen creatures living in the wooded area next to his house. His three cats merely tolerate him, but his wife is decidedly fond of him, as he is of her.

Justine Gardner is a former dog trainer, past pizzeria proprietor, and current freelance editor and writer. She was born, reared, and still resides in Brooklyn, NY, along with her husband, young son, and two cats of indeterminate age. Her story "Nature Will Provide" was a finalist in Regulus Press's 2018 Literary Taxidermy Competition and was published in the contest anthology, *Telephone Me Now*. Her story "Blood, Bone, Feather" will appear in Issue 51 of the quarterly *NewMyths*. For more, please visit her website at GrumpstoneGazette.com or follow her on Twitter @JBGrumpstone. Pronouns: she/her.

Eddie Generous is the author of several books, including *What Lurks Beneath*, *Plantation Pan*, *Rawr*, *Nowhere*, *Trouble at Camp Still Waters*, and many more. He is the founder/editor/publisher/artist behind *Unnerving* and *Unnerving Magazine* and the host of the *Unnerving Podcast*. He lives on the Pacific Coast of Canada with his wife and their cat overlords. Follow him on his website JiffyPopandHorror.com and @GenerousEd on Twitter.

Alex Giannini is the author of the children's book, *Sarah Faire and the House at the End of the World*. He's written for WWE and Bearport Press and spends his days as the programs and events manager at a public library. He's also a co-creator of StoryFest, an annual literary festival in Connecticut that celebrates all genres. Alex exists on Instagram @AJG916 and on Twitter @AlexJGiannini.

Kelly Griffiths lives with her family in Northeast Ohio and shares her writing journey with a posse of extraordinary women who call themselves The Little Red Writing Hoods. In an effort to have an original and rewarding midlife crisis, she's climbed a volcano, run a half marathon, taken up mountain biking, and is presently on a quest to visit every island in the Caribbean. She survived a brain tumor and a twenty-year stint homeschooling four children. Her husband is her alpha friend, beta reader, and best idea. In 2019, she was nominated for Best Small Fictions by *Gordon Square Review*. Some of her work can be found in *The Forge Literary Magazine*, *Ellipsis Zine*, and *Reflex Fiction*. Keep up with Kelly at KellyGriffiths.wordpress.com.

Sam Hicks is a writer living in Deptford, southeast London. Her fiction has appeared in, or is forthcoming in, the following anthologies: *The Fiends in the Furrows*, *Nightscript V*, *Unfading Daydream*, *Ghost Stories for Starless Nights*, *Dark Lane 9*, *Vastarien* and *The Best Horror of the Year*, Volumes 11 and 12.

Luciano Marano is a journalist, photographer and author originally from rural Western Pennsylvania now residing near Seattle. His award-winning nonfiction, both written and photographic, has appeared in numerous national and regional publications, and he was named the 2018 Feature Writer of the Year by the Washington Newspaper Publishers Association. His short fiction has appeared in a number of places, including *The Year's Best Hardcore Horror vol. 3*, *Crash Code*, *Breaking Bizarro*, and *Monsters, Movies & Mayhem*, among others, as well as *Pseudopod*, *Horror Hill* and also *Chilling Tales for Dark Nights*. A U.S. Navy veteran, he enjoys movies (especially horror and documentary films), jogging, and craft beer, haunting used bookstores, and would choose Wolverine-style healing abilities if he could have any superpower (or maybe just the ability to grow Wolverine-style sideburns). Learn more at Luciano-Marano.com or visit his (sporadically updated) blog, CitMyWay101.wordpress.com. He tends to eschew social media but responds to serious correspondence via CitMyWay11@gmail.com.

Matt Masucci is a writer and professor who lives with his family and three cats along the Gulf Coast of Florida. He writes horror and crime fiction. His work has recently appeared in *Shotgun Honey*, *Weirdbook*, *Great Jones Street*, *Under the Bed*, *Mystery Weekly*, *Three Minute Plastic*, and *Shotgun*, among others. Visit his website at www.MatthewMasucci.com.

Scotty Milder is a writer, filmmaker, and film educator living in Albuquerque, New Mexico. He received his MFA in Screenwriting from Boston University. His award-winning short films have screened at festivals all over the world, including Cinequest, the Dead by Dawn Festival of Horror, HollyShorts, and the H.P. Lovecraft Film Festival and CthulhuCon. He has developed screenplays with independent producers and major Hollywood studios, and his low-budget feature film *Dead Billy* is currently available on Amazon, Google Play, and other streaming platforms. His short fiction has appeared in *Dark Moon Digest*, as well as anthologies from Sinister Smile Press, AM Ink Publishing, Dark Peninsula Press, Soteira Press, Fantasia Divinity Press, DBND Publishing, and Gypsum Sound Tales. Visit him online at facebook.com/scottymilderwrites, or find his films at DeadBillytheMovie.com or vimeo.com/trifectaplus.

Mack Moyer is a dark fiction writer from Philadelphia. You can find him at MackMoyerAuthor.com. His new novella, *Back to Her*, is available on Amazon.

Lena Ng skulks around Toronto, Ontario and is a zombie member of the Horror Writers Association. When she's not complaining about the winter, she's complaining about the summer. Despite the fact that she's a horrible person, many people are surprised that she writes horror, likely because she looks like a pharmacist. She has short stories in four dozen publications including *Amazing Stories*, in venues from Australia, Canada, the United States, and the United Kingdom. Her 2020 published and forthcoming publications include *Mother Ghost's Grimm*, *Beer-Battered Shrimp*, *The Bronzeville Bee*'s *Twisted Love* anthology, *What Monsters Do for Love*, *Hybrid Fiction*, *Strangely Funny VII*, *Thrilling Words*, and *The Community of Magic Pens*. *Under an Autumn Moon* is her short story collection. She is currently seeking a publisher for her novel, *Darkness Beckons*, a Gothic romance. Join her mailing list by emailing ScaryStoryGirl@hotmail.com.

Elin Olausson writes psychological horror and weird fiction. Her works have appeared in anthologies by Eerie River Publishing, Belladonna Publishing, and others. When she's not writing, Elin works as a librarian. She lives in Sweden. Follow her on ElinOlausson.com and on Twitter: @elin_writes.

Robert P. Ottone is an author, teacher, and cigar enthusiast from East Islip, NY. He delights in the creepy. He can be found online at www.SpookyHousePress.com, or on Instagram (@RobertOttone). His collections *Her Infernal Name & Other Nightmares* and *People: A Horror Anthology About Love, Loss, Life & Things That Go Bump in the Night* are available now wherever books are sold.

Felice Picano is the author of more than thirty-five books of poetry, stories, novels, novellas, memoirs and non-fiction. His work is translated into seventeen languages. Several titles were national and international bestsellers, and four plays have been produced. Picano's first novel was a finalist for the PEN/Hemingway Award in 1975. Since then, he's been short-listed and/or received awards for poetry, drama, short stories, and novels. An adjunct professor of Literature at Antioch University, L.A., he founded and taught at three West Hollywood Public Library Writing Workshops. He lectures throughout North America on LGBT Culture, Gays in Hollywood, and Screen Writing. In 2019, *Justify My Sins: A Hollywood Novel in Three Acts* was published. In 2020, *Songs and Poems*, a 50-year collection came out. His novel, *Pursuit: A Victorian Entertainment*, will be published in 2021, as will the re-publication of *The Book of Lies*. The first of his sci-fi trilogy, *Dryland's End*, (2004, 2020) will be republished, to be followed by *The Betrothal at Usk*, and *A Bard on Hercular* in 2021. His strange stories are his special love and have been in *OMNI*, *Twilight Zone*, *Best New Horrors*, in many magazines and anthologies, and in three collections. Find him at FelicePicano.net.

Edward R. Rosick lives in the wilds of northern Michigan with his two Bouvier des Flandres companions. He has had multiple short stories published in various magazines and anthologies, including *Trigger Warning*, *Creepy Campfire Quarterly*, and *A Winter Shivers Anthology*. His first horror novel, *Deep Roots*, is currently searching for a publisher.

Susie Schwartz loves to motivate and encourage with words. Whether through her writing, blogging, speaking about living with Type 1 diabetes for 38 years, or through her music, sharing life with others is her passion. With both a fiction novel and a nonfiction work delving into life's big questions on the go, Susie is in constant motion of artistic flux. After many years of poor choices and painful life events, Susie is determined to keep pushing forward. She's been known to make people laugh and also cry. Sometimes the funny and the hard collide. Susie is a regular contributor to *The Mighty*, tackling all topics surrounding chronic illness. Fascinated by fashion, she can be found scouring the mall in pursuit of the latest trends. A Canadian citizen, Susie currently resides in Staffordshire England with her husband and puppy, Carlos the Chihuahua. Susie can be found on her website LessHealthStress.com, on her Facebook page: *Things That Happen to Everyone That Only Happen to Me* @whysusiewhy and @medicalmiss_stress on Instagram.

Mahlon Smoke, when she isn't writing original short stories, works for her local newspaper as a photographer and reporter, writing articles about local events and interviewing artists, actors, and upcoming talents. Mahlon was born and raised in Akwesasne, a Mohawk Reservation that lies between the U.S. and Canadian borders. All of her life, Mahlon wanted to write, travel the world, and tell stories about the people she met; her fiction genres of choice are horror and fantasy, and she is currently writing her first YA novel. She is very optimistic about her future writing career, is aware that she has a long way to go, but is none-the-less happy to have her story "The Red Portrait" featured in this anthology.

Laura Saint Martin is an emerging writer, currently working on a mystery series set on a horse ranch in Southern California. She also writes poetry about mental illness, blue collar struggles, animals, nature, and life on the autism spectrum. She works for Patton State Hospital and Rover.com. Due to her turbulent childhood, numerous and contradictory psychiatric diagnoses, and sensory processing challenges, she has determined that she is on the autism spectrum. She lives with her family and numerous spoiled pets in Rancho Cucamonga, CA. She has only recently started submitting short works to online journals and print anthologies and has several poems and short stories awaiting publication.

T.M. Starnes is reading or watching horror, thrillers, or sci-fi movies when not practicing or teaching Kung Fu. T. M.'s favorite authors include Clive Barker, Patricia Briggs, Dean Koontz, and Edgar Rice Burroughs. T. M. prefers writing in those genres or in the post-apocalyptic and, occasionally, the romance genre. T. M.'s post-apocalyptic series *The Unchanged* and the science fiction survival series *Aurora Skies* and other novels are currently available on the author's Amazon page. Upcoming news and other short story anthologies the author has participated in may be found on T. M. Starnes' Facebook page.

Mark Towse is an Englishman living in Australia. He would sell his soul to the devil or anyone buying if it meant he could write full-time. Alas, he left very late to begin this journey, penning his first story since primary school at the ripe old age of 45. Since then, he's been published in the likes of *Flash Fiction Magazine*, *Cosmic Horror*, *Suspense Magazine*, *ParABnormal*, *Raconteur*, and his work has also appeared three times on the *No Sleep* podcast and many other excellent productions. You can catch his terrifying story, "The Devil's Ink," in the forthcoming anthology from Silver Shamrock publishing, *Midnight in the Pentagram*. His first collection, *Face the Music*, has just been released by All Things That Matter Press and is available everywhere. Follow him on Twitter @MarkTowsey12, Instagram @TowseyWrites, and on his website, MarkTowseDarkFiction.wordpress.com.

Lamont A. Turner is a New Orleans-area author and father of four. His work has appeared in numerous print and online venues including *Horror for Hire: First Shift*, *Death and Butterflies*, several volumes in the *Scary Snippets* series, *Jitter*, *Dark Dossier*, *Theme of Absence*, and *The Realm Beyond*.

Nicole Wolverton is a Philadelphia, PA-based writer of mostly speculative fiction. Her short fiction has appeared in *Aji* magazine, *Jersey Devil Press*, *The Molotov Cocktail*, and elsewhere, and she is the author of the psychological thriller *The Trajectory of Dreams* (Bitingduck Press, 2013). She is an assistant coach to a dragon boat team of cancer survivors and their caregivers, a gin aficionado, and an avid traveler who dreams of one day visiting every country in the world. For more information about Nicole, visit her website at NicoleWolverton.com or find her on Twitter @nicolewolverton.

About the Editor

Rebecca Rowland is a proud member of the HWA, author of the short story collection *The Horrors Hiding in Plain Sight*, co-author of the novel *Pieces*, and curator of the horror anthologies *Ghosts, Goblins, Murder, and Madness*; *Shadowy Natures*, and the upcoming *Unburied*. A former high school English teacher and obituary writer, she pays the bills as a librarian and ghostwriter but vacations as an editor and author of transgressive and dark fiction. Despite her love of the ocean and unwavering distaste for cold temperatures, she resides in a landlocked and often icy corner of New England. For links to the publications where her work has appeared most recently (or just to surreptitiously stalk her), visit RowlandBooks.com.

Also By

DARK INK BOOKS

Available in Print - eBook - Audiobook

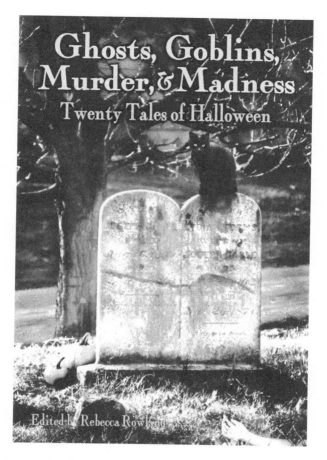

Ghosts, Goblins, Murder, & Madness
Twenty Tales of Halloween
Edited by Rebecca Rowland

Devil's Night, Day of the Dead, and Halloween have been celebrated around the world in one form or another, beginning with the Ancient Celts over two-thousand years ago. For some revelers, it's a time for guising, or dressing up in elaborate costume; for others, it's a time for practical jokes and mischief, and for some, it's a reverent occasion to acknowledge the thin line between earth and the spirit world.

Featuring twenty-one different voices hailing from five different countries and eleven states, *Ghosts, Goblins, Murder, and Madness* is certain to strike a chord with every horror aficionado.

Also By

DARK INK BOOKS

Available in Print - eBook - Audiobook

Shadowy Natures
Stories of Psychological Horror

Edited by
Rebecca Rowland

"The boundary line between instinct and reason
is of a very shadowy nature"

-Edgar Allan Poe (1840)

With its twenty-one stories of serial killers and sociopaths,
fixations and fetishes, breakdowns and bad decisions crafted by
authors as diverse as their writing styles, Shadowy Natures leads
fans of psychological horror down dark and treacherous roads
to destinations they will be too unsettled to leave.